ALSO BY STEVEN SHERRILL

Visits from the Drowned Girl

The Minotaur Takes a Cigarette Break

The
Locktender's
House

The Locktender's House

a novel

STEVEN SHERRILL

RANDOM HOUSE

New York

The Locktender's House is a work of fiction. Apart from any well-known actual people, events, and locales that figure in the narrative, all names, characters, places, and incidents are the products of the author's imagination or are used fictitiously. Any resemblance to current events or locales, or to living persons, is entirely coincidental.

Copyright © 2007 by Steven Sherrill

Published in the United States by Random House, an imprint of The Random House Publishing Group, a division of Random House, Inc., New York.

RANDOM HOUSE and colophon are registered trademarks of Random House, Inc.

Library of Congress Cataloging-in-Publication Data
Sherrill, Steven
The locktender's house: a novel/Steven Sherrill.
p.   cm.
ISBN 978-1-4000-6153-2
I. Title.
PS3569.H4349L63 2007
813'.54—dc22

Printed in the United States of America on acid-free paper

www.atrandom.com

246897531

First Edition

Book design by Jo Anne Metsch

FOR MY WIFE, LEE,
WITH ABIDING LOVE

The
Locktender's
House

I

The bomb that blew a hole in Wednesday morning and in Private Danks as he walked barefoot—barefoot despite the recent disciplinary write-up—through the desert sand, back from the commissary with a tube of anti-itch cream and a bottle of hypoallergenic shampoo, the explosion not only wreaked its upward havoc upon him but also surged through the earth's web of tectonic capillaries, pulsed from beneath the great bodies of water so uniformly that the schools of damselfish and chubs dithering at the various coasts turned en masse, and simultaneously, toward some primordial idea of safety, the ensuing waves lapping and licking at the remnants of a pier in Pamlico Sound, off the North Carolina coast, with just enough vigor to rouse the baker's dozen of plovers or gulls or pelicans clacking their beaks or squawking atop the creosoted pylons, the flap of wings and the shuddering that followed coinciding with a gust of salty wind that stirred the sea grass then rode the tops of the skinny pine trees inland, across the Piedmont, traveling 6,347 miles away from the dead boy in the desert, where, as if coming home, the percussive essence of that bomb climbed two flights of stairs in the middle of a sprawling apartment complex on the outskirts of Greensboro, then, without pause, rattled unit 33's door in its jamb, and shook the interior wall imperceptibly, but with all the force necessary to jostle Private Danks's dusty, out-of-tune banjo hanging from its peg head by a thin leather strand on a nail above his Easy-Boy recliner.

The brittle strand broke. The banjo fell, the twang and clang upending the sleep of Private Danks's girlfriend, Janice, on the other side of the shared wall. Janice bolted from the bed and ran headlong into the worst migraine of her life.

The headache knocked her to the ground. Instantly. Blurred her vision. She fell, with the faintest cry, and curled into a tight ball beside the bed. The pounding pounding pounding filled her head. There was no space for questioning the noise from the next room. Had she imagined it? Like buckets of thunder pouring over her, the pain drenched Janice's trembling body from her skull to the soles of her feet. Movement equaled pain, even slight movement. A ligament in the fingers going taut, pulling against bone and muscle, became a heavy rope squealing and biting against a wooden mooring post. The eyelid's soft closure rang out like a cell door slamming shut, steel against steel. She tried not to move.

Was there someone in the apartment? Janice hurt too much to worry about possible intruders. Did something really fall in the next room? Or did the thump and discordant clanking—so loud it even penetrated the earplugs she'd taken to wearing not long after moving in—did those sounds originate inside her own body? Janice wanted, wanted badly, to reach up and pluck out the dense foam plugs from her ear canals. They'd failed her that night. Whether or not the noise of the falling banjo had insinuated itself into her head, now the earplugs seemed to stop tight the flow of blood surging through the locks and channels of her veins. Pounding, pounding, pounding against eardrum, vitreous humor, cranium.

She'd had migraines before. She knew the pain would subside eventually. Would ebb and flow. She just had to endure. Janice lay motionless on the floor beside the bed. Some time later, hours maybe, she tried to look at the clock on the night table, but the blocky red numbers threw too much light. She couldn't sit or stand, or pull herself onto the bed. The phone, beside the clock, was within reach, but Janice had no one to call. Janice mustered her strength, reached up, through the pain, and grappled until she was able to drag a pillow and a blanket down to the floor. She covered her head, and lay as still as possible for the next two days.

For the next two days pain stormed around her mind, kicking open and kicking closed doors of semiconsciousness, doors of nightmare. Here, the bomb exploded again and again. There, the banjo pot struck the floor over and over; its strings grated against the bridge and the goatskin head. She lay, chilled and sweating by turns. She smelled bread. Biscuits. No, not just biscuits. Burned biscuits. As a teenager, Janice had lost her sense of smell, and so, even through the pain of the migraine, she was grateful for this olfactory gift. The phone may or may not have rung, several times. And if it had, would it have been anyone but her boss, and would he have made anything more than cursory efforts to find her? She couldn't stand, couldn't eat, couldn't make her way across the floor to the bathroom. Sometimes the sound took shape, becoming an umbral presence moving through the apartment and her sleep. Sometimes it became Private Danks plucking away on the old stringed instrument, furiously chasing, but never catching, rhythm or melody. Sometimes it was nothing more than stampeding, hooves against wooden planks. Still other times, the sound droned without source or form. Janice dreamt of walking, so much walking. She walked through strange landscapes, equally unknown and familiar. Had she been there before? She walked along a narrow channel cut through dark, brown earth, the sides damp, cold and muddy. She walked alone, in and out of dream. It may or may not have rained, in the dream, or outside her apartment. The pin oaks lining the parking lot may or may not have iced over in the night, may or may not have shivered and shucked off their cloaks of ice in the morning sun. Janice didn't know.

Janice knew, in those moments of cognizance, that Private Danks wasn't in the next room. But she didn't know he was dead. That he'd died the instant the bomb exploded, and stayed dead. She didn't know that the bomb had stripped away his insignia, his uniform, along with his skin, that it blew out the cracked molar he'd scheduled an appointment to have capped that very afternoon. In fact, she'd never know about the bomb itself, whether it was an improvised explosive device, or a rocket-propelled grenade, or if it was friendly fire, or even if it had been intended for him in particular. She'd never know whether his death was regarded as banal or heroic by those who witnessed it, or by the others he left behind. She'd never know about the brief and soft shower of blood that fell, and its imperceptible hiss as it seeped into the Iraqi sand. Janice would never know any of these things, because the National Guard was only obligated to contact next of kin. And Janice didn't know Private Danks's next of kin.

Janice lay on the floor and dreamed herself through the migraine. The pain began to diminish, each pulse less debilitating than the last. She was walking, walking along a dug-out path, walking in half light, or less, the world sepia toned. Somewhere in the distance, farther along the channel, a weak light bobbed and swayed. Never getting closer, never farther. Janice, walking somehow just beneath the earth's surface. Afraid to stop or to go back. Afraid the walls might cave in upon her. Upon her, mucking through the shadowy slough.

But the walls of earth didn't fall, and after two long nights the smothering pain began to lift. To rise like fog off the surface of Janice. She was able to open her eyes, to look at the clock on the night table. Almost seven a.m. The early winter morning just barely prying up the dark lid of night. By seven-fifteen, she'd pulled the earplugs from her ears, allowing the potential for sound to rush in. She sat up against the bed. Weak, nauseated, and so dehydrated she felt brittle. But at least the migraine had subsided. Janice didn't know what day of the week she'd woken into, but even in her misery she considered trying to make it to work on time. Two hours in which to stand, bathe, and feed herself seemed barely doable.

At seven-twenty, just as Janice struggled to her knees, her body weary to the marrow, the bomb from so far away and so long ago exploded one more time. The telephone rang.

"Janice . . . Janice Witherspoon."

As if she spoke through cotton batting, the words snagged in her mouth, leaked out messy and damaged.

"What . . . ?"

The words coming in splintered and fell apart.

"What . . . ?"

And that was all.

She didn't even know Private Danks had a brother, and by the time she'd come to terms with that fact, the brother had already told her the boy was dead, that he and their parents were coming down from Virginia, after the body arrived stateside, coming to clean out the apartment, and that they'd appreciate it if she was gone by then.

"What," Janice said, not *why*; but the line was empty.

"Okay," Janice said.

She held the phone to her ear for a while anyway, hanging on the emptiness, knowing intuitively the faint buzz in the line would be more soothing than the silence to follow.

2

After a while, the nausea subsided. A weak equilibrium staked its claim. Janice was able to walk into the living room without holding on to the walls. From the door, she saw no signs of burglary or vandalism. She couldn't bring herself to look behind the Easy-Boy, but the wall where the banjo had hung, bare now but for the faint dust-ghost of the instrument and small dark head of the twenty-penny nail, told her enough. Whatever presence, whatever intruder had come into the apartment nights ago, it must have limited its damage to the instrument and to several days of Janice's life.

Private Danks was dead.

She had to be out of the apartment before his family arrived.

Janice stacked half a dozen saltine crackers neatly in the center of a saucer, poured a glass of juice. She tried to eat some crackers and drink.

How did she get to this point?

Janice asked versions of the question over and over as she cleaned herself up, made the bed, and sifted through the closet looking for clothes that she could bear the weight of. Flayed by the migraine, mauled by the news, her entire body felt raw; her spirit, dull. She moved slowly, deliberately. Outside, the winter morning revealed itself by degrees, as if to see the whole day at once would be unbearable. Janice listened as her neighbors began to stir: the slamming of doors, the heavy footsteps echoing in the concrete stairwells, the cars sputtering out to join the throngs headed to work. To work. Her neighbors? Strangers, all. How did she come to live in that apartment: four boxy, lifeless rooms, in a boxy, lifeless cinderblock building, in the middle of fifteen buildings exactly like it, more than three hundred apartments, all rented, and everyone pretending the exotic theme names of the buildings, the halfhearted landscaping, the shallow overchlorinated pool behind an eight-foot chain-link fence, and the proximity to the beltway made it worth the expense? How? Janice could barely remember *when* she moved in.

How could she live with a man for nearly three years and not know that he had a brother? She knew his parents were still living, and suspected that they didn't like her, but wasn't exactly sure why.

Maybe she'd imagined the call too. Maybe it was a continuation of the migraine-induced nightmares, those images still fresh in her mind. From where she sat, on the high chrome chair at the bar dividing the small kitchen and the living room, Janice could see the other telephone, and its message light blinking like an irrefutable visual metronome. There were nine calls.

How could she be so much a part of a man's life, have him be so much a part of hers, and not cry at the news of his death? The migraine. The migraine must've rendered her numb. She'd cry later, Janice promised herself. For now, it was all she could do to figure out where to go. She'd been too addled by the brother's call—his brusque tone as much as his message—to ask whether he meant for her to just be away while they gathered the dead boy's things, or if he meant she should leave and stay gone. Where to go, in either case? Should she simply go to work for the day?

For a very little while, Janice allowed herself to be angry at the brother and the parents. Who the hell were they to just push her aside? She had rights, too. She had feelings, too. Or did she? Janice tried for a minute to cry about Private Danks. She tried to hold on to her anger at his family. Neither effort worked.

It wasn't that she hated him. But she didn't love him either. Love, like the other hard troublesome emotions, required too much investment, for too little return, the risk of loss so high.

Private Danks was dead.

Janice found it best to just do the days of her life as they came to her, without letting emotion rile things up. Bad spells, she took minute by minute. Janice needed to subdue the noise in her brain, to make some basic decisions about the next couple of days. Years ago, before Private Danks, even before her job at Biggers & Twine Wholesale Foodservice Distributors, she'd succumbed to an infomercial pitch and bought an absurb quantity of fancy yarns, needles of different sizes and styles, and a series of knitting instruction videos. For the next few years Janice was embarrassed by how enthusiastically she embraced the craft. She wouldn't knit in public; not on the bus, nor the bench while waiting for it; not in the park near the duplex where she used to live. For a while, she'd order her patterns and skeins of yarn online, then eventually she braved the trip to Victoria's House of Needle Arts. And hundreds of dropped stitches, and dozens of scarves, shawls, and sweaters later, after she'd endured Private Danks's teasing, after the women at Victoria's started calling her by name, Janice found the rhythmic click of the needles in her fingers, and the constant attention to pattern, to the thing at hand, she found these to be the perfect distraction for any moment, public or private, needing such.

At lunch, while sitting at her desk in the online catalogue division of Biggers & Twine, Janice regularly took out her current knitting project to help ward off the gossipy eyes of the older women in the office, the ones who handled all the packing envelopes and postal materials, and who found Janice too naturally thin and healthy looking, if somewhat aloof and dour, to invite her to join them at the regular diet and wellness seminars hosted by the Human Services office. The project—whatever its color, texture, or sequence of stitches—also kept her somewhat immune to the indifference of the other, younger, hipper girls in the office. Even the webmaster—a surly young man with expressed disdain for anything not "cutting edge"—had seen her knitting, and Janice barely cared.

Private Danks was dead. She'd cry later. For now, Janice needed to think. To sort out her feelings, or their absence. She retrieved the lime-green foam earplugs from the bedroom, pinched one tight and tucked it into her right ear canal, and while the foam expanded, sealing out the sound incrementally, she did the same to her other ear. Janice had bought a supply of earplugs during one of Private Danks's irregular, and always fruitless, attempts to teach himself banjo, an enterprise undertaken without books, tapes, or other instruction. And, seemingly, without any inherent talent. Janice thought it charming the first few times he pulled the instrument down off the wall. Janice didn't know what kind of music was supposed to come from a banjo, but she was damn sure that Private Danks didn't make it.

Quickly, she came to like the feeling of the soft dense foam blocking her hearing. She liked the feeling in both the physical and emotional senses of the word. The bullet-shaped plugs not only blocked out the noises of the thin-walled apartment building, and the sounds of her day at work—the

chattering office women and the incessant clicking of computer key-
boards—but the plugs somehow kept the messy noise of her own mind
from spilling out and taking over. Janice wore her earplugs a lot.

Still weakened from the migraine, Janice had to rest a while and drink
some water before situating the silk brocade knitting bag by the couch,
resting her feet on the coffee table, then fingering the television remote
until she found both a news channel and the mute button. Almost noon.
By now, going to work was out of the question. Should she call? And if she
called, should she call in sick? How would she explain her absence the
past few days? Should she tell them about the headache? Or should she
tell them that Private Danks was dead?

Ideally, she'd be able to sit, watch the silent news broadcast, and finish
the second sleeve of the heavy wool pullover while deciding where to go,
what to do. Janice laid a magazine over the answering machine, covering
the blinking message light completely. One sleeve to go, then she could
graft the pieces of the sweater together. Janice was casting on when the
realization hit. She was making the sweater for him. For Private Danks. As
a gift. As protection from the desert's cold night air. She'd resisted the urge
to buy the richly colored yarn, resisted the fancy cabled patterns, choosing,
for him, the plain, the serviceable, the durable.

There. She almost cried. Janice felt it. Almost.

She set to work on the final sleeve with the same determination that
drove the garment's first stitch, months ago, back before she knew what the
Middle East weather was like, or how long he'd be away.

Who was this boy, killed in a foreign place? Foreign. Janice had no real
idea where Private Danks was. Or where he'd been killed. The more she
thought about it, Janice realized that even before he'd become Private
Danks, even when he was in their windowless bathroom with all those
plastic bottles of cream and wrinkled tubes of ointments scattered over the
sink and cabinet, or when sitting with her at their kitchen table, in their
shared, all-utilities-included apartment, in the middle of North Carolina,
the boy was foreign to her. The fervor and suddenness with which he'd
enlisted in the National Guard was no more or less understandable than
anything else he'd done in their time together. The truth was, most
humans seemed foreign to her. The acceptance of this condition, this per-
meating quality of her life, a truth that had tripped her up for longer than
she could remember, made Janice sadder than the news of Private Danks's
death. In fact, there was something not at all surprising to Janice about his

death. She couldn't put her finger on the reason for her lack of surprise; there was nothing definitive, nothing palpable, but Janice anticipated bad news nonetheless. Like a low-grade fever, a nebulous niggling dread hung just beneath the surface of her consciousness. Hung there regardless of the circumstances. Had always been there. Before Private Danks. And after Private Danks. Had the soldier not been blown to gristle by an anger-forged bomb, had he not enthusiastically signed on the dotted line in the recruiter's office, he would've been hit by a sheet of ice falling from the window of Greensboro's only skyscraper, or he would've choked to death somehow, strapped in the Tilt-a-Whirl at the county fair, or found any other of the unfathomable number of ways to be killed. No surprise to Janice.

She busied her head with stitches. Slips. Crosses. Purls. These were predictable. The rhythmic shhhcck shhhcck, shhhcck shhhcck of the needles comforted. She thought of nothing else. The bobble stitch. The bind off.

Come see me.

What? Janice almost said it aloud.

There was no one there, of course. Janice forced a little smile. It happened often enough, when the needles were working back and forth, in the give and take of yarn, and the soft clicking of wood against wood — she heard things. Sometimes voices. Sometimes pure sound.

Come see me. Come to the body.

It was clearer this time. Clear enough that Janice stopped her hands in midstitch. Clear enough that, through the earplugs, through the silence, Janice felt her heartbeat quicken. Janice closed her eyes, took some deep breaths, and blamed the migraine for the tricks her mind played.

A yogurt commercial on the muted television made her hungry. She'd finish the row, then go to the kitchen and find something that her fragile stomach could tolerate. She needed to eat, and to rest. Janice looked toward the TV, struck up the needles.

Come. Come to the body.

This time, when Janice heard the words, she was looking at the television. Something about the war. Always something about the war. Over the shoulder of the newscaster — always that large toothy smile — in a silent video box, an Associated Press file archive of undated stock footage chronicled the gaping belly of a military transport airplane birthing a succession of flag-draped caskets into the waiting hands of crisply dressed soldiers.

Come to the body.

That's it, Janice thought. I'll go. I'll go to see him arrive home. I'll give him the sweater.

Taking the voice, its decree, as a moment of inspiration coming from inside herself was uncharacteristic—Janice was seldom moved into action without much mulling and stewing—but grabbing hold of the idea and claiming it as her own was easier than speculating about where else the words might have originated.

She'd take the finished sweater to Virginia. Wasn't that where he'd deployed from? Wouldn't he return there as well? She'd be there when the body landed at the airport.

In the hours that followed, other questions pressed upon her. Some relevant, some not. Janice looked over the ziplock bags arranged, in order of size and contents, on her bed. Bras and panties, seven each, packed separately. Seven pairs of socks in neat balls. She'd wear tights, for the chill. She'd wear a pair of corduroys, pack another and some jeans. How could she have come through twenty-seven years of life and be able to pack almost everything that was important to her in one oversized red suitcase—scuffed, dented, and practically as old as she—and a couple of duffel bags? Janice looked around the bedroom once, then again to convince herself. She walked from room to room in the small apartment, and in each the truth was clear. Almost nothing belonged to her, solely to her. She felt rushed. Hurried along by the combined conditions of Private Danks's now irrevocable absence, his family's animosity, and some other unquantifiable, but no less pressing, urge.

Janice had moved in with Private Danks a few months into their relationship, and after a year and a half, after boot camp, after his long absence and even death, the apartment was still very much his. Or, at least, not very much hers.

In the bathroom, Janice packed toiletries and a few cosmetics (not, certainly not, out of vanity) into a single see-through case. She studied her face in the mirror, looking for signs of mourning. Looking for signs of most anything. True, except for her knitting stuff, there were hardly any possessions she cared about. The one exception was a toy tomahawk, which she kept wrapped in a scarf and hidden away. Danks never knew about the tomahawk. Janice never showed it to anyone, and didn't unwrap it when she stuck it carefully in the elastic pocket of her suitcase. As time droned on, Janice had carried fewer and fewer memories of her past with her. She studied that face—its wide, open features awash with freckles, the slight asymmetry of her full lips when she, reluctantly, smiled—and wondered what traits she got from whom. Where the broad nose and the jawline? The hazel eyes, flecked with yellow? And the dark, unruly hair?

Sweaters, of course. Janice packed more than needed, even though she didn't know exactly where she was going, or how long the trip. She spent several minutes deciding between two rayon dresses, chose the one that always made Private Danks whistle. A nightgown and—because motel floors are always cold and dirty—slippers. A couple other just-in-case things. All the knitting supplies, projects, and pattern books, including the welcome-home sweater for the dead boy, filled one of the large duffel bags. Shoes and two pairs of boots in the other duffel.

Janice arranged and rearranged the contents of the suitcase, the task allowing her to ignore or deny the lack of any solid plan for the trip. From the one-sided conversation with his brother, she had a vague idea about where Private Danks's body would land, and when. Janice, without deliberation, and in stark contrast to how she ever did anything, planned to go in that direction.

Her laptop, some of her clothes, and an unopened box in the bedroom closet—a box, taped shut, with *miscellaneous* scribbled on its top (one she'd packed during some move even before the duplex), the contents long forgotten—Janice left behind. Whatever remained when she returned to the apartment, she'd claim for her own. There were no plants to water. No fish to feed. No reason to leave the light on over the sink. Janice locked the door behind her. Because she hadn't fully recovered from two days of not eating or drinking, two days of pain, she wrestled the big red suitcase down the stairs with much effort, each thudding step rattling her teeth and bones. It took three tries to heave it into the rear hatch of her Subaru. Janice dug the scraps of a road atlas from beneath the driver's seat, checked for the Virginia and North Carolina pages.

Friday? Saturday? Janice didn't know for sure what day of the week it was. She'd let the subscription to the paper lapse when Private Danks went to boot camp, and she'd been too fuzzy-headed to pay close attention to the television that morning. While she had no intention of going by Biggers & Twine to explain her absence to the office manager, Janice struggled with her decision not to call. She'd always considered dependability one of her best traits. But she couldn't bring herself to pick up the telephone and call in, or even to listen to the nine messages on the answering machine. The thought of the voices, making sounds, forcing words, her own voice, those of her coworkers or bosses, or anyone else who might have left a message—any one of these seemed unbearable. The migraine. Janice blamed her behavior on the migraine. And the loss. She promised herself to call when she got to wherever it was she was going.

Janice held her breath and turned the key in the Subaru's ignition. But holding her breath didn't prevent the engine backfire that preceded the cranking; not that time, nor any other. A couple months ago the car had started backfiring every time Janice cranked or turned it off. She'd taken to wearing the earplugs whenever driving. The earplugs. She remembered standing them on end, side by side, next to the television remote.

When Janice, leaving the car running, went into the apartment one final time to retrieve the earplugs, the quiet rooms already seemed more foreign. As if, in her nascent absence, some *other* had slipped in and taken up residence. As she stood just inside the doorway, reluctant to move deeper into what used to be her home, a fresh and unfamiliar fear surged through the woman's body. She wasn't wanted in this place. Leaving the door wide open, Janice hurried through the dimly lit hallway and into the living room, where she bent over the arm of the couch to snatch the earplugs from the table. In doing so, she noticed the neck of Private Danks's banjo angling out from behind his recliner. She couldn't tell if or how much it had been damaged in its fall. Janice, without forethought, and with no good reason why, clambered into the tight space, grabbed hold of the instrument up near the peg head, and ran back to her car. She lay it carefully on the back seat. Releasing her grip, she looked at her palm, traced the four evenly spaced lines indented into her flesh by the steel strings.

Rusty Scupper. In the rearview mirror, Janice read, in reverse, the name of her building one final time before shifting the car into gear. Right turn out of the parking lot onto Cockatiel Way, past the combination laundry and gym facility, past the apartment complex office—hurriedly, with her head down and looking away, and trusting that the big red slab of her suit-case went unnoticed—to the first stop sign. Left on Topsail, to the second right on Catamaran. Bear left at the juncture of Orchid Trace, Rumrun-ner Avenue, past the Ketch, past the Yawl, the Trawler, and all the other buildings named for boats. Janice had done it so many times, she could probably find her way out of the labyrinthine tangle of lineless asphalt roads, all with watery, exotic floral or tropical bird names, with her eyes closed.

At the entrance to the apartment complex, Janice let the car idle. She looked over at the sign, COCONEY BAY: AFFORDABLE LUXURY. And despite the misleading, almost silly, name, she found comfort in the sprays and stands of ornamental grasses that rose up, and cascaded down, their winter shades of ocher, around the faux-weathered wooden marquee. *Coconey Bay.* It suggested something tropical. Rum and strange fruits and sunshine. And water. But the entire apartment complex was built around a murky retention pond.

Janice turned right onto Dunyhill Road, toward the beltway. She'd turned right coming out of the apartment complex so many times she wasn't sure what lay in the other direction. Rote. Sameness equaled stability.

It didn't matter that the apartment complex name, the road and building names, promised so much—lives of salty adventure, beauty, modest opulence, and reasonable debauchery—and gave little more than two parking spots per tenant, reliable garbage service, and central air-conditioning instead; Janice liked the forced order of life at the complex. She loved the grasses greeting her at the entrance, equally beautiful in yellows against the sunless winter sky, and in their full spring greens. She loved, expected even, the bank of black-eyed Susans at the rear of the community building every spring, and the beds of poppies throughout the complex, despite the fact that she'd never been able to smell them. She loved, too, the dumb names of the individual buildings, in part because they prevented her, on those tired evenings after work, from wandering into some neighbor's apartment, some stranger's life, and taking up residence. Janice loved where she lived. Loved the façade of exotica, and on those rare occasions when asked, she would answer with a little pride: *Coconey Bay.* So, it was with no small anxiety that she pulled out of the protective confines of the apartment complex that morning, still weakened by a horrible migraine, still in shock over the death of a man who used to be her boyfriend, turning vaguely north, beckoned by an unfamiliar instinct, and unsure when she'd return.

3

The modest Greensboro rush hour must have either run its course or not yet begun, so Janice eased onto the beltway around the city without braking even once. She still didn't know what day it was, nor, with the sun unable to show itself through the hard gray sky, was she sure about the time. Nearly every other day, Monday through Friday, as she drove this same stretch of road, a heaviness would settle into Janice's body and mind. Each mile that she drew closer to Biggers & Twine heaped more and more intangible weight onto her shoulders, and with it a dull roaring, which swelled in her ears. By the time Janice, on any normal day, pulled into the parking garage—promptly at eight-twenty a.m.—she was already tired. The steady stream of cars coming into the garage, the doors opening and slamming shut, the Biggers & Twine employees saying their good mornings, or not; so much noise there, that if Janice didn't have her earplugs in when she parked, they were solidly in place well before the elevator door opened to the fifth floor—where the catalogue division occupied three cluttered and practically windowless rooms in the northeast corner—and they often stayed lodged in her ears until the morning break. Practically windowless, because in the manager's office she could occasionally tell if it was sunny or overcast through the dirt-caked rectangle of frosted safety glass behind his desk. And Janice was fairly certain of the presence of a window or two hidden behind the several faded posters—one a photo of a kitten clinging to a bar by its forelimbs, and dangling over a motivational platitude; three showing carcasses of meat (veal, beef, and pork) segmented into the various cuts offered by Biggers & Twine; and one that she couldn't make any sense of—taped up along one wall.

Despite the drudgery, and the unappealing environment of her work-place, when Janice drove past her normal exit, exit 34, where the ramp passed within feet of the Piedmont Community College billboard, she felt a pang of loss. If in fact she was quitting her job, she'd miss it, miss process-ing the orders, and the dependability of numbers and quantities and sums. A customer has either paid their bill, or they haven't. There were no gray areas.

She'd miss the billboard too, and the fantasy she harbored about return-ing to school one day. Maybe it was the loss of that dream she felt while merging onto the northbound interstate. Janice reached over to the pas-senger seat and traced her finger down the open page of the atlas, but the act did little to quell the unease inside her. Janice had no idea where she was driving to. Other than the Virginia coast, she had no clear destination. Foolish. If she thought too much about what she was doing, thought about how foolish it was to drive to the ocean and wait for a body . . . Janice forced herself not to think about anything other than the straight stretch of pavement tethering her toward a darkening sky. Darkening. She hadn't eaten anything since the crackers and juice earlier that day. Hunger welled up to share her inner space with fatigue, and doubt, and the resid-ual weakness and confusion from the migraine.

Why had she left so late in the day? Why not get one night of sleep before beginning such a journey? She couldn't remember what she'd packed in the suitcase. Less than an hour on the interstate, Janice passed a rest area, thought of pulling off for a nap. But thoughts of sleep brought images from her dreams of the past days—the roar of traffic became surg-ing water, something raked across the banjo's strings, and the sound of hooves stamped over the Subaru's roof. A blaring air-horn brought Janice harshly and immediately back to the moment. She braked hard and swerved to avoid the tractor trailer.

She'd missed the rest area. Couldn't see it in her rearview mirror. Had she fallen asleep? How many miles? The thought of it happening again, of lapsing into sleep at highway speed, terrified her, but the thought of sleep itself, and the possibility of the dreams recurring, scared her more. Janice decided to drive all night, but at the very least, she had the presence of mind to get off at the next exit for a large coffee, and maybe some food.

The beacon of the BP sign rising into the evening drew her off the high-way. Of the two gas stations there, Janice decided the BP was the more effi-cient choice, for its proximity to the exit and easy-off-easy-on layout. Janice took pride in her efficiency. But when she pulled the Subaru to a stop beneath the illuminated green super-awning, and the car backfired, she realized she hadn't spoken to or interacted with another living soul in several days. And there, under the wash of fluorescent light, and in the wake of the ambient high-energy music, with everybody looking her way because of the backfire, Janice couldn't bring herself to get out of the car.

Mercifully, there was no engine noise when she restarted the car. Going against many crucial elements of her nature, Janice crossed several lanes of traffic before whipping into the half-lit, pothole-riddled parking lot of the much less busy CC's Gas & Gro. She parked near the door, put the car in neutral, and yanked up the emergency brake. Janice sat in the idling car. She was more concerned about whether she could form words in her mouth, should she actually have to speak to the clerk, than she was about anyone stealing the Subaru.

"Thank you."

"Thanks."

She practiced some possibilities.

"That's all, thanks."

Except for the irregular clicking of the clerk's pricing gun, the store was quiet. Janice felt suddenly conflicted. She wanted to make her purchases and get out of the store before anyone else came in. Janice reached deep into the front pocket of her corduroys to check for some folded bills, and flushed with embarrassment over her sudden hope for an inadvertent touch from the clerk when the money exchanged hands.

Will you come see the body?

Janice almost dropped the Styrofoam cup of coffee she didn't remember pouring. The hot liquid sloshed into the crook of her thumb. How long had she been standing at the health and hygiene shelf?

"What?" she said, looking toward the cash register.

"I said can I help you find something?"

Janice must've misheard.

The clerk, a girl with skin the color of fresh-cut poplar wood, stood behind the counter tugging the zipper of her CC's smock up and down. Boredom vying with manners in her voice.

"Ummm, no," Janice mumbled, reaching for napkins to mop up the spilled coffee. "I've found what I need."

And to prove the point, she stood and reached out to the eye-level circular wire rack, and took off the closest thing, hoping that it wasn't emblazoned with a Confederate flag. Janice grabbed a candy bar, then stepped up to the narrow clear space in the midst of the displays and advertise- ments cluttering the countertop and placed the coffee, the candy bar, and a plastic vial of aspirin between herself and the clerk. She stared at the nametag pinned over the girl's right breast, worried because she couldn't understand the letters.

"It's Laurel," the girl said, then smiled and winked when Janice looked up.

Once Janice realized the nametag was upside down, she smiled too. The last purchase, the thing she'd taken from the wire rack, Janice laid, with hesitation, on the counter. She didn't look at it and kept it covered with her palm until Laurel cleared her throat. Janice had no idea what she would reveal upon lifting her hand.

It was a key chain, the fob a large safety pin encased in clear acrylic with the words *diaper-head secret weapon* embossed around the edges. Janice didn't understand the message. Laurel, laughing, apparently did.

"That's one of my favorites," she said, putting Janice's things in a bag. "Did you see our bumper stickers?"

Laurel gestured to the red-white-and-blue poster hanging on the wall behind her, and two columns of bumper stickers with messages either pro- American or anti something or other.

These Stripes Don't Run

Going to War Without France Is Like Going Hunting Without Your Accordion

Skin Bin

God Bless America

If I'd known this, I'd have picked my own cotton

Democrats: Making The World Safe For Terrorists

"We got some the boss won't let us keep out in the open," Laurel said. "Want to see them?"

Janice had little time to answer before the girl behind the counter pep- pered her with other questions and proclamations.

"Where you headed, hon? Been on the road long? Lord knows it's cold enough out there."

The girl talked and talked, holding Janice prisoner with a couple of bills, a receipt, and some change that never quite made it across the counter. Janice had little energy for resistance. The girl's litany washed over her, saturated her. Janice tried to keep up, tried to look Laurel in the eye, but couldn't. Instead she focused on the angled shelves beneath the checkout counter where the topics of weight loss, secret sex techniques, war, and movie star gossip weaved a patchwork quilt across the covers of the magazines and newspapers. There, in the top corner of the *Mocksville Standard,* the local paper, a story about a dead soldier captured her attention. His young face, ready and trusting, juxtaposed with the same AP file image of coffins being removed from a military aircraft Janice had seen that very morning.

"Hey, did you see our new CDs? This one here has eleven different bands doing 'Proud To Be An American.' It's great! You should get it for your trip."

And so, bullied by Laurel's enthusiasm, Janice did.

"Stop by again on your way back, hon."

So disconcerted was she by the exchange with the clerk, and by the newspaper article, Janice forgot she'd left the Subaru running. Nor had she seen the other car pull into CC's Gas and Gro—pull, despite the empty parking lot, into the space right beside her car. The lean young man standing between the two cars, one hand on his own roof, the other too near the handle of Janice's passenger door, frightened her.

She paused.

He spoke.

"You play?"

Janice had no idea how to respond. She scrambled into the driver's seat, fumbling with her purchases and with the automatic lock, clicking it several times before truly believing that the man wasn't going to open the door and climb in beside her. She put the car in gear, held tight to the cup of coffee, backed up, crushing the new key chain she'd unknowingly dropped in her haste, then sped out of the parking lot without ever looking back at the man.

"What the hell?"

She might have actually said it aloud. Who was that crazy man? And what did his question mean?

At the turn from the access road to the on-ramp, Janice finally looked out the passenger window, for verification that the lunatic wasn't clinging to her car. No lunatic, but in the hurricane fence separating the weedy CC's property line from the right-of-way, plastic cups—red cups, white cups, and blue cups—were wedged into the wire holes to form something like an American flag.

Five miles up the road, heart still pounding in her throat, Janice realized the boy was asking about the banjo lying across the back seat of her car. In fact, if she remembered correctly, wasn't he wearing some kind of music T-shirt? She reached back, grabbing for the neck of the instrument, wanting to put it on the floor, to avoid another such incident. On second thought, it felt wrong, somehow, to put the banjo behind or under the seats. Janice tried to wriggle and squirm out of her coat, the car weaving back and forth on the highway; afraid of crashing, she reached behind the passenger seat, pulled the nearly complete sweater from her knitting bag, and draped it over the banjo, covering as much as possible.

Janice almost laughed at her misinterpretation. Almost. But she'd rather err on the side of caution than take unnecessary risks. Especially where men were concerned.

Over time, much time, and enough life experience, she'd come to an instinctive distrust of men. Not that Janice had ever been physically harmed or abused, but it seemed that every time she allowed herself to get close to anybody, they would eventually and inevitably go away or die. Always. For better or worse, this way of believing, of living fearfully in the world, was so much a part of Janice's personalia that it dictated her actions at an involuntary level. Men leave.

Private Danks for example.

She still hadn't cried over his death. Janice decided she would try to later, after the coffee kicked in. Janice wished she hadn't forgotten her wristwatch. The LED clock in the Subaru's dashboard never worked.

Driving north into the night, with little traffic to help illuminate her journey, in the confines of that darkness, the confines of her small car, Janice thought about the most recent man to leave her. She wondered if he'd felt that kind of angry patriotism, the self-righteousness of those bumper stickers. She wondered if, in the seconds it took for him to die, his patriotic pride was displaced by fear and doubt. Janice couldn't know, because Private Danks was dead. And they didn't talk about anything substantial when he was alive. Before he'd enlisted, Janice, in her knitted cocoon of work at Biggers & Twine, then at home on the couch, paid little to no attention to the war, or to any other events shaping the larger world. Once Private Danks was in uniform, in the desert, thousands of miles away, her only concession was to watch the news while knitting. With the mute button on, it was impossible to tell if the news anchors were talking about atrocities or miracles.

Janice didn't love Private Danks. Liked him, for the most part, but love felt like too much of a risk. Fortunately for her, in their mutual stasis, they never talked of a future together. Moving in together had happened with no real discussion. With neither hesitation nor enthusiasm. They had no plans. So much so that beyond its immediate effect on her, Janice wasn't likely to question the rightness or wrongness of his death too deeply. Driving through the night, North Carolina flattening itself out on either side of her for miles and empty miles, driving further and further into her fatigue, Janice struggled to remember why they'd been together in the first place. What held them together for nearly three years?

Nothing. She recalled nothing, beyond their first meeting at a mandatory "time management" conference in Atlanta, that explained the longevity of their relationship. He'd sat down beside her in the second-to-last row, arriving late to a seminar on telephone etiquette and efficiency. And, despite her inherent interest in the topic, and historic aversion to men, Janice couldn't keep the boredom at bay, and allowed herself to be distracted by the short, overcologned (even Janice smelled it) fellow who couldn't seem to settle comfortably in the next seat. Not five minutes after arriving, he nudged her leg with his clipboard, pointed at the note scribbled on the legal pad.

Could I look at your conference schedule?

When she inched away and ignored him, the man wrote *Please?* circling the word three times, and then—after Janice reluctantly handed over the information booklet—*Thank you!* with a double underline.

The man must've taken her surrender as an invitation. He continued to write notes to Janice.

What time is it?

Will this torture never end?

I have a cramp in my foot!

I always eat while talking with customers on the phone! Doesn't everyone???

Speaking of eating, when's the break?

He wrote incessantly throughout the seminar, and passed increasingly ridiculous notes. While Janice never offered a single response to him, his persistence paid off. She couldn't remember the last time a man had paid such attention to her. The man wore down her defenses. Janice moved, slowly but decidedly, from wariness, through annoyance, and was butting up against the other side of amusement when he wrote the next note.

Let's sneak out and have lunch.

And in the most spontaneous moment of her life, before or since, Janice said yes.

She felt practically criminal, exhilarated, walking down the sidewalk with this stranger.

"Let's eat here, Janice Witherspoon."

They sat at a picnic table, outside the Big Pig BBQ, and ate pulled pork and coleslaw from paper trays.

"Have another hush puppy, Janice Witherspoon."

Turned out, he worked for Biggers & Twine's competitor, their offices and warehouse pinning down the business on Greensboro's south side.

"Come with me, Janice Witherspoon," he said.

And before she had time to protest about getting back to the seminar, he was already lining up her ball on the first hole of the miniature golf course across the street from the conference center.

"Bounce it off the buoy, Janice Witherspoon."

The man kept calling Janice by her full name at every hole, the scent of his cologne wafting throughout the fake palm trees and the very real stands of pampas grass, the sharp green blades keening with each breeze. Hidden speakers surrounded them with the sounds of garbled birdcalls, waves rolling ashore, and incessantly beach-y music. As she was about to tee off on the surfer-themed ninth hole Janice realized she'd been wearing her conference nametag the entire time.

They were the only players, despite the sunny day. He got more and more excited as they approached the thirty-foot-high concrete and faux basalt volcano that was the eighteenth and final hole.

"Watch what happens, Janice Witherspoon."

Janice didn't know what to expect. But when his orange golf ball, propelled by a confident stroke, charged up the steep green-carpeted ramp, and ricocheted off the bamboo bumper directly into the gaping mouth of the Tiki figure at the top, she followed his gaze to the mouth of the volcano and held her breath. And held her breath. When the insipid flame sputtered out above them, when the audiotaped rumbling ground to a halt and the array of lights flickered once and only once, Janice wished she had more breath to hold.

The pimpled kid handing out putters, balls, and scorecards blamed the power outage on some grackles nesting in the generator housing, and gave Janice and her sullen companion coupons for two free games apiece.

A month later, after the lease on her duplex expired, with more resigna-
tion than trepidation, Janice moved into the one-bedroom apartment at
Coconey Bay, and hung her clothes in the closet beside those of the now-
dead Private Danks. Three years later she passed over the Virginia state
border and the midnight line, the border of day, with no fanfare, unaware
of either, driving toward the body of a boy whose face she couldn't recall.

There must have been something pleasant, or at the very least, satisfying
about those first few months of living together. As she drove deeper into
the neighboring state, bound for the coast—spindly pines and black
swamp water creeping ever closer to the highway—time unhinged itself,
like the jaws of a great serpent, to swallow up past, present, and future all at
once. Janice thought about her relationship with Danks, how its trajectory
had been set in place by the mechanical failure of a fake volcano. Danks:
boyish even in manhood. Janice thought about the boy's childish enthusiasm, how it waxed and waned, bouncing randomly from one focus to the
next. Two months prior to enlisting, he'd obsessed over tournament bass
fishing with the exact same fervor that propelled him through the door of
the recruiter's office. Janice wondered if bass fishing would eventually
have killed him, had Danks stayed with it long enough. Janice tried to list
the things she liked about him, about them together, but in the confines of
her Subaru, in the confines of her memory, she found nothing but sounds.
Early on, she'd come to hate the sounds of Private Danks: his wet, toothy
eating; the bone that cracked in his left foot with every step; the chronic
sinus troubles, and their noisy medications; and, most of all, the banjo.

Had they fought, about the noises or about anything else, the interaction between Janice and Private Danks might have been more fulfilling.
But fighting required an intimacy that neither of them was capable of. Janice resigned herself to a life of intrusive sound, and she had no real idea
what compromises Danks felt he made.

Surface. While Janice had never articulated the thought before, the solitude of the drive, the road all but trafficless, her mind pared down to raw,
reactive instinct by fatigue, shock, and pain—the slow recovery from that
pain, the miles of travel brought her close to an understanding. Until the
past couple of days Janice Witherspoon had always skimmed along the surface of the earth, the world she inhabited, rarely, if ever, penetrating experiences and relationships to any substantial depth. But the intensity with
which she felt Private Danks's death, the subsequent dreams, and the ban-
ishment from her living space was different. New. She still hadn't cried,

but Janice's emotional aquifers had been plumbed to record depths. And she knew, beyond certainty and without knowing how, that a nascent energy quaking her life to its core had taken root.

Janice shuddered in the driver's seat, and toppled the nearly empty Styrofoam coffee cup cradled between her legs. She thought she'd drunk all but a few sips, but the tepid black liquid seeped beneath and dampened her thighs, wicked up by the corduroy. The Subaru swerved into the passing lane; the semi charging up to pass flicked its headlights, and the air horn sounded out the full Doppler effect as the truck passed.

Janice pulled onto the shoulder, jabbed at the switch for the emergency blinkers. It was all she could do to keep her eyes open, despite the caffeine and the snacks. How long had she been awake? Janice couldn't remember. Outside the car, the night segmented by window glass, Virginia looked exactly like North Carolina in the dark, and she had no way to tell where she was in the state. She had a cell phone in her purse, but the battery was probably dead. Even if it were fully charged, who would she call? The State Patrol wasn't likely to come rescue a woman from her tiredness. The cell phone's Contacts list consisted of the knit shop, the dry cleaners, her work numbers, and Private Danks's number before he'd left the country. No friends that she could call up and talk with to stay awake. No friends to tell that she was worried about getting lost. No family to help her deal with seeing Private Danks's coffin. She'd spoken with him twice during boot camp, and two, maybe three, times during the few months of his deployment; with each call the distance between them compounded. And now, en route to see him—his lifeless remains—one final time, she feared for her own life. Afraid that she'd fall asleep at the wheel and plummet off the road, or plow into oncoming traffic, Janice toggled the window down, sucked in the winter air, and eased back onto the highway.

By the time she pulled beneath the overhang where the two larger-than-life Civil War soldier replicas stood guard at the front door of the Manassas Bull Run Motor-Lodge, Janice was so cold she couldn't feel her fingers or her face. The Subaru engine dieseled, continued to sputter and cough, even after she'd removed the key from the ignition, and didn't completely stop until Janice stepped up to the motel door. The combined sounds of the engine backfire that rattled the safety glass as she stepped through the doors and the automatically triggered sensor that played "Dixie" whenever anyone entered the lobby disturbed a small and very skittish Indian man who flew out from a back room clutching, in long thin fingers, a pepper-spray canister sheathed in leather. From it dangled a ring of keys. His glance darted around the lobby, empty but for Janice, and when it finally settled on her face, he didn't lessen the grip on the self-defense weapon.

Neither of them spoke, until Janice began backing up against the door.

Are you coming to see the bodies?

When he said it, a bolt of fear ran the length of Janice's body, nailed her to the worn-carpeted floor.

"I say, would you like a room, please?"

"Oh," Janice said, slumping a little.

"Excuse me?" the desk clerk said, finally putting the keys and the pepper spray on the counter.

Distrusting both her ears and the sluggish tongue in her numb face, Janice nodded and reached her wallet up to the chest-high surface. The clerk spent several minutes flitting, sparrowlike, between Janice, a filing cabinet, and a photocopier. Over his head, Janice saw into the back room, dark but for the flickering of a television somewhere out of sight. The erratic pattern of blue-gray light playing across a bare wall threatened to rekindle her migraine. Janice closed her eyes. Although he didn't seem to ask enough questions, after they'd worked out the details, after the requisite signatures, he handed her a key. But when she started to go he spoke again.

"One moment, please."

The voice a potential hurdy-gurdy of sound. She had the fleeting hope that the nervous brown man wanted to make conversation. Maybe ask about her drive, where she was headed. Anything. Janice readied herself to answer any question.

When she looked up, the man was holding something out toward her.

"Complimentary," he said.

Reluctantly, Janice reached out to accept the offering.

A bullet. A ceramic bullet, dirty white, ringed, drilled through, and tied with a piece of ribbon to a small card that on one side identified it as the bullet of choice for the Confederate musket. The other side of the card welcomed guests to the Manassas Bull Run Motor-Lodge.

"Thank you very much continental breakfast in the lobby from six until ten-thirty have a pleasant evening enjoy your stay," the man sang, then returned to his dark nest before Janice had even turned to leave.

At least she didn't have to worry about him seeing the coffee stain on the back of her pant legs.

It didn't occur to Janice until after dragging her luggage in, closing the door of room 19, on the backside of the motel's second floor, and turning the deadbolt, that she should have asked the desk clerk for a room closer to the office, and on the first floor. Something less isolated. Too, she wanted to know how far she was from the coast. While going all the way back down the stairs and around the building seemed impossible, given her weary condition, Janice wanted a more human interaction than the telephone could offer. But after moving her suitcase onto the folding stand crammed between the bed and the night table, she saw the clock: 2:30 a.m. The room would have to do, and her other questions could wait until daylight.

The room was small and boxy, as perfunctory as possible within the generous limits of the Civil War theme décor. The front door and the broad expanse of the window that consumed the rest of the wall stood opposite an unadorned bathroom mirror nearly as large as the window. There seemed to be no escape from either inspection or introspection. Janice had no real choice but to look at her own tired pale reflection, barely recognizing the face in the mirror. Sleep. She needed sleep. Whatever Janice was headed toward would still be there when she awoke.

In her nervous haste Janice dropped the Do Not Disturb sign twice before hanging it in place on the exterior doorknob. The absence of any other cars in the parking lot comforted little. She checked and rechecked the locks. The heavy curtains gaped open several inches no matter how many times Janice tugged on the double pulley cord, and wouldn't stay closed until she propped a lamp against them and the window. She didn't bother unpacking, and by the time Janice got out of the damp pants and washed her legs with the coarse and overly bleached cloth folded neatly by the sink, she was too worked up over the possibility, real or not, of intruders to sleep. In an effort to dispel the unsettling feeling that the *intruder* was already there with her, Janice looked under the bed twice, and in the cramped shower stall she'd just stepped out of, before curling up under the stifling fabric of the bedspread, her mind hurtling through the unmappable terrain of fear. Calm. How to find a place of calm?

She'd find calm where it always dwelt. Janice got up and arranged her knitting bag on the floor beside the bed. Laid the needles and the last sleeve of Private Danks's sweater on the pillow while she dug the earplugs from her coat pocket, squeezed them into place. In no time at all, Janice Witherspoon stitched herself into sleep.

4

Three little darkies lying in bed
Two was sick an' the other 'most dead.
Send for the doctor, the doctor said,
"Feed dose darkies on short'nin' bread!"

Mammy's little baby loves short'nin', short'nin',
Mammy's little baby loves short'nin' bread.

Slip to de kitchen, slip up de lid,
Slip ma pockets full of short'nin' bread.
Stole de skillet, stole de lid,
Stole de gal to make short'nin' bread.

Mammy's little baby loves short'nin', short'nin',
Mammy's little baby loves short'nin' bread.

Dey caught me wi' de skillet, dey caught me wi' de lid,
Caught me wi' de gal makin' short'nin' bread.
Six dollars fo' de skillet, paid six dollars fo' de lid,
Spent six months in jail eatin' short'nin' bread.

5

And slept for twenty-nine straight hours.

The bomb that changed Janice's life when it exploded in the desert also knocked her circadian rhythms completely out of whack. The body lost its reference point in the time frame. Fortunately, if Janice dreamt anything at all in that span of hours, she remembered nothing. No dreams of hoofbeats, or surging water. No endless paths through dredged earth. No screaming. And no dreams of Private Danks.

Janice slept through the first tentative knock by the housekeeper, a woman—darker and smaller than her counterpart at the front desk—who practically hid behind the overflowing cart of bedding and cleaning products while she tapped on the door. A whole day passed behind the Do Not Disturb sign, and the hotel staff fully expected a dead guest when they opened up room 19. It'd happened more than once at the Manassas Bull Run Motor-Lodge, and when the clerk told everyone how sickly the freckled American girl looked when she checked in, there was little doubt she'd died.

Nevertheless, when the shift manager stood behind the maintenance man and urged him to slip the special tool into the gap of the open door and lift the security chain from its position, which he did so carefully and quietly, they all held their breaths.

When Janice screamed and yanked the twisted covers over her bare legs, they all let their breaths loose in a barrage of Hindi and Urdu and pidgin English, the cacophony penetrating her earplugs. Everyone but the manager scurried out of the room. And once they'd come to terms with a couple of things—that Janice was in fact a living guest who intended to

rise up and pay her bill, that this pecan-colored man was not a rapist nor
killer, a source or continuation of the horrible thing that stormed around
her head all those days ago—the manager offered to get Janice some of the
food left over from the morning's complimentary breakfast.

Ravenous. Janice, wide awake and relatively calm, was hungrier than
she'd ever been in her life. And with that hunger came clarity. Lying there,
beneath the covers, the unfinished sweater bunched on the floor where it
fell, the relieved motel staff gone back to their duties, the afternoon sun, a
winter sun, leaking into the room around the curtain's edges, Janice realized the absurdity of her situation. She'd left her apartment in Greensboro
with no notion of when she'd return. She had no idea what Private Danks's
family planned to do with all the stuff. Even if the boss at Biggers & Twine
allowed for all her unused sick days and vacation, he'd probably fire her.
She'd packed her car and driven away, driven into the night. Beyond the
Virginia coast and some idea of a military plane full of coffins, Janice had
no real destination.

She packed. She packed her bullet. But, without too much forethought,
she retrieved her needles and left the unfinished sweater and the unused
yarn wadded in a loose ball in the drawer on top of the Gideon bible. Not
able to deal with the likelihood of a backfire just yet, she loaded her few
bags into the Subaru, then walked around to the lobby. As she checked
out, the manager spoke to the other clerk in his native tongue. The woman
disappeared into the back room, and when Janice signed her bill the manager gestured over her shoulder.

"Help yourself, please."

It was during the second blueberry muffin that Janice decided to quit.
To stop heading east, toward some improbable reunion with the dead soldier. She ate Raisin Bran from a small box that became a bowl when
opened just right, which she did but there was no milk and because the·
hotel staff seemed a little apprehensive about her, Janice didn't ask for any.
She ate the cereal dry, with her fingers. She picked sticky tidbits from a
cup of fruit cocktail, leaving the pears, tried to tune out the game show
blaring from a TV console, and tried to figure out where to go next. Hadn't
come up with anything by the time she went back to the kitchenette to get
salt and pepper for the boiled eggs. And wouldn't have seen the little display stand for the Natural Bridge brochure had she not knocked it over
reaching for the shakers. Janice took the glossy ad back to her table and
read it over while she ate. She couldn't go directly back to Greensboro.

The Virginia Natural Bridge was only a few hours away, due west. And the *Drama of Creation Sound and Light Show* projected onto the rock face nightly promised to be "spectacular."

The change in plans felt right. As if the decision were made for her. Climbing into the car, Janice saw the undraped banjo on the back seat, had the brief impulse to leave it lying in the parking lot. But even though she meant the trip to be the end, both symbolic and literal, of her connection to Private Danks, abandoning his banjo seemed too extreme. She was, inexplicably, moved by its mere potential for music.

After two days of sitting unused in the parking lot, the Subaru cranked without backfiring. Janice opened the road atlas for a cursory look, then drove into a gray afternoon where, after so much time but not so many miles, she, at last, cried. She cried over Private Danks. His death, as well as the lifeless years they spent together. Janice cried because, at twenty-seven years old, she had no real friends to help her through this crisis. Janice cried because she didn't understand how she'd gotten to this lonely point. For the past several days *destinations* had been enough of a distraction. Life was about leaving one *place* and going to another *place*. Now, for whatever reasons, the destination of the Natural Bridge, one of the seven wonders of the world, held some promise, however vague.

Open once and for all, the sluice gate of her sorrow poured forth. It was as if her body purged itself of a lifetime of hoarded tears. Janice cried and drove, and drove and cried. Given the opportunity, the body always seeks balance. Janice Witherspoon's body was coming back to plumb. Level. Janice went so fully into her sadness that she stopped paying attention to the road signs. She'd missed a key junction, taken an unintended off-ramp. Realized her mistake only as the lanes of traffic funneled into the single open tollbooth at the entrance to the Pennsylvania Turnpike. With no clear way to turn back, Janice took her ticket from the automatic vendor, waited for the green light, chose her lane and sped toward it.

Truth was, she'd never felt at home in Greensboro anyway. Like so many towns and small cities in the South, Greensboro's history—its past, present, and foreseeable future—was shaped by the insidious politics and business practices of the textile industry. The well-tended machine of social stratification spat out generations of mill-hill workers, all with slippery "good" manners and no sense of self-worth. Janice's lack of confidence had different origins. She wasn't a native. But the idea of giving up her home, however tenuous the label, frightened Janice. She wanted to go to the Natural Bridge. To see the hundred-million-year-old wonder. To cross it, if possible. The turnpike took her in the right direction; she hoped the setback was brief.

Janice stopped crying. Or, more likely, cried herself out. She figured it to be midday. Her idea was to drive west for a couple of hours, then head back down into Virginia. If she could just get to the Natural Bridge, to rest, to think, and gather her wits. From there, the future would surely be more clear. Janice pulled the folded brochure from her purse and positioned it where she could see the road over the top as she read.

Two hundred fifteen feet tall.
Ninety feet wide.
During the night pageant the mountainside becomes a vast stage . . .
Scenes move and change with the mood of gripping music in a
    spectacle which takes onlookers back into the eternal ages.

As the Pennsylvania landscape became mountainous, the turnpike hemming her in tighter and tighter as it cut through the stone, Janice read how, historically, visitors to the bridge could be lowered from the top in a steel cage while, on the crag above, a violinist played. The first time the horn blared from the next lane, Janice thought she'd veered across the centerline. She tucked the brochure between the seats and held tight to the wheel. The highway had narrowed. On either side the mountains encroached, squeezing the four lanes—separated by nothing more than a string of concrete dividers—impossibly close together.

The second time she heard the horn, Janice knew it must've been intended for someone else. She checked her mirrors. She wished the lanes would widen. She wished the curves weren't so sharp. She wished the traffic would slow down. Finally, the third time the horn blew right beside her, Janice looked out the window at the converted U-Haul panel truck in the passing lane, which was keeping an even pace with her car. And her looking was encouragement enough for the three young men in the cab of the truck. The driver, whom she couldn't see, began tapping out insistent rhythms on the horn.

The turnpike's bare stone faces, sheared flat decades ago by unrelenting machinery, climbed into the sky on her right, glared down upon all that passed, and regularly littered the narrow shoulder with shards of rock, some the size of her car. In the rearview mirror, an irregular line of traffic stretched out behind her. Janice sped up a little to see if the truck would drop back. But the boys took it as a challenge. When the boxy truck pulled alongside, then ahead by half a length, she saw the ghost of the U-Haul logo, muted but visible, through the slapdash paint job advertising HOLY SMOKES: BBQ AND BLUEGRASS EXTRAVAGANZA. The crude rendering of a pig dancing over a fire while three cartoonish men, barefoot and wearing overalls, played instruments told Janice enough. They must've seen the banjo in the back seat.

Janice tried slowing down. She wanted nothing to do with the truck or its contents. But the truck decelerated as well. She wished she'd left the banjo at the motel. Maybe she'd chuck it into the trash at the next rest stop. Until then, all she could do was drive and try to ignore the idiots in the truck. But that too became impossible when the two passengers, both bearded and grinning, hung insanely far out of the open window, and waved down at Janice, who'd never seen anyone die and felt sure she was about to. The two jockeyed for position, elbowing each other, pounding on the door, and yelling things Janice didn't understand.

"Hey baby, can I see your clawhammer?"

"How 'bout that three-finger style?"

Hurtling along the Pennsylvania Turnpike, through the gray afternoon, through the tight deep shadows cast by mountain and massive stones, Janice felt trapped. Together, the Subaru and truck rounded a sweeping curve and began moving up a steady incline. The men hooted, they whistled. Janice heard them even through closed windows, wished she hadn't forgotten the earplugs. The road steepend, and as they climbed, both vehicles slowed. Janice eyed her gas gauge with concern, then stared out over the hood, refusing to look any other direction until something caught her vision on the right. What were those irregular bursts of white dotting the dark rock walls along the highway? Ice. Spring-fed from deep within the mountain, or rain runoff from above, trickling through tight crevices, along rivulets in the earth, spilling or dribbling out from splits in the rocks. When the water met the cold winter air it solidified. And as more water escaped from the warmer ground, the ice began to build and drape itself over the rocks. Although she knew it couldn't be possible, Janice felt surely that the encroaching ice and rocks were reaching out to catch her. To consume her. Janice, in her Subaru, struggling in the cold thin air to climb, could not escape the flow she was caught up in. The stupid men, in their stupid truck, unrelenting in pursuit, the highway itself, everything in the world seemed to be squeezing her tighter and tighter.

The Subaru sputtered, stalled, then backfired, but didn't stop. Why hadn't she filled the gas tank earlier? Janice twisted the knob for her wind-shield wipers. Swore at the sudden rain. But, wait. Rain doesn't come at you from the side. How could she not have looked to see the man hanging so far out of the truck window that he could have climbed into Janice's, hanging there by one thin arm, and in the other hand clutching a squirt gun aimed at the Subaru.

She slapped frantically at the door lock. She heard them laughing. From behind, horns blared as the other drivers struggled around them in the passing lanes. Then the man changed tactics. He put away the water gun and began pounding on his door and gesturing between Janice's car and the high panel side of the truck, pausing the action occasionally to lift the hem of his T-shirt over his pale belly. When they crested the hill, the truck eased ahead of Janice just far enough for her to see what the man had been pointing at. She hadn't seen the sign duct-taped to the truck when it passed her miles back. Was too focused on the gaudy childish scene painted over the U-Haul logo to notice the cardboard with its message, its plea, scribbled in black marker.

Attention All Ladies:
We're A Poor Tired Band Of Merry Men
On The Road Two Months Already
With Three Months And Thousands Of Miles To Go.
Help Us Make It To The End.
Show Us Your Boobs!

Beneath the sign, on the metal siding of the truck itself, tick marks, in increments of fives, kept a running tally of responders. Five. Ten. Elven, twelve, and thirteen. Janice looked from the sign to the man protruding from the truck window only because she was so baffled by the whole expe-rience, she didn't know what else to do. He knew she'd read the request; the look in his eyes said so. She knew, from that same look, what he wanted. Lunatic. Janice was afraid of even normal men or boys in groups. Lunatics terrified her. And this particular lunatic seemed about to climb out of his moving vehicle and into Janice's window. She knew it. She couldn't stop him. The glass wouldn't stop him. Nothing would stop him from getting what he wanted. Nothing, except the siren that began whipping the air behind them.

Janice watched the truck pull onto the shoulder of the road, saw the trooper's headlights and flashers chopping furiously in her rearview mirror. A mile and a half later, at a random, unfamiliar exit, Janice, having had enough turnpike for the time being, and hoping to find a gas station soon, veered right. The exit ramp narrowed quickly from two lanes to one, looping around an outcropping of graffiti-scarred rocks. What did that say? Something about *bodies*? Janice passed by too quickly to read. She slowed, the vibration of the rumble strips chattering her teeth, and headed into the narrow covered passage at the single toll collector's booth, stopping short to fish the ticket from between the seats. Janice was so grateful to have escaped the fools in the truck she almost said a prayer of thanks. But who would she pray to? If the toll collector looked friendly enough, she'd tell them what just happened. There wasn't another car anywhere in sight; maybe Janice could tell the whole story.

She found her ticket, dug the wallet from her purse, and put the car into drive. She hadn't noticed the Have You Seen Me poster adorning the visible wall of the booth. The smiling child, in grainy black-and-white, had been missing since September 8, 2004. Her name was Samantha. She was last seen wearing a God Loves Me T-shirt. She is ten years old. She blinked at Janice.

The little girl's mouth gaped, closed, gaped, closed, and she blinked at Janice.

Janice shut her own eyes tight, crumpled the toll ticket in her hand.

Breathe. Just breathe. Hunger and fatigue and duress, all these things can affect the mind.

Janice had to move. She couldn't sit at the tollgate all day. Her jack-in-the-box heart sprung and sprung and sprung. Janice clutched the steering wheel. If, when she opened her eyes, the face on the poster still moved as if alive, Janice planned to drive through the gate as fast as her dilapidated Subaru would go. Without paying. She revved the engine, took a deep breath, and looked. Right into the two-dimensional lifeless eyes of a poorly rendered photograph.

Janice pulled up to the window. Awash in soot from engine exhaust, and tinted against the sun, the tollbooth windows were nearly impossible to see through. Janice couldn't tell anything about who was inside. She wanted only to pay her toll, find the way to the Natural Bridge, and decide what to do with her life. Up ahead, the mountains stepped back from the pavement, fell away in places. The world widened just a little. Up ahead, she'd catch her breath. She just needed to get through the tollgate. She'd sit for one more minute, and only one. If the attendant didn't open up, Janice would blow the horn once. If that got no response, Janice, both numbed and irrational, wracked by life, swore she'd break the orange gate from its hinge. She traced a tentative finger around the embossed black horn panel, and tried not to look back over her shoulder. She sat through her signifying minute and was halfway into a second, without putting any pressure on the horn, when the tollbooth window whooshed open.

Janice hoped the transaction would go quickly. But the current of air that spilled from the tollbooth window down into the car was so cold and damp she felt like she could drown in it. Sounds of rushing traffic, even though there were no other cars around, or was it water? and the smell — wet, mossy, surely the smells of a thing submerged for years. From the dim shadows of the booth's interior, a figure leaned into view. A woman, eyes sunken, loose in their sockets. Thin. Flesh soft and sallow on its bones. Its bones and flesh clothed in coarse brown fabric. Wet, dripping, even. Some type of uniform, maybe. Her matted hair dripping as well. Janice thrust the ticket toward the woman, meaning to drop it quickly on the narrow stainless-steel counter, but the toll collector moved faster. Before Janice could pull her arm back, the woman had her tightly by the wrist. The left wrist.

She screamed. No, she meant to scream, but sound refused the charge. Janice pulled against the woman's grip, to no avail. The woman pulled against Janice, would have lifted her from the seat if not for the belts across her chest and lap. No matter how hard Janice yanked, she could not break free of the woman's hold. She'd had no expectations before pulling up to the tollbooth. And now, she expected to die there. To pay for this increasingly absurd journey with her very life. When Janice's body resisted, held back by both fear and straps, the toll collector leaned out of the narrow window. Bending at the waist, bending at the neck — both angles so extreme — until her damp face was only inches from Janice's; the water dripping from the woman's hair and clothing — so, so cold — trickled down Janice's arm, spilled into her lap.

Janice's quick breaths contrasted with the woman's labored inhale, exhale, each suck of air wet and constrained. Each sour breath washing over Janice, who couldn't move, couldn't find enough air for her own hot lungs. When Janice looked into the eyes, so close, readying herself for this strange death, she didn't expect the tenderness found there. Not malice. Not evil. Rather, a pleading. A wanting. A sadness. And a deep familiarity. Janice saw reflections of herself, past, present, maybe future—if the future can be reflected—but she lost track of time in all of its permutations, and when she, at last, returned to awareness, still in her car, still held in the toll collector's grip, the fear had subsided a little.

The woman was speaking to Janice. Hissing, softly, the same words over and over.

"Soon, sweet girl. Soon."

"Soon."

And while Janice's fear of the woman—fear of the moment—lessened, comfort did not take its place. She wanted to be released. She wanted this wet cold face away. She didn't want to hear what the woman said. And when the woman turned Janice's wrist up, the toll collector's ragged sleeve slid along a pale forearm to reveal a crude tattoo, no, three raised and ragged welts—///—crossing over the tendons and veins of her own wrist like a brand, and fear came storming back.

And when the toll collector drew Janice's trembling limb in close, pressed with her bloodless thumb-tip, the ragged nail digging and twisting into the thin white flesh of Janice's wrist—the move deliberate and precise, as if drawing with her nail—then whispered again, *Soon, sweet girl,* and let go, something surged between them; something from that touch coursed through Janice's veins. Janice drew back her numb arm, frantically stabbed at the window switch. The toll collector stood erect, eased back into the shadows of the booth, its window hissing shut. The mechanical gate, a thin orange board, rose partway, fell with a bounce, rose partway, fell again, then climbed slowly to vertical. Janice sped away.

At the bottom of the exit ramp, the highway abutted, unceremoniously, a rural two-lane road. Janice could go either right or left. She sat, idling, at the stop sign. Surely, she must've imagined what just happened. It wasn't real. It couldn't be real. But when Janice saw the damp circle spreading out on her pants leg, when she looked at her wrist where the woman had touched her so intentionally, when she saw the bruise there—the size of a thumbprint, the shape almost familiar, the wound throbbing—Janice suddenly had to vomit, and barely got the door opened and seat belt unbuckled in time.

Janice leaned against the Subaru's rear wheel, head on her knees.

Careening. Literally. Metaphorically. She had no idea how to stop. Anything. No idea what to do next. No idea what the woman meant by *Soon*. Was there some grand conspiracy against her? Karmic retribution for things she'd done in past lives? Janice refused to give up her goal of the Natural Bridge, but she'd had enough of interstate highway travel. It was afternoon. The sun lay to the left, propped like a milk-glass saucer on the shelf of an unslakable gray sky. Janice turned toward it.

Drove into the wide mountainous belly of rural Pennsylvania, where the landscape crunched up and up into laurel-covered crags for miles, then lay flat and grassy for still more miles. The physical world she drove through mirrored the emotional terrain she'd traversed since the news of Private Danks's death. Janice drove through the empty countryside, watching the needle of her gas gauge fall until it lay against the pin by the foreboding E. She'd passed nothing but farmhouses and the occasional group of two, three, or four small dilapidated homes clumped in a tight hollow, always too close to the road, and empty fields, and abandoned farm machinery. Janice didn't want to deal with any more strangers that day. But if she ran out of gas, there'd be no choice but to knock on one of those unwelcoming doors. Surely she'd have to pass a store soon; even reclusive hicks need gas for their cars and tractors.

In the distance, on a short straightaway, Janice saw what she hoped was an intersection, and maybe a store. But when she pulled up, and the big orange sign warned her that the Dumb Hundred Road Bridge was closed for repairs, the detour arrows stabbed left, down Knob's Furnace, where as before, the earth crowded up against the twisting and turning road. She followed directional arrows through several more turns, onto increasingly less maintained roads, losing any sense of orientation. The warning light blinked its gas-pump shape from the instrument panel. With each mile that passed, turning around made more sense, but became less likely. Good common sense is often scarce in times of crisis. The stretch of road she drove kinked and knotted back and forth through dense woods; turning around on the blind curves was too dangerous. Janice looked for a turnoff, a dirt road, anyplace to safely change direction. But the Borough of Gesseytown sign came first. And just past it, the dirt parking lot for Chunk's Market.

Janice pulled up to the two ancient gas pumps standing on a concrete island directly in front of the door to the windowless building. Where the windows must have been once, painted plywood advertised weekly specials. A fat rusty signpost stood high between the pumps, a yellow marquee aimed at passing traffic and missing several black letters. As best Janice could tell, it read, HOME OF THE WINKY DINK. PRAISE THE LORD! A different day, she might've smiled. She didn't really expect the old pumps to take charge cards, but when there were no Visa or MasterCard icons on the door, Janice got worried. One thing she'd forgotten was to get cash. Aside from a pickup truck and a car with no windshield parked at the side of the building, the Subaru was the only vehicle in the lot.

Janice got out and locked the doors. Because she had no other choice, she went into the store, not meaning to let the storm door slam shut behind her.

"Sorry," she said, to anyone who might be listening. Not wanting to rile either the Winky Dink or the Lord.

"Don't worry about it, honey."

Inside the windowless store, fluorescent light fixtures ran, front to back, the length of the low ceilings. Janice could see over the tops of the wide, open shelves—the sparsely stocked merchandise washed free of shadows and much color by the sterile lighting—could see to the checkout counter dead center on the rear wall, could see the woman by the register look up from her magazine and smile.

"That old door's been slamming shut since before me and you was born."

From the entrance it was impossible to tell her age. Once standing directly across from the soft round woman, Janice still doubted she could guess within a decade.

"I can't stand the way he treats her," the woman said, closing the glossy cover of a *People* magazine, and lining it up neatly atop an *Us* magazine. "It's sinful."

Janice smiled awkwardly.

"Do you take charge cards?"

The woman sipped a red beverage from a straw in a cup bigger than any cup Janice had ever seen.

"Well, yes and no," she said. "We do when our machine works, but it's been busted for the past few days."

Janice fingered the bill compartment in her wallet. Not enough there to fill the tank and get something to eat. She was suddenly so hungry.

"Is there an ATM?"

"Lord no!" the woman laughed. "We do have a dinosaur of a Xerox machine over yonder. Maybe you can run off a few copies of your twenties."

The woman thought this very funny.

Janice was, at least, relieved that the clerk seemed relatively normal. Safe.

"Could I use your restroom, please?" she asked.

"Sure thing, honey. It's over there, just past the ice-cream cooler."

The woman opened her magazine and buried herself in a story even before Janice had turned around. Down a narrow hallway, and across from a tile mop basin that stank of bleach and sour water, the door to the single bathroom stood open. And wouldn't close completely once Janice was inside. Even if the door did close, there was no lock, nor bolt, nor even hook to hold it shut. No matter. Who else would come in?

Who else? The boys in the converted U-Haul truck. Janice suspected them, sensed them, even before the storm door slammed shut. One of them mentioned "girl" and "banjo" and "cop" in the same sentence and they all started laughing. Janice sat on the cold cement floor, her back to the metal door, and jammed her feet against the base of the toilet. She put her fingers in her ears, and waited. And waited. Wanting to cry. Wanting to keep quiet. Eventually, inevitably, someone jiggled the doorknob, pushed against the door itself. Janice braced herself, ready for the force. But none came. They were all there. Even with her ears plugged, she could hear the three different voices, their laughter, their cooing to her through the thin metal. With one final halfhearted shove against the door, the men just left. They left her alone, and after some playful rowdiness with the cashier, they left the store as well. Janice stayed in the bathroom. Stayed until the cashier waddled back and tapped softly on the door.

"You all right, honey?"

"Yes," Janice said, without standing up.

"Your friends paid for your gas," the woman said. "They pumped your tank full. Bought you a couple Winky Dinks too."

"They did?" Janice said, then more to herself, "Why?"

"I couldn't say, sweetie," the woman answered. "I can't even figure out the boys I know."

"I'll be out in a minute," Janice said.

Maybe the boys in the truck were just that. Harmless boys. She tugged her sleeve down over the nearly gone bite-mark. Maybe all the weirdness of the past few days was random, and not the predestined path into hell that it seemed like at the moment. Janice missed her apartment. Missed her job. Even missed Greensboro. She wanted to be somewhere still and quiet, full of predictables, and away from this life of strange commerce.

Janice gathered her wits as best she could, and left the bathroom.

The sandwiches of thick dark cookies with too much white frosting globbed between them, wrapped obscenely tight in cellophane, must be the Winky Dinks. Everything else that lay by the register—a bottle of water, a stick of beef jerky, a foil pack of aspirin, a glow-in-the-dark condom—Janice could identify.

"How much do I owe you?" Janice said, reaching out with a handful of bills.

The woman took Janice's hand, put her finger on the bruise at Janice's wrist.

"Wow," she said. "I thought that was a tattoo of a bird . . . You don't owe me nothing, honey. I told you, your friends took care of everything."

The woman released Janice's arm and pushed a small brown bag across the counter and smiled.

Janice paused at the door, feeling like she needed to clarify things. Like she needed to ask more questions. To ask for help.

"If you're in the neighborhood," the woman said. "Come by the Church of the Brethren Fellowship Hall next Friday night for chicken and dumplings."

Janice wanted to yell at this woman, to let her know in no uncertain terms how far away from this place she planned to be by next Friday.

"There's a map tacked up to the bulletin board right by the door. And a phone number too."

Janice held tight to the doorknob, the bruise throbbing at her wrist, and scanned the peeling corkboard. Found the map, obscured by a Free Puppies sign, and a note scrawled on a scrap of yellow paper advertising *House for Rent—Sabbath Rest Road.* She left the store without replying, carelessly pushed Danks's banjo onto the floorboard of her car, threw her coat on top of the instrument, at once striking and muffling the discordant notes, then climbed into the driver's seat.

Janice traced her finger lightly around the spot on her wrist. Saw no discernible shape, no matter what the clerk said. No bird. Only a purplish bruise. But the fact of the clerk's notice, it meant, didn't it, that Janice hadn't imagined the encounter at the tollbooth. There, at her wrist, throbbing proof that something had happened.

She opened the atlas across her lap and tried to find herself among the jumble of black and blue lines. No luck. The atlas contained only the major county and state roads. She couldn't concentrate anyway. But with a full tank of gas, even gas bought for her by those lunatics, Janice knew she had more choices. To continue on toward Gesseytown—or whatever the town's name—while the right direction, meant possibly encountering those men in the truck. Janice wouldn't risk it. The thought of finding her way back through the detour to the turnpike also filled her with dread. Maybe, if she went back toward the highway, there'd be a road she overlooked. She could find a motel, rest for the night, plan her life.

How hard could it be? She was in Pennsylvania, for God's sake. Not the Dakotas. Civilization couldn't be that far away. Janice looked for the sun, but the gray sky denied her. When the Subaru backfired, Janice hit the gas too quickly, too firmly. The back end of the car whipped around in the gravel, spraying rocks across the storefront. Any other time, she'd go back in and apologize. This time, she drove on down the road.

Drove in the direction she'd come from. Drove into landscape, the word's two syllables careening through her cerebellum. She drove, ruminating on the word. And took the first right onto Black Bottoms Road, which she didn't remember passing. Intuition, instinct, or some other vague instigator led her to believe that heading right would take her more or less to the south. Toward the home she used to have. Toward, relatively, the Natural Bridge. But Black Bottoms Road held no loyalty to the compass. The road ran willy-nilly through the ridges and folds of the region's topography, hiding stretches of flat land behind the mountains, the mountains rising up, riblike, a stony heartless cage. Janice flipped on the headlights, but the added light was useless. The pocked macadam narrowed quickly, and meandered down into a wide valley, an earthy sternum, following the sweeps and curves of a creek bed Janice caught occasional glimpses of through the window.

Down and down, the grade gentle, away from daylight and toward the evening, and at the bottom of the hill the stream and the road parted ways. Janice drove—the road dead center—through a vast field of corn stubble. The damp earth, dug, turned, blacker than any she'd ever seen and crept right to edge of the pavement. Rising up, one on either side of the road near the end of the field, Janice saw two thin high crosses. Crosses? And what were those things hanging from the wide crossbeams? Janice slowed, a little afraid of what she might find.

Gourds. Dozens of gourds, dangling from not one but two crisscrossed beams high atop the vertical poles. Hollow, painted, with holes bored into each one, making them suitable houses for purple martins during their spring breeding season. Janice passed the birdhouses, their emptiness striking a hard chord in her heart.

Where was she? Where were the detour arrows to direct her? Janice was so tired of being in the car. So, so tired of being lost. She passed through the field, the barren farmland, and just on the other side a copse of spindly buckeye trees shrouded the juncture of Black Bottoms and Sabbath Rest Roads.

She'd seen that name before. Sabbath Rest. Sabbath Rest.

Faith or fate? Dubious guides, both. Nevertheless, Janice followed.

She followed Sabbath Rest Road even deeper into the coming night. As the road narrowed to a lane wide enough to accommodate her car and her car alone, so did the evening pull its blinding quilt over the heads of everything behind her. By the time she rounded that last S-curve and pulled up to the road's dead end, there was just enough daylight sifting through the clouds and dense woods for her to make out the funny little whitewashed house and outbuildings that faced away from the road toward nothing.

"Shit!"

What now?

No light shown through the few small windows at the house's rear. No sign of cars in the drive. Should she put the car in reverse? Should she retreat? Backpedal time and geography, looking for a moment in the past where she was, if not happy, at least stable?

Sabbath Rest. She'd seen that name before. Sitting in the Subaru, at the dead end of Sabbath Rest Road, watching the house's white plaster color shift to blue-gray in the fading light, she remembered where. On a scrap of paper thumbtacked to the bulletin board in that store. *House for Rent— Sabbath Rest Road.* Janice hadn't passed another house along the way. This must be the one.

Janice rolled the window partway down.

"Hello?" she called out, too tentatively for anyone to hear.

She turned the car off and opened the window a little farther, started to speak again—but the rush of cool air, and the sounds of flowing water off in the distance, chilled her. Fear overwhelmed Janice, wracked her body in hard waves. She banged at the window, hoping to make it rise faster. Reached to lock the passenger door. And in reaching, knocked over the bag of food from the store. Became ravenous. At the mercy, now, of pure body, hunger blended with terror. She tore open the packaged cakes, shoved them into her gnawing mouth. Then, without bothering to wipe the mess from her face, did the same with the candy bar and the Slim Jims. All she wanted in life was to be back at home in her Greensboro apartment sleeping. To be back in dull, predictable stasis. To sit on her couch, watching the muted television, knitting. Janice draped her arms over the steering wheel, laid her forehead against them, and wept.

6

Still. Stillness. And pitch black, pierced only by the insipid yellow beams of her dying headlights, which spat weakly into, but could not penetrate, the dense brush at the end of the drive. Janice reached for the ignition, reached out of confusion—had she been dreaming?—reached even before she was fully awake, and her own piteous moans all but drowned out the engine's one useless effort to crank. At the second turn of the key, the solenoid's dry click click click chipped away at any remaining façade of control. Janice feared another migraine. Janice feared everything outside the car. Janice feared death.

The headlights flickered, flickered again, then went dark. Nothing penetrated the moonless and cloudy night. Nothing but cold, and the sounds of Janice raging against her fear, pounding the steering wheel, over and over, stifling the urge to scream. But when she accidentally slammed her palm down on the horn, and the device trumpeted, its thin electronic notes rending the whole of night, Janice stilled herself. The horn might as well have been an invitation to any deranged creature, in the house or in the woods. Here she is. She can't escape. Come kill her.

Janice was a city girl, to her core. Less than a week ago, the orbit of her life had been tight and predictable, and all held within the well-paved and populated confines of Greensboro. But some cosmic jokester had tugged the rug of familiarity right out from under her mired feet. Knocked her off course with the death of Private Danks, set her spinning, at the mercy of momentum and occurrence, and dropped her unawares in the dark, with a dead battery, and no heat, in the woods, somewhere in the middle of Pennsylvania, at the dead end of Sabbath Rest Road.

In a moment of hopeful clarity, she dug the cell phone from her purse. Turned it on, cupping it tightly in her palms to mute the maddening tune she'd never figured out how to stop from playing whenever the phone powered up. And, while there seemed to be sufficient battery strength for at least one call, the No Signal icon glared in the corner of the small illuminated screen. Useless. Just before mashing the power button, Janice checked the time on the phone's clock, but she had no way of knowing if three a.m. was correct. Didn't matter, anyway. She tried the car radio, found only hum and static. Hum and static.

And memory. Funny how terror stokes the synaptic fires. Janice remembered her birthday two years ago, when Private Danks gave her a Deluxe Emergency Survival Kit, with a heavy-duty flashlight snugged between the jumper cables and the official Red Cross First Aid Kit. He helped Janice wedge the whole shebang into a storage compartment in the Subaru's rear. Then they ordered pizza, which Private Danks poked a few candles into before serving.

With the impenetrable night pressing in all around, keeping Janice prisoner at the end of Sabbath Rest Road, she was too afraid to get out of the car and go around to its back to retrieve the flashlight. Despite the tight squeeze, Janice pushed and pulled and contorted her lean body through the narrow space between the front seats. She'd forgotten about the banjo on the floor and couldn't bring herself to look and see what broke when she put her foot down on it—the discord of its protest syncopating with the clank and rattle of her fears. Janice draped across the back seats and yanked at the emergency kit until it came free. She dumped the contents out, clutched the flashlight tightly, and scrambled back into the driver's seat. Then, as an afterthought, climbed back for the spool of medical gauze. Janice wrapped her wrist, bandaged the place where the toll collector had touched. Didn't want to look at it. Didn't want to think about it. She sat with her thumb poised on the flashlight switch.

Janice didn't press the switch, though. Strangely, just the potential for light brought comfort. And as she sat there, lost, ungrounded, in no less dark than before, her topsy-turvy world began to settle. A calmness crept into the car, into her belly, her heart, her brain. Not that she felt safer, in any significant way. Rather, Janice sensed that whatever threat came her way, she'd survive. Probably.

There were maybe four hours until daylight. She could sit in the car for the rest of the night. She could get out, with the flashlight, and walk

around, walk to the house. She could knock on the door. And if, as she suspected, or hoped, no one answered, she could try the knob. If the door
opened, she could go inside and wait. For what, daylight? If the door didn't
open . . . or if it opened because someone was inside the house . . . Janice
sat in the car.

In the still dark, the winter air turned malicious. Janice began to shiver,
her teeth chattering against her will. Greensboro, however lonely, never
got so cold. After a while, she leaned again into the back seat, retrieved the
suitcase, and put on all the layers of clothing she could stuff her body into.
She wondered what it would feel like to freeze to death. Wondered, with
genuine curiosity, and surprisingly little fear.

It wasn't the first time Janice Witherspoon had sat afraid, alone, in the
dark, and waited. She remembered, most clearly, the last time they took
her mother away. Janice could tell—she'd experienced it enough times by
the age of seven to know—that her mother had, once again, gone somewhere, somewhere deep inside her self, or far far outside herself, leaving
behind a wide-eyed babbling creature, prone to laughing and weeping
and biting by turns, a creature in the shape of her mother that Janice could
not keep up with. Could not count on. They'd driven for hours, driven
into a beautiful dawn on Grandfather's Mountain all those years ago. Janice slipping in and out of sleep on the back seat. Her mother, yammering
away about something. A campground. The Highland Games. Sheepdogs.
All the men in *kilts*. Kilts, which young Janice misunderstood. Misheard.
Kilts. Killed. Kills. Young Janice, certain they were driving to watch men
die, held back her tears. But there were no dead men at the Highland
Games, only hundreds and hundreds of loud and living people—too
many for Janice to count—cheering and laughing and jostling them at
every step. Janice was hungry. They'd stopped at a roadside diner on the
way up the mountain, but her mother had only ordered coffee. Nothing
for Janice. She didn't know what was cooking in the cast-iron pot at the
back of the concession tent, but it smelled so good—Janice still remembered the smell—that she lingered there by the entrance. When she
turned around her mother was gone. She'd disappeared into the crowd.

What happened in the hours that followed, Janice had lost memory of.
Something like screaming. Her mother. Humiliation. When the man with
the gun and badge found her, Janice was cowering in the dry red dirt in the
crawl space beneath one of the wooden shacks scattered throughout the
campground. She rode, hungry and quiet, in the back of the police car all

the way down the mountain, all the way into a decade of shuffling from one great-aunt, or step-uncle, or willing neighbor, to the next. Janice never spent any real time with her mother again after the day in the mountains, outside of random and supervised visitations. As for her father, he'd died shortly after Janice's birth, and she was ashamed that she didn't know how or why or exactly when. She remembered nothing of him. Nothing at all. Remembered only the averted eyes and the hushed talk the few times his name was mentioned. She learned to seek the path of least resistance. No trouble. No trouble. She learned not to expect much. Not to be surprised by the fickle, often frightening, nature of grown men and women. And while there dwelt a scant handful of pleasant childhood memories in rivulets and folds of her mind—sitting in the bleachers at a church softball game; fishing in an indoor pond at a sportsman's show (but whose safe strong arms helped her cast?); the night it rained at the drive-in movie, the movie *Gargantuans*—mostly Janice Witherspoon remembered waiting in dark closets, in cupboards, in basements, behind or under things, waiting for storms to pass.

So while Sabbath Rest Road, and central Pennsylvania, and the strange song about *short'nin' bread* stuck in her head were all new to Janice, waiting in the dark felt so familiar it was almost comforting. She hummed that absurd tune until the sun came up.

The sun came up. Reticently. Lazily. Creeping in, through trees and clouds, from the back of the car. And as the bats and raccoons and other nocturnal creatures slipped into their dens for sleep, as the insipid morning light finally took responsibility for the day, Janice Witherspoon relaxed her grip on the flashlight and began to look around.

Not quite brave enough to leave the safety of the car, she craned her stiff neck first one way, then the other. One house and two small outbuildings, nothing more. The drive she'd followed the night before spilled out of a dense copse of leafless trees rising up at the top of a slope—more or less east, judging by the sun—and angled across an unmown hill, terminating in the misshapen gravel cul-de-sac now occupied by her lifeless Subaru.

The house itself, two narrow stories of whitewashed stone and a stubby little front porch, stood near the edge of an uneven rectangular plot; what looked to be an outhouse and a small barn marked the back border of the property, and the weedy remnants of a garden lay between.

How strange, Janice thought, that the house faced away from the road. Faced south, she recognized, although it wasn't a detail she'd normally notice. Not enough suitable land for this to have been a farm. Even she could see that. And stranger than the placement of the house was a clearly defined path Janice noticed as daylight settled in: slightly elevated, wide, wider than her car where it wasn't overgrown, choked and constricted by weeds and brambles, abutting the drive and running the length of the property in front of the house and disappearing into thick laurels in both directions.

With her head resting against the glass, Janice's breath fogged the window. The cold winter chill, which she'd somehow, and mercifully, forgotten for a few hours, came storming back into her body with a vengeance. Her body quaked from within its cocoon of sweaters. Out of instinct, with no small degree of hope, she turned the ignition. Nothing. No heat, then. Nor could she roll down the electric window to get a better look around.

While the morning sun did little to abate the cold, the lessening of shadows and darkness did ease her fears a bit. Janice opened the car door—the squeaking hinge crying out like a cyborg raptor—and held her breath. When nothing, no creature nor human, responded to the sound, she opened the door the rest of the way.

"Hello?"

Janice barely recognized her own voice.

"Hello?"

Only a little louder that time.

No reply. No surprise. Janice got out of the car and looked toward the house. Given the craziness of her life over the past few days, she half expected to see curtains flutter in the upstairs windows. That, or some other horror-movie cliché. But there were neither curtains to flutter, nor ghostly images in those windows. Only dark. Only blank.

Leaving the car door open, she walked, not toward the house, but to the edge of the drive, where she stepped onto the footpath. Stepped up the slight rise and put her boot down on the packed earth, grassless still, and stood there, letting the hard undocumented histories of everyone who'd trod that path surge around her. Familiar. Janice had never been there. Ever. But she couldn't deny the deep sense of familiarity.

She couldn't see it while sitting in the car, but once on the footpath Janice saw that the trail bordered a channel in the earth. Fifty feet, maybe more, across the top, the channel sloped down on both sides to a depth of at least six feet, as best she could tell. Its bed was stony and blanketed with yellow winter grass.

Six feet. Fifty feet. Numbers. Funny how easy the estimates of scale came to her.

This is a man-made thing, Janice thought. And uniform. That was clear enough, despite all the places where the banks had caved in, or tree roots had breached the walls. She looked down the channel, away from the house, wondering what purpose the whole thing could have served. Back toward the house, the expanse narrowed. The far bank angled in sharply, to a width—directly in front of the house—of little more than fifteen feet. That altered dimension ran twice the length of the house itself, and was defined on both sides by thick stone blocks: a fortified passageway of sorts. Janice walked along the footpath to the mouth of the sluice. She knelt at the lip of the steep walls, by the remnants of some kind of wooden gate apparatus, knelt with the shards and gravel digging into her knees, knelt partly out of sudden vertigo and partly out of an inexplicably strong desire to *see*. But the weak winter sun couldn't penetrate the channel's deep shadows. Janice couldn't see any more than a few feet into it, even though the channel was only ten feet deep inside the stone walls. She wanted to see. Wanted, at that moment, more than anything, to see what was at the bottom, what was in the middle of the hewn ditch. Janice lay on her belly, felt the cold of the stone seep in through her sweaters, and hung over the edge.

Roaring. A wet roaring filled her ears. A clopping. Hooflike. Echo. Echo. Wood against rock. And something almost voicelike. So strange. And so strangely familiar. Closer. Janice wanted to get closer. She inched forward, digging in with the toes of her boots, digging in with her fingertips.

What passed through this cut in the earth? Who passed? When? Why? Closer.

Janice wanted to get closer. Deeper.

Wasn't that water? Water, flowing somewhere in the distance?

Water made Janice nervous.

Was it water?

A voice?

The body is here.

Janice scrambled backward, like a big gangly insect, fighting more than gravity to keep from falling into the trench. When the door slammed behind her, she screamed. Except that no sound came out. Janice got to her knees, turned to confront her fate, but when she saw a small something scurry beneath the old outhouse, its off-kilter door slamming again, she almost laughed.

Death by opossum, or raccoon.

She realized she could simply walk into the stone passageway by climbing down the dirt banks beyond its mouth. Later. She'd do it later. Maybe.

There was no lock on the front door of the house. No keyhole anywhere. That was the first thing Janice noticed when she stepped onto the porch, the planks sagging a little under her weight. From the outside, the house looked, not abandoned exactly, but decidedly empty.

"Hello."

She said it first to the closed door, then again with her hand gripping the knob and her lips pressed to the thin crack, the sliver of opening.

"Hello?"

The air inside the house spilled over Janice's face through that narrow trespass. Warmer somehow than the winter morning. But Janice couldn't bring herself to go inside. Not yet. Her back hurt from sitting in the car all night. Neck stiff. Janice halfheartedly attempted a few stretches she remembered reading about in *Knitter's Monthly*, but gave up too soon for any benefit. Even out there in the woods, all alone, at the end of Sabbath Rest Road, Janice was self-conscious about her body.

Maybe this was an old farmhouse after all. Didn't she pass empty fields on her way in yesterday? Maybe they only use the house during the day. Maybe, if she just waited a while, some old farmer would drive up on his tractor, help Janice start her car, and send her safely home.

Home. Where was home? Where would she go, now?

The other alternative, of course, the one she worked hard to keep at bay in her imagination, was that deranged killers lived in the house and were simply waiting for the right moment to make Janice their next trophy. To make knickknacks from her bones, oily stew from her muscles and organs, things too perverse to think about with her flesh.

She pulled her knitting bag from the car and sat at the edge of the porch, in all the sunlight the sky could muster. She'd wait a while, then start walking. Janice dug deep in the canvas bag for a pair of needles and a ball of yarn. After leaving the unfinished sweater at the motel, she had no project, nor pattern to follow, but it didn't matter. She wanted only the comfort of the needles moving back and forth in her hands. Click click, click click, click click. Like bone against bone. Like wings. She cast on a heavy gray wool and set to work.

By midday a scarflike swath pooled at Janice's feet, and she'd momentarily forgotten the spooky voice and *the body* it spoke of. Momentarily forgotten the horrific encounter at the tollbooth. Could not forget entirely; her wrist ached and burned. She peeked under the gauze to find that the color of the bruise had deepened—nearly black—and the edges had sharpened.

Hunger. An undeniable hunger churned in her belly. Janice had come so far from her safe, dull life of routine in Greensboro. Her sleep cycle was out of sync. She couldn't remember her last proper meal. She was, at that moment, more hungry than afraid. And, as if that weren't enough, she really really had to pee. Few things could override demands on the psyche like the demands of the body.

She'd seen pictures of outhouses. And, on the way to work—back when she had a job—she passed one that had been painted, quaint-ified, and turned into a bus stop for schoolkids. But she'd never been inside. And this outhouse in particular, its planks as gray as the winter sky, its lightless interior no doubt full of spiders and whatever it was she witnessed crawling beneath it earlier, listed visibly to the right, way back in the corner of the yard near a dense thicket. So, while she was certain of the closet-sized building's function, Janice couldn't bring herself to follow the still-visible path leading from the back door of the house.

She circled the house once, then again, halfheartedly calling out hello, halfheartedly looking in the four narrow, shutterless, curtainless windows on the ground floor, avoiding both the outhouse and the other dark shed, then squatted awkwardly behind a waist-high line of cordwood and, for the first time in her adult life, peed outside. The hot stream steamed as it seeped into the cold red dirt. Its smell embarrassed Janice. And she almost fell over trying to keep her shoes out of the puddle.

This is ridiculous, she thought. Ridiculous. Was she just going to stay there all day? Another night? For all she knew there was a telephone inside the house. Later, she noticed the absence of creosoted poles.

Courage is a funny thing. It's often shored up by extreme fear. Or avoidance. Or numbness. Or fatigue. Or all of these, and more. Janice pushed open the door of the house and crossed the threshold, ready for anything. Anything but the déjà vu. The musty stale air, bound tight by closed windows, couldn't mask the sense of familiarity—a feeling that practically displaced her fear. Janice had never been in the boxy house. Never stood in that austere open room—crude kitchen at one end, a nearly empty living space with chairs and a table at the other, a fireplace between them—with its low ceilings, its bare plastered walls. She'd never been up the tight, steep stairs centered along the back wall to the two bedrooms crammed beneath the pitched roof, nor down the other stairs—the dark, inverse twin—to the dank, earthen-floored cellar. But she knew it was all there. And the familiarity soothed her.

"Hello," Janice said again. She stood there, just inside the wide-open doorway, waiting for the consequences of her trespass. None came. Nothing but her own voice cracked the caul of silence that time had draped over the abandoned house.

"Is anybody home?"

Stupid question. Stupid silence. Somehow, she knew that silence, the specific quiet of that empty house.

To go up, or down.

Janice knew the house was empty. Knew it in her bones. Winter daylight badgered its way through the curtains, but did little to illuminate the spartan living room. Unadorned white walls, whitewashed—all other colors kept secret—and plank floors, unobstructed but for an upholstered settee years beyond comfortable, a rocker, and a thick plain table between them. Low ceilings pushing down. Forcing Janice either back outside or farther into the house.

"Hello?"

Janice made her way around the double fireplace, ash stirring in the pit as she passed.

"Hello?"

She called up the stairs, and down the stairs.

"Is there . . ."

She didn't complete the sentence.

In the corner of the narrow kitchen, crowded at the end of the house by the fireplace, a cookstove, and another purely functional table with two straight-back chairs, stood a dark wooden cupboard nearly spanning the wall, floor to ceiling, window to door. Its tin-punch doors—a swirl of stars, a bird in flight—the only visible decoration.

Without hesitation, Janice opened the cupboard doors, and the unexpected beauty of the jars and jars of vegetables—beans, tomatoes, corn, and more, all unlabeled—took her breath. By the time she sat at the table and pried open the still-tight seal on a quart of green beans, Janice was crying real, unencumbered tears. She didn't bother draining the liquid from the beans. Didn't bother looking for a fork. Paused only long enough to sniff at the contents. When no foul odor penetrated her nearly defunct olfactory organs, Janice began to pull the beans out of the jar with her fingers and shove them into her mouth.

She ate practically the entire quart of overcooked beans, including the rubbery strip of fatback near the bottom. She wiped her fingers on her pants, her mouth on her shirt. She decided to stay the night.

When anybody finally showed up at the house, she'd just explain what happened. She'd tell about getting lost, about the men in the truck. Maybe even about Private Danks.

Private Danks. He was probably in the ground by then. Janice sat at the cramped kitchen table and wondered who'd attended the funeral. Wondered if he had all the pomp and circumstance the military liked to muster up as filler for the void left by doubt and sorrow.

Thanks for dying. Here's your twenty-one-gun salute, and a seriously folded flag.

She wondered about the apartment they'd shared. Had his family taken everything? She wondered why she couldn't remember what his duties were in the Guard. She wondered about her job. How many days of work had she missed? How many days of no TV, no radio? How many days completely shut off from everything, everybody, she knew? How to find her way back?

But the thought of going *back* to that life spun Janice like a top. She felt sick. Needed air. Rushed into the cold afternoon, letting the door slam open then shut behind her. Janice leaned against the Subaru until the dizziness passed, looked around again for any human presence. None. She took only her big red suitcase and knitting bag in the house, and had to consciously stop herself from saying hello when she opened the door. Sat everything in the middle of the floor. That's when she remembered the sign—*House for Rent—Sabbath Rest Road*—thumbtacked to a bulletin board at the store.

Then she remembered the voices too. The voices she'd first heard while sitting on her couch in Greensboro.

Come see the body.

The body is here.

Was there a connection between the voices and the sign? Janice acknowledged her fear, but didn't back down. The Janice Witherspoon of last week would've run. Would've run then and there, run up the road, abandoning her meager possessions—the car, the banjo, the knitting needles—without looking back. But the Janice left after the death of Private Danks, after the nightmarish journey back and forth across the eastern seaboard—that Janice grew less timorous by the day. This empty house, deep in the woods, was, for whatever reasons, less frightening than the rest of the world.

The day passed, without need for Janice's approval or engagement in it. The minutes did what minutes do, and in the clockless house, Janice drifted along on the Möbius strip made up of her emotions and memories.

Eventually, a tepid blade of sunlight cut clean the top edge of the kitchen curtains. Janice looked out the window, saw the shadows of the outbuildings laying claim to the yard as the sun made its laborious tumble down the mountain slope, ticking off degrees of visibility as it sank. She went to reach for a light switch, and wouldn't believe the house had no electricity until she'd looked at every wall on the ground floor. No plugs. No sockets. No switches.

The season, the time of year, the latitude, the topography, all conspired to make for stingy daylight. She was willing to stay the night, but wanted to look the whole house over before full dark came.

It's funny how sometimes a person doesn't see a thing until it's truly needed. How a person can look right at something, for hours—days, years even—and not even register its presence. The kerosene lamps, for instance. Janice had never used one in her life. Never seen one lit that she remembered. But there it sat, against the wall, at the edge of the very table where she ate her beans. Nor had she seen the other one on the living room table.

Janice worked her fingers, still sticky from the beans. She jacked the pump over the sink until it spat cold water, muddy first, then clear. Rinsed her hands and opened the only drawer under the sink, where she found some utensils and, mercifully, a brick-sized box of Blue Diamond strike-anywhere matches.

She picked up the lamp from the kitchen table, noted its wick coiled like a thin bleached snake in a nearly full fuel reservoir. Twisted the wick, first down to wet it, then up, and took off the glass globe. The kitchen match lit with the first swipe across the strike plate, and for the briefest moment set the brightest place in the whole world at Janice Witherspoon's fingertips.

Upstairs? Or downstairs? Which first?

She cradled the lamp's bowl in both hands and made her way to the second floor, where a skinny, windowless hall split the halves: one room on either side, both doors closed. Janice took a breath, turned the knob without knock or pause. The room could not have been emptier. No furniture, no bed, no rug. No air. She closed the door, crossed the hall, and pretended to be brave one more time. Expected nothing. Would've accepted much. But the dead crow demanded more fortitude than Janice could produce. There was a bed, a narrow cotlike thing. A nightstand. An oval rug just by the bed. And a dead crow just by the rug. It lay, wings outstretched, beak canted toward the closed window. Dead so long the bones had relinquished their hold on the feathers. Dead so long, there was only a trace of smell. Smell. Janice actually smelled the rot.

She almost dropped the lamp on her way back downstairs.

It was just a dead bird.

It was just a dead bird.

She stood at the top of the other set of stairs and peered into the cellar's dark. If only for the sake of knowing, she wanted to go down. Janice pushed at the door, but it was swollen against its jambs. She pushed harder and the door gave way with a catlike yowl. Cool damp air boiled up from the dirt floor around Janice, hushed the squeaking hinges. Rose up the stairs and left the whole house in utter stillness. Janice stepped into the black space beneath the house. Its darkness so insistent that the lamp sputtered and dimmed, thin wings of flame whipping at the dark.

One quick look around. Burlap sacks lined up on a pallet against the nearest wall. Dried beans in one. Rice in another. Cornmeal and flour and sugar in crocks. Coffee too. And various tools that she couldn't name stood at attention on the opposite wall. Odd, given that there was no heat upstairs, that the cellar was the most comfortable room in the house. The idea of sleeping down there tried to crawl into Janice's consciousness. She killed it.

By the time she opened the back door and found the stack of cordwood, the sun was tipping the brim of its gray hat to central Pennsylvania. Janice struggled in two armloads and a handful of kindling, and using half a box of matches, built the first fire of her life.

It hadn't been a life with much opportunity to face a challenge and then feel good about the outcome. Janice felt good about the hot orange and yellow flames licking the sooty hole of the flue and warming the room. She'd sleep downstairs, in the living room. The middle ground, between the dead corvid and the dark larder.

Janice lay on the lumpy settee, testing. While her small frame fit okay within the upholstered arms, the cushions were sprung and dilapidated to the point of causing pain. Janice went into the kitchen, found a fork, stood over the sink and ate a jar of tomatoes. Nothing had ever tasted redder. She paced the floor, picking tomato skins from her teeth, and noted with no small worry the lack of locks on the doors. She dragged the settee into the path of the front door. It was something, anyway. As for the back door, she chose not to think about it.

Janice liked this new person, fear and all.

She opened up her suitcase, made a pallet of clothing on the floor in the corner as far from the windows as possible. She remembered there were other sweaters in the car that could make her bed softer, but decided that leaving the house in the dark wasn't worth it. She could tolerate discomfort for one more night. Janice wished, again, that she hadn't lost her earplugs.

She put the open suitcase between herself and the barred door, the toy tomahawk tucked securely in its pocket.

She lay down. She waited.

She waited through the fear. Waited through sadness. Waited through alternating waves of doubt and near giddy elation. Heard the possums and the other nocturnal creatures nosing around the outhouse. Heard them scribbling paths across the porch. Janice waited through those sounds. Heard other sounds. Waited through those. Waited out the night. Waited until she heard, finally, nothing. So much nothing.

7

De boatman dance, de boatman sing,
De boatman up to ebry ting,
And when de boatman gets on shore
He spend his and works for more.

I wen' on board de odder day
To see what de boatmen had to say;
Dare I lets my passions loose
And dey cram me in de calaboose.

When you go to de boatmen's ball,
Dance wid my wife or don't dance at all;
Sky blue jacket and a tarpaulin hat,
O' look boys for de nine tail cat.

De boatman is a thrifty man,
Dars none can do as de boatman can;
I neber see putty gal my life
But dat she was a boatman's wife.

When de boatman blows his horn,
Look out old man your hog is gone;
He cotch my sheep, he cotch my shoat,
Den put em in a bag an toat em to de boat.

8

That sound? Was it music? Was it water? Water flowing over rocks? Music underwater?

Morning snuck in like a guilty child, not wanting to be caught. Janice woke, not because of the light, but because of what she heard, or thought she heard. Woke stiff, curled in a ball in the corner of a cold room. She'd kicked off the layer of sweaters in the night. Janice felt as if she hadn't slept at all. As if she'd run all night. Or danced. Except that Janice Witherspoon never danced.

If it was music that woke her, it meant someone was there playing the music, someone who could help her. But by the time Janice loosened her muscles and joints enough to stand, by the time she rubbed the sleep from her eyes and stood by the window, there was nothing to hear. Nothing to see. Nothing but woods and fields. In the distance a mountain shouldered in, nothing more than a blue-gray mass on the horizon. Between them, she couldn't tell what. No vistas from this house.

Aside from the obvious, evergreen or deciduous, she couldn't place any of the trees. Couldn't name them. And despite hearing things scurry around the yard throughout the night, there was not a bird nor creature staking its claim in the morning.

Janice stoked the fire, which came to life easily. The shock of the cold water pumped into her cupped hands, then splashed on her face, caused Janice to cry out so loudly she flushed with embarrassment. She traced her finger along the Mason logos embossed on all the glass jars, but the contents of the labelless jars, while easy to see and quite beautiful in their range of colors, weren't all identifiable. Janice chose a jar of corn for breakfast. By midmorning the fog had loosened its grip on the mountain. Or the reverse. Wherein lies the power: the mask, or the masked? By noon, all the mountain's leafless soldiers stood at attention, ready to charge. Janice couldn't bring herself to open the curtains.

Was another night in the house possible? Janice recalled the miles of empty road she'd driven to get there, decided more rest was necessary before she'd try walking out. Emboldened by the daylight, her new brave self, and the fact that nothing had come up, or down, or in and killed her while she slept, Janice thought to look thoroughly through the house. Maybe she'd find something to help her get back on the road.

What she found, instead, were reasons to stay. In the cellar, more jarred and dried food. A half-full can of kerosene, three gallons or more, for the lamps. Candles. Before going upstairs, Janice stabbed at the embers in the fireplace with a lead pipe that was propped against the brickwork for just that use. She threw in a fat handful of kindling, laid two logs crisscross atop it all, jerking back to avoid jettisoning sparks.

Poker. She stood the make-do poker back against the bricks. Voiced the word. And, because memory is nothing if not opportunistic, recalled that stupid hat Danks wore home, and all weekend, on his only furlough. A ball cap with LIQUOR IN THE FRONT, POKER IN THE REAR embroidered across the front.

Stupid hat. Stupid Danks. Stupid dead Danks.

Janice shuddered at the depth of her own animosity.

Because of the crow, she hadn't noticed the wooden chest at the foot of the narrow bed in the furnished room. She stepped carefully around the carcass, opened the chest, and found two rough wool blankets—as gray as the morning—nothing more. Janice took them, along with the pillow on the bed, downstairs.

So little in the way of goods and furnishings; even a single human seemed too much. Janice wondered if the house had ever been more cluttered, more occupied. She'd found a tin of gingersnaps at the back of the cupboard, and though they were stale, she welcomed the dry breadlike texture in her mouth. She'd stay a few more nights; it was a conscious decision. After lunch, she dragged the settee out of the way and retrieved the rest of her stuff from the Subaru. All but the banjo.

She arranged her things in a corner, made a more substantial bed with the wool blankets. Then, for some reason, tossed the Natural Bridge brochure into the fire. Then, for an altogether different reason, snatched it out again just as the ink began to blister on the cover. It pleased her to be able to smell singed hairs on her forearm. Janice stuck the brochure between two random pages of the tattered atlas, and buried both in the bottom of her suitcase. By nightfall she'd read the knitting magazines cover to cover several times. Nothing else to read. Reluctantly, she pulled the atlas from its hiding place and began to travel. She wanted to see where she'd come from. To trace her path, her trajectory through this newfangled world. She thought to spend a while planning future trips: south, or west, or north. But Janice couldn't bring herself to leave pages 94 and 95. She couldn't get out of Pennsylvania. Took her tired finger and tried again and again to locate herself on the grid. Never did.

~

O ole Zip Coon he is a larned skolar,
O ole Zip Coon he is a larned skolar,
O ole Zip Coon he is a larned skolar,
Sings posum up a gum tree an' cooney in a holler,

Posum up a gum tree, cooney on a stump,
Posum up a gum tree, cooney on a stump,
Posum up a gum tree, cooney on a stump,
Den over dubble trubble, Zip Coon will jump.

O Zip a duden duden duden zip a duden day.
O Zip a duden duden duden duden day.
O Zip a duden duden duden duden day.
Zip a duden duden duden zip a duden day.

~

Another morning. More music? Maybe she dreamt it.

She woke, sore again, and with one pure thought. "Scary" wasn't upstairs or downstairs. The real "scary" was inside, her fearful heart pounding away at the bars of the osteal hoopskirt she called her rib cage. Be damned if she'd spend another night on the floor. Janice opened the curtain wide. She opened all the curtains. In the cellar she'd found an old straw broom, its whiskers ragged and uneven, but stiff enough to push the crow bones and feathers into a battered dustbin. Janice took them out to the edge of the yard, back where the border of the untended garden was losing its battle with thistles and brambles, and was just about to scatter the whole black-and-white mess, when something caught her eye. The crow's eye. Its empty socket, anyway. There was a striking quality to that nearly featherless head—the beak, so strong and defiant even in death, looked about to caw. On impulse, Janice slipped two fingers around the dead bird's neck, held its skeleton still, and tugged. The head came free with such ease—no more effort than breaking off a loose thread. Janice was both frightened and impressed by the ease with which she succumbed to the strange desire to take the head.

She put it on the nightstand while she swept the rest of the upper rooms. Left it there while she swept the stairs and the ground floor as well. She fashioned a sort of mop out of an old T-shirt wrapped around the broom head, shaved off a few slivers of dense soap from one of several bars stored on a shelf in the cellar. Swabbed the floors. As she worked to clean the small house, time itself seemed to change, to loose its patina of regularity. Janice Witherspoon moved into the upper bedroom, and lost count.

She ate. She slept. She ventured out into the cold only to gather more firewood and to empty the chamber pot she'd quickly adapted to. She cleaned the house. Nobody came that next day to charge her with trespassing, or to demand she sign a lease. No one came the next day, or the next day, or the next. After a while, she forgot the pain in her wrist. After a while she forgot the bruise, the dark bird there, wings stretched across her thin pale skin. How long had she been in the clapboard house at the end of Sabbath Rest Road? How far away from the migraine that laid her down? A week? Two? More? She'd stopped counting, and didn't miss it. The counting. All she ever did for Biggers & Twine was count. No more.

Janice sat a lot. Just sat. In the house. With her thoughts. Watched, from the window, one snow blanket the whole visible world—the useless car a beautiful white box—then melt away. And another snow. The question of whether or not to stay in the house, without permission, without all the other things she did without—that question and its attendant anxieties and doubts came and went, tidelike.

Janice Witherspoon would not pretend that her passage through this non-time was easy, was painless. She had the knitting to keep her fingers occupied when the dark desires crawled, oozing and nasty and insistent, out of their holes somewhere in her belly. In the rare, darkest moments, when the one sharp butcher knife in the kitchen caught and held her eye in the glint of its blade, Janice had the knitting to keep her busy. In the merciless night, when the fear cajoled and taunted her, when the urge to hurl the lit kerosene lamp against the wall, the curtains, seemed almost overwhelming, she kept those thoughts and their retinue of destructive urges at bay by the steady clicking of her needles.

Loneliness wasn't the problem. She'd spent most of her life lonely, even the few times there was a boy around. Danks, the most recent, was no exception. Even before he'd joined the military, little charges of isolation detonated in their daily lives. She tried to recall his face, pre-uniform, pre-haircut. Janice never knew what Danks did as a soldier. Except die.

As for friends to miss, to be missed by, Janice came up empty-handed when she tried to name one. The women in the knitters group came close to being friends, but not close enough. She never could figure out how to get close to people in the first place, so maintaining closeness wasn't an issue. No model. She thought back over the grown-ups in her life and realized there'd never been anyone sufficiently stable enough, around long enough, to teach her about friendship. Eventually she just stopped thinking about it. She couldn't care less if the neighbors at Coconey Bay Apartments didn't know her name.

Truth be told, boredom took a much higher toll than loneliness.

There was the music every morning, in her head. She brought the banjo in with the half-cocked notion to teach herself to play. Except that the banjo head was punched through, and the neck was loose, probably cracked. First Janice stuck it under the bed, then she put it back in the car so she wouldn't have to see it. Then Janice learned that boredom, like everything else, passes too.

Nor was this seamless river of days and nights completely without joy.

It didn't take long for Janice to notice that the heaviness, the oppressive weight of her orderly, safe existence, so present back in her Greensboro life, was clearing. In turning toward doubt, her mind felt clearer. In stepping into uncertainty, her breath came easier. She smiled when she realized how long it had been since she'd jammed a wad of expandable lime-green foam into her ear canals to block out sensory input. And there were smells. She was coming upon smells again. The musty cellar. Burning wood. Sometimes she built fires. Sometimes she accepted the cold on its own terms. Her job at Biggers & Twine had made her mind race, the thoughts displacing all concerns of intimacy and closeness and pleasure.

On the job, she gave no pleasure to the people she interacted with. Took none from them. Her whole life had been about eliminating pleasure, given or received, or justifying its absence. There in the woods, Janice began to reclaim pleasure. She discovered quiet. She recovered smell. Even the smells of the chamber pot satisfied.

Janice spent an entire afternoon watching, through the kitchen window, a box turtle the size of a frying pan traverse the property. She remembered once, as a little girl, finding a dead turtle jammed in a crack at the base of an old stone barn foundation. She couldn't recall where the barn stood, who it belonged to, nor how old she was, but she remembered that some-one had painted a crude red heart on the turtle's back. She remembered the bullet hole in the center of the heart. Janice spent the afternoon with the turtle and the memory. She tried to imagine the scene: Who painted the heart on the turtle's back? Who fired the gun that killed it? Were they one and the same? In the end, she decided that there was a lot about love and target practice that overlapped.

Then three whole days disappeared into the simple act of cleaning the ash from the cookstove and giving it a coat of blacking from a can and brushes she found in the cellar. The first thing she did after lighting the stove was to boil the remaining bits of gristle from the crow's head. Janice didn't question where the impulse came from. When it was clean, she strung a loop of jute twine through its occipital cavities and hung it on the wall over her bed. The whole house stank of odd flesh for days. Then, she taught herself to cook rice and beans and grits. She tried several concoctions for bread without milk or eggs, eventually making something edible. Never before had she taken the time, or had the desire to find and explore the pleasures in food and eating. For much of her life she'd struggled enough for mere sustenance, sometimes metaphorically, other times more literally. Now, simple food. Pure tastes.

Sooner or later she'd have to go outside. She'd have to look in the smokehouse. She'd have to come to terms with the outhouse and its stealthy residents. Sooner or later, she'd have to walk out to that channel again, out and into the massive stone aqueduct, the last place she'd heard the voice.

The body is here.

9

—Come up, mule!—Hemp rope cinches against the snubbing post. The rope yowls as it tightens—Morning. Hot. Morning. Already hot and not even six a.m.—The babies asleep in the cabin, beneath the woman's feet. The woman, young enough, but hardened by birthing and hard life, steers the slow boat into a rising sun—Whoa, mule!—The man ties off—The mules shuffle against their harnesses. The boat low in the muddy water, full of coal, or flour, or corn—Ties the narrow vessel behind a dozen similar boats, waiting to unload, all the mules hoofing the towpath—The man on the deck swats at flies big as nickels, pinches his straw hat at its peak, lifts the hat and drags a lean forearm across his forehead—Morning, like so many others, waiting to unload, turn the boat around, harness the fresh mules and go back upstream—The babies asleep in the cabin. The hatches closed— The woman scratches at a chigger bite, wonders how many biscuits are left over from supper. She walks the plank deck as quietly as her heavy brogans can manifest quiet. Her babies are sleeping in the straw-tick bunks at the stern—The second team of mules hoofs anxiously in the covered bow, the mule shed, knowing they'll soon be working—The woman sings softly. Not babies, really. Two boys, two girls. Another year and the boys will be old enough to walk the towpath. Won't get to sleep so late. Not babies, really. The girls learning to make turtle soup. Bean soup—

Morning. Hot—Tied up with all the other boats, along a stone wall, waiting to unload at the dock—The man unhitching his mules, takes time to scratch at their muzzles and ears. Takes time to whisper to them—The woman goes quietly down the narrow stairs, so familiar with the boats' soft bobbing that *balance comes naturally. Goes into the cabin for the night jars, which she empties overboard—All the boats bobbing gently in the wake—Tied along the seawall, as they'd done countless times before. So many times they'd stopped noticing the big cast-iron pipe protruding from the stone wall. Six inches in diameter—The man fetches the race plank, readies his mules to walk the narrow board into the dark berth—Steady mule. Steady, now—The woman, wanting to give her babies a few more minutes of precious sleep before she lights the stove and clanks the pots for breakfast, stands on the deck and rigs the awning against the coming heat of the day—Another year, and the oldest boy will have to sleep in the hay house, the amidships cabin—Stopped seeing the heavy pipe, and certainly had no idea where it led to. Neither its purpose nor origin—Six a.m.*

Six a.m.—The fat pipe practically tapping at the closed window hatch of the cabin where the babies slept—Six a.m., and that day the powerhouse up the river blows the steam off its massive boiler—all that hot steam let loose through the discharge pipe—the discharge pipe aimed directly at the windows of the boat's cabin—The man hears it coming. Hears the whistle, feels the rumbling in the ground. Holds tight to his mules—The woman hears it. Smoothes her skirts—The steam. The sleeping babies hear nothing—The steam discharges directly into the cabin, knocks the windows out the other side—The heavy boat rocks against the force—The woman almost falls overboard—The boiling steam fills the dark cabin instantly—Scalding. Scalding—Strips the sleeping babies of their clothes. Their white flesh going pink then red—Hissing and screaming. Hissing and screaming—The mules, at the other end of the boat, wild-eyed, stamp their hooves in protest—

ot. No music, but fever. Janice woke, her bones aching, her
thoughts mired in the syrup of a feverish mind. Her skin, tender
to the touch, seemed about to pull apart from her bones and muscles. Her bowels seized and twisted; her stomach roiled. Janice felt as if she
were floating on a raft. She reached out from the narrow bed, put her hand
against the wall to steady herself, but the act took too much strength. What
had she eaten? It was meat of some kind; several jars in the cupboard.
She'd opened one the previous night, picked the irregular cubes of stringy
flesh from their tiny vat of gristly brine with her fingers, ate without heat-
ing it. Could've been cow, or deer, or pig. Those were the options she gave
herself. Not bad, whatever its source. The taste was just a little off, but it
had been so long since she had any meat. The fever, going up and up. Janice moved in and out of consciousness.

~

*—It was state law. All the boats had to stop when there was a body in the
water—The woman, the mother of the dead babies, lies decimated, inconsolable, in a hospital ward bed—The boats had to stop. You couldn't run
over the body—Four plain wooden coffins in a row. Too small. Too small.
Four graves side by side—Everybody had to help search. You take off your
boots and overalls. You jump in the water, feel around the bottom with your
hands, with your feet—They asked the woman if she wanted to go to the
funeral. They gave the woman laudanum. Enough—When they find the*

man, the father of the dead babies, the husband of the distraught woman,
they follow the letter of the law. Never take a body out of the water until the
authorities arrive—The man had cleaned up as best he could, but when he
attended the burial of his sweet children, there was still mule dung in the
tread of his boots, still the stink of coal and sweat about his person—You
break the law, you pay a big fine—They found the man, the father and hus-
band, not too far from where he'd jumped in. They dragged him up onto the
sloping banks of the canal, left his feet—bare now, and so pale—dangling
in the tepid water. That was okay by the law—The boatmen went back to
work—

~

Too much light. Too much dark. Whenever Janice opened her eyes, raised
her head, the house, the plot of land at the end of Sabbath Rest Road, was
too much. Her head spun, throbbed. Filled with strange, foreign images.
Emptied. Filled again. She wanted water. Couldn't fathom making the
journey downstairs. She'd vomited, in the night, or the day, her bile
crusted across her chest and the bed. Janice reached, swept weakly
beneath the bed for the chamber pot.

   Knocked it over.

~

—Purty, they all said. The woman, childless and newly widowed, was too
pretty to go to waste—She can steer good as a man—Cook up a fine pie—
Everybody up and down the canal whispered about the tragedy—Everybody
knew her plight—One hundred eighty-five miles of gossip—And the men,
the boatmen, knew the face of opportunity no matter how sad the mask it
wore—Had she been black, the commerce would've been more explicit—
Still got some breedin' years left in her—They bargained slyly with one
another. They lied. They plotted—The dead man's boat went back to the
company—His suffering wife had nowhere to go—A baker's dozen of ragged
half-wits vying for possession of the woman—She could steer a boat. Cook
well enough. Sing, too, but none of the bidders knew nor cared—What she
never liked, what she never grew accustomed to, what she feared, were the
mules. The whites of their eyes. The noisy lips and nostrils—The man who

finally led the woman, frail, whipped, done in, but most of all, compliant, down the race plank of his own boat couldn't care less how she felt about mules. He hated walking the towpath. He hated switching mule teams. He hated stepping in mule shit. This was his boat. He was the captain. Until they raised up some children, she'd do whatever he told her to do—Got to fatten you up, he said. Too damn skinny—Within a week, a dun-colored mare kicked the woman solid in the forehead as she tried to bridle the animal down in the mule shed—The man left her, bleeding and unconscious, at night, on a mercantile pier at Dunbar's Landing—

~

Janice. Mind thick with fever. Janice. Up ahead, out in the distance, out in the dark, a dim light sweeps in small arcs, back and forth, the width of an arm-span, back and forth, scooping out bowls of night. In the distance, the dim light recedes as Janice walks toward it. Toward it. Janice walks beneath the earth's surface. Walks an endless channel through black dirt; steep walls looming up on either side. Beneath her feet, the dry ground begins to change. Begins to change. Dust. Then damp. Then a trickle of water in the center of the path. Swells. Janice walked. Janice walking. No past, no present, no end of either. The light, up ahead, the light. In the dark, her feet wet now, and the sound of pouring water. Cold. So cold, the water at her feet. And the light goes away. Simply stops being light. Janice walks, in the dark, arms up, hands out, palms to the night. The air in the deep channel, cold, colder with each tentative step. Her hands, her palms, touch it first. A wall, an end, a terminus, of ice, rising above her, rising up overhead. A wall of ice. Sheer, vertical. Slick to the touch. Janice looked back through the dark channel. Janice looked to the sky: no moon, no stars. Janice, mind thick with fever, squirmed her feet in the cold mud, laid her hands on the wall of ice, pressed her forehead between them, against the ice, and looked into the blackness. Looked. Waited. Looked. Overhead, no moon. But, looking. Deep inside the glacial river, at its core, at its heart, a glow. Softer than moonlight. Janice looked, with patience, and began to see. Began to see. The sticks and twigs and stones, the suspended detritus of centuries the glacier carried with it. Carried with it, a body of light. Janice opened her arms and let her whole body press into the cold wall. The sticks. The stones. And the grasshoppers. As she looked, deeper, with more patience, Janice saw the grasshoppers. Hundreds and thousands of grasshoppers, caught, trapped, captured, their bodies brilliant green jewels, hinged legs hung in the ice.

~

—Unconscious and bleeding. And bleeding. The woman lies on the rickety pier, her head now as cracked and battered as her heart, her hand dangling in the tepid water, the bream and sunfish nipping incessantly at her finger-tips—Ain't got no use for her—Worthless as a sack of shit—Get more use out of a dead nigger—Oughta pushed her off in the water—All but one. All but one. All but the locktender. Didn't care if she couldn't cook anymore. He could boil his own cabbage. Didn't care that she, perpetually dizzy, couldn't walk a straight line. The locktender didn't care. Paid no mind to the ridiculous smile that rarely left her mouth once she come to. Paid no mind to the lopsided quality of her face, the forehead creased and sloping, the one eye slightly askew—Still purty. Awful damn purty—The locktender paid no mind to what the rest saw as flaws. He had other plans—The locktender cleans her up as best he can. The locktender gives her some cornbread and a tin cup of potent homemade liquor. The locktender drags an old tick-mattress out to the smokehouse, makes room amid the hams and side-meat—

~

Janice turned in her fever, turned away from the wall of ice. Walked back through the path cut deep in the earth. Walked without the benefit of light. Walked until the ground beneath her feet grew slippery. The rime crackled then thickened. Rising up. A swelling. The world swelling. Walking now atop a river of ice. No traction. No traction. Janice tried inching forward, a little at a time, without lifting her boots. Hard to keep balance. As if the ice beneath her moved. Falling. Janice fell. Lay on her belly, on the ice. Began to pull herself along. Crawling, on her belly, her arms her breasts and thighs damp and so cold. Stopped to rest. Wanted to cry. Wanted not to feel the ice beneath her chest. The ice beneath her. And beneath the ice, something more fluid. Movement. A thumping against the crust of ice, a thumping she felt in her bones. Janice and her bones lay on the ice. She cleared, with both hands, the ice beneath her face and looked in. Looked to find the current, the flowing water not so far under the frozen surface where she lay. Watched first one, then another, then another, child float by, float under her. Children. In the current. Flowing. Beneath the ice. Each one, belly up. Each one, eyes open. Each one tapping, knocking softly at the ice. Each one mouthing something. *The body.* How many? So many. Mouthing what? *The body is here.* Gape. Gape. Knock. Knock.

~

—*Respite. Brief respite. Eat, sleep, heal. She'd lost something, the woman, but couldn't tell what. Where is she? Doesn't like the smell—heavy, smoky, oily—Dark, but for thin ribbons of sunlight between the planks of the dark walls—The dark. She likes the dark. It comforts. It brings her things. Food, sometimes. And sometimes, hints of what she lost—Laughter—The boat tied for the night—Mules fed and stabled—Boys swimming, catching turtles—The girls tying a string to a june bug, spinning along as it flies a slow orbit over the man and woman on a blanket on the towpath—The man working a jaw harp—The woman singing—Laughter—*

Respite. From the dreams, respite. Janice slept. Janice woke. Befuddled by the fever-driven nonsense in her brain. Woke weak, filthy, but, most important, woke hungry. A good sign. It took hours to get down the stairs, cleaned, and fed. It took hours to make the small bedroom livable again. She could've died up there. Out there. Who would've known? How long before some unwitting soul would've opened the door and found her like she found the crow? Splayed out, caved in, and reduced to the elemental. She hoped, at the very least, they'd boil her skull too, and hang it on the wall.

For the next three days she rested, packed and repacked her smallest duffel, searched the house for the weapon easiest to carry, and made a plan of action. She'd hitchhike. There was no other choice. Finally, she felt strong enough to walk up Sabbath Rest Road, her first venture beyond the yard. Where to go? Which direction? The store, maybe, where she saw the sign. Where she got the Winky Dinks. Another house, a neighbor? Worry over food supplies, and now food quality, had crept into her days. With no real sense of how far she'd have to walk before finding another human, nor what she planned to do beyond that meeting, Janice set off, with the duffel bag—and the thick-bladed butcher's knife wrapped in a sock hidden inside—hanging from her shoulder. No matter, the lack of plans. Janice had misjudged her strength. By the time she got to the top of the sloping drive that spilled out of the woods and down to her front door, she was dizzy and exhausted. Couldn't go on. A tree, old, an oak she guessed, had years ago began a slow tilt away from the eroding drive. A mass of thick interlocking roots swirled from the exposed edge, jutting out over the lip of the drive. Janice sat in the crux to catch her breath.

She wouldn't allow fear to take hold.

She tried to piece together the sounds and images and feelings from her fever-dreams. Tried to string together some sort of narrative. She recognized herself in some of the dreams; in others, though . . . all strangers. But Janice couldn't make sense of any of it. No surprise there. Janice knew all too well that the workings of her psyche, even when not affected by food poisoning, were rarely clear and understandable. She didn't know how to travel that inner landscape. She realized, too, that she had no idea what condition her larger world was in. The one she was so isolated from. When she'd exited the turnpike, long long ago, there was war and dying. And all those sad, scary forms of male chest-pounding. Janice assumed, rightly or wrongly, that if something drastic had happened, that if the president—whom she'd come to distrust even in her apathy—was ultimately slow on the draw, and another cowboy, in a different uniform, waving a different flag, and telling the same lies in a different language, got to the trigger first, if there'd been a (not wholly unexpected) nuclear exchange, she felt pretty sure she'd know it, even though she was completely cut off from the media. She'd know it by the change in sunsets, or sunrises. Or the sky itself. Maybe birds would drop out of the sky in flocks, dead and featherless. Except that she never really saw any birds at the end of Sabbath Rest Road.

Maybe all the killing and warring was necessary. Just like the president said. Or maybe the dearth of women's voices being heard at the top of the military chain of command ought to suggest something else. Stupid Danks. And his kind. Allowing that it was always much easier to formulate an opinion about external things, big or small, than to judge and assess, with any degree of honesty, internal things (always huge), Janice felt satisfied at her insightful conclusion.

Janice held no illusions, however, that she could be such an emissary for her gender. Would prefer that Armageddon pass her by, unnoticed. As for her dreams, they were just *dreams*. Right? She got up from her seat of roots and headed toward the house. Two steps later, she figured out what took the box turtle so long to crawl across the yard. The big, plodding reptile pulled the whole of spring behind it. Janice saw the crocuses, in the shade of the oak. Didn't know the flowers by name, and thought they looked like tiny praying hands, purple praying hands. She'd call them prayer plants. She'd stay. Soon enough, the forsythia would explode all along the fence lines. She'd name them butter-stars, and giggle when she said it. She could endure the dreams. She believed, in that moment and with all her heart, that in the spring the garden would offer up its residual wealth. Sustenance. Soon she'd be able to open her windows wide at night, and sleep in the breezes spilling down from the mountain in the distance. She'd stay, and when she felt brave enough, strong enough, she'd name the mountain too.

Not yet, though. More cold nights to come. In the time she'd been there, Janice had used only the living room fireplace, but she did her minimal cooking on the woodstove as well. She'd burned through nearly all the cut wood stacked behind the house. What she needed was an ax, or a saw.

She found both in the cellar; carried one in each hand out the front door.

The trees, standing and fallen, were closer to the backyard, but Janice headed toward the weedy channel just beyond the driveway, and the woods beyond it. She tossed her tools down the bank, turned sideways, then backward, and did a splay-legged back-step down to them. She reached to grab the ax, and her mind flooded with flashbacks from her strange dreams. This! This channel! She'd walked the channel in her dreams. To her right, the wide pathway kept going, no end in sight. To her left, the massive sluice, its stone walls cool and dark. The sounds of flowing water. Janice hurried past, kicking up dust as she went.

Went up the other bank even less gracefully than her entrance. Janice wandered a semi-perpendicular route through brush and brambles, low trees with kinked trunks and limbs, humps of leafless sumac, wandered a hundred yards, two hundred yards until she came to the river.

Dread. The water, shallow, slow, its bed of stones visible all the way across, and quite beautiful, filled her with dread. Janice turned around, rushed back into the woods, deep enough so that she didn't have to look at the river, found a small dead tree on the ground, and swung her ax.

Swung her ax.

But no matter how many times she swung the ax, she never seemed to make headway through the thin trunk. The dull blade refused to bite into the dense white flesh. Janice swapped the ax for the saw, and found accord with the rhythm. She cut the tree into logs, then cut another. She cut until her hands blistered, stopping only after the pain became unbearable. She carried logs by the armful—three heavy loads—to the lip of the channel, where she tossed them in, then pitched them, one log at a time, up to the opposite bank, three heavy loads to the back of the house.

That night, Janice slept, exhausted. A night without dreams, the first in longer than she could remember. For days, she cut and hauled wood to the point of exhaustion, reveling in her fatigue. Her body grew stronger. The routine, mindless and immediate, allowed her imagination a new freedom. And while she felt, in body and spirit, more than capable of walking up Sabbath Rest Road, of walking all the way out of Pennsylvania if necessary, her imagination took another turn.

She pictured herself a pioneer woman, toughing it out in the Wild West. Battling the elements, the Indians. She imagined herself in the aftermath of a crisis—a blizzard, a hurricane—making do. She imagined herself working this small, stony plot of land hidden away in a forgotten valley. Scratching out a life. Chopping wood. Carrying water. Surviving.

Too, in the settling of her mind, in the lessening of her fears, there came memories. A "vacation" with her mother. Her mother using the word again and again, like it was a piece of delicious candy in her mouth.

Vacation.

Vacation.

They went to Cherokee, a little town in the North Carolina mountains, where there was a cable car and a merry-go-round. They saw a cowboy-and-Indian gunfight that made Janice cry until her mother explained that it was all play. Janice got a rubber tomahawk for being brave. On the way home, they ate peanut butter and scallion sandwiches at a scenic overlook on the Blue Ridge Parkway. *You can see for miles, all around,* her mother said. *You can see what's coming.* Janice remembered her mother's head wrapped in a scarf, as green and iridescent as a june bug's wing. Janice knew, then and there, that her mother was the most beautiful, exotic woman in the world.

Let's go see the caged bears, honey.

But they didn't make it to the bears. Mama sped home, mumbling over and over to herself, *Leave me alone! Leave me alone! Leave me alone.*

Janice loved the rhythms of the saw. Like breath. Like heartbeats. Like music.

Back and forth, she cut. Contentedly, she cut.

Until the day the saw teeth whispered to her through the sawdust.

—Comes the body—comes the body—

Back and forth. Back and forth.

—Comes the body—comes the body—

She left the saw in the woods. Left it swaying, in midstroke.

Enough firewood. For a while, anyway. The jarred food and the kerosene were another story. Janice walked the still-visible rows of the garden. Truth was, she didn't know weed from vegetable sprout. Spooked by the food poisoning incident, she felt the rash confidence that fueled her earlier fantasies wither. Janice didn't trust herself to pick something edible. She decided, skeptically, that there might be something in the other shed—not the outhouse, the bigger building. Maybe not food, but possibly seed packets. Or fuel.

Janice approached the building with caution. Not knowing what to expect. She'd been in the house for a few weeks now, and had adamantly avoided the shed. Practically denied that it stood there. She'd invested so much energy in her avoidance that when she walked up to the door and grasped the looped piece of chain serving as the handle in her sweaty hand, Janice's heart beat so hard she felt as if her eardrums would rupture any minute.

The pounding didn't stop her from hearing the door of the outhouse slam shut.

She turned, just in time to see . . . what . . . a possum? A raccoon? Some brownish thing scurried out of sight beneath the privy.

Deep breath. Stupid animals.

Janice yanked at the chain with way too much effort.

The smokehouse door slammed back, jerked against its hinges.

Light spilled into the narrow cramped room. The stink of cured meat, thick, heavier than air. Light flowed in; the dark spilled out in a cool rush over Janice's face. Light lay down on the filthy, stained, tick-mattress bunched in the far corner.

~

—In the dark, the woman rests. Eats and sleeps—The dark is still. The floor, the walls, don't move—A man brings her things to eat—A man takes her to the pumphouse, to the well, makes her wash—Cold! Water too cold—The dark smells—But mercifully, the dark is still—Heyyy Lock!—Git up!—The man makes her stand, makes her leave the dark—Purty little thang, ain't

she—What happened to her head?—The man leads her through the grass, each blade sings its song to her bare feet—Goddammit! Let's go!—The man yanks her by the arm—Another man waits—waits by the—by the boat— No!—The woman yells it in her head—No boat!—Her mouth won't make the words—No boat! She tries to run, too dizzy—The men laugh when she falls. Then slap her—She kicks and fights, tries to bite—The men slap and slap and slap her—Until there is no more fighting—The man, the other man, not the man who brings her food, the other man opens the boat hatch, drags her in by the hair—Put your money in the bucket, the man says, the man who brings her food—Put your money in the bucket on the porch when you're done—

~

The next morning, spring hurled its green self against her window.

Janice woke. Held to the bed. Felt the wall with her palm. Making sure she was home.

In the night, there'd been a sound, metal against metal. A hammering. Tchink, tchink. Tchink.

The arrhythmic heartbeat of some part-human, part-machine thing living in the river. In the night, she'd imagined herself walking the riverbank, back and forth, after a storm, the river water frothy and raging, walking back and forth, calling out across the water, calling out to that sound. Janice kicked her covers off, to discover muddy wet sheets. Thin brushstrokes of blood on the pillow and sheets. The wound at her wrist had opened. The bruise no longer held the bird captive. Across the floor, muddy tracks, muddy footprints, led from the stairwell to her bed.

Why was that filthy mattress in the outbuilding? What if someone had been sneaking in there to sleep at night? And Janice, with no locks on her doors. Janice worried. About the possible intruder, and about the weird daydream she'd had opening the shed door. And now, sleepwalking.

One time, in a motel with her mother, Janice got up and stood at the mirror hung on the closet door, stood with her nose touching the silvered glass. *What are you doing, honey? Come back to bed.* One time, staying with an aunt and her new husband, Janice walked, wide-eyed but sound asleep, into their bedroom, climbed between them and under the covers. Him snoring, her snoring softer, both naked. The man flew into a rage. Strapped Janice to her own bed with belts strung together.

Janice thought she'd grown out of the habit.

Outside, the trees on the distant mountain had begun to bud. Their green shimmer, so reticent, practically glowed in the morning sky. Janice went through the house, opened all the windows, invited in the energy of blossoming. She cleaned the muddy footprints from the bedroom floor, from the stairs, and from the living room. That night, she moved the settee against the door once again, but not to keep anyone out. In the morning, the muddy tracks led from the back door. Janice, exhausted from the non-sleeping sleep, cleaned yet again. In the backyard, where she went to empty the pail of mop water, she saw, and even in seeing hoped it wasn't true, her own footprints leading, making a repeated path, the grass clearly flattened as proof, back and forth from the smokehouse to the outhouse.

How do you run from yourself?

~

—A pound of coffee, I'll swap you a pound of coffee—Put it in the bucket— Will you takes these hen eggs? They's fresh—Put 'em by the bucket—Every time the man tries to lead the woman into the dark cabin of a boat tied off and waiting for her, she fights—She's a damn wildcat, they all say—Makes her more appealing—Every time she fights, they slap her down and slap her down—Heyyyy Lock!—She fights—In the boats, it hurts—It hurts every- where—These bad men—You boys got any money, the man asks—Our daddy give us a dollar apiece, they say—Put it in the bucket—The boys aren't strong enough to fight her—The man ties her to a post—The boys laugh—In the bucket, he says—

~

Tracks. Every night. Tchink, tchink. Tchink. Every night. Every night she went to sleep to this sound. Every night she prayed for a different outcome, but every morning the muddy footprints betrayed the path she'd taken in sleep. Every morning her wrist tender and raw. Janice remembered little to nothing. Didn't remember, never remembered, how her sleeping self managed to untie, or move, or go under or over, the increasingly complex obstacles her waking self constructed in order to keep both selves unified and safe in the house. Sometimes it seemed as if her barriers went undis- turbed, with only her footprints in the morning as evidence that she'd been out that night. How do you run from yourself? Tired. Janice was too tired, too hungry, too weak to leave. Janice worried that the thing on her arm was cancerous. Weariness clouded her mind. Just stay. Endure.

~

—The man brings an old rag and a jar of kerosene to the building—Washes her between the legs—Burns! Stings!—To get the nigger off, he says—The man does this every time a dark man puts money in the bucket—Move your arm, goddammit! he says—Let me get them titties, he says—In the lightless building where she sleeps, where she waits—naked, mostly, sometimes in a thin smock—in the building the woman has a secret—The goats—When she cries, the goats come to her—when the man isn't looking—They bleat softly—like whispering—and when she sticks her fingers through the cracks between the boards, the goats nuzzle and lick them—

~

Tchink, tchink. Tchink. In the dream, it is day. Or night. Janice, her circadian rhythms out of sync, had begun sleeping at odd times, waking at odd times, dreaming at odd times. The waking world and the dream world begin to merge. To meld. Tchink, tchink. Tchink. Janice walks, bodiless, embodied, following that sound. In the dream, it's hard to tell the source. Janice walks the perimeter of the property, as if orbiting the house, the outbuildings, her loose nightgown billowing. She dreams both a past and a present. Tchink, tchink. Tchink. The sound comes from the shed. Tchink, tchink. Tchink. It comes from beneath the outhouse. Tchink, tchink. Tchink. In the dream, Janice follows the sound in circles. Cool air, morning or evening, penetrates her thin gown, rises beneath it as she walks. In the dream, Janice wears the skull of a crow on a string around her neck. Walks, weapon in hand. Tchink, tchink. Tchink. Janice holds the tomahawk tight in her fist, rings of paint on its dowel handle worn and faded, the rubber blade cracked and brittle. In the dream, Janice follows the sound through the woods, comes to the river, its stony bed visible. In the dream Janice fords the river, almost falls, her cotton gown wicks the cold water up past her thighs, her belly. Tchink, tchink. Tchink. In the dream, she follows the sound across the water, up the bank, and into unknown land. In the dream Janice comes to a barbwire fence; tied to its top strand, tied with baling twine, dead muskrats sway, rotting. In the dream, a sunlit moment, the ground beneath her feet is suddenly spongy, is suddenly alive. Janice steps up to the ankle in a thriving yellow-jackets' nest. In the dream, the bees begin to sting her foot, her bare legs. In the dream, she does not scream as the bees crawl up her legs, stinging and stinging. In the dream she swings at the swarming insects with her toma-hawk. Tchink, tchink. Tchink. Each time she kills a bee there is the sound. In the dream, when the bees seem about to consume her, Janice wakes. Janice woke.

Woke, soaked through, thin gown clinging to her wet flesh; woke clutching the tomahawk; woke outside, looking into the windows, tall and wide windows, of a well-lit building, a studio of sorts; looking at a man who struggles to move a huge stone onto a table—a stone not unlike a grave-stone—looking at a man, who looks back at her. Awake, Janice ran. Ran, on pure instinct to guide her back across the river. Ran through thorn bushes and scrub. Found herself at home, wet, with bleeding legs. Was that man, the man with the gravestone, real? Was he a figment of the dreams?

~

—Boys and men—The things a body is capable of doing—The things a body is capable of enduring—Ain't got no use for it, the man says to the man who likes to take the woman to the mule shed and put a bit in her mouth— Cain't play, ain't gonna learn—It's a fine instrument, the man says. Keeps tune real good—I cain't eat it. I cain't drink it. I cain't spend it I got no use for no hog fiddle. You want to crawl up in that girl's hole, you bring me some-thing for my bucket—The man clutches his unwanted barter to his chest and spits—He thinks about busting it across the old man's head—The woman knows this man for his special meanness. The woman fights extra hard when he comes to the smokehouse door—The man drags a thick yellow fingernail across the four strings—Discord rings throughout the valley—Everywhere but in the smokehouse—The woman pushes the door open with her feet, slides out, looking to the source of the sound—Both men see this—The man strums the instrument again—The woman smiles, walks unsteadily toward him, hands out—Leave it in the shed with her when you're done—

~

How long had she been standing there? How long had he been looking at her? Janice wrestled these questions and others like them as she cleaned herself, attended to the scrapes and scratches on her body. How long would these lunatic dreams and the sleepwalking go on?

The question of just how much of what she saw and experienced was a product of her fatigued mind and weary psyche, as opposed to being very real, palpable manifestations of forces outside of the confines of her body and spirit—that question went unasked. That question had been avoided. Avoided numerous times throughout her young life.

Janice inspected the tomahawk for damage, then carefully wrapped it in the green scarf and tucked it back into the suitcase. She wished, in that moment, that she had someone to talk to, to ask these things. To assure her that it was all okay, was all going to be okay, that it was just a normal part of living. Once, the Human Services office at Biggers & Twine held a mental health fair. She'd planned to go, until Danks mocked her and made fun of the whole idea.

If she could only find a way to lock the doors securely before nightfall. How much day was left? Janice stood on her bed and hung the crow's head back on its nail. She turned to look out the window, to gauge the remaining sunlight. Saw him, that man, come up out of the channel, walking toward her door.

12

This mule he am a kicker
He's got an iron back
He headed off on a railroad train
And kicked it off the track.
He kicked the feathers off a goose,
He pulverized a hog,
He kicked up three dead chinymans
And swatted him a yellow dog.

Whoa there, mule, I tell you
Miss Liza you keep cool,
I ain't got time to kiss you now,
I'm busy with this mule.

When I seen Miss Dinah the other day
She was bent all over her tub,
And the more I asked her to marry me
The harder she would rub.

Whoa there, mule, I tell you . . .

—*Sometimes song*—*Sometimes nonsense*—*The woman worked her fingers*
up and down the fretboard whenever she wasn't in some man's boat. She
plucked at the strum hollow, notes and chords of her·own devising—
Sometimes nonsense—*Sometimes song*—

I'm crazy 'bout my light-bread
My pig-meat on the side.
Say I'm crazy 'bout my light-bread
And my pig-meat on the side.
But if I taste your jelly roll
I will be satisfied.
Tell me, is your jelly roll fresh
Or is your jelly roll stale?
I say, is your jelly roll fresh,
Or is your jelly roll stale?
I swear I'm gonna buy me some
If it lands myself in jail.

—He beat her—The man beat her for some songs—*You keep playin' that nig-*
ger music and I'll fetch my ax and bust that goddamn thing to splinters—
She'd go to the boats without fighting—The woman would take all their
meanness, all their hurting without shedding another tear—*Just don't take the*
dulcimer—The woman, in the dark smokehouse, curled on the tick-mattress,
holds the instrument as if it were a baby—Finds the drone note. Coos. Cries.
Whispers—Begins to sing softly—Just outside the walls, the goats gather, sit,
with their goat ears cocked, their goat eyes nearly closed, ruminating—

'Member one thing an' it's certainly sho'
Judgment's a-comin' an' I don' know.
Up on the mountain, Jehovah he spoke
Out of his mouth come fire and smoke.
I tell you once, I tell you twice
My soul's been anchored in Jesus Christ.
My Lawd spoke in a 'ponstrous voice
Shook the world to its very jois'.
Rung through Heaven and down in Hell
My dungeon shook and my chains, they fell.
Wade in the water, wade in the water chi'ren,
Wade in the water, God's gonna trouble the water.

13

"Hey!" he said. "Heyyyy Lock!"

There was no lock. Nothing blocking the door. Nothing preventing the man from coming inside the house and killing her.

"Hello?" he said. Then knocked.

Do killers knock? Janice didn't take a chance. She grabbed the first thing she could find, her knitting needles, ran as quietly and quickly as possible down the stairs and wedged her body against the door.

"Hello?" he said, softer that time.

Janice trembled. Sweat, the sweat of fear, trickled into her eyes and stung.

Was there time to run out the back door and up the road?

"Listen, I know you're there."

Janice could tell that he'd put his hand to the door, palm flat. She just knew it.

"You . . ." he started. "I think you came by my house earlier. You looked . . . you looked like you were in trouble."

"Go away," Janice said, with as much force as she could muster. The first words she'd uttered to another human in months were *go away*.

She could hear him breathe, hear him step back from the door.

"I just wanted to see if I could help," he said. "I tried to find you when you ran. But . . . I had my hands full."

Janice thought of the gravestone.

"I don't need anything from you!"

"Well . . ."

He seemed to be at a loss for words.

Janice heard his footsteps in the gravel. She leaned into the corner of the window to see the man walking around her car. He was tall and lanky. When he knelt to look at something under her car, pulling his hair—a little too long and well into gray—out of his face, Janice was struck by his handsomeness. Handsome despite, or because of, his goatee and mustache.

Killers are often good-looking.

Then he came back to the door.

"Look," he said. "I know you might be scared, but . . . you were the one who showed up in my window, soaking wet and carrying a hatchet . . . I just . . . your car . . . if you need some help . . ."

Janice was torn. Torn asunder. Divided then subdivided. All the things she wanted contradicted one another.

He stood quietly—figuring, Janice was sure, how to dispose of her body.

"My name's Stephen. Stephen Gainy. I guess you know where I live. If you . . . please, if you need some help, come find me."

He was practically back to the stone mouth of the channel before she opened the door.

"Stay over there!" Janice commanded, pointing the knitting needles at him.

Stephen paused.

"I'd rather be chopped up with your hatchet than knit to death," he said.

Despite herself, Janice smiled. And the smile took some of the tension away. She tucked the weapons in her back pocket. Clinched her sweater closed, to keep her hands busy.

She stood in the doorway. He stood by the lip of the channel.

She didn't know what to say.

"Well?" Stephen said.

Nothing.

"What's your name?"

Janice tried to recall the last time someone asked her name.

"It's Janice," she finally said. "And I'm sorry if I scared you."

"I'm sorry if I scared you," he said.

Janice, the old Janice, the woman who spent her days shutting out the world with earplugs, always turned inward in the presence of a man she thought was too good-looking to notice her. She shut down.

"You . . . have you been here long?" he asked.

A long and awkward pause ensued while Janice remembered all the things she'd endured and overcome since driving out of Greensboro. The new Janice answered his question.

"Just a couple days," she said.

Stephen looked at the weeds growing up around the wheels of the Subaru.

"You're not a very good liar," he said, picking a long blade of grass. He measured a length of the grass along his finger, broke it off at both ends and positioned the remaining piece, reedlike, in the tiny gaping mouth made between the knuckles of his two aligned thumbs. Stephen put his cupped hands to his mouth and blew.

The sound—part cry, part horn, part squeal—resonated throughout, seemed to bounce off the distant mountain and echo back. It frightened Janice with its volume, then made her laugh aloud.

"That's the call of the rare and nearly extinct barefooted-hatchet bird . . . the Native Americans called it . . . whoo-aka-wickwick . . . which translates into . . . something like . . . *pretty-white-lady-gets-wet-in-river-then-runs-through-the-woods* . . ."

Again, Janice laughed, despite herself.

Killers are often charming.

"Really," Stephen said. "I'm not joking."

He sat on the hood of her car.

"Are you stuck here, Janice?"

To confess would take great faith in the fact that, beneath his soft demeanor and handsome face, there dwelt a kind soul. A leap made less frightening by the odd sense of familiarity that seemed to lie behind her fear of Stephen. Had she met this man before?

"No," she said.

"No," she repeated.

"Well . . . maybe," she said. "My battery is dead."

"That's easy," he said. Then he left.

The only surprise about Stephen's return, half an hour later, was that he rode up out of the channel on a muddy all-terrain vehicle. Janice watched him do a little wheelie as he crested the steep bank's lip. Stephen skidded to a stop directly in front of the Subaru.

Janice came out of the house. He grinned at her, didn't seem to acknowledge that she'd changed clothes, which was fine by her. But his gaze lingered for a moment on her bandaged wrist.

"Is that how you travel?" she asked, easing closer by slow degrees.

"Depends," he said. "This house is a quarter of a mile away from me, through the woods. It's ten miles, maybe more, if you take the roads."

Stephen unstrapped a heavy toolbox from the rear of the ATV, dropped it with a thud.

"I didn't know they'd restored this old place," he said.

"Yeah . . . well," was all that Janice could say.

"Got your keys handy?"

"There're no locks," she said. "On any of the doors."

Then she realized he meant car keys.

"Your secret's out," he said. "Better sleep with your knitting needles under the pillow."

Janice blushed, feeling stupid and vulnerable.

"Hey," he said. "I'm sorry. That wasn't funny at all."

She retrieved the car keys, and when he reached for them, she noticed his hands. Big. Big hands. Heavily callused. Cuts and abrasions on his knuckles.

Stephen popped the hood, took jumper cables from the toolbox and attached them to the car battery and the four-wheeler's battery.

"Do you want the honors?" he asked, offering her the keys.

Janice smiled, an insipid, nervous little smile. Shook her head, no.

The cold engine struggled through one revolution, then gained momentum with each successive pump of the crankshaft. Fourth time around and the ignition sparked, and the Subaru backfired louder than Janice had ever heard it.

"Wow," Stephen said over the sputtering engine. "That'd wake the dead."

"Sorry, I should've warned you."

"Does it happen often?"

"Only every time I crank it, or shut it off. I'd forgotten how loud it can be."

"Hmm."

Stephen tugged at his goatee, bit his top lip, then spoke.

"Do you have a quarter?"

"What?" Janice asked.

"A quarter? Do you have a quarter in your pocket?"

Janice had no change, knew she had nothing in her pockets, but made the effort to check because he was looking at her so intently.

"Maybe inside," she said. "But why?"

"I used to go out with a girl who ran the parts counter at a Subaru dealership. She taught me lots of tricks."

"Did she have a goofy Native American name too?" Janice asked, surprised by her own uncharacteristic wit.

Stephen laughed. She went inside, pleased with her quickness, to fetch the coin. By the time she returned he already had the air filter off and was removing the carburetor. As he worked, Stephen explained what he was doing, something about intakes and vacuums, in part to fill up the quiet. Janice was content to let him work and talk. The questions came later on, presented as afterthoughts.

"How'd you find this place?"

"A sign," she said. "Tacked on a bulletin board."

Partly true.

"You're not going to make me listen to eleven different versions of 'Proud to Be An American,' are you?"

"What?" Janice asked. She'd forgotten about the CD she bought, under duress. "No."

Stephen changed the socket on his wrench, then tucked a screwdriver into his back pocket.

"You play that banjo?" he asked.

"Not really. I wish I could. Give me something to do out here. It's broken, anyway."

"Hmmm," Stephen said. Her answer betrayed more than she intended. "Well, that's a good thing. The world surely doesn't need another banjo player."

Smiles, again. Both of them.

Within the hour, Stephen closed the hood and started the Subaru several times to prove that he'd fixed the backfiring.

"Thank you," Janice said. "A lot. I wish . . . I don't really have anything to offer you . . . food, I mean. Or . . . really, nothing. Would you like some water?"

The rambling quality of her speech made Janice feel young and silly, but Stephen's very genuine smile countered the embarrassment.

"I tell you what," he said. "You can pay me by being my dinner guest. I'll cook for you."

Real food? Real human company? And such a handsome killer making the request.

"You know, I think I'm going to be leaving this afternoon . . . Sorry."

"Oh well," Stephen said, cinching the straps on the toolbox. "Next time you're stuck in the woods, look me up."

He cranked the ATV, winked at Janice, and rode out of sight in the channel.

She listened until distance took the sound of the engine away from her.

She filled the vacuum, the absence, with a near-manic sense of new-found freedom. Janice started the car, left it running while she packed. She packed hastily, stuffing the suitcase, and throwing other things directly into the back seat. Pulled out her atlas, and the Natural Bridge brochure fluttered to the ground. Janice picked it up, traced her finger over the charred faces of a picnicking family, and stuck it in the glove box.

Janice counted her money. She wondered if her final paycheck had been deposited. She wondered over many small and useless things, until she had no choice but to wonder where she should go.

Late afternoon brought heavy winds, the currents charging over the mountains and gaining speed on the downslope. Janice wished she'd asked him for directions. Asked Stephen for directions. She wished she'd gone to his house for dinner.

The old car resisted her tug at the gear lever, and when it finally clunked into drive, the wheels and brake pads made their own loud complaints. Janice drove, slowly, to the top of the drive, noting the oak where she'd sat weeks ago, in full leaf now. Janice realized she had absolutely no idea which direction she'd come from. Nor which direction to go.

The Natural Bridge, vaguely south, vaguely west, had been a destination.

Lacking a better alternative, she found the sun up to the left in her side window. Janice turned left at the first road she came to. She passed, and remembered, the barren fields, and the empty martin houses. All those gourds, with their single black holes, like empty eye-sockets, whipped in the high wind. The fields . . . odd, she thought, it was spring and the fields bore the marks of plowing, but nothing grew. Janice drove the narrow road as it meandered, first along, then away from the river—the same river she'd crossed to get to Stephen's house?—and back again.

She'd gotten used to solitude. Couldn't imagine living again in a place like Coconey Bay Apartments. She did, however, allow space in her imagination for a good-looking companion. Somebody who would be nice to her. Somebody smart. Somebody who . . . who would replace, or better yet, supersede Private Danks. The return of sadness, guilt-tinged now, over the dead boy took Janice by surprise. As did its brevity.

Janice had been so deep in her fantasy she nearly ran into the orange-striped traffic barrel sitting dead center in the road. A thick wooden post rising at an angle from the middle of the barrel held a caution light with very little will to flash, and two signs: DANGER — BRIDGE UNDER REPAIR and WAIT FOR LEAD VEHICLE.

What day of the week was it? Janice saw no signs of workmen. No flags, no trucks. She thought of simply driving past the sign, but then she thought about driving off a bridge. Janice rolled down the windows, sat and waited.

What was his last name? James? Garvey? Gary? Gainy! That was it. Stephen Gainy.

Janice wondered how the man's life had led him to handling grave-stones and rescuing lost souls in the woods of Pennsylvania. Such big hands. And kind eyes, for a killer. She smiled. She'd given up thinking of Stephen as a threat, and wished they could've shared the joke a little while longer.

Janice was about to say something to Stephen in her mind. Was about to be bold. About to take a risk. But the bells made her lose the thought. Broke her spell of imagined bravery.

Bells. Janice heard bells. Small, jingling bells.

Maybe it was the "lead vehicle" on its way.

On either side, the gravel shoulders were nearly as wide as the road itself. Close-mown banks led into sparse pine woods on her left and leafy cattail swamps on the right. She saw no lead vehicle up ahead, nor in the rearview mirror. And the bells drew closer.

Janice locked the doors, and was about to roll up the window when she saw the first goat. A tawny male with one cracked horn, a bell tied around its neck with baling twine, passed within inches of her arm in the window. When it passed, the size of its testicles embarrassed Janice. She laughed and looked away. Looked out the passenger window to the pair of white goats walking by. Their soft bleating a gibberish Janice couldn't under-stand, but she couldn't help feeling they were commenting on her. More goats, on both sides of the car, flowing around her, spilling off the road and into the pines. All kinds. Black. White. Horns. No horns. No hurry. The goats ambled, their bells chiming willy-nilly, around the parked car and down the road. Some looked her way, the sweep of their necks as they turned, beautiful. The sliver of white rimming their dark eyes, terrifying.

No way to count. But there had to be a hundred goats. Maybe more. Just walking down the road. Unattended. Unconcerned. Walking in the direction Janice was headed. Before she could get lost, get even more confused, Janice turned around and sped back to Sabbath Rest Road. Sped back home.

14

When she waded through the river the next day, Janice, wide awake, held her shoes up high in one hand, and a scarf in the other. There'd been no dreams that night. No sleepwalking. She felt more rested than she'd been in weeks. She was grateful to Stephen for it, and emboldened by her gratitude. She'd thought of driving to his house, but quickly calculated the number of reasons why she shouldn't.

Given the circumstances of her only visit to and exodus from his property, Janice surprised herself at how accurately she judged the direction and distance. The conscious and intentional trip brought her to Stephen's from a slightly different angle, but she recognized the peaked roof of the studio, and its high windows. In full daylight, the place was stunning. A packed gravel drive looped around an island of beautiful blooming bushes. Rhododendrons, he'd tell her later. The flowers, white explosions over thick green leaves. Janice thought she heard music, or water flowing, but with the calls and chirps from all the birds feeding at various stations around the yard it was hard to tell. Beyond the studio stood a house so well integrated with the environment—the colors, the scale and lines—it seemed as if it grew there, along with the trees or was hewn from the boulders. From one side of the house a low deck without a railing jutted several yards over a shallow ravine. On the deck, facing away from Janice, and as naked as any human ever was, Stephen Gainy stood perfectly erect, with his arms extending heavenward, palms together, fingers straight.

Jesus Christ Almighty! What was Janice supposed to do with that?

Stephen didn't give her time to decide before he moved.

He moved. Arched his back, so that his body was one fluid curve, then bent completely forward so far that his nose had to be touching his knees, and his hands were nearly flat on the deck boards. Which meant, much to Janice's riveted distress, that his bare, bifurcated, quite white, and incredibly muscled ass was aimed directly at her.

She wanted to look away. Really. Truly. It was just that . . . she'd seen naked men before, but . . . but, Stephen moved again. Lunging out with his left leg, one giant step, dropping his right knee to the floor, right foot extended. He put his hands parallel to the left foot and looked to the sky. This move too, proved troublesome, because it put all his male stuff on display. Hanging there, nearly dragging against the planks. Janice wanted not to look.

It took two more equally intense, and revealing, positions before Janice realized he was doing yoga. Three positions later, when she'd finally resigned herself to watching, a crow winged by, inches from her head, cawing cawing cawing.

Janice screamed. The crow lit on her back, cursing in her ear.

"Clyde! Get off!"

Somehow, Stephen had found his way into some shorts, and stood shooing away the big black bird with a towel.

"Sorry," he said. "That's Clyde. My watch-crow."

Janice tried to smile, but she was so embarrassed that it probably seemed more a grimace.

"Are you okay?" Stephen asked.

"I just . . . I've only . . . I didn't see anything," she said with way too much emphasis.

"Okay," he replied, completely and genuinely unconcerned. "Can I make sure you're not bleeding, at least? Clyde's a sweetie most of the time, but his talons are sharp."

Janice stood perfectly still while Stephen traced the imprint of the bird's perch on her back.

"What's that?" he asked, eyeing Janice's hand.

"It's for you," she said, reaching the scarf out toward him. "It's a scarf."

"Well, thanks. It's . . . really . . . beaut . . . it's . . . what, seventy-five, eighty degrees out? Is there a cold front coming through?"

"I made it," she said, heaping a little attitude behind the statement. "I wanted to thank you for helping me yesterday."

"I'm just teasing you, Janice. It's a really great scarf."

He paid close and real attention to the handiwork, as if acknowledging the level of craft.

"Beautiful," he said. "And now I've got a head start on winter. Did you decide to stay an extra day?"

Stephen walked to the deck, gesturing with his head for her to follow. Clyde flew in, ruffled his feathers, and cocked a black eye at Janice.

Was it possible that the bird knew about the skull hanging above her bed? Her bed.

"No," she said. "I came back. I left and came back."

She neglected to mention the goats, or the fact that she didn't even make it five miles.

Stephen looked about to ask her something, probably how long she planned to stay. Janice quickly filled that space.

"I like your place."

"You're just in time for dinner," he said, opening the sliding glass door from the deck.

"I don't want to be any trouble," Janice said, sure that the saliva was already dribbling down her chin.

"Do I need to search you for weapons?"

Janice laughed. She liked this man. Comfortable. Easy. Familiar.

"Let me get a shirt," he said, hanging the scarf on a coatrack as he passed.

Janice perched at a high barstool, feeling ridiculously young and awkward, until Stephen returned and began pulling things from the refrigerator. His house was funky. Eclectic. Now she could say that she'd been in a genuinely eclectic home. But Janice was so enthralled with Stephen that she mostly just watched him cook.

"Can I help?" she asked.

He handed her a cutting board, and an oversized knife—handle first. When Janice reached for both, Stephen looked at the bandage on her wrist.

"Are you okay?" he asked. Then added, "There?"

The location of her bandage, and the wound that might or might not lie beneath, could easily have been misinterpreted.

"Yeah," she said. "It's . . . it's a new tattoo."

"Can I see it?" Stephen asked, genuinely excited.

"Nope. Not yet."

Stephen laid a pack of hotdogs by the cutting board.

"You're going to have to trust me on this one, okay?"

"What do you mean?" Janice asked.

"I promise it's going to taste good, despite first appearances. Will you cut the hotdogs into little coins?"

Stephen was right on both counts. When he spooned, then spread, a generous layer of homemade guacamole onto thick homemade flour tortillas, added a layer of sauerkraut and the little oddly tan hotdog discs, Janice had her doubts. But when he heated the tortillas on a griddle, flipping them to a perfect golden brown, and she tasted a small wedge from his fingers, it might have been the best thing she'd ever put in her mouth.

Hunger. Real, deep belly-hunger.

Janice ate without speaking, until she noticed Stephen watching her and smiling.

She wanted to tell him about the goats, but couldn't think of a way to bring up the subject.

"Sorry," she said.

"I'm glad you like it so much," Stephen said, opening the door to toss the bullet-shaped end of a hotdog onto the deck. Clyde pounced immediately.

Janice told him that all she'd eaten "recently" were the canned goods she'd found in the cupboard, and rice and beans.

"So you're the new locktender, huh?" he asked.

"What do you mean?"

"You're living in an old locktender's house. I thought those were all state park property. It's cool that you were able to rent it."

"Yeah," she said, in full denial. "Yeah. But what's a locktender? Do you mean like a locksmith?"

Stephen affected a combination of some deep-hillbilly and hybrid German-Mexican accent.

"You are not from these parts, are you, lady?"

Janice was too concerned about being busted as a trespasser to laugh at his attempt, which Stephen mistook for disapproval.

"Sorry," he said. "Some jokes just don't get off the ground. Can I come by tomorrow, and show you what I mean by lockhouse?"

YES! YES! YES! The word stormed in triplicate around Janice's brain. She'd been bereft of human company for so long, and this particular human, in whose presence she forgot all about Danks and the dreams and the sleepwalking and the spooky tollbooth attendant, and all the nonsense of her recent past, this particular human was more genuine, less an emotional swindler, than any man she'd ever met.

"Maybe," she said. "Let me see what I have planned . . ."

Stephen opened two bottles of beer.

"I make it myself," he said. "It's a little hoppy, but not bad."

Janice took a drink, and the potent herb sent a tingle straight up between her eyes and down her spine.

"Wow . . ."

He asked about living in the house.

"Is there electricity?"

"Nope."

"How do you cook?"

"The woodstove," she said. "It's a pain. I wish there were another way."

Stephen moved two deck chairs out to the porch. They sat facing the mountain.

"So you're this mystery pioneer woman, retreating to the wild, and surviving by your wits and your knitting needles alone?"

"I reckon," she said, wanting to change the subject before revealing too much about her status as a resident in the house. "What about you? You live way out in the woods, carve gravestones, eat hotdogs with guacamole, *and* practice yoga?"

Stephen gave her a one-eyebrow-raised look and said, in mock shock, "I thought you didn't see anything."

Janice felt her face and neck glow bright red.

"I . . . uh . . . no . . . well, I just walked up. I didn't mean to."

"It's okay," he said. "I forgive you. Besides, now we're even."

"What do you mean?"

"Well, you did show up outside my window the other day in a soaking-wet white gown . . ."

If it were possible for layers of delicious embarrassment to be heaped one atop the other . . .

Stephen rescued her by graciously changing the subject.

"What did you mean by gravestones?"

"I saw you in the window moving a huge tombstone."

"Ahhhh," he said. "Come with me."

Janice followed Stephen out to the studio, where he opened a set of bay doors and stood back like a proud father.

Evening sun filtered through the trees, flowed into the open workspace, and spilled over the wide heavy tables in the center of the room—tables holding chisels and hammers, rasps files and calipers. The sunlight spread across the far wall and the strange gridded drawings tacked along its expanse. The sunlight penetrated the depths of the room, hurling its warm fearless presence against the most beautiful stone carving Janice had ever seen.

"Wow."

Janice didn't know what else to say.

"It's an altarpiece," Stephen said. "A depiction of the Passion of Christ, in low-relief granite. Byzantine style."

He sounded like he was reading from a brochure.

"Or, the Passion of Christ captured in stone? Which sounds better?"

Janice was too overcome by the magnitude of the work to pay any attention to his question.

"What?" she asked. "This is so amazing. These are definitely not grave-stones!"

"Which sounds better, 'a depiction of the Passion of Christ in low-relief granite,' or 'the Passion of Christ captured in stone'?"

Floor to ceiling, a thick wooden frame held the series of stones at a barely detectable angle against the wall. The three panels across the bottom—all five-foot-high rectangles, the center stone twice the width of the two-foot-wide sides—seemed almost finished. The two arching caps for the side stones were also in place, but the middle arch lay on the work-table. That was what she'd seen him moving the other day. Janice walked up to the table, reached out and traced her finger along Christ's beautifully tortured face, the crown of thorns. Put her dusty fingertip to her mouth.

"Oh my God, I'm so sorry," she said, genuinely appalled by her action. "I didn't mean to touch it without asking!"

Stephen laughed.

"It's granite. Your finger isn't likely to do any harm."

He stepped around the table, took her hand, and placed it on the rough, uncarved brow of a robed woman on the side panel.

"Mary Magdalene," Stephen said, then told Janice all about the work, panel by panel, chisel mark by chisel mark. He picked up his tools and made several strokes.

Tchink, tchink. Tchink.

Janice recognized the sound she heard some nights. Was it possible? Could this conversation between stone and chisel carry all the way through the woods? It had to be.

"I've been carving this for about three years," he said. "I'm on sabbatical until fall, and I want to finish before then."

"What's a sabbatical?" she asked. "You work for a church or something?"

"Nope. I teach in the art program at Penn State University. Once you're tenured, once you've given enough flesh and blood to prove something to half a dozen useless committees, they let you have a year off."

"Paid? A yearlong paid vacation?"

"Well, you have to have a project. This altarpiece is my project. What the campus doesn't know is that I'm trying to sell the work to the Orthodox diocese in Philadelphia. And, in my dream world, that leads to commissions for more altarpieces. I'm working on the copy for my promo stuff."

"Why wouldn't you tell the university?" Janice asked, sitting on a backless stool near the worktable, picking up the chisels and hammers as if gauging the weight of each.

"If I sell this piece and get commissions for two more, I'll never set foot in another classroom. I'll hold a ceremonial burning of my tenure letter on the steps of the provost's office."

"Six more years of carving stone . . ." Janice said, mostly to herself. She'd never known anyone who'd been so devoted to anything.

Stephen narrated the short walk back to the house by pointing out all the flowers in bloom and naming the visitors to his bird feeders.

"Bluebells over there. Arbutus. Daylilies, of course. Last night, right at dusk, I saw a hawk take a mourning dove off that tree limb. A little puff of feathers, and they were both gone."

"It's so peaceful here," Janice said.

"Like your place is party central?"

"It's quiet, you're right. It's just . . . I'm having such a hard time sleeping. Crazy, crazy dreams. And lately . . ." Janice paused, unsure if she should tell.

"Lately what?"

"Sleepwalking. Almost every night."

"Really?" Stephen laughed. "That sounds fun . . ."

"No, I'm serious . . . There's no locks and . . . You're not going to believe it, but I was sleepwalking the first time I came here."

"Wow, you crossed the river?"

"Yes! I woke up watching you move that stone."

"You could tie yourself up. Or maybe I should leave out some cookies and milk. Or . . . leave my door unlocked."

"It's not funny, Stephen. I'm worried."

Stephen. It was the first time she'd called him by name. The word felt good in her mouth.

"Sorry," he said. "Sometimes I don't know when to quit. You know what I think?"

"No, what?"

"You should try yoga."

"What?"

"Yoga. The thing you didn't see me doing today."

"I know what yoga is," Janice said, looking away so that he wouldn't see her blush. "But why do I need yoga?"

"If you do ten Sun Salutations every day, morning or night, doesn't matter when, you'll sleep like a baby. Your mind and body will be right with the world."

"And Sun Salutations are?"

"It's a sequence of twelve positions, *asanas*, done in a certain order. It's what I was doing on the porch, although you don't have to do them naked."

There was fire in Stephen's eye.

Janice forced herself to the flame.

"And if I do them naked will I get right with the world even quicker?"

Janice was in full blush even before she finished the sentence. Stephen just grinned.

"No doubt about it."

Neither of them knew where to take the conversation after that. Janice asked where his bathroom was.

"Such a beautiful place," she said, coming back. "Running water, a tub, and all."

"Yeah, I'm not as tough as you," he said.

Clyde landed just outside the sliding glass door, tapping three times with his beak. Stephen let him in.

"I . . ." Janice felt suddenly, inexplicably, nervous. "I should be going. I don't want to cross the river in the dark."

"Let me give you a ride back."

"No, no . . ."

"Come on, it's quick and easy. Just climb on the back of . . ."

"No. Really. No."

"Well at least let me take you partway and show you something."

Stephen held out his hands, palms up.

"No tricks," he said, then swung a leg over the ATV's seat.

In a few short minutes—with Janice trying to hold on to him, trying not to seem like she was holding on to him, or at the very least pretending that straddling the same seat as this good-looking man was no big deal, with her legs V'd and locked tight so that the random and regular bumps in the path didn't force her body completely against his, locked out of fear of falling off the back; locked in place, consciously or not, close enough to guarantee at least a little touch—Stephen skidded to a stop at a point not too far upstream from where she'd crossed before. The banks were steeper, but Stephen took her to a fat old willow tree and showed her the rope bridge: two parallel cables, one for walking on, another chest-high one for balance, spanning the river between the willow and another tree on the opposite bank.

"Now you can come see me without getting your feet wet."

"What makes you think I'm gonna come back?"

15

Another night without dreams. Another night without the muddy footprints of her nocturnal twin to greet her in the morning. Janice, however, didn't sleep all that well. Could've been the potential for escape: the Subaru and its charged battery. Could've been the lack of yoga in her life. But, more likely, she couldn't sleep because Stephen Gainy said he was coming over the next day.

There'd been no discussion of when, though, and once Janice rushed through a meager breakfast and chilly sponge bath, she tried everything she could think of not to be *waiting*. She sat, for a while, in the driver's seat, holding on to the steering wheel. Even cranked the car once, even shifted into drive. Then, after several hours of not waiting, she actually gave in and sat on the front doorstep knitting. Finally, Janice decided he wasn't coming.

She misheard.

He misspoke.

She scared him away.

He lied.

He came over the lip of the channel without a wheelie this time.

"Hey," he said.

"Hey," she said. "Don't you ever wear a helmet?"

"Listen now, if you're mean to me I won't give you your presents."

Stephen climbed off the ATV, shook the wind out of his hair. His face was still so new to her that it took Janice a moment to reconcile the gray hair and the taut youthful skin.

Janice tucked her knitting into its bag, stood up, and brushed the dust from the seat of her skirt.

"Just trying to keep you safe," she said, then immediately wished she hadn't.

"Well, my head is harder than the rocks I hammer on all day. Might knock some sense into me if I fell off this thing. Hold out your arms."

Janice did as she was told, and he turned and handed her an olive green, two-burner camp stove.

"I've got some fuel here, too."

Janice laughed.

"You don't know how much I appreciate this."

"Yes I do," Stephen said, following her inside.

It made her nervous for him to be poking around while she brought out the dish of preserved pears and some lukewarm tea.

"I'm sorry I don't have much to offer," Janice said, and meant it far more than he knew.

"This is just right," Stephen said. "You know, I didn't think they could rent these out to the public, it being government property and all."

"They?" Janice answered without thinking.

"The Parks Department," he said, confusion in his voice. "Isn't that who . . ."

"Oh, yeah yeah," Janice interrupted him. "I didn't know you were talking about the house. It took some finagling."

Change the subject. Change the subject.

"Plural," she said. "Presents, with an *s*?" holding out her arms again.

"Okay, then. Sit here at the table."

"Should I close my eyes?" Janice asked.

"Yes, yes. Good idea."

Janice heard him move the dishes from the table, heard him wipe it, heard him pull something from a backpack. Paper. It sounded like paper. Untying. Unrolling. She felt the presence of his hands as he positioned the gift in front of her.

"Okay," he said.

Janice opened her eyes, blinked twice at the drawing.

"It's the Sun Salutation," he said. "All the positions."

"Did you draw this?" Janice asked, stunned by the beauty and accuracy of the twelve figures, the perspective slightly above, slightly oblique, figures caught in charcoal, each snared in the critical moment of a stretch or step or bend or turn.

"Yep," he said. "Did it last night."

Janice reached out to touch the drawing, but pulled back.

"You can touch it," he said. "I put a fixative on it."

"It's too beautiful to touch," Janice said, but traced her finger a scant millimeter above the perfectly rendered back, the naked back, of a naked woman, in a circle of unabashedly naked women . . . no, woman, they were all the same woman, all with the same body, sometimes front, the belly soft but proportional, the breasts not idealized, but about the same handful Janice found during her occasional checks for lumps and such, the limbs lean, hips full and round enough, a woman's body, the face, when visible, the same open face, hair just so, the smile a little crooked, and the freckles.

"Is this . . . this is . . ."

"Yep," he said.

"How?"

The faintest tinge of worry crept into Janice's voice. Is this when the *killer* emerges?

"I'm good at what I do," Stephen said. "The human body is my subject, in stone, or on paper. And despite our culture's never-ending attempts to warp and reshape both the bodies of the world and our ideas of what bodies are, I've got my own notions, and I'm not giving them up."

Okay, no killer.

"And you," he added. "You have such an interesting mouth."

Janice instinctively put a hand to her face. She looked for a while, looked only at the drawing because, although it was awkward to see herself portrayed so nude, so accurately, so generously, and so flexibly, she couldn't meet Stephen's gaze.

Keen to her embarrassment, he defused the moment.

"Hey, do you have any more of those pears?"

Janice took an unopened jar from the nearly empty cupboard.

"Last one," she said, handing it to Stephen. "Weren't you going to tell me some stuff about this house?"

Stephen paused, midbite.

"It's strange that they didn't tell you about the house, and the lock, when they rented it to you."

He stabbed a piece of the soft, colorless fruit with a fork, ate it, then handed both the jar and the fork to Janice.

"I'm sure they knew that some industrious stone-carving, peeping-Tom-ish hermit would charge out of the woods to do that job," Janice said.

"That's the pot calling the kettle black."

They walked to the lip of the high stone wall.

"You're living in the locktender's house," he said, then made a sweeping gesture over the deep stone channel at their feet. "And this is the lock."

They sat down on the cool stone and ate the rest of the pears while Stephen explained the history and operations of the canal system to Janice. Told her about this ambitious but short-lived and ill-fated predecessor to the railroads. Talked with genuine excitement about the man-made, often hand-dug, series of waterways crisscrossing the Northeast, for trade and commerce. An industry that peaked briefly in the mid-1800s, and by the turn of the century had been all but obliterated by the railroad system.

"So many people died in these ditches. Standing all day in knee-deep mud. Men started getting sick with cholera, and the canal bosses told them it wasn't contagious. Men died within twenty-four hours. Turned black."

Stephen told Janice, in more detail than she would have asked for, horror stories about the lives and deaths of the men who built the canals.

"All this water, miles and miles of water, goes over land that changes in elevation. They built the locks as a way of accommodating the elevation shifts. It's like a hoist, like a water-driven elevator that lifted the canal boats up or lowered them down to the next water level."

Stephen pointed out where the massive wooden sluice gates were hinged into the stone at both ends of the lock. They stood, and he led her to the end where the lock key and the swing beam would have been.

"This is where the locktender stood to open the gate."

"So the gate-man lived here?"

"Yep. The locktender. It was a 24/7 job. The man practically had to sleep with his hands on the gate. If memory serves, I think you're living at Lock 33."

Janice loved the stories. There was a strange familiarity to all that he talked about. As if, when he told her about a particular step in locking through a canal boat, she wanted to say, *well of course.* Janice loved, even more, the passion with which Stephen told the stories. She wished she could think of other questions, many more questions, to prolong his telling.

"Wait a minute," she said. "Now I remember. When you came to my door the first time, you hollered . . ."

"Hey Lock!" he interrupted. "It's how the boatmen called to the lock-tender. Either a yell or a horn. At night, they swung a lantern from the bow of the boat."

A swinging lantern. Back and forth. Scooping out shallow dishes of night.

"Hey," Stephen said, tugging her sleeve. "Where'd you go?"

"Sorry," Janice replied. "Just spaced out for a minute. Tell me something, how do you know so much about all this canal business?"

"Come on, I'll show you."

Stephen scrambled halfway down the canal's dirt bank, just past the lock, and held his hand out for Janice to follow.

To follow.

Janice couldn't bring herself to reach out, to step down, to follow.

"I . . . um . . . do you . . ."

"You got to come in with me if you want to know the secret."

Still, she hesitated.

"Chicken?"

Janice shook the fog from her head and back-stepped into the canal without taking his hand.

Stephen walked into the shadowy stone channel, and even he was dwarfed by its scale.

Janie stepped up, stepped in, and the surge of cold air nearly knocked her down. Took her breath, chilled her to the core.

—*near, the body is near*—

"Did you hear that?"

Whispers. Or wing beats.

Dizzied, Janice reached out to the walls, the cold stone biting at the flesh of her palms.

"Hear what?" Stephen asked. "Are you spooked? Worried about the canal ghosts?"

He smiled at her.

Janice wanted to leave the lock. Janice wanted to tell Stephen about the dreams, the crazy things in her head, to tell him about voices and the goats and the migraine that started it all when Danks was killed. And she wanted Stephen to listen without laughing.

"What are you going to show me?" she asked.

"Here," he said, drawing her attention to a perfectly square cornerstone.

"What?"

Stephen wiped away dust and creeping mosses for Janice to see the letters: SJG.

The initials were incised with hard exact lines, curves, and angles, into and along the bottom edge of the stone.

"Stephen James Gainy," he said.

"That's not you, is it!"

"No, it's my great-grandfather. He helped build almost all the locks on this canal. My grandfather was a mason too. They emigrated from the Ukraine, and inhaled rock dust in the land of the free until it killed them."

Janice felt light-headed. She wanted to go back.

"Don't tell anybody," Stephen said, pointing to the opposite end of the lock, where the walls gaped from several missing stones, like a snaggle-toothed mouth.

Janice conveyed her question wordlessly.

"This," he whispered, looking around with exaggerated concern. "This is where I get my stones for the altarpiece."

She tried to smile and look either accusatory or understanding, succeeded at neither.

"Let's get you out of here," he said.

When Janice turned, the toe of her shoe caught on a thin rock shelf at the uneven floor of the lock. Off balance, she grabbed at the wall, pulling out a loose shard, then sat down painfully.

"Ummph!"

"You okay?" Stephen asked, moving the loose stone aside.

Janice nodded yes, got to her knees, and was about to stand when she saw something else.

"What's this?"

Stephen crouched to look at a spot by the shard Janice had yanked from the wall.

Scratches. Crude scratches. A jumble of letters, some reaching up, some down, that neither of them could make sense of.

"Maybe a name?" Janice said.

"Probably kids. Vandals," he said.

"Maybe a name," Janice repeated. Then she vomited. Then her eyes rolled back.

Then she awoke in the bed, in the locktender's house, with Stephen sitting on the floor looking at her.

No jokes. No teasing. Only concern in his eyes.

"Hey," he said.

"Hey," came Janice's weak reply.

"I think we need to get you to a doctor," Stephen said.

"No."

Then again, with as much force as she could muster.

"No! It's only . . . it's just food stuff," she said with an attempt at conviction. "I've gotten sick before, eating from the jars."

Janice closed her eyes. Sitting up was out of the question.

"I'm taking you to my house tonight," he said. "You can have my room, and I'll sleep in the studio."

"No, Stephen."

"I do it all the time. I work late at night, then sleep there. Besides . . . it's ridiculous. You have no food, no way to take care of yourself."

"No. No. No."

"You can't . . ."

"I can do whatever I want. I appreciate your concern. I really do. But I'm fine. I just need to sleep awhile, then I'll eat something better. I want you to go home. Thank you for the offer, but . . ."

"I don't feel right about leaving you here."

Obstinate. Embarrassed. Whatever the case, Janice would not be swayed.

"All right, I'll go on one condition. And I mean it. If you don't agree, I'll just sleep downstairs."

"What?" Janice asked.

"Tomorrow, I'm going on a grocery run. I want you to come to my house . . . I want you to make a list tonight and bring it over tomorrow. Put everything you need on the list."

"I don't have . . ."

"I didn't ask you about money," he said. "I'll be gone for several hours. I want you to stay at my house while I'm gone. Eat some decent food. Sleep in a real bed. You can even take a bath."

It all sounded wonderful to Janice. Her only hesitation was the fear that she'd lack the energy to cross the river.

"I'm coming after you around noon," Stephen said.

"Okay. Okay."

Alone in the locktender's house, exhausted, Janice worked at the meager list of groceries and supplies for hours. Adding to, then napping, erasing from, then napping. The undertaking of each letter, each syllable, each word put down on paper required a team of mules, a hammer and chisel, ropes and pulleys.

16

Cold blows the wind to my true love
And gently drops the rain
I never had but one sweetheart
And in green wood she lies slain

There's one thing that I want, sweetheart
There's one thing that I crave
That is a kiss from your lily-white lips
Then I'll go down from your grave

My breast it is as cold as clay
My breath smells earthly strong
And if you kiss my cold clay lips
Your days they won't be long

Go fetch me water from the desert
And blood from yonder stone
Go fetch me milk from a young maid's breast
That a young man never had known

The stalk is withered and dry, sweetheart
And the flower will never return
And since I lost my own sweetheart
What can I do but mourn

17

S he'd made the list. Slept horribly. Dreamt strange songs. Mournful, sad songs. The notes, plucked and strummed, so real in her mind, in her ears.

But Janice couldn't trust her ears.

—*the body is near*—

What happened in the lock didn't feel like food poisoning.

Lying there in the narrow bed, afraid to look at the floor for fear of the damning footprints, Janice wished she could go home. But where would *home* be?

Certainly not Greensboro. Once, aeons ago, the Natural Bridge had been her destination.

Janice looked at the floor, the mercifully clean floor. She sat up and her equilibrium went topsy-turvy. Each thought, an oarless canoe in mad water. Each slight movement, a carnival ride. Common sense notwithstanding, this place, the locktender's house, felt as much like *home* as anywhere else. Despite the dreams. Despite the footprints.

The list. Did she put eggs on the list?

The dreams. Had the nightmares returned to torment her after a maddeningly brief hiatus?

Batteries. A cheap flashlight.

She could leave, but—

"Do you play an instrument?" she asked.

The tampons? Did they end up on the list after all the false starts?

"What?"

"Do you play an instrument?"

Anything in a can.

"No. Look at these fingers. Listen, do you have a can opener?"

"Stephen?"

Stephen. Comfort. Reason to stay?

"Yes?"

How long had he been there, sitting in half-lotus on the floor by her bed?

"I heard a banjo . . . or something stringed . . ."

"Doesn't surprise me," Stephen said, but didn't say why. "Maybe we should take you to a doctor?"

"I'll be fine. I just need to eat better."

There was neither conviction nor convincing in the statement.

"Well . . . if you're not any better in a few days you're going to the doctor, even if I have to shanghai you."

Janice smiled weakly. How'd he get in? When did he come?

"I want to take you to my house before I go for groceries. Is there anything else you want to add to this list?"

Stephen held the paper up for Janice to look at, but her eyes wouldn't focus.

"Next time you can go with me," he said. "I'll wait downstairs while you get dressed."

Bread. Cheese. Did she put batteries on the list? Aspirin?

"Do you drive this thing to the store?" Janice asked, climbing with great effort onto the back of the ATV.

"No, I have a pickup, too. I guess I should've come after you in it, but I just wasn't thinking. Anyway, by the time I get around to Sabbath Rest Road, I'm about halfway to the store."

Janice, licensed by fatigue, let go all pretense of distance and lay fully against Stephen as he puttered slowly back across the dry canal and the shallow river to his house. After some coffee, a hard-boiled egg (abundantly salted), and buttered toast, served by Stephen, who sat patiently—elbows anchored on the table, chin perched on his hands—while she ate, Janice felt like she could approximate coherent speech.

"Why don't you want to teach anymore?"

"What?"

Not the question he was expecting. Nor was it one she'd planned to ask.

"You said if you got commissions for more altarpieces, you'd never set foot in the classroom again."

Stephen chuckled.

"It's a long, boring story," he said. "And no doubt full of my own paranoid biases. I guess the short and sweet version is that they don't want me on the faculty any more than I want to be there."

"But why," she asked. "Those carvings are incredible. And . . ."

"Incredible? Yes. And incredibly outdated. I'm a dinosaur. A lumbering, ungainly, loud, messy creature who's overstayed its welcome. An unnecessary appendage that evolution is about to lop off and discard."

"I don't understand. I'm sure your students love you."

"Students," he said. "A small doe-eyed pack of devotees isn't much to bank on."

Stephen went to a low bookshelf under a wide clear window and retrieved a thick leather pouch, the size of a family bible. He laid the pouch on the table, nodded for Janice to unzip it.

Tools. Chisels, hammers, rasps and files.

"What do you see?" he asked.

"Besides the obvious?"

"What's obvious," Stephen said. "What's obvious is there's no keyboard here. No USB ports or firewall cables. No hard drive. No program icons to double-click. No mouse to click with. No cut and paste, redo, step-back. You fuck up with the chisel and you've fucked up, plain and simple."

The intensity of Stephen's mini-tirade spooked her. She realized she hadn't known this man for very long.

"Sorry," Stephen said. "Didn't do my Sun Salutations this morning. They help keep the bile in check."

"That's okay," Janice said, tracing patterns in the salt left on the plate with her finger. "I just don't understand what you're talking about."

She licked her fingertip and looked at the plate. Were those letters she'd made in the salt?

"Oh, I'm just complaining about growing old. The whole art department, in fact the entire academic art world, is moving toward *new media*. Most of the studios are now computer labs, and the painting and sculpture classrooms have been moved into an old maintenance building with only two windows. The *tactile* is becoming unnecessary. So . . . *new media*," Stephen said again, with an exaggerated "quotation" gesture. "Are you sure you'll be okay here while I'm gone?"

After he left, Janice continued sitting at the table as the not-quite-muffled sounds of his truck disappeared in the folds of topography. She wondered where the road went.

Temptation almost got the best of her. She wanted to look around. Look for pictures, letters from other girlfriends. Pictures of ex-wives. Something to explain why such a kind, smart, good-looking man lived like a hermit in the woods. She wanted to find something that would belie his secret, illuminate his dark quarter. But decency held sway. Janice restricted her curiosity to the bookshelf, where her fingertips traced a path from right to left, touching each spine as she went, whispering the titles.

"*Beginner's Mind.* Brancusi. Giacometti. Rumi . . ." and on down the line, to the shelf below. So many books. As if on cue, the late morning sun found safe passage through the dense copse of birch trees along the edge of the property and laid a warm yellow-white plank across the room to a shallow alcove in the far wall. Janice hadn't noticed the Buddha before. But there, with the sunlight playing over his lidded eyes, the sweep of the brows mirrored inversely in the many folds of his robe, the dense grain of blond wood so polished there was no doubt it would feel like fabric to her fingertips, sitting with his hands in his lap, as if cupping a delicate egg, sitting thus illuminated, the Buddha was the most beautiful thing Janice had ever seen.

She wanted to reach out and touch his face. Couldn't. And couldn't say why.

Janice stepped past the sliding glass door onto the deck where she'd seen Stephen in all his naked yogic glory. She hadn't looked closely enough at the chart to remember any positions from the Sun Salutation. She tried a tentative lunge, placing her right foot far in front, bending into the move. But her jeans were cinched tight in the waist, the knee, the seat and groin.

Janice stood and looked around, into the woods, and up the narrow drive that disappeared in the trees. Trying as hard as she could not to seem nervous, Janice slipped out of her jeans, folded them neatly, laid them just by the door, and tried the stretch again. Then the other side. It felt good, the blood flowing, sunshine, and bare skin. Emboldened, Janice yanked her T-shirt over her head. Took a deep breath. Felt herself to be the bravest woman in the world, standing there in her bra and panties, in the open air.

Well, maybe not *the* bravest. She turned to face the house, then arched her back, the way she'd seen Stephen do. She bent forward, legs together and straight, unsure if she could actually touch the plank deck, and was doubled over so, hands clasping ankles, semiexposed, and vulnerable, when Clyde cawed from a nearby branch.

Janice fell forward, skinned her knee on the deck. Got a splinter in her palm. Clyde cawed again. Then again. Laughing. Cursing. Or both.

Janice's face burned with embarrassment. She grabbed her clothing, covered herself, and not so unlike Eve in her exodus from the garden, rushed through the door, closed it tight behind her.

Stupid bird. Stupid bird.

Janice ran a bath, sat on the toilet seat pushing at the splinter in her palm with her thumbnail.

Stupid bird.

How long had it been since she'd lain in a tub of hot water?

Having drawn the bath as hot as she could possibly bear, she settled into the deep old tub slowly, letting her skin acclimate by reddening degrees. Once comfortable, legs stretched fully, back perfectly cradled by the warm porcelain, she reached for the book on meditation, the most basic one she could find on his bookshelf.

Breath.

So much about breath and breathing.

The warmth began to seep into her muscles, her joints, even to the marrow of her bones. Janice opened up and welcomed the cleansing heat, hoping it would purge those dark dreams from deep inside her.

Breathe. The simplest, and most profound, meditation is to follow one's breath.

In. Out. The point of entry into the body . . . the point of exit. All things start and stop with the breath.

Janice read. Through the open bathroom door she watched a band of sunshine slowly consume the bedroom floor.

Breathe. Be present with the breath. Accompany the breath down into the belly, the breath pulling the unflinching light of awareness into the body, where it radiates out into every vessel, every pore. Breathe. Be present with the breath as it leaves the body, carrying with it all the pure unqualified love the body is capable of generating. Breathe. Breathe. Breathe.

~

In the dream—or is it memory—in the dream, the mother and the little girl. The mother and her child, her Janice, in the tent, and the preacher walks back and forth, a bible held aloft in his big hand, the book perched up there like a black bird. In the the dream—or is it memory—the girl is scared of the bird. The preacher cries. Whispers *nigger blood*. Whispers *mongrel*. The congregation, the flock, cries. An organ. Or maybe it's just her mother. In the memory—or is it the dream—the dark preacher calls them to the altar. Forgiveness. Redemption. The mother drags the girl down the muddy aisle. The congregation, the flock, laughs. Or maybe it's just her mother. In a galvanized tub, the preacher scoops her up, like a baby, tilts her head back to dunk it in the tub—the water, cold against her flesh, her clothes—the water, searing, burns up her nose, down her throat—breath, nowhere to be found—the mother, or maybe it's the congregation, weeps, wails—tongues—tongues—echolalia—her mother babbles to God—too hard, this business of souls—too exposed—in the dream, in the memory, the little girl is ashamed of the mother—the preacher's big hands—the bible takes flight—its black cover whips the air overhead—the congregation laughs, or cries, or maybe it's the mother—so much crying—laughter clinks and clanks in their throats—tchink, tchink, tchink—the baling twine knotted at her wrists, cuts deep—you have to stay here, honey—you have to stay here, honey—I'm sorry—says *watered-down nigger blood is still nigger blood*—tchink, tchink, tchink—the water comes, slowly at first, fills the canal—fills it up—submerging everything in its wake—

Tchink, tchink, tchink—they can't run, or crawl, fast enough—the man comes, who makes the noise—in the dream, he touches her ribs and muscle and bone fall away—tchink, tchink, tchink—in the dream, with only his hammer and pure love, he reshapes her face—tchink, tchink, tchink—chips a small and necessary passage into her chest cavity—in the dream, the man slips two fingers into the hole, plucks out a key, hands it to the woman—in the dream, the woman stands at the bank of a raging river—in the dream, she clutches a key in her palm—in the dream, she hurls it into the torrent—caw—the bible flies—tchink, tchink, tchink—in the dream the chisel in all its perfection—wet—the sex of her body, denied, forgotten, ignored, sealed—the chisel in all its glory, knows the way—caw—in the dream—caw—or is it memory—the man chisels himself inside her—down there—the caw—down there the metal is cold the metal is hot—down there the woman is torn asunder—cries out—down there—laughter—down there—weeping—wanting—caw—tchink, tchink, tchink—

~

Janice woke, with a start. The water completely cold, her mind reeling, her body goosefleshed, bluing, her thighs still trembling from the first wet dream, the first orgasm, she'd had in years. Despite the chill, it took quite a while before she had the wherewithal to stand and drape herself in a coarse towel. Janice stood at the sliding door, forehead resting against the thick glass.

How long had she slept?

How long before Stephen returned?

Clyde, his coal-black crow, sat high at the peak of the studio roof.

Looking at her? Was the bird looking at Janice?

When the crow stretched his wings and fell into flight, Janice took a step back from the door. When it cawed that pitiless, merciless caw, she almost ran. When it flew, without hesitation, into the closed glass door, the fine bones of its crow-neck shattering, fluid ruby-red jewels of its crow-blood dotting the site of impact, when it fell without bouncing, wings back and behind, in supplication, on the deck, Janice didn't know what to do but run.

18

Run. Her first impulse was to run, back across the cable bridge, back across the dry and empty canal, back to the locktender's house, to her car. An image from the dream flashed through her consciousness; she laid two fingers against her breast, the flesh over her heart tender and sore.

Run. She didn't know this man, in whose house she stood naked, whose ink-black bird lay limp and dead on the other side of a thin glass door, its life, its death both a million miles away and so close the feathers caught in her throat. Gag.

She'd never seen Stephen angry. He could kill her, out there in the woods, with the acres at the ready, ready to take her body. He would blame her. How could he not? And Janice, in the recent and rare moments of restfulness, of lucidity—moments between the dreams and the sleepwalking—Janice had allowed herself to feel for this man, this stone carver, this Stephen Gainy. To feel, at the very least, a potential between them. Potency. To hope, if not quite believe, that he too recognized the potential. And now, goddammit, the bird was dead. She killed his bird.

Janice dressed hastily. Carelessly. As if being watched.

She slid the glass door open. Afraid to step out, afraid to step over the dead bird, Janice got to her knees. She could take the crow's carcass into the woods and hide it. Clean the window. He'd never know. She could pretend to be asleep when Stephen returned, pretend she hadn't witnessed anything. She could tell Stephen the truth, but she wasn't sure what that meant. She knelt and looked at the dead crow. A single black eye, open and cocked toward her, refused entry, denied reflection. The beak, its twin tips splintered, gaped on the deck planks. Black tongue, still and lifeless. Silent. Janice left the bird where it lay.

Back at the locktender's house, Janice, frantic, rifled through her suitcase, her knitting bag, all her belongings dumped to the floor.

"Fuck!"

She said it aloud.

The key. The key to the Subaru. She'd lost the car key. Or had he taken it? Stephen. While she slept. The key. The key to her car. The key in the dream? The muscles over Janice's heart spasmed, a white-hot needle of pain shot her through.

She grunted and strained, pushing the settee in front of the door. Moved the kitchen table up to block the back door of the house. Upstairs, in her room, Janice dragged the bed over as a barricade to that door, built a meager fire despite the summer heat, sat in the corner farthest from the room's entryway, sat with her knitting, sat with her suitcase open, the gray rubber blade of the toy tomahawk visible in its pocket, sat wishing she had earplugs, sat humming a song she didn't know, sat, waiting, for whatever came next.

Came next. What came next, came rumbling slowly down the drive. A car, truck maybe, engine idling as it rolled over the gravel, the crunching swoosh growing louder by degrees. Could be Stephen, probably was, but Janice had no plan to get up and look. She hugged her knees to her chest and listened. Honeysuckle. The scent of honeysuckle wafted in. Janice had forgotten to close the window. The window became a funnel for sound. The engine shutting off. The vehicle's door squeaking open. Squeaking shut. Footsteps on the crushed stone driveway. Footsteps on the loose boards of the porch. A pause in the sound, hesitation. A brief silence, held in place by distant birdsong. Then the knock.

"Janice?"

Stephen.

"Hey Lock!"

Was that anger in his voice? He knocked again, more vigorously.

"Janice, are you here?"

Anger? Or impatience?

"Is everything all right?"

Janice kept still. Kept quiet. Kept listening.

Stephen jiggled the latch and pushed gently at the door. Janice heard the settee do its job downstairs.

"Janice? Are you . . ."

He must have decided against repeating the question.

No apparent anger, but maybe the lack of detectable rage was a trick. Maybe once Janice went out to greet Stephen, he'd have the dead bird in his hand ready to lay blame and dispense justice. Janice heard him step off the porch, listened to his footsteps circle around the house, pausing at each window. She heard the back door latch shake, heard the door balk at opening, heard Stephen complete his orbit, walk back to the truck, and open its door. But no closure. Stephen must be sitting in the truck. Waiting. Waiting for Janice.

Waiting.

The waiting for certain death was excruciating to Janice. Stephen sat in the truck, its door gaping open, singing to himself, while Janice crunched herself as far as she could into the corner of the nearly empty bedroom upstairs.

Maybe he hadn't been home yet. Maybe Stephen came straight from the store to the lockhouse. Maybe he didn't know yet of Clyde's death. Maybe that's why he didn't seem angry. Maybe, but she still didn't want to face him.

When Janice could sit still no longer, when it felt like the silence was crushing her, smothering her, she stood, half-crouched really, and peered out of the bottom corner of the window.

"Janice?"

She ducked.

"I thought you were out walking," he said.

Janice heard the truck door close.

"Were you sleeping?"

Heard him push against the door of the house below.

"Janice? Is there something blocking this door?"

When no answer came, Stephen stepped back into the drive and talked up to the bedroom window.

"Janice, are you all right? Do you need help?"

Sounded genuinely concerned. Not like he wanted to kill her.

"I'm all right," she said, probably too softly.

"Janice?"

She stood up, fully, looked out the window.

"Janice? Can I come in?"

He carried no weapon. His face, his posture, bore no evidence of rage.

Janice saw the several boxes of groceries and supplies in the bed of Stephen's truck. Surely he hadn't been home yet.

"I'm coming," she said.

Stephen unloaded all the boxes onto Janice's porch.

"Did you have the door blocked?" he asked, after she finally dragged the settee away and opened up.

"No," she said. "Yes . . . I got scared."

"Of what? Something at my house?"

He picked up a box and nudged Janice out of the way as he carried it through the door.

She selected the smallest box and followed him. She didn't answer his question.

"You certainly left in a hurry," Stephen said, the accompanying look either teasing or accusatory.

Janice moved so that the table stood between them.

"Are you mad?" she asked.

"Mad? Me, mad? Well . . . yes. Nothing in this world makes me angrier than . . . than finding cold, used water in my bathtub, and . . ."

With exaggerated effort, Stephen pulled something from the front pocket of his jeans.

". . . a pair of panties crumpled on the floor."

He smiled, extending his arm out across the table, her underwear bunched in his hand like a pale white flower. Janice plucked them from his grasp, turned around so that he couldn't see her reddened face, certain that evidence of her scary and erotic dream in his tub was apparent.

"I meant to wash them for you," he said. "But I wanted to get your food and stuff over before dark."

"Sorry," she said. "I didn't mean to . . ."

"Hey, I was kidding. I don't care about the bathwater. And, as for those unmentionables, I just thought you were . . . it was . . . well, anyway, of course I'm not mad."

Stephen unloaded the boxes as he spoke.

"I got everything on your list, then decided your list was ridiculously too short."

Stephen stacked can after can, box after box, until there was no more room on the table.

"I practically emptied the shelves," he said.

He said nothing about the dead bird.

"Your batteries," he said, emptying another carton. "And these."

Stephen held a battery-powered radio in one hand, and two flashlights in the other.

"You didn't have to do all this," Janice said.

"One last thing," he said, and from the final box he pulled a book and a couple of magazines. "I looked for the *Hot Knitters Gazette*, or *Drop Stitch Monthly*, but all they had was *Purl Two*, the one with the naked pictures; I didn't think we knew each other well enough."

Janice fanned out the issues of *Time*, *People*, and *Harper's*.

"Thanks. Much."

"This," he said, holding out a familiar book. "This you left on the bathroom floor. If you're really interested in meditation, it's a great book to start with."

"You really didn't have to do all this."

"Well, I'm going to take it all back unless you tell me what spooked you."

Why? Why had he not mentioned the broke-neck crow? The blood beaded on his glass door?

"I meant to clean up," she said.

Janice put away the groceries while Stephen wandered around outside. She was about to call his name, when he walked back into the house carrying the banjo.

"I don't . . ." Janice began, but was interrupted by Stephen's attempted song.

"I'll fly away, oh glory, I'll fly away . . ."

Voice off-key. Instrument out of tune. At least one string broken. The resonating head punctured. Stephen's rendition of the song was more hell-call than hymn. She tried not to laugh. Tried in vain.

"Oh," he said, heading toward the door with the banjo. "I brought you one more thing."

Janice wanted to ask him about the bird. She wanted to ask him about her car key. Instead, she asked about the cushionlike thing he carried back from his truck. Brown, shaped like an aspirin tablet, and as big around as a jack-o'-lantern.

"What is it?"

"A zafu," he said. "A meditation cushion. It'll help you sit up straight. Look in the book."

Stephen handed the cushion to Janice, who clutched it to her chest, as if it were a life jacket.

"Are you sure everything is all right?" he asked.

Janice nodded her head. Yes. Yes.

"Well, I have to go get some work done. If I keep hanging out with you, I'll never finish my altarpiece."

Janice stood inside the door and waved as Stephen drove away.

Why was this man being so nice to her? Why was she not more suspicious of him? His motives? Janice shook the doubts from her head.

Upstairs, she fed the radio its batteries, put her thumb against the toothed on-switch, but then chose silence instead. She opened the meditation book to the page she last remembered reading in Stephen's tub. According to the book, there were two ways to sit on the zafu. Janice chose to straddle it.

19

T hus astraddle, hands cupped in mimicry of the serene figure demonstrating correct posture on page three of the book, Janice sought her breath. Breath. Tidal. Orbital. The ongoing charge and retreat, the whole world as battlefield. A tug-of-war between the body and soul. To the victor, go . . . To the victor . . . Breathe in from the diaphragm. Pull the breath deep inside. Exhale. Inhale. Exhale. Exhale. Exile.

~.

I've often heard it said ob late,
Dat Nawf Ca'lina was de state,
Whar a handsome nigga's bound to shine,
Like Dandy Jim of Caroline.

~

—Black as pitch, breath sweeps its dark wings—the heart is the truest abattoir—sit still! sit still!—mama's coming back soon—sit still, Janice—don't move—black as tar, hard as coal—memory and dream converge in the mouth—sit still—hold it tight—tight—not so tight mama—come back soon mama—the magic door—ankle and wrist—the rest—in shadow—hungry—

~

For my ole massa tole me,
I'm de best looking nigga in de county oh,
I look in de glass, as I found it so,
Just as massa tell me, oh.

~

—In the dark, in the breath—words rise from the shadow—lullabies—lullabies—it's okay sweetness—what's it mean, mama, *nigger blood?*—in the breath, in the dark—daddy rises from the shadow—goes, forever, away—don't cry baby girl don't cry baby girl don't cry baby girl don't cry baby girl—*them's just words*—words come and go—like prayers—

~

—Nigger music! *What'd I tell you about playing that goddamn nigger music—the man in the door—light spilling around him on all sides—halo—god—god, the man yanks the instrument from her hands—the woman, the dulcimer—cry out for each other—clubs—the man clubs the woman—her sole comfort in splinters—dragged bleeding into the boats—the man laughs—makes her do—makes her do—cost extra, he said—put it in the bucket—*

~

—naked—mama's dress—I told you to stay in your goddamn room—the slap and burn—shame and naked—hungry—whose house—the room too dark—and noises—the weeping bird—I told you to stay in your goddamn room—the slap and burn—tuck me in mama—will you tuck me in mama—it's okay sweetie—don't say nothing sweetie—the sheet wrapped like a church robe—this'll help you sleep—this'll help you sleep—

~

—*the man swings hard—the mule kicks—the babies scald—wailing—in the boat—face grinding into wet splintering planks—mule shit—blood—and the men—their grunts and snorts—their issue burns—the men who throw her back onto the bank—the men who carry her back to the shed—all fill the bucket—the man who empties the bucket—the man who broke her sweet dulcimer across her face—nigger music—the pale woman dreams the strings knotted around his throat—dreams his bleached ribs noting the fret-board—the man sometimes drags her from the dark shed—makes her do—makes her do—chains her ankle to a stob in the yard—makes her do—laughs—empties the bucket—*

> *De bull dog cleared me out ob de yard,*
> *I taught I'd better leabe my card,*
> *I tied it fast to a piece ob twine,*
> *Signed "Dandy Jim of Caroline."*

~

—so many words slipping through the mouths—swimming in and out of her ears—padlock soapbox dung-beetle matchbook jackdaw toadflax mag-pie johnsongrass bootblack lullaby monkey-wrench straw-dog treadmill gallows-tree good-egg muckrake dither-fish highfalutin auction-block landlord lullaby lord god bended-knee new-broom pickax ill-will dirt-dauber butterchurn cudweed dogbane titmouse bobolink mule-skinner johnboat lullaby lullaby lullaby—so many words—corncrib fruit-fly pig-iron brickbat tongue-tied cotter-pin spit-shine rattail cottonmouth ten-penny pawnbroker homesick funnel-cake cowbell bluetick dry-mop buckeye cattail inhale exhale shoehorn sinkhole shoehorn sinkhole coon-hound nigger-toe nigger-heaven nigger-blood nigger-blood nigger-blood—

~

—empties the bucket—eggs and butter and milk and okra—the man grows nothing anymore—his weedy garden—the bucket provides—everything comes from the bucket—everything disappears into the bucket—the woman—her loss, her rage—the woman—hungry and cold—sometimes old bread—sometimes she sucks the sweet goat milk—the goats lick her wounds—nuzzle nuzzle—one time, the woman—one time in the floor of a boat—one time she found half an apple—one time its peeled surface wiz-ened—like a face like a face—one time she bit into it—one time he beat her extra long extra hard—sometimes the man makes her sing—sing me a hymn—sometimes he cries—

~

—Breathe. Breath. Each breath a gust of hot wind. Count the breaths. Each a bellows to the wings, the lazy lumbering wings. Follow the breath. The bible lies open on the pulpit. Breathe. Each breath stirs the pages more and more until the great bird takes flight. The bible rises, its leather cover flaps and flaps and flaps, with each undulation a hot wind washes across her face. Sears. Seers. The bible in flight. In search of prey. Of carrion. The bible lifting, heavenward, in a widening gyre, is joined by other bibles, the bibles rising in a widening gyre, a black vortex of consonants and vowels, maelstrom of commandments, condemnations, filling the sky. The bibles in flight, the bibles in flight, began to swoop down at her, the girl and her breath, wailing with each pass, screeching cawing out their bitter psalms, cawing cawing, part angel part harpy, talons out and eager for blood, eyes black as redemption, beaks keened on the whetstones of faith, of fear—

~

—*the woman dreams of babies cooing in her lap—the woman hears the roar before the steam breaks through—some great lusty belch straight out of Satan's mouth—boiled the skin right off her babies—the woman beats her head against the stone wall—her blood trickles into the carefully incised initials—the woman dreams an old bone whetted sharp against a rock—dreams the man's jugular opening, then bone—dreams the spray of his blood a flock of stillborn starlings—the man beats her when she cries—when she dreams of her dead babies—the man—the woman, despite hardship—the woman is ripe—like any good animal—the woman is ripe—bears fruit—*

> An ebery little nig she had,
> Was de berry image ob de dad,
> Dar heels stick out three feet behind,
> Like Dandy Jim of Caroline.

~

—so many words—so much loss—so much rage—

~

I took dem all to church one day,
An hab dem christen'd widout delay,
De preacher christen'd eight or nine,
Young Dandy Jims of Caroline.

—too soon—he takes them from the tit too soon—throws her back in the boats too soon—the babies die—the man rages—drops their stiff bodies, as lifeless as turds, into the outhouse—beats the woman—scrubs her with kerosene—drinks until he's blind—makes her do—makes her do—heyyyy lock!—

~

"Heyyyy Lock!"

Janice rose out of meditation, to the call coming from somewhere beyond the windows and walls. Rose through the slough of dream, of daydream, of nightmare, rose into consciousness, rose besmeared by the dregs and filth of her journey.

20

"Janice?" Stephen said as he climbed the stairs. "Are you here?"

"Yeah . . . be out in a second . . . don't . . ."

Stephen pushed the door open before she finished the sentence. "You okay . . . God, Janice! What happened?"

Janice tried to shake the muddle from her head.

"What? I don't know . . ."

But then she looked around. Looked at the floor. Looked down at herself.

Janice sat on the meditation cushion, just as she remembered doing earlier. It was the last thing she remembered. She sat, shoeless, her feet scratched and covered in mud. Her pants, torn at the knees, dripped cold water onto the floor. The floor bore muddy footprints, from her bare feet, that came in from the stairs and circled the room, circled the zafu. When Janice stood, her sore thighs and calves ached. She reached out for Stephen, clung to him with filthy bleeding hands.

"Janice, what happened?"

He helped her to the bed.

She lay back, and the room spun. No, the room bobbed, up and down, side to side. As if afloat.

"Where did you go?" he asked. "Who . . ."

"No . . . nowhere. I didn't go anywhere. Just ss . . . just meditated, like the book said."

"You meditated this morning?" he asked.

"No. This afternoon. Today. You brought the cushion over today, right?"

"That was yesterday, Janice. I came over yesterday evening. You've been . . ."

Stephen didn't know how to finish.

Neither did Janice.

He went for a pan of water and a cloth.

"Let me get you out of these wet clothes, and cleaned up."

But when he came back and reached for the button of her stained shirt, Janice drew back.

"No! I can do it myself! Leave me alone. Please!"

"Don't be ridiculous, Janice."

This was it, Janice thought. Now he's going to strip me and rape me and kill me.

Stephen did none of those horrible things. He draped Janice with a sheet and helped to get her soiled clothing off without exposing her body.

"Janice," he said, wiping the mud from her face. "I should look to make sure you don't have any cuts that need attention."

Janice shook her head, mumbled something about doing it herself, but within moments fell deeply enough into sleep that Stephen's kind, gentle hands and the cool washcloth ceased to scare her, and brought, simply, comfort.

When she woke, hours, maybe, later, Stephen sat at her bedside reading the meditation book.

"Hey," she whispered.

"Hey."

Stephen laid the book at the foot of the bed, leaned to look into her eyes.

She looked back, but then thinking she saw the black crow fly across his pupil, turned away.

"I almost see a person in there," he said. "Here's a question—how do you sleep with that thing hanging over your head?"

Janice rolled her eyes up to look at the crow's skull.

"He protects me," she mumbled.

"Riiiight . . . Listen, tomorrow I'm taking you to the doctor. If nothing else, to get that tattoo looked at. It should've healed by now. There's a clinic in town and . . ."

"I'm all right," she said, trying to sit up.

"Won't take no for an answer," he said. "We'll make a day of it. Besides, it'd do you good to get out in the real world."

Janice lacked the energy to argue.

"I want you to come home with me, but I know you won't, so, I'm staying downstairs tonight."

"You don't need . . ."

"It wasn't a request."

Stephen heated some soup, and they ate together up in the bedroom. He asked questions about the sleepwalking, and Janice could tell he wanted to ask more, but she was unwilling to reveal the few fragments of those horrible dreams that lingered in her mind. Nor was she willing to fully concede that her body had been so beyond her control. He probably wouldn't believe it all anyway. And Janice herself had lost whatever scant ability she'd had to differentiate between the real and dream worlds she inhabited.

Stephen told her that the muddy tracks had come in the back door.

"It's like there's a path worn between the two outbuildings and the back stoop."

She changed the subject.

"Did you work today? Carving, I mean."

"Too busy taking care of you. And looking for my bird."

Janice shivered at the mention.

"He goes off sometimes," Stephen said, and Janice heard both hope and concern in the statement. She kept quiet.

Stephen tried to teach her a high-energy card game called Egyptian Ratscrew.

"I don't get it," she said. "There's nothing about Egypt, or rats, or . . ."

"Right," he said.

An hour later, it was clear that Janice's mind and body were too weary to keep up the pace necessary for the game.

"Bedtime," Stephen said, and before Janice had time to register any concern or worry or expectation over what that meant, he bid her good night and closed the door. Janice lay in the dark, comforted by the sounds of the stone carver moving about, one floor beneath her.

She slept, in peace, and without stirring, until a raucous mockingbird brought the morning sun into her eyes. Janice stood, on legs still sore, and tender feet, and looked out the window where Stephen had just finished his yoga routine, the territorial bird cutting, with its gray wings, sharp slices of air around him.

Janice blushed at her spontaneous disappointment over the presence of Stephen's shorts. She hobbled downstairs as he came in the door.

"Morning, sunshine," he said. "I've packed us lunch."

After coffee and her minimal protest, they drove up Sabbath Rest Road. When they passed the old tree where Janice sat on her earliest attempt to leave, the invisible bonds holding her in place tightened noticeably, constricted just enough to make breathing a little more difficult.

"You okay?" Stephen asked.

She nodded yes.

As they drove, Janice watched the mountainous land fold and unfold upon itself, a continental origami, each epochal crease spanning aeons; holding, spawning, devouring, generation after generation of lives. She tried to keep her eyes on the road, out of the woods, for fear of seeing the goats again.

"Maybe you should just take me to a Greyhound station," she said, not fully meaning it, but with enough seriousness to make him respond seriously.

"I can help you through this," he said. "Whatever is happening. But if you really want to leave, let's get you healed up and rested, then I'll take you wherever you want to go."

Wherever.

Stephen meandered along the back roads, pointing out landmarks and local legends, talking about everything and nothing. Janice rode and listened, rode and listened. Happy. Miles later, the empty fields and woods gave way to houses and buildings. Janice felt like an explorer discovering a new part of the world. They turned from one road to another. Left or right, made no difference to her. They passed other cars, other trucks, with increasing frequency. When Stephen pulled to a stop in front of a gas station-cum-post office, its façade painted, windows darkened, flagpole erect, and asked if she wanted to go in with him, Janice instinctively leaned her elbow on the lock button.

"No," she said, not fully sure of what she feared.

"The never-ending ex-wife saga," he said, then disappeared into the building.

Stephen was gone only long enough to buy a stamp and post the envelope, and though brief, his absence provided ample time for a complete (overblown, illogical, melodramatic) escape narrative to run its course through Janice's mind, and for her to make a decision.

"I don't want to go to the doctor," she said when Stephen slid behind the steering wheel.

"Janice . . ."

"Look, I don't have any insurance, and I don't have the money to pay for a visit."

"I'll be hap . . ."

"No, Stephen. Besides, you were right. I just needed to get out in the real world for a while."

Janice hoped the lie held water.

"Janice, those dreams . . . those cuts and bruises on your legs . . ."

"Let's just stop at a drugstore. We'll get some Neosporin and some over-the-counter sleeping pills. Once I get a few good nights' sleep . . ."

"I have money for the doctor, Janice. It's not a problem."

"I'm not going," she said. "I'm just exhausted, and a little stir-crazy. I won't pay a doctor to tell me what I already know."

He didn't ask her why she was so willing to go back.

She didn't ask herself, either.

Stephen cranked the truck, and they sat without speaking or moving for several long minutes.

"Damn, you're hardheaded," he said, finally putting the truck in gear. "I'm not taking you straight home, though."

"Don't worry," she said, trying to sound light. "I didn't expect complete victory."

Nor did she argue when he pulled to a dusty stop by the only open picnic table, at the far end of the gravel lot at PawPaw Landing Historic Park.

"Popular spot," she said.

"It's Saturday. Folks like to come out and play."

Janice had all but forgotten about weekdays and schedules. She looked out of the truck windows at the array of people, old, young, and in the middle, coming and going along crisp sidewalks defined on either side by knee-high stanchions and plastic link chain, leading through and into a series of old buildings and structures, people pausing to read, or completely ignoring the plentiful signboards and placards on the way, people interacting with, listening to, or trying to avoid the ubiquitous actors in period costumes.

"What is it?" Janice asked, feeling suddenly both out of place and strangely at home. Of late, even cognitive dissonance was familiar territory.

"Why it's the PawPaw Landing, of course."

"And what lands here? Spaceships? Helicopters?"

"Canal boats," Stephen said. "It's a restored boat landing, with some re-created businesses from the time. And, best of all, a lockhouse and a functioning lock."

Janice appreciated the gift, however quirky. Stephen's thoughtfulness touched her.

"Let's eat first," he said. "Before we look at everything. I'm hungry."

Janice slid onto the picnic table bench facing the parking lot, hoping Stephen wouldn't notice. It had been months since she was out in public, and the crowd—the families, the kids, the couples, the noise—overwhelmed her. Stephen spread the sandwiches, chips, pickles, and cookies, along with a gallon jug of tea, on the plank tabletop.

The sun warmed her back, felt good. The salami and mustard sandwich was more delicious than anything she'd ever tasted. Even the happy laughter and bickering children in the background seemed okay. Janice opened up, just a little.

She told Stephen a few of the details from her meditation nightmare, and some from her sleepwalking dreams as well. He told her what he knew about meditation. How the mind is devious and tricky. How the cunning subconscious would do all in its considerable power to remain in control.

"You just have to push through," he said. "Stay with the calm and quiet."

"It's not as easy as you make it sound," she said.

"I never said anything about *easy*. It might be the hardest thing you ever do."

Stephen pressed the open package of cookies to his nose and inhaled deeply. Janice rolled her eyes in response.

"Do we get to actually eat them?" Janice asked. "Or are they for huffing only?"

Working. Working. Forcibly driving the disquiet from her mind.

She told him a little about the trip that brought her to the lockhouse.

"The last line on the sign was 'Show Us Your Boobs.' "

"Did you?" he asked.

"Don't be ridiculous!"

"Why not," he said. "It would've been good for you and them."

"That's no way for a Christian man to talk."

"Whoa now." Stephen feigned seriousness. "Who are you accusing of being Christian?"

"The person who is, even now, chiseling out 'a Byzantine depiction of the Passion of Christ, in low-relief granite.'"

"A-hha. So you like that better than 'the Passion of Christ captured in stone'?"

Stephen told her he thought of himself as about seventy-five percent heathen, and the other twenty-five as misguided seeker.

"What's with all the Christian symbols and stuff then?"

"I went to Catholic school, from kindergarten on through the twelfth grade. It gets in your blood. You know what I remember most?"

"Nope."

"The dances. There was a rule, strictly enforced, that you had to stay the width of the bible away from your dance partner."

"Have you ever been to the Natural Bridge?" Janice asked, the question spilling out of her mouth with no link to conscious thought.

"Natural Bridge, Virginia?"

"Yes," she said, another fictional narrative running its furious course through her mind, where the chasm between synapses can span years. "Yes."

She could travel with this man. This man who turned the horribleness of her yesterday into a picnic today. This Stephen Gainy. And in her mind, in that instant, named the distant mountain, the one she looked at from her bedroom window, Gainy's Knob.

"What are you laughing at?" Stephen asked.

"Nothing," she said. Then, "You and that bible."

"Well, to answer your question, no, but I've heard about it."

Janice almost told Stephen that she was staying in the lockhouse without permission from anyone. That she got stuck there months ago, because of the dead battery, and just never left. Stayed now, in no small part, because of him. Janice almost said these things.

"I really like your altarpiece," she said instead. "A lot."

"Thanks. Listen, I've been meaning to ask, are you . . . did you . . ."

Stephen hemmed and hawed at the question.

"Yes?"

Janice hoped for more than the question, when it finally surfaced, contained.

"Are you, like, independently wealthy? Or between careers? Or, I just . . . you know all this stuff about me, and you're still the woman of mystery."

"No great mystery," Janice said, then elaborated, and exaggerated just a bit. "I did, I guess most recently, the web-based catalogue design and sales for a wholesale food distributor."

"Hmm," Stephen said, clearly trying to reconcile that detail with her presence way out in a central Pennsylvania lockhouse with no electricity, and hoping for more details.

She gave none.

"Let's go see this place," she said, standing.

Stephen began stuffing the empty sandwich bags and napkins into the empty cookie package.

"You know," he said. "If I had a slick website for my altarpiece, this one and future pieces . . . maybe you could show me how to set that up?"

"I'd like that," Janice said. "Very much."

Honeysuckle. There was no mistaking the scent of honeysuckle in the air. Janice took it in greedily.

Stephen was much more interested in telling her all that he knew about the locks and canal systems than in wasting any time reading the plethora of informational signs. They wandered deep into the faux village armed with his considerable knowledge.

"They always had a blacksmith on-site," Stephen said, leading Janice under the sweltering roof of the smithy's workshop. The roar of the bellows drowned out sounds from beyond. "The canal boats delivered big slugs of pig iron, and the blacksmith made shoes for the mules, and all the gate and lock hardware."

Janice crinkled her nose, waved a hand in front of her face.

"Too hot," she said. "Too loud."

And as soon as they stepped back onto the sidewalk, the song filled her head.

> *Willie, little Willie, I'm afraid of your ways*
> *Willie, little Willie, I'm afraid of your ways*
> *The way you've been rambling, you'll lead me astray.*

Janice grabbed Stephen by the arm. The look of terror that surged over her face frightened him.

"D . . . Do you hear that?"

"That music? Of course I hear it. She's sitting right over there."

Stephen held Janice's hand in place on his forearm, and pulled her to the front porch of the ersatz general store, where a woman of indeterminate age in a long gingham skirt and a starched white bonnet sat on the steps playing an instrument and singing.

> *Polly, pretty Polly, you're guessing 'bout right,*
> *Polly, pretty Polly, you're guessing 'bout right,*
> *I dug on your grave for the best part of last night.*

> *He stabbed her to the heart and her heart's blood did flow,*
> *He stabbed her to the heart and her heart's blood did flow,*
> *And into the grave pretty Polly did go.*

The music sounded so familiar to Janice. Like the music that played through her dreams and nightmares. The wooden instrument lying across the woman's lap she didn't recognize, but something about the sweet drone that spilled from its narrow body, the heart-shaped sound holes, something about the rhythmic strum and the short stick she used to press the four strings up and down the fretboard, something about these things penetrated Janice to the core, ran like lightning up and down her spine, out the nerve-rivers of her limbs, and left her fingers and toes tingling.

A small crowd grew around the performer. The woman looked from beneath the bonnet, and winked at Janice as she began the final verse.

> *He threw the dirt over her and turned away to go,*
> *He threw the dirt over her and turned away to go,*
> *Down to the river where the deep waters flow.*

"Do you know 'Stairway to Heaven'?" a bearded man spilling out of a Harley-Davidson T-shirt asked. Almost everybody laughed.

Janice tugged Stephen down the sidewalk.

"Philistine," he said.

"Me, or the biker?"

"Both of you. You don't like music?"

"No, I do. I really do. The song was beautiful. But the woman gave me the willies."

"You'd get weird too, if you had to spend your days pretending to be a floozy from the 1800s."

Yes, Janice thought, the kinship of pretense between herself and the costumed woman not lost on her. Yes indeed.

Nor did she miss the similarity between the PawPaw Landing locktender's house and the one she'd squatted in. She read from the larger-than-life overpixeled photomontage filling the back wall while Stephen bought tickets for a canal boat ride. Then they both spent time peering into the waist-high glass display cases in the center of the room. Stephen seemed more genuinely interested in the unearthed artifacts, the grainy enlarged photographs mounted beside the decaying books from which they were copied, and the discovered documents than Janice. By the time he reached the midpoint, she'd already circled around and stood opposite him.

One series of photographs did capture her attention. The book—*Canal Life: Legends & Lore*—lay closed in its airtight glass tomb, surrounded by half a dozen eight-by-twelve-inch pictures, all monochromatic, all shades of gray. Some of the scenes were explained, some of the subjects were identified by name. And while all the faces—enlarged and also overpixeled—were hard to make out, Janice felt as if she'd seen them before. So strangely familiar. She lingered there, able to see Stephen's reflection in the glass.

"Hey," he said. "Did you see this?"

Stephen pointed at a tattered logbook lying open in the case.

"What is it?" Janice asked, not moving.

"You have to come see. I'm not telling."

She circled the glass case and stood beside Stephen. The ink was smudged. The page had either been burned or waterlogged. But several names were still semilegible, listed in a column down the book's left margin.

"What?" she asked, daring to shove him out of the way with her hip.

"There," Stephen said, tapping on the glass. "Read that name."

"Ridenhour, comma Ezekiel?"

"Two down."

There it was.

"Witherspoon."

"Same spelling, right?" Stephen asked.

Void. Empty. In that brief instant, Janice felt completely emptied of all thought, of all emotion. As if she'd lost consciousness standing there. But the feeling, or the lack of feeling passed just as quickly. She held tight to the glass case. Shook her head.

"You okay?" Stephen asked.

"Yep," she answered, said nothing about what'd just happened. "I can't make out the first name. Can you?"

"No. Looks like Eunice or Eliza. Something with an E. Whatever it is, she either earned or owed fifteen dollars. Reckon it's your kinfolk?"

"*Reckon* it's my *kinfolk*? Is it legal to expose that much fake Southerner? To tell you the truth, I don't really know if we even could be related. I have no idea where my *kinfolk* hail from."

The information card with, presumably, history about the book had tipped over in the case, so its source and identity went unknown.

Janice shrugged, palms up. He mirrored the act.

"Let's go catch a boat," he said.

The boat was much like an amusement park ride. The crowd of people waiting to climb into the canal boat processed through a series of narrow lines defined by a railing of welded steel tubes that doubled back and forth from the sidewalk entry to its exit on a short covered pier that hung no more than a foot or two over the canal bank.

"I hate these things," Stephen said. "These lines and the weird mini-relationships you have to have, or avoid, with the people one rail away."

"And I thought I was asocial," she said, as they stepped up behind a family of six. They watched a dad and two boys with sweaty flattop haircuts; a mom and two girls awash in Avon products; all clad in green camouflage shorts and red Jesus Loves Me T-shirts; the lot of them pasty-white and rotund in precise decreasing scale, like nesting dolls gone bad.

"You have to do the talking with these guys," Stephen whispered into Janice's ear.

But they had to curtail the joking right away when another family—equal in size, if not makeup—stepped up close on their heels.

"Y'all ready for the tunnel?" the father in the family ahead of them asked.

While he faced Stephen and Janice, and everyone behind them, the man wasn't looking at anyone in particular. Much to their chagrin, the grandfather of the family breathing down their necks took the conversational bait.

"It's something, ain't it."

Thus sandwiched, Stephen and Janice learned, as they shuffled and waited and shuffled and waited, all there was to know, and more, about the tunnel the boat would take them through a mile into their trip.

At the midpoint during the wait in line, a placard hanging from a post promised "Only   minutes from here!" but both hands had been pulled from the painted, smiling clock face. Janice looked out at the still water in the canal. So flat. So perfectly at the mercy of gravity. And seen obliquely, holding no reflection whatsoever.

With all the perfume, bug-spray, and sunblock odors emanating from the family ahead of them, Janice almost regretted the return of her sense of smell. Then again, if she stood close and downwind, she could smell Stephen. A healthy, male scent, unencumbered by product.

The boy sitting on a stool taking the tickets seemed unconcerned that the onyx-colored Celtic tattoo circling his neck didn't match his costume.

"Have your tickets out please hold on to small children hands and feet inside the boat at all times no smoking don't throw anything overboard remain in your seats while the boat is in motion have your tickets ready please."

There was nothing remarkable about the wooden boat, nor its painfully slow arrival and docking. Nevertheless, every single ticket-holding soul in line watched with rapt attention as the man on deck snapped his suspenders, then tossed a thick hemp rope around the snubbing post and cinched it tight. The hull nudged against the pylons, and a wide plank thudded into place, bridging the three-foot span between the boat and the pier. The boat bobbed each time a passenger disembarked. The first family, the fat loud ones, boarded with far more caution than was necessary. Settled in, bickering over the best seats.

Janice handed over her ticket. Paused. Stephen hadn't anticipated the pause and almost tripped over her.

"Should I carry you across the plank?" he asked, in jest, and put his hands on her waist.

—*get up bitch—unnngh—a man in the dark—and the boat won't stop swaying—and the man hits her again—bleeds—in the belly of the boat— the moonlight falls through an open window hatch—winds her hair around his fist—moonlight falls on white flesh and black blood—the man—his make-do branding iron—the nasty man—three times, the flesh of her wrist seared, gave way—the nasty thing—teach you to bite me—filthy harlot—*

unngh—bitch—teach you to sass back—unngh—milk white moon—milk white flesh—the man and the pliers—the taste of metal and mule shit—the pulpy little fish of her tongue flopping and twitching and swimming in a pool of beautiful moonlight on the floor of the boat—

In jest, he put his hands on her waist.

Stephen moved Janice one step closer to the plank, to the boat.

"No!!"

Janice cursed. Screamed something unintelligible. Pushed back against Stephen.

His arms encircled her.

"Goddamn you!" she shrieked. "No! No! No!"

She spun, from within his grip, and swung, and swung, and swung.

"Hhrrrrrrr," throat tight, breath clawing its way in and out. "Hhrrrrrrr . . . Hhrrrrrrr."

In less than a minute, Janice hung limp in Stephen's embrace. Conscious, but confused. All the children on the boat were crying, and the family in line behind them stood far away, the adults in a tight worried circle around the young ones. And Stephen's face bore the deep bleeding evidence of her fingernails.

"We don't give no refunds," the boy said, his voice quavering.

When Stephen lifted Janice into his arms to carry her back to the sidewalk, the herd of voyeurs parted silently to let them pass through, then went back to noisily chewing their cuds of curiosity. The mumbling and speculation starting before Stephen and Janice were out of earshot.

"I bet she's on dope . . ."

". . . loony bin."

"My daddy had fits like that when . . ."

Stephen found a bench in the shade, out of sight, out from under the chopping-block eyes of those who'd witnessed the incident. He sat her down, touched his cheek and stared at the fat bead of blood on his fingertip.

"Janice, what the hell?"

It was, apparently, all the question he could muster.

"I'm so . . . Stephen, I'm so sorry!"

She reached for his face. He pulled away.

"I don't know what happened," she said. "There was . . . I . . . no . . . no control. Something horrible flashed inside my head . . ."

"What do you mean? A dream? What?"

"No. Yes, maybe. No pictures, that I can remember. Just a sick scary feeling. I'm so sorry."

This time, when she reached, he didn't back up quite so much.

"You need to take care of this," she said. "There's probably a first-aid office here."

"No," Stephen said. "I'll just wash it in the bathroom and we'll go."

Stephen headed down the sidewalk without looking back. Shift. Change. The whole tenor of the afternoon had turned, topsy-turvy, for the worse.

Janice sat on the bench, leaning forward, head in her hands, watching yellow jackets come and go in a pool of spilled cola. She heard someone huffing and struggling for breath coming up behind her, but had neither the energy nor desire to look back.

"Late!"

Janice felt the bench shift as the man leaned against its seat back.

Go away go away go away go away go away . . . Janice repeated the mantra in her head. Even in her best moments, Janice never really trusted role players or re-enactors. To participate in such an absurd interaction now was unthinkable.

"S'posed to be here yesterday!"

Clearly the man was talking to someone else.

Janice looked up and down the sidewalk, for Stephen, or for the other person that this man spoke to. But the walks were empty. She looked over her shoulder just enough to see his arthritic hands gripping the bench. Clawlike. Talonlike.

"Yesterday!" he said again, and shook the seat.

Janice wanted to turn and face the man. She wanted to be rude, blatantly mean. She wanted to tell this old man to take his drunken self straight to hell. To leave her alone. She wanted to threaten him. To threaten to report him in the park office. To make him lose his job.

"The thang was breech!"

Janice didn't have to turn and face the man. He came around the bench. Janice pressed her body into the seat back, clung to the planks. No escape. No escape. The man snatched her left arm free, gripped her hand in his hand, crushing, crushing, dragged the sleeve up her forearm—his fingers dry and hard and bloodless—twisted her arm, glared at the mark on her wrist. Spat. Cursed.

"S'posed to be here yesterday!"

No one. There was no one else around for Janice to call out to. No children. No parents chasing them. No park officials. No Stephen. Only this lunatic leaning into her face and shouting at her.

"Breech! All twisted up inside there! I had to do it myself. Cut it out myself! It come out all blue!"

He stank. He stank of clay, and moss, and stagnant water. He stank of liquor, beans and fatback. His costume was filthy, threadbare. Missing buttons. Stained. Torn. No hat. The skin of his face furrowed and sallow. Few teeth. His rheumy eyes augering into hers.

"Blue! All that mess! I done it myself. Then the big hole in her belly. I couldn't . . ."

The crow landed before the man confessed his shortcoming. Landed on the seat back, right by Janice's head. Whispered across its split black tongue, into her ear.

— *Come see the body* —

Janice screamed and screamed and screamed.

Fought against the man who held her by the shoulders.

Screamed and screamed. Struggled and screamed.

"Janice!"

No!

"Janice!"

The man who gripped her shoulders.

"Janice!"

Stephen.

Stephen?

"Stephen?"

Janice opened her eyes and fell, weeping, against him.

Between racking sobs, she tried to tell him about the man who accosted her. And despite her protests, Stephen led her to the park office to report the malefactor.

"Nobody by that description works here."

Janice amended her story, looking for more specificity.

"Sorry ma'am," the officer said, not making much of an effort to hide his irritation. "There's nobody on the park grounds that fits the description of your 'bad guy.' Maybe you've been out in the sun too much today. Maybe you're getting over last night's party. Maybe you need to see your doctor."

These were not questions.

Couldn't they see the damp handprints on her shoulders? Couldn't they smell the old man's stench lingering in the air?

The ride home was painful in its hard silence. But, mercifully, quicker. Stephen took the most direct route. Janice recognized landmarks. Chunk's Market. Stephen pulled into the lot, went in without saying a word. Came back with a bottle of peroxide and some Band-Aids for his face.

Stephen sped up the on-ramp for the turnpike, and when they exited many silent miles later, Janice recognized the tollbooth. Her heart clanged and clanged against the mute bell of her sternum throughout the entire brief and thoroughly normal exchange of coins. And Stephen didn't utter a sound until they sat, with the truck running, at the end of Sabbath Rest Road.

"You know," he said. "If you're not willing to help yourself, I sure as hell can't help you."

Janice had no idea how to respond. Anger? A plea for understanding?

"You don't believe me, do you!" she said. "About the man?"

"I'm not sure what to believe."

"Your bird," she said. "Your crow was there today. It landed on the bench."

Stephen shook his head. Looked away.

"I've got enough problems of my own, Janice."

He put the truck in gear.

"Just . . ."

"Make sure the door closes," he said, gunning the engine.

21

Alone and afraid.

By day's end, after the exhausting, possibly psychotic, humiliating nightmare at PawPaw Landing, after the long ride home, its impenetrable silence, after Stephen dropped her off and sped angrily up Sabbath Rest Road, the truck's muffled rumble disappearing and reappearing as the road wound through hills and hollows—the realization of deep loss coming in fits and starts—by then Janice had nothing but fear and loneliness to keep her company.

While day and night were no longer reliable demarcations for her— sunlight as the mind's peacekeeper; darkness tipping the scales toward lunacy—Janice couldn't fathom the idea of driving away that evening. Her body weary, the muscles and their attendant ropes and pulleys ached, resisted each step toward the door; her hyperstimulated nerves whipped and careened through their micro-trajectories, each thought, each sensation a subcutaneous carnival ride.

Tomorrow. Tomorrow she'd pack her car and leave. Destination didn't matter. She'd think about it on the road. On the road. Tomorrow.

Mortared by fear, night stacked its black bricks around Janice. Hemmed her in.

Janice's body wanted nothing more than sleep. Delicious, inexplicable, restorative sleep.

In her mind, however, the sleep-state had been robbed of all its gifts. She'd come unmoored, lost her psyche's tethers. Thus, at the mercy of memory's tempest, Janice feared where she might drift to in sleep. She resolved to stay awake, all night, then drive as far from the locktender's house tomorrow, as far as she could get, to drive until sleep caught up with her.

For a few hours, knitting mindlessly calmed her anxious mind. But only for a few hours. After a ragged swath of coarse and bluish yarn pooled at Janice's feet, the steady shhhcck shhhcck, shhhcck shhhcck proved too soothing. Her head bobbed down, snapped up, sleep pounding at the door of her consciousness.

Janice boiled water, made a quart of instant coffee, bitter and black. She paced the downstairs, sipping at the huge mug until the coffee was cool enough to guzzle. Three full mugs later, the caffeine ringing in her ears all but drowned out the crow's cawing. The crow. Was it a crow? Outside, in the night, near the lock. Was it his crow? Or was she imagining the crow sound altogether? Hard to tell. So awake. So much coffee. In fact, maybe she'd imagined the whole thing. The madness at the park. The madness in her dreams. The turnpike. The tollbooth. That dead boy, what was his name? Danks? Had she imagined him? His life *and* his death? The loss felt real enough. And Stephen? The loss of Stephen, the loss of the potential of Stephen, hurt so much more than Danks's death. Had she imagined them both? Conjured them up out of the bowels of . . . what? Her own sad mind? Where did such darkness originate? Janice lit all the lanterns in the house. The outhouse door slammed shut, then again, then again. The crow outside, real or otherwise, cawed incessantly.

Janice brought the radio down from upstairs, rolled the dial through the hiss and static until she found a weak signal, so broken that she couldn't tell what genre of music she heard. Janice went from window to window, working the dial with her thumb, searching the spectrum for company. Pulled the chamber pot from under the bed. Peed. The coffee burned. Upstairs, in the closed room, by the window, the right side of the window, the telescoping antenna tapping at the pane, Janice found a signal. A talk show, maybe? Men talking. A softer voice in the background. Janice shifted back and forth trying to keep up with the conversation. The radio waves. Men talking. *Mongrel child.* Arguing even. Haggling. In the background, a softer voice. A woman? Was she crying? Possibly a talk show. Didn't matter. Janice wanted only contact with the larger world. Assurance of its existence. Men's voices, their aggression made only slightly more palpable rendered through the small tinny speaker, bickered. Something about a bucket. Something about goods and services. Systems, barter, and honor. Something about law or no law. And the voice, in the background, whispered over it all—*she's come to see the body—the body—come see—the body*—Janice threw the radio to the floor, stamped it until her bare heel bled, and when the speaker would not cease hissing—*come see see see*—anger displacing fear, Janice took the handle of her toy tomahawk and drove it through the perforated plastic cover, through the speaker's gray fabric, stabbing again and again until no further sound escaped. Escape. Can't leave. Want to leave. Tomorrow. Wait until daylight. Janice found the medical supplies Stephen had added to her shopping list, bandaged her foot, dug the cotton wadding from a new bottle of aspirin, balled it into tight pills and pushed one into each ear canal, blocking all but the high-pitched ringing inside her skull. More coffee, and a swig of milk of magnesia. Some crackers. More pacing. Janice took the batteries from the only clock in the house, turned it face down on the nightstand.

Even if she had made it all up, what then? The hospital. A hospital. There are places that can help. Or, at least, hide you away, and in hiding, help the others. The ones that stay behind. Janice. Her mother. *Mama, don't. Please don't, Mama. She'll be good. I promise. Take those off. Don't do that. Take those off. Don't do that. Take. Don't. Take.* Janice shook the bitter memory from her head. In the morning, she'd find a doctor. In the morning. How far away, the morning? The room smelled of moss and dank clay. Mama's room smelled. The last smell Janice remembered. The room, the locktender's house, smelled sour. Keep moving. Stay awake. So loud, the ringing inside. So loud. Janice, keeping busy, Janice, looking for something to eat, pulled a folded piece of paper from behind the cans of food stacked in the cupboard. The chart. The Sun Salutation. Each of the twelve moves demonstrated by her own naked form. Had she imagined it all? His kindness? His refusal to judge her? His physical beauty? The crow? The crow's death? The songs? The chart? The chart, she laid flat on the floor, smoothed its creases. Janice studied the moves, forced herself to look at the small versions of her nude body until the shame subsided. Janice stripped. Janice laid a blanket on the floor. Janice began. Upright, palms together, prayer position. Inhale, stretch arms up, arch back, hips pushed forward. Exhale, hands to the floor, fingertips and toes forming a line, head tucked in toward knees, close to touching. Inhale, right leg stretched behind back, knee to floor. Hold the breath, left leg extended back to meet the right, straighten the body, the push-up position. Exhale, bend the knees, place knees, chest, and forehead on floor. Inhale, slide hips forward, arch head, chest up, into the cobra position. Exhale, keep hands and feet locked, hips up high, the inverted V. Inhale, right foot between the hands, drop knee to the floor. Exhale, bring feet together, straighten knees, forehead down toward legs. Inhale, stretch up, arch back, arms up behind. Exhale, return to upright prayer position. Inhale deeply, repeat. Janice, honoring the sun from within night's black backside. Janice sweating. Movement. Blood keening her body. And hungry. And more coffee.

And, still naked—*Dear Stephen*—decided to write a letter . . . *some things I have to tell you* . . . *first, to thank you* . . . Sitting on the blanket . . . *meant so much* . . . Sitting on the floor . . . *if only we could have* . . . With her back to the small couch, she'd explain everything . . . *lies I have told* . . . Confess it all . . . *secrets I have kept* . . . No more secrets. Pencil it down. Erase. Pencil it down. Erase . . . *when I was a little girl* . . . She'd deliver the letter in the morning . . . *and since meeting you* . . . Then drive away . . . *more than I could've imagined* . . . Drive away . . . *so sorry* . . . Drive to Natural Bridge . . . *so sorry* . . . Six scribbled pages later, Janice put the pencil down, laid her head against the couch, and wept. Cried and cried. The tears, seeking the path of least resistance, rolled down the slant of her nose, hooked around her mouth, dripped from her chin, landed on her sternum, the thin bone channel that lay between her breasts, the tears, cooled there, pooled there, slowed by the attritus from the eraser, the dusty rubber raspings littering her chest and belly, hung in the fine blond hairs, mixing with her tears, the graphite darkening with her salty lacrimae. Janice, purged of both words and tears, looked around the room. The walls constricted; the ceiling oppressed. Janice, her back against the settee, looked down at her own naked body, began to wipe away the mess with her fingertips, found in wiping, quite unexpectedly, the flick of her thumbs against her nipples stirring. Satisfying. She wiped her belly, coming back again and again to her nipples, hardened now, and expectant. Before long, Janice abandoned the pretense of cleaning herself, cleaning her body, and simply took hold of both breasts. Heartbeat, in her fingertips. Breath. Breathe. The softest pinch. And tug. Janice, mind and body at odds, the caffeine and fatigue, the fear and the pleasure, all doing battle inside. Outside. Had she imagined them all? Stephen's hands, capable of shaping stone? Janice let her knees fall open. She'd been beaten for this as a girl. As a girl. Beaten for the body's curiosity, the body's instinctual desire to know itself. Janice let her hands ease down the shallow dome of her belly. Let them go despite fear. Despite guilt. Open. Knees open. Janice, at last, Janice found the other opening and the mute mouth was not without song. Not without song.

Harmony—*comes, the brown-skinned woman with soft fingers, with strong hands—the woman, in the dark, gravid, again—the men, their constant seeding of fecund ground—the babies—and the brown-skinned woman who brings them into the world—bites through the yolk stalk—comes the brown-skinned woman, both mother and lover, every time—beckoned or drawn—sweetness—cooing comfort—opens her up—reaches inside—plucks them like ripe fruit—the babies—cleans her—soothes her—eases the pain—strokes her hair—her face—helps her on the pot off the pot—not like the man—his rough rags and kerosene—the babies cry—and the tit—and the man comes—and the man takes the babies—and the babies stop crying—and the tit—and the milk—so full it hurts—and the brown-skinned woman comes—takes the milk—sweetness—that mouth—* and when Janice succumbed, and when Janice came, morning came with her. When she cried out, no name but *I saw you do it! I saw you do it!*—her mother's voice—the sun answered back. Clean white shafts of daylight drove hard into the opposite wall, spilled over the room, illuminating naked Janice, her letter, her deed.

Janice cleared the cotton from her ears, dressed hastily, burned the yoga chart, washed her hands. Washed her face, slapping the cold water again and again over her nose and eyes and cheeks and mouth. Slapping away the guilt. Welcoming the rage. Goddammit! It's her body! Her mind! Her life! Goddammit! She would not give them up. She would not give the small pleasures of the body up to guilt, that prehistoric carrion bird perched forever on her shoulder, urging her toward death. She would not allow every hope, every want, to be chased away by the hardworking scarecrow that was doubt. She would not be a scapegoat for the sins—real or otherwise—of her mother. Or the sins of anyone else. Janice, having endured much, readied herself for the rest.

Under the steam of anger, half-deluded, she carried the letter across the empty canal, through the cockleburs and beggar-ticks, through the ankle-deep river, not bothering with the cable bridge, and up to Stephen's property. But each step closer cooled her heels by scant degrees, and when his studio came into sight, Janice almost turned around. Almost. A few more steps and she saw that his truck was gone. And with it, she presumed, Stephen. The apology in absentia she could handle. Janice paused, listened carefully for the truck, or the crow, then stepped onto Stephen's deck. She tugged at the handle of the glass door and was not at all surprised when it slid open, unlocked.   .

Janice walked around inside his house. She took her time. She dawdled, half-hoping he'd come home and catch her. Looking for nothing in particular, she opened all the cabinets, all the drawers, but was unwilling to dig further for any secrets. She sat on Stephen's bed, looking at the nightstand. An unadorned lighter, a small glass pipe, and a ziplock baggie with enough marijuana to fill the pipe several times took up most of the surface. Inside, nothing but a box of condoms, some squeeze bottles that Janice wouldn't touch, and several magazines that she had even less interest in. No saint, this man she owed an apology to.

Janice wondered if this was the extent of his roguery. Janice wondered where he was. What he was doing. Janice wondered why there were no photographs in Stephen's house. None. Not of him. Nor anyone else. She looked through the house one more time, searching for pictures. Found none. Odd.

At the kitchen table she propped the letter, in an envelope, against the saltshaker. Picked it back up. Sat down and looked at it for a while, unopened. At the kitchen table, the preponderance of her fatigue bore down upon Janice. Heavy. She felt so heavy.

Just go. Go lie in his bed. Close your eyes. He'll come home soon. He'll take care of you. Just go. Go. Janice knew, if she didn't go then, didn't leave the house right then and there, she might never. She left the letter and ran back out through the glass door. Through the yard. But not toward the river.

Janice went to the studio. Found it, too, unlocked. The cut stones stood against the far wall, ponderous in their heavy casing, in shadow, radiating the cool of the prior night. Through the residue of caffeine Janice could almost hear the hammer's peen strike the chisel. Squinting, she watched sparks dart from the holy faces. Janice picked up a chisel and a hammer, approached the altarpiece. She dragged the wedged end along Stephen's cuts, outlining the folding robes, the suggestion of limbs, the exposed granite flesh. One panel left to complete. One face. One figure. One. One small strike. Just do it. Take the hammer. Chip here. Or here. Make your mark. You deserve it.

Janice didn't stop running until she'd crossed the river. It took every shred of energy in her body to resist the urge to vandalize Stephen's work. By the time she'd crossed over, her fingers had gone numb, the chisel still clutched in her hand. Janice stopped to catch her racing breath, sat on the bank until the light-headedness passed. Pack the car. Go. Don't stop until you are miles and days from this place.

Back through the weeds and underbrush, Janice approached the canal, stumbling on roots and rocks. She could see the roof of the house, her house, the locktender's house, rising up beyond the canal's berms. Down one steep bank, sliding across the rutted base, the seat of her pants filthy—*don't look toward the lock*—and up the other side to the towpath that ran parallel to the canal from one end to the other, every wretched mile.

She knew it was called the towpath, because Stephen had told her so. He'd explained it all. Mules pulled the boats along, boats filled with coal or corn, or empty. One team of mules walking the towpath, one team of mules in the bow. One person leading the mules: boy, or man, or girl. Walking all day, most of the night. Locking through. Stopping for supplies. Stopping for . . .

"Hey Lock!"

Had she imagined the voice? For the briefest instant she hoped it was Stephen.

No truck in the driveway.

Janice looked up the towpath to where it disappeared around a bend fifty yards away. Nothing. She cocked her ear, listened close. Nothing. No voice calling out. No sound.

She slipped the chisel into her back pocket, was about to step off the path. No sound. She'd imagined it. Or . . . wait . . . Janice hadn't walked the towpath before, not awake, not consciously. The only times she left the property she went straight across the canal, or up the drive. She had no clear idea what lay around that bend, or beyond that stand of pin oaks. But nothing would surprise her. As near as she'd verged into craziness these past few days, Janice knew the music she heard coming from down the towpath was real. That drone note, the slippery chords, those were not figments of her overtaxed imagination.

So pretty. She should be afraid, shouldn't she? The song wove in and out of the trees, as airy as light itself, the sound waves dappled. Maybe it was the woman from the park. Crisp and clear, then mute, nearly silent. Maybe it was the strange, crazed man from the park. So pretty. The music was so pretty, so soothing, Janice abandoned any notions of danger. So pretty. So familiar, she thought as she walked down the towpath, toward the song, toward the music, toward the music maker.

22

Shady grove, my true love
Shady grove I know
Shady grove, my true love
I'm bound for shady grove

Beautiful, the song. So peaceful. So unlike the night she'd just endured. The week. Months. An unknown song, familiar nonetheless to Janice's ear. Sweet. Incantatory.

Peaches in the summertime
Apples in the fall
If I can't get the girl I love
Won't have none at all

Janice walked the towpath slowly, not out of fear, strangely enough. Rather, she walked so as not to disturb. Walked, not thinking of the sonic connection to her dreams, both waking and sleeping, nor the madness found there. Walked slowly, deliberately, as if between the beats, as if pulled along by the drone notes. Not out of fear. The fear washed away by the music. Thaumaturgy.

If I had a needle and thread
Fine as I could sew
I'd sew my gal to my coattails
And down the road we'd go

Wish I had a banjo string
Made of golden twine
And every tune I'd pick on it
Is "I wish that girl was mine"

She sat just off the path—the music maker—with her back against a poplar trunk, facing Janice. Facing Janice, eyes closed. Janice could not help but look. Could not help but listen. Could not help but close the distance between them. So pretty, the song, and simple. And pretty, the singer, her bare feet crossed like mislaid parentheses, marking time at the frayed hem of her red calico dress.

I once had a mulie cow
Mulie when she's born
Took a jaybird forty year
To fly from horn to horn

She smiled when she sang, and why not? The words themselves, silly, and the voice that cradled the melody, rapturous. She strummed and noted the instrument in her lap, her thin limbs conjuring magic out of the strings and sound box. Janice stepped closer, certain, sure she'd be able to see the music take flight from the woman's mouth. Woman? Barely. Pretty. Dangerous? No, no danger. A lean face, oddly lopsided, the long thin scar angling across her forehead and disappearing into thick black hair at the temple and widow's peak.

Higher up the cherry trees
The riper grow the cherries
The more you hug and kiss the girls
The more they want to marry

The face. Janice knew that face. But from where? Common sense told her she ought to be afraid. Given the nature of her encounters with other strangers over the past few months, why wouldn't this woman, this strange woman, strangely dressed, sitting and singing way out in the woods, why shouldn't she turn on Janice like the rest? She remembered a similar instrument at PawPaw Landing. The music itself felt old as salt and just as pure. Necessary. Janice ought to be afraid. If the dead hummingbird that hung, like a beautiful pendant, on a piece of twine around the song maker's neck, its eyes sewn tight, if that odd necklace were any indicator, Janice ought to turn and run before the song was over, before the singer opened her eyes.

> *Every night when I go home*
> *My wife, I try to please her*
> *The more I try, the worse she gets*
> *Damned if I don't leave her*

Could turn, in an instant, this beautiful song. Turn monstrous. Become a discordant scree, a searing tumble of consonants and vowels that crushed and scorched everything in its path. Or, worse, even, could stop altogether. Could disappear. Leaving nothing. Janice feared the vacuum. She hung in the balance between want and need. The song touched her. And, the song traced to its source, the song maker, too, held sway over any fears welling up inside. Janice wanted to reach out, to touch this manifestation of beauty. To make sure it, the body, the face, the voice, were all real. Real flesh. Real blood. Real breath in that melodic throat. The eyes of the hummingbird were stitched shut. The eyes of the song maker opened. She smiled at Janice, winked, kept singing.

> *Fly around, my bright-eyed girl*
> *Fly around my daisy*
> *Fly around, my brown-eyed girl*
> *Nearly drive me crazy*

No torrent of fire. No rattling bones. No cataract eyes spinning madly in their sockets. No spook's tongue-cum-noose to yank tight at Janice's gullible neck. The singer simply opened her eyes, looked at Janice, and smiled. She *was* real. She had to be real. She sang. The song and the smile warm and welcoming. Forgiving, even.

> *Shady grove, my true love*
> *Shady grove I know*
> *Shady grove, my true love*
> *I'm bound for shady grove*

"You like my hog fiddle?" she asked, and in speaking, broke open the spell that had lured Janice down the towpath. The voice—the speaking voice—though sweetly intoned, languorous and curdled.

Janice didn't respond. Didn't know how. She smiled back, but little beetles of fear darted through her mind.

"Some folks call it a scattlin," the woman said. "Or a dulcimore. Or devil's box. I prefer hog fiddle."

She lifted the instrument with both hands, as if it were a baby presented for baptism, offered it to Janice.

"You want to pluck it?"

The dangling hummingbird swayed ever so slightly between her breasts.

Janice had no answer. She took a step back. Wanting to run, and wanting to stay, equally.

No. She shook her head, softly. No.

And just as she was about to turn and walk away, *walk* away, the woman spoke again.

"Come by here tomorrow, I'll play you another song," she said.

23

There was no conscious decision to stay. But for the life of her, Janice couldn't recall how she'd spent the remaining hours of the previous day and night. And was both surprised and relieved to wake, fully rested, with no muddy tracks on the floor. She woke lying in bed, pleasantly chilled in her T-shirt and underwear, looking up at the crow's skull hanging on the wall, its beak aimed down at her. Woke with the tune to "Shady Grove" so clear in her mind that she got up hurriedly and looked out the window, expecting, almost hoping, to see the woman.

The woman? Had Janice imagined her? If not, where had she come from, and did Stephen know her? Janice craned to look up and down the towpath from her window. Saw no pretty woman. Saw instead, the goats. Heard not "Shady Grove," sung and strummed on the dulcimer, the hog fiddle—but instead the clank and rattle of the goats, their collar bells, the dour clappers whose flat notes laid the herky-jerky percussive background for the chorus of throaty bleats. This, she mistook for "Shady Grove," these goats, their thick tongues stabbing between thick teeth as they trotted up out of the canal, as they meandered the towpath; a goatish call and response; goat heads shaking; goat ears flapping; black goats, white goats, tawny goats; some heavy-boned and squatty, others with their bloated udders or their walnut-sized goatballs swinging between longish legs. The herd of twenty or thirty goats squabbled noisily as they nipped at the long grass growing up around Janice's car, as they butted one another out of the way to taste the marigold blooms that sprouted in clumps by the house. Janice looked on, amused at their antics, not—surprisingly not—afraid, and when the goats wandered around to the back of the house, she went downstairs, without dressing, to watch them from the back door, pausing on the way out to pick up a bag of gingersnaps, another of Stephen's purchases.

When Janice sat on the steps, settling into the gritty coolness against the bare flesh at the back of her thighs, and opened the package of cookies resting between her feet, all the ears of all the goats twitched. Pricked up. And, one by one, the animals turned to look at her. What she wouldn't give for a camera, a picture of this moment, her half-naked at the center, at the heart, of a ragged half-moon of bleating goats.

A big ram came first, a billy with a white, dished face and hooves the hard flat-black of mussel shells. He stepped up cautiously, the little ditches of his nostrils sucking in the sugary cookie smells.

Janice bit into a cookie.

The goat lifted his head and mumbled something.

"Sure," Janice said, laughing. And the laughter surprised her. The laughter momentarily eclipsed the weariness and distress of the past few days. "Yes, of course," she said to the goat, then reached into the bag and offered the animal a gingersnap.

A moment later the entire herd crowded around Janice on the back step. She giggled at their capric snuffling, at their greedy, rubbery lips pulling cookie after cookie from her open palms. Laughed out loud when, cookies all gone, the goats licked at her hands and fingers.

"I wish I had more," she said, dumping the crumbs out at her feet, and practically swooning every time a fleshy goat tongue curled across her toes and arches.

Then the goats left suddenly, as if beckoned by some distant goatherd. The big billy cocked his head toward the woods, and they all trotted off, parting around the smokehouse and scattering up the hill, taking with them all the urgency Janice had felt the night before. She watched until the animals were deep into the trees and brush, until she no longer caught glimpses of goat fur between the trunks and brambles. She'd go. She'd miss Stephen, no doubt, and miss finding out more about that strange woman with her hog fiddle and songs. Nevertheless, she'd go that day, but there was no rush.

~

Janice felt certain that Stephen had read her letter by then, and she wondered if *he'd* miss her at all. The goats' visit had brought Janice real pleasure, and they took with them some of her embarrassment, a little of the shame she felt over the weird things Stephen had seen happen to her.

She embraced some small pleasure in believing that, at least, Stephen wouldn't forget her. And, she had the chisel taken from the studio to remember him by. The chisel and the Sun Salutation chart. Not much, but enough. Funny, though, she couldn't recall putting the chisel away. In the house, Janice searched the bedroom first, under the mattress, under the pillow, in her suitcase. No chisel. Had she dropped it crossing the river? Downstairs, she looked everywhere the chisel could possibly be. As she stood at the mantel, trying to retrace her steps from last night, an odd object caught her eye.

It was early summer. She'd cleaned the ashes from the fireplace a month ago, and hadn't built a fire since. But there, between the dog irons, the crumpled black remnants of a piece of paper.

Janice knelt, and the smell of soot, tinged with the scent of more recent burning, washed over her. Very little white remained of the paper, only its balled core, bitten away on all sides by gray-black teeth. Janice poked the paper with her finger, shattering the ash surface. She picked it up, and by the time she'd opened it up to see the small drawing of her own backside and legs stretched fully into the cobra position, all her fingers were filthy.

The violation enraged her. Who else but Stephen, Janice thought. She talked out loud, angrily. Who else would've come into her house while she was asleep? He'd done it before, under other pretenses. The nerve! The gall! He'd burned the gift, the yoga chart, and didn't even bother to take away the remains. Then, fear crept in to chip away at Janice's anger. What else had Stephen done while she lay asleep?

Janice wanted to leave then, more than ever. To get in the car and drive away from the locktender's house. Pick her destination later. To drive away, and not even say goodbye.

The tears that came as she packed surprised Janice. She hoisted the heavy suitcase so that it balanced upright on her thigh, then labored down the stairs and out the door. Standing behind the Subaru, Janice shook the cramp out of her hand and reached for the latch. Locked. As were the doors.

Panic didn't fully set in until Janice had practically turned the house inside out looking for the keys.

"Goddammit!"

But her rage was tempered by more worry and fear.

Unless . . . unless she'd somehow dropped the keys, unknowingly, on the way over to, or from, Stephen's house. The keys and the chisel. No. He did it. He took them. No other explanation fit. The keys and the chisel. The keys . . . the dream. A sharp twitch where the pectoral muscle meets the sternum—the domain of the breast, the heart—and Janice recalled her dream—tchink, tchink, tchink—the chest cavity breached—fingers in the hole—the bank of a raging river—a key hurled into the torrent—tchink, tchink, tchink.

Once again, she was stuck at the locktender's house. Trapped. But unlike the first few months when, in the dead of winter, the tight confines of the old house were Janice's whole claustrophobic world, she knew all too well now that Stephen's house stood a quarter of a mile through the woods. With little notion of what she'd do, beyond looking for her car keys, upon arrival, Janice pulled on a skirt, buckled up a pair of sandals, and headed toward the canal.

Oh I fall on my knees and I pray to thee
To come and stand around with me, little girl
Come stand around with me

Janice heard the music as soon as she stepped onto the towpath.

Turn and run. Turn and run. Twice the thought crossed Janice's mind before being displaced.

—Come by here tomorrow, I'll play you another song—

How could she have forgotten the woman, the song maker, and her promise?

Look up, look down that lonesome old road
And it's hang down your little head and cry sweet girl
Hang down your little head and cry

Janice paid little attention to the words. Wanted only to hear them sung, to watch the mouth of the singer shape them. How could she have forgotten the striking face, the voice of an angel? And how was it possible that the rage and fear of a few minutes earlier were so quickly displaced by this singer and her song? It was as if the droning strings of the dulcimer stretched over the strum hollow, up the fingerboard, through the peg box, out and down the towpath, where they wound themselves around Janice's sternum and ribs.

Drew her in. The woman sat against the same tree. Wore the same calico dress. The same dead hummingbird hung around her neck.

> I wish to the Lord that I'd never been born
> Or died when I was young, little girl
> Or died when I was young

> I never would have kissed your red rosy cheeks
> Or heard your lying tongue, little girl
> Or heard your lying tongue

Janice no longer wanted to cross the canal bed, to climb the other side and seek out Stephen Gainy. She wanted nothing more, in that inexplicable moment, than to hear a song. The gravel crunching beneath Janice's sandals heralded her approach. The singer smiled, threw more fire into the final verses.

> You told me more lies than the stars in the sky
> And you'll never get to heaven when you die, little girl
> You'll never get to heaven when you die

> My suitcase is packed and my trunk it's done gone
> Now it's goodbye, little woman, I'm gone gone gone
> Goodbye, little woman, I'm gone

"Hey there," the singer said.

Janice waved, stepped a little closer.

"Sit yourself down," the woman said. "I promised you a song."

Nothing in the world, not even her own very palpable fear, could have prevented Janice from plopping down cross-legged and smoothing out her skirt on the edge of the towpath. No apparition, this. No fear. Mercifully, no fear.

The woman sang a song about cornbread and molasses.

The woman sang a song about a groundhog.

> One old woman was the mother of us all
> She fed us on whistle-pigs as soon as we could crawl
> Tan-a-rig-tail, paddle link-a di-de-do

When she stopped singing, the woman picked up a stick and scratched something in the dirt.

"My name's Addie Epps," she said. "It goes like this."

Janice leaned and tried to read the childlike scrawl.

The woman, Addie Epps, poked at the hard consonants.

"These two feet reach up to heaven; these two feet dangle in Hades."

Then she crossed and crossed out the names, not stopping until she'd dug a little ditch with the end of her stick. Not stopping, in fact, until Janice, wanting to get her attention back, spoke.

"Your singing is so pretty. Your playing, too."

Addie Epps grinned, as if Janice had said just the right thing. With a flourish, she hit a chord on the instrument. But didn't speak.

The silence nettled until Janice broke it.

"Do you live around here?"

"Close by," Addie said, then played a while without singing. "You ready to try it?"

Again, Addie offered the dulcimer to Janice.

"No, I . . . no. I have to go . . ."

She remembered her lost key, her destination. She worked it through her mind. Maybe she could stay another day?

"Tomorrow, I'm leaving. I'm leaving. Tomorrow."

Maybe this woman, Addie Epps, could make the day more bearable.

"What you want to do that for?" Addie asked, grinning. Always grinning.

"I have to go," Janice said.

The woman, Addie Epps, reached out toward Janice, palm up. Janice could not miss the three rough bars of raised flesh cutting across her wrist. Janice wondered where she'd seen those before. Janice, without really intending it, took Addie's hand in her own, felt the scar tissue beneath her fingertips. Addie grinned. Addie turned their joined hands over; Janice's palm now up. Addie pressed her thumb-tips into the bruise on Janice's flesh; traced the small bird exactly, and without looking.

"Come see me tomorrow and I'll teach you a song."

"I have to go," Janice said, and somehow—momentarily—released, she turned and walked back down the towpath, and was about to cross the canal and head over to Stephen's house when his truck rattled to a stop in her drive.

"Speak of the devil," she said, but not loud enough for him to hear.

Janice puffed her chest out a bit; tried to work her anger back up.

Stephen looked at her for a long silent moment, as if gauging her frame of mind, as if settling on his own response. "Been out for a walk?" he asked, from within the truck.

"Where's my key, Stephen?"

The question rang with accusation.

Of course, she also wanted to ask about his reaction to the letter, ask if he'd ever seen the goats, ask what he knew about their strange neighbor.

"What?" Stephen said, genuinely perplexed. "What key?"

"The car key," Janice said, but already the rockets of her anger had been disarmed. "I can't find my car key."

Stephen got out of the truck, looked at the suitcase behind the Subaru. "You going somewhere?"

Janice avoided the question. She stepped around the Subaru, to keep the car between them.

"Did you . . . I mean, it seemed like someone had been in my house. Now, I can't find my key."

Stephen leaned against the bed of the truck and chewed his lip.

"Janice . . . I'm really sorry about the things I said the other day. I was wrong."

He said nothing at all about the letter she'd left in his house. Nothing at all about the stolen chisel. She said nothing at all about his—deeply appreciated—patience in dealing with her outrageous behavior.

"Hell, maybe Clyde took the key. I haven't seen that damn bird in weeks."

"No sign of him at all?" Janice asked, the question more loaded than Stephen knew.

"None. I'm actually pretty worried. It's always crow season around here. Legally, any hunter, any farmer could shoot him anytime."

"I don't think . . ." Janice began, but didn't finish. She came around from behind the car and leaned against the tailgate.

"I brought you a peace offering," he said, then added, "but it comes with two conditions."

A peace offering? It was Janice who ought to be humbly asking for forgiveness.

"What?"

"What, what? What are the conditions, or what is the gift?"

What makes you so kind? What brings you back to me, after . . . ?

"Both," Janice said.

Stephen plucked a tin of breath mints from his shirt pocket, popped two in his mouth, and handed the tin to Janice.

"I'm not even going to show you the present until you agree to the first condition."

"Okay," she said, the syllables made more open as she rolled the mint on her tongue.

"Promise that you won't go anywhere, at least until tomorrow afternoon."

Janice paused, then with mock disdain said, "Duh, my car key is lost."

"Well, you could take a cab. Or, you could dupe me into giving you a ride to the bus station. Nevertheless, no agreement, no present."

"All right. I promise I won't dupe you into anything until at least tomorrow afternoon."

She put her hands out, waiting for the gift, which he made her wait for until the silence and stillness were almost unbearable.

Finally, Stephen reached into the truck and took the gift off the seat.

"Close your eyes," he said.

She did so, reluctantly.

"What is it?" she asked before looking, and in a million years she would not have guessed the gift to be a handmade gourd banjo.

Janice laughed and strummed the instrument, and they both realized it was in dire need of tuning.

"You know I can't play this thing at all."

"That's the other condition," he said. "You have to swear never to practice within several hundred yards of me or my house."

Janice wished, more than anything at that moment, that she could throw herself so fully into a sweet song, it'd make Stephen's head spin.

"I found it at a flea market," he said. "And remembered your broken one."

"It's really cool. Thank you. I mean, a lot."

"Can I give you a hand with this?" Stephen asked, taking hold of the suitcase's handle.

She nodded. Stephen headed for the house. Just before reaching the door he turned to speak and saw Janice standing on the towpath looking off in the distance.

"You trying to escape?"

"I thought I heard something," she said.

They sat for a while on the front porch, with Janice trying to pick out notes and chords on the banjo.

"See," he said. "Already you're reneging on your promise."

The gourd bowl of the instrument was as big as half a basketball, with a thin skin head stretched tight over the opening and tacked in place. The five strings ran up a polished, fretless fingerboard. Janice plucked, each note rich and round. No sustain.

"All right, you can make noise in my general vicinity if you do one other thing for me."

"What?"

"We had so much fun the other day, until . . ."

"I don't want to talk about it," Janice said, wrapping her hand around the banjo's neck. Stopping the sound. "I'm sorry. About . . . all . . ."

"No, no, I'm sorry. Neither do I. But I don't want that to be the last experience we have out in the real world together. Especially if you're leaving."

"So . . ."

"So, I want to take you somewhere."

"No more surprises, Stephen. Tell me where, or I'm not going."

"A boat ride," he said, and immediately saw the hackles rise. "But before you have a spaz, not a canal boat, and not on a river. I have a pontoon boat. I made it myself, and it's docked on a lake a half an hour from here."

Janice looked at Stephen. One unruly long gray hair had escaped the flow pattern of his goatee, and curled straight out from his chin. How could she say no to his request?

"Now?" she asked.

"If you're ready. Bring a swimsuit; I have everything else."

"I don't swim," she said.

"We can float; I have inner tubes."

"I don't float."

"You don't have to bring a bathing suit, Janice. You don't even have to look at the water."

A dozen times on the ride to the lake, she wanted to ask Stephen questions. About his meditation practice, if that's what kept him so even-keeled. She wanted to ask him about the letter, whether he'd read it. And about the goats, and Addie Epps. Resisted every time. The missing key, the burned yoga chart, the chisel, these things, on a merry-go-round of rationalization and illogic, Janice decided, were all her own doing. It was the safest explanation.

"My ears are stopped up," she said when they pulled onto the gravel access road. The half-hour drive had been all switchbacks and climbing elevation.

"It's so pretty up here," Stephen said. "Too far out for it to be crowded during the week. And the lake is about two thousand feet above sea level, so it's always a little cooler than down where we live."

There were no other cars in the parking lot. A bank of upturned canoes and kayaks chained to a log fence defined one edge of the open waterfront. In the middle, there was a floating pier with a paved boat-ramp on either side, and at the other end, a single picnic table and a fire pit guarded a small sandy beach. Across the lake, dense woods encroached on the shoreline as far in either direction as Janice could see. The green of the leaves and needles, and the gray-brown of the trunks gave way to impenetrable shadows within feet of the water's edge.

"What's all that?" Janice asked, watching Stephen unload a cooler and several camp-style storage containers from the bed of his truck.

"I'm a growing boy," he said. "You don't expect me to spend all this time on the boat without nourishment, do you?"

Janice looked at the canoes, and the pier.

"What boat?" she asked, with just a hint of suspicion.

"It's tied up in a little cove down that path."

He pointed to an opening in the brush beyond the picnic table and hoisted the cooler onto his shoulder.

"Now I know you're not going to make me carry all this stuff by myself," he said.

Janice grabbed what she could carry and followed him down the path.

"Wow," she said, more relieved than she should have been to see an actual boat in the water.

"You okay with this?" Stephen asked, after laying the gangplank in place and putting his cooler on deck. He reached for her hand.

"Yes," she said, with little hesitation. "But . . ."

"But what?"

"Do you have a life vest?"

"Sure," he said. "But you know the maximum speed on this boat is just a little slower than walking?"

"It's just that . . ."

"No problem," Stephen said.

After he helped with the zipper and adjustable straps, they loaded their gear beneath the flat roof that covered nearly half of the carpeted deck, Janice pausing to press her fingers into the vivid green faux-grass.

"Classy, isn't it," Stephen said.

"You didn't really make this boat, did you?"

Nothing about the watercraft—not its fifteen-by-ten-foot covered deck fenced with rectangular aluminum tubing, nor its semitransparent corrugated roofing, nor the small enclosed cabin at the stern, and the engine and railless platform behind that, nor the pontoons themselves, twin rows of fifty-five-gallon drums welded together and sealed—none of this was remarkably well-crafted, but the mechanics and engineering of its construction were outside Janice's realm of experience.

"Did so," he said, yanking the cord once, twice, before the small outboard motor sputtered to life. "My first college experience was a welding program at Portage Technical Institute. I've got a diploma to prove it."

Janice sat on a backless bench by the cabin door while Stephen maneuvered them into deeper water.

"And you built a boat?"

"Yep. It was my final project. Feel these beads."

He came from behind the steering wheel, took Janice's index finger and pulled it over the joints where the aluminum railing uprights met the horizontal posts.

"What am I feeling for?" she asked, very willing to go along.

"Nothing," he said. "If you can't feel the welds, then they're perfect. Lucky for me, you're sitting on the end-of-the-semester side. My beads are much messier on the other side of the boat, where I started."

When he pulled her hand away from the rail, Stephen held her arm up and studied the mark there.

"Such a strange little tattoo," he said. "Does it mean anything?"

"Nope," she said.

Nope.

Janice sat, the collar of the life vest bunched up around her face.

For a long while, they puttered along the shoreline, the silence broken by a jumping fish or the call of some waterbird.

"You were right," she said. "It's so pretty here. And big. Bigger than I expected."

"I've been coming here since I was a boy. My great-grandfather owned the property before it was a lake."

"It's man-made?"

"Yep. They damned up Gainy's Bog in 1926. Or maybe '27."

"What kind of fish are those, the ones that keep jumping?"

"Bass, probably. At least the ones that jump in the middle. Closer to shore the sunfish and the humongous carp sometimes have an altercation. You hot, yet, in that vest?"

"Not hot enough to take it off."

Stephen got a cold jug of tea and some apples and cheese from the cooler. After they snacked, Janice took her shoes off and let one foot dangle in the water. She lay back and closed her eyes, but then grew self-conscious, and when she sat up and looked over, Stephen was sketching her.

"Can't you find anything better to draw?" she asked, making a face at him.

"Well, it was either you or the big old turtle coming through the water after your toes . . ."

Janice pulled her feet onto the deck.

"How's your altarpiece coming?" she asked.

"You know, I'm going to have to stop doing so many of these apology-to-you trips if I want to get it done."

Janice reached down and wet her hand in the lake, then flicked the water at Stephen.

With no one at the helm, the boat drifted close to shore.

"Come here," he said, getting behind the wheel.

"What?"

"I'll teach you to drive."

Janice, the new Janice, stepped up without hesitation and took over steering the boat. Her body, her emotions, had ricocheted back and forth between extreme distress and unexplained serenity over the past few days—weeks, maybe—and standing up at the helm she felt in a precarious balance.

"It's not like there's much to learn," Stephen said. "Just watch out for the speed bumps."

As he spoke, Stephen stripped off his T-shirt, and before Janice could protest, dove from the bow.

"Hey!"

Where did he go?

Water. Janice never liked the water. Even good swimmers made her anxious. And Stephen, she had no idea how adept he was in the water.

"Hey!" she called out, her voice rolling over the surface of the water and disturbing a heron fishing on the opposite shore. "Damn it, Stephen!"

Could a person hold their breath so long?

Just as Janice was about to leave the helm and go to the front of the boat, there came a ringing thud from underneath. The pontoons must've hit something. Or, something hit the pontoons.

Seconds later, Stephen hauled himself up onto the platform, shaking the water from his hair and wiping his goatee and mustache.

"That felt great!" he said. "Did I scare you?"

"No," Janice said.

"Want to go for a dip, while I steer?"

"What did I tell you before we came?" she asked.

"Oh right, you don't dip."

Stephen unrolled a towel on the exposed deck, lay on his belly in the sun. Janice leaned against the rail behind him, pulled her skirt up enough so that the sun spilled over her thighs. Pulled it back down when he stirred. Again, the boat had drifted near the bank.

"Okay," he said. "If I anchor the boat in the middle of the lake, will you take off the life jacket?"

"If you anchor the boat in the middle of the lake, and I sit in the middle of the deck, I'll unzip it."

He did, so she did.

"What time do you think it is?" Janice asked.

"Six, maybe seven. You gonna be late for work?"

"Not likely."

"Got a date?"

"Hush," Janice said. "I'm trying to enjoy the peace and quiet."

"Hmmm," he said. "Now you're getting it. You know that's why I come out here. I mean, in addition to using the boat as the official boat of apology, sometimes I get so discouraged that I need to shut it all out for a while. Shut it out and recuperate."

"*It* being work?" she asked. "You get discouraged with your carving?"

"Sometimes," he said. "But that's one area of my life where I'm pretty confident and clear. Usually it's everything else that frustrates me. Campus politics. Ex-wife politics. Girl trouble, although it's been so damn long . . ."

Janice cleared her throat, and it was louder than she intended.

"How long . . . I mean, have you been divorced for a while?"

"Not long enough," he said. "Lately, it's the state of the world that's getting to me."

"What do you mean?" she asked.

"Do you get the . . . no, there's no paper delivered to your house. Or mail, either, right?"

Stephen was caught up for the moment in the logistical problems of Janice's isolation, until she redirected him.

"I keep up," she lied. "The radio, remember? What are you talking about?"

"Well, we've got a monkey in a cowboy suit leading us all to hell, and grinning every step of the way. It's been what, three years now? I have students without arms. Students without legs. Kids, I mean. I just wish there was something I could do, something besides hammer away at rocks."

Janice wanted to reach out and put her hand on his shoulder. Didn't.

"My ex's nephew leaves next week. He volunteered. He wants to go. Thinks he's doing good."

"I'm sorry," she said. "I can't . . . I don't know too much about what's happening. It's not that I don't care how the world works. It just closes me down. Scares me."

She started to tell Stephen about Private Danks. Didn't.

"The scariest thing," Stephen said. "The scariest thing is that there's no real order to how the world works. Not at the tiny, human scale. But all these people, sometimes in the form of whole countries, spend so much time building all these fires and pissing on other people's fires and blaming everybody else for the fires that get out of hand . . . there's nobody in charge, not in any way that can make a difference."

Stephen went into the cabin. Janice, thinking he might be upset, followed.

"But then," he said, untying and unrolling a small quilted pouch. "Then I come out here to the most peaceful place on earth, smoke a big old bowl, and I realize that even if the idiots-that-be destroy the whole fucking planet, after a while something will crawl out of the smoldering bog and stand upright. The whole cycle will start again. It ain't about the human scale. That's where I find my peace."

Janice watched him pack the bowl of a little, ornately colored glass pipe.

"And now, I get to share my place, and my pipe, with such a pretty girl."

These last words he spoke with a constricted throat, with fine jets of smoke curling out of his nose.

How could she not? How could Janice not take the pipe, the lighter from him, and inhale deeply? How could she tell him that she'd only smoked one other time in her life, and that was a decade ago? How could she refuse him after that comment, the one about a pretty girl? How could she not hold the hot smoke in despite the burn, the biting in her lungs? Stephen lit the pipe again for himself. How could she not share it that second time? Not hold it in until a strange fog rolled across her eyes? They sat in the shade smoking, and how could she not have noticed before all the fine red-blond hairs on his arms and legs? How could she have missed the scar in the shape of the heron's wings in flight, the small scar over his right eyebrow? How could she not have seen that the trees were stacked perfectly straight, their thick trunks like the teeth of a comb? A comb standing on edge, atop a narrow band of bare earth? And all that holding in place a hard vertical plane of water? Janice noticed, with some concern, the fine dividing lines drawn around everything. Everything. Everything was separate from everything else. She said it out loud.

"Everything is separate from everything else."

Stephen laughed so hard he couldn't get out any words.

They lay, side by side, on the fake-grass carpet, tried to speak, giggled, tried to speak.

The high crept stealthily over her consciousness and body. Sometimes a physical sensation, as if her head were swelling, balloonlike. Painless, but disconcerting. Sometimes, purely cerebral, the nugget of a thought snowballing, gaining momentum and size and complexity as it tumbled through her gray matter, then scattering and disappearing at the most inopportune moment.

In the entire history of human culinary endeavor, of people eating and drinking, nothing ever tasted as good as the chocolate chip cookies that Stephen brought out. In short order, and with only monosyllabic ceremony, they devoured the entire bag, two trays each, then went at the bag of shoestring potatoes with equal fervor.

"I can't believe you're still wearing that life jacket," he said. "Safety orange is a good color for you."

And this cast them into another fit of laughter.

"Let's take the edge off this enhanced-brain moment, shall we?"

Stephen uncapped a quart-sized demijohn of wine and tipped the red liquid into two plastic cups.

"You have to know, before you drink, that I'm no wine connoisseur," he said. "Cheap and red are my two criteria. It has to go well with cookies. That's not a deal-breaker is it?"

"I consider myself forewarned," she said.

At full dusk, when everything was in hard silhouette, or hued in purple, Stephen told her to lie down on the deck and watch the sky.

"I've arranged a performance," he said.

The first bats that flew by the boat—some mere inches away before turning hard and sharp against the sky—those first dozens scared Janice. But Stephen convinced her that their aim was precise enough to pluck mosquitoes out of the air in flight, and that the bats had no interest in either his big head or hers. So by the time the spastic airborne ballet was in full swing, hundreds and hundreds of brown bats winging overhead, skimming the water's surface, Janice, in her altered state, agreed. "Very fucking cool."

Deal-breaker? What deal? The wine warmed her in more familiar ways than did the smoke. The wine soothed the swarm of locusts that was her nerves. Janice finished her cup first and poured another. They lay, as the pontoon boat drifted in slow circles around its anchor, orbiting in silence. Phase two of the marijuana buzz was softer. Janice let her mind play. Let her mind fill and go blank, fill and go blank, at its own pace, with its own erratic contents. Fill and go blank. She was so comfortable there, with Stephen, she let herself, her imagination, drift into a future with him.

Of course, he'd need to know all about the house, about the tollbooth, and about Addie Epps. He'd have to know about these things, these experiences, and maybe even help her determine how real each of them were. Janice tried to put together some sentences to begin the conversation. But her mind was fuzzy from smoke and drink, and the mood was wonderfully, mercifully, light.

"Chuck roast, rib roast, porterhouse, sirloin, round steak, rump roast, tenderloin, flank steak, short ribs, brisket, stew meat, shank."

Janice spoke out of the blue.

"I think that's all."

"What the hell are you talking about?" Stephen asked. "Do we need to smoke more? Or maybe less?"

"Cuts of meat," she said. "Beef. Where I worked, at Biggers & Twine, there were posters covering the windows. One showed a picture of a cow, with a diagram drawn on top of the photo showing all the cuts of meat that come from the animal."

"No wonder you have a bird skull hanging over your bed."

Stephen got up, went to the front of the boat, opened a gate in the rail, stepped onto a narrow platform that jutted out inches above the still water, sat down, and hung his feet over the edge. Janice joined him, tucking her skirt under her knees to keep it dry.

They talked about the website she was going to design for him.

They talked about Biggers & Twine, her dissatisfaction there. Not prying, but out of genuine curiosity, Stephen tried to get an idea of how she supported herself at the locktender's house, but Janice deflected all the most probing questions.

"Maybe I should get a job up here," she said. "Keep me from going stir-crazy."

"Good luck," he said. "This part of the country is threadbare."

"I could be your model," she said, blushing at her own suggestion.

"You could, but I'd have to pay you in cookies and pot. And you'd probably insist on wearing that damn life jacket."

"It could be a whole series," she said. "Drawings and carvings. *Woman in Life Jacket.*"

"It sounds good," he said. "You could become an itinerant banjo player. One of those unshaved, unwashed, tie-dye-wearing, patchouli-smeared retro-folkies who go from school to school terrifying young children with your spooky songs about killers and drunks and dead maidens."

"I could," she said, and her mind turned to Addie Epps, the singer, the woman on the towpath. Janice almost asked Stephen if he'd ever seen her, ever heard her sing. She had the words in her mouth, knew their weight on her tongue, felt them bump against her teeth.

"Speaking of unwashed," Stephen said, and then he fell forward into the water.

Janice dodged the splash, and when he rolled over and floated on his back she asked if he planned to do that all night long.

"That depends," he said. "Are we staying here all night?"

"I can't," she said.

"Aw, come on. I'll sleep at one end of the boat, and you can sleep at the other. I promise, promise, promise not to cross whatever line you draw. Besides, we've had too much to smoke and drink. That's not the way I'd go into . . . well, you can trust me."

It hadn't occurred to Janice that he might ask her to spend the night. With the smoke and the drink, she didn't pay attention to the time, nor to the ebb and flow of their energies, nor to her other needs.

"You can trust me, Janice."

He sounded like a little boy. A little, sincere, boy.

"It's not about trust, Stephen. I do trust you. I just . . . it's just . . . I have to go home."

"Will you tell me why?"

The new Janice spoke up.

"I have to pee."

"That's it? You're going to end our good night and make me take you all the way home because you have to pee?"

"I told you it wasn't about trust."

Stephen swam to the end of the boat, treaded water; she left her feet hanging over, jolting subtly each time his hand or his own foot inadvertently touched hers.

"That's silly, Janice. By the time we get back to your house, on that curvy, pothole-riddled mountain road, you'll have wet the seat of my truck."

"Is there a bathroom close by?" she asked.

"Yes," he said. "Two, actually."

But before Janice could get her hopes up, he pointed.

"You see all those woods? That's one option. Or, the better is this two-hundred-acre lake."

"I can't . . ."

Janice, despite the buzz, despite the playful flirtatious nature of the exchange, grew visibly anxious. The sun had all but packed up and clocked out for the day. The dense woods looked even darker.

"Why's the lake better than the woods?" she asked.

"Well, squatting out there in the dark, with all the possums and raccoons and foxes and bears and snakes, not to mention the mosquitoes and ticks and chiggers, your chances of getting bitten are much greater. If you hang your behind out over the boat, the most you can get are nibbling minnows, or a catfish barb. Or, there is that snapping turtle. Or, the legendary Gainy's Bog razor-tooth gar. Or . . ."

"Shut up, Stephen! I'm not hanging anything over the edge of the boat! No way."

"Then you'll just have to come in with me."

"I'm not peeing in the lake with you floating there beside me. Besides, I can't swim."

"Janice, you're wearing a flotation device that would hold up a small nation. You don't have to swim, and believe you me, I'll get out of the way of whatever you do."

The conversation went back and forth. Janice really didn't want to go home—they both knew it—but neither did she want to humiliate herself. Staying the night, on the boat, with Stephen was definitely within the realm of possibility. But any kind of intimacy, including urination, she wasn't ready for.

"What if I float away?" she asked.

Stephen's patient insistence, and her full bladder, convinced Janice to agree that, if he knelt on the boat's platform and kept his eyes closed the whole time, she'd pull her skirt up high around her waist, hold on to his hand, and climb into the lake and float until she relieved herself.

"Better?" he asked, pulling her back onboard.

"Did you keep your eyes closed?"

"They're still closed."

"Then, yes, much better."

Stephen got out a smoked sausage, some grapes, and vegetables.

"That calls for a celebration," he said. "Or at the very least, dinner."

She dried her legs with an already damp towel while he sliced the vegetables and meat on a little round cutting board.

"Did you have a boyfriend down there?" he asked. "At Biggers & Twine."

"Private Danks," she said. "He was killed in the desert last year. Thought he was doing a good thing."

"I'm sorry, Janice. I didn't know, earlier, I didn't know . . ."

"It's okay," she said, snatching a quarter-sized piece of sausage.

"Danks," he said. "That name is from this part of the country."

"I don't want to talk about it," Janice said. "How many girlfriends have you had?"

"Too many for my own good," he said. "And not enough to learn how they work."

They spent the meal talking about past relationships, Stephen divulging far more than Janice. She, offering nothing at all about Danks.

Stephen took a folding table and two chairs from a low storage chest in the cabin. Told her about his ex-wife. Told her about the guy she left him for. Told her about sending his first pitiful pubic hairs to a girl one grade ahead of him, with a note expressing the depth of his love.

"That's both pitiful and gross," Janice said. "My first boyfriend, or the first guy I thought, or even said, the word *love* with, I met him the last day of church camp. Everybody else had gone home. The preacher and deacons had moved an old double-wide mobile home onto the grounds; they were going to convert it into the chapel and Sunday school rooms. So there were two halves of this house, each strapped down on its own trailer. The trailers sat side by side, out in a clearing, with maybe ten feet between them. The whole side gaped open, and you could see everything. I stood in one half, he stood in the other, and we spent a whole afternoon tossing lit firecrackers at each other across that gap."

Stephen argued that this was much crazier than his pubic hair fiasco.

"His daddy owned a fireworks tent out by the interstate. For the longest time, I thought it wasn't real love if my ears didn't ring."

"Did you stay in touch?"

"No," she said. Then, after much thought, "He died. Some freak winter lightning strike while he was doing inventory in the tent."

"Damn."

"This other guy, I was in junior high and he'd just gotten his driver's license. We didn't even really call it a date, but he was supposed to come pick me up in his mom's car. Never showed. The next day, they found him."

"Found him where?" Stephen asked.

"Kids used to park behind the screen of this abandoned drive-in theater. They'd drink, and smoke, probably kiss and stuff. The next morning, they found him. The whole screen had fallen over. He was by himself. He was crushed, him and the car both."

"You're making this up, Janice."

"No," she said. "I'm not. I'm really not."

"Remind me not to get involved with you," he said.

"I don't want to talk about it anymore."

Janice changed the subject. "I should've brought my banjo."

Stephen broke the peace of the night, singing at the top of his lungs.

"Well I come from Alabama, with my banjo on my knee / I'm going to Louisiana, my true love for to see / It rained all night, the day I left / The weather was bone dry / The sun so hot, I froze to death / Susanna, don't you cry . . ."

"Hush," Janice said. "You're scaring me and all the other wildlife."

Stephen just sang louder.

"Oh, Janice Witherspoon, don't you cry for me / For I come from Alabama with, my banjo on my kneeeeeeeeee!"

The woods and the shoreline were stone silent for a long time after his song.

He smoked a little more. Janice declined, the chemical chicanery from earlier still very present in her brain.

"Do I need to tie you to the railing?" Stephen asked. He'd arranged some blankets and pillows for Janice just outside the cabin door. When he carried his own bedding to the bow of the boat she told him to stop acting ridiculous. She lined her sandals up, toe to toe, two feet from her pallet.

"That's your border," she said. "Trespassers will be shot."

"I'm going for a final dip," Stephen said. "It's your turn not to look."

Janice listened to him strip, listened to him ease into the water, listened to his slow strokes all the way around the boat.

"Close your eyes," he said, just before climbing back onboard. She wouldn't tell him whether or not she did.

Stephen and Janice lay in the dark, their talk growing more and more quiet, less and less reciprocal.

"Do you believe in God?"

"What do you think happens after you die?"

"Did you ever see anybody die?"

Janice loved the looping conversation. She didn't want it to end, fought hard against sleep. She wanted to tell Stephen that she hadn't been away from the locktender's house at night since arriving. She wanted to tell Stephen that she'd never talked like this with anybody. Anybody. Ever. Janice fought the encroaching sleep.

"What's the prettiest thing you ever saw?" she asked, and when Stephen told her about hiking in the mountains with his grandfather, somewhere in the Northwest, and seeing all the grasshoppers embedded in the ice, at the terminus of a glacier, a vague recognition of the image almost roused her.

"Pretty," she mumbled.

Then the summer night laid its rich bounty out on the sackcloth sky. The scents of steeplebush and laurel. The cicada's heated ratchet. The bullfrog's lament. A gibbous moon climbed its invisible ladder.

—In the dream a pale woman sings to her babies, in the dark—in the dream, babies—in the dark, she sings to soothe them all—in the dream, no buckets no fists no hemp rope knotted tight around her ankles—wrists—in the dream her backside isn't bared again and again—no pawing no pinch-

ing no biting—the bit—the mule-slick bridle—in the dream, her babies at her tit—the milk runs sweet—the brown-skinned woman—her softness—got to get the milk, honey—the brown-skinned eases the slick babies through the birth canal—prods and pulls—inside, the brown-skinned woman reaches inside—comes back, the brown-skinned woman, with her mouth—hush child—strokes her belly—all the soreness—hush child—we won't tell him nothing about this—in the dream—such a pretty thing—such a sad, pretty thing—lay still, now—don't fight it—in the dream, the brown-skinned woman goes—the pale woman weeps and wails—in the dream, no other void is as black and empty as the brown-skinned woman's absence—in the dream—

In the morning, Stephen shook Janice gently by the shoulder.

"Hey," he said, softly. "Hey, what's the matter? Why are you crying?"

Janice woke enough to see him propped on one elbow, reaching over to her.

"What?" she said.

"You were crying."

"I was?" She reached instinctively for her face, found her cheek and the pillow wet.

"Actually, you've been crying off and on throughout the night. I just didn't . . . I didn't know what to do."

"I'm really sorry, Stephen. I must've been dreaming. But I don't remember anything about it."

Janice wiped her face with her sleeve. She saw the life vest in the space between the two sleeping pallets. Didn't remember taking it off either.

"That's embarrassing," she said. "You probably think I'm truly crazy now."

"Oh please, I'm sure it was the wine and the dope."

They had a pleasant breakfast on the pontoon boat. Watched the sun come up.

On the way home, Janice suddenly, and adamantly, decided she wanted to walk from Stephen's house.

"There's no need to take me all the way," she said. "It'll save you half an hour, and I really don't mind crossing the river."

"Are you sure?" he asked. "You sure you're up to it after . . ."

He didn't finish.

She didn't ask him to. Once she was out of sight of his house and studio,

Janice hurried across the cable bridge, but slowed when she came to the empty canal. Slowed, and listened. She took a few steps down the towpath. Listened. Nothing. No singing. No playing. She walked the rest of the way home.

What's that? Something on the porch, by the front door. Had she been paying a little less attention, Janice would have stepped on the object, small and unexpected as it was. Could have easily mistaken it for a leafless tree branch. Fortunately, she looked down in time, then knelt to get a closer look. No bunch of twigs, this. It was a chair. A model of a chair. A six-inch-high, simple ladder-back chair, made of bones. Fine, white bones, tied with thin strands of reed or grass. Bird bones, maybe. Something delicate. And in the seat a flower, the edges of its petals still sharp, the orange and yellow color still vibrant. Touch-me-not. Maybe the one flower that Janice could identify easily. A single, beautiful, red-orange touch-me-not—the jewelweed—laying in the bone-slat seat of a miniature bone chair. Janice looked in the direction of the towpath and smiled. She lifted the object with utmost care and took it into the locktender's house.

24

Janice spent the morning in and around the locktender's house, reliving, replaying the previous night's events, but coming back and back to the bone chair and its occupying flower sitting on the mantel. So odd, the little osteal totem, and its gravitational pull. Exquisite in its construction. Both immediate and ancient. Cryptic in its very existence. She looked at the chair from all angles, lifted it as if she were an entomologist handling tissue-thin wings of a rare specimen.

Stephen? Or Addie Epps? Janice knew no one else. And of the two, Addie Epps was the least known and most likely suspect. But Stephen was clever, and might have found a way to sneak the gift onto Janice's porch. Except that she'd been with him all night.

Gift? Janice refused to let her mind entertain the other possibilities. Caveat. Omen. Thundercloud. Handwriting on the wall. Refused. Janice refused.

She'd told Stephen she was leaving today. But that was before spending such a great night on his boat. He'd probably forgotten. And besides, she still hadn't found the car key. One more day, and one more night. Janice decided to give herself this much time. It was so unlike her to be absent-minded, to misplace things. But maybe forgetfulness was part and parcel of the new Janice. She'd clean the house a little, probably come across the key. Maybe she'd meditate, or do some yoga. She'd pack sometime the next morning. She'd drive over to Stephen's house and tell him how much she'd miss him.

What if he asked her to stay?

What if he didn't?

Then there was the song maker, Addie Epps.

I'll teach you a song

The Sisyphean quality of Janice's indecision took hold of the next several hours. She turned to knitting, returned to the familiar for comfort, for guidance, but soon found each stitch excruciatingly dull. She heated water on the camp stove, sponged off the residue of lake water and night air from her body, then strangely regretted doing so. She pushed, pulled, stretched, and compressed her body through five halfhearted Sun Salutations. She sat cross-legged on the zafu, trying to stay focused, until every fiber of her being embodied the word *antsy*. She thought about writing Stephen another letter, a letter informed by their closeness on the pontoon boat, but a letter saying goodbye nonetheless. Then she thought of that same letter turned inside out, the inverse, the opposite of goodbye, but couldn't find the words in her head. No clear vocabulary for staying there, with him, or for him.

I'll teach you a song

Janice picked up the banjo Stephen gave her, cradled the bulbous gourd in her lap, and plucked shyly at the strings. While each note that resonated down the fingerboard and through the taut skin head was round, sounding almost wet, and potentially beautiful, nothing about the assorted plinks and plunks she made resembled music. Janice persisted through her self-consciousness, looking around shyly from the overlit stage of her own awareness, and got louder by slight degrees. She fingered two or three random frets, brushed across the strings with her fingernails, and tried to match the chordish thing with her voice.

In short order the small rooms of the locktender's house filled to overflowing with discordant noise. The low ceiling and narrow windows oppressed. Janice took the banjo onto the front porch, sat on the step, and set about making her haphazard music. Plunk and twang. Plink and thump. Janice, through trial and error, found a series of note combinations that sounded good together, or at least okay. She closed her eyes and tried humming along. The flexibility of her human voice, weaving up and down, in and out of scales, belied her lack of confidence.

"You just got to cut loose!"

The voice startled Janice into silence. She kept her eyes shut, hoping it'd been a figment of her imagination. No such luck.

"You have to give yourself over to the music. Let it show you the way."

Janice, who'd never even whistled a tune for family, looked, through her embarrassment, at Addie Epps standing on the towpath, the hog fiddle cradled in the crook of one arm. She stood, backlit, the whole of the afternoon sun in an aural blaze around her. Her hair, her skirt, even her skin and bones seemed to glow from within.

"You got a pretty voice," Addie Epps said. "But you're holding on too tight. Way too tight."

Janice still hadn't uttered a word by the time Addie Epps walked, with an unsteady sashay, down the gentle slope and across the drive, and stood swaying, grinning, toe to toe, in front of her. A cool, damp, almost mossy presence.

"What's the matter?" Addie Epps asked. "Crow got your tongue?"

Janice jolted.

"What?"

"I said cat got your tongue?"

"Sorry," Janice said. "I mean, hey."

Janice sat looking up at Addie Epps looking down. Addie Epps smiled, if it was possible, even wider, and the warmth from her lopsided, animal-like, and ultimately lovely face melted away any of Janice's remaining embarrassment.

"You want to sit?" Janice asked.

Addie Epps sat down, heavily, at the other end of the step, positioned the dulcimer on her lap.

"Hit a chord," Addie Epps said, gesturing at the banjo with her head.

"I don't know how," Janice said, circling the neck with both hands, making sure to stifle all sound.

"Just strum it one good time."

And when Janice did, while the air was still ringing with the cumbersome notes, Addie Epps put her fingers in place on the dulcimer's fretboard and played a series of perfectly harmonious chords.

"Wow," Janice said. "I wish I could do that."

"You can, girl. I know you can. You just got to remember how."

Janice wanted to ask what she meant, but Addie smiled and the question got lost.

Under Addie's patient prodding, Janice tried out a few more notes, adding barely perceptible speed and a jerky attempt at rhythm.

"Watch my hands," Addie said, then launched into a slow lamenting tune.

Janice tried—she tried hard to focus on the pale scarred fingers, the thin wrists, *and where had she seen those scars before?* three ragged bars across the wrist—but Addie, singing with her eyes closed, embodied the song with the whole of her being. Janice couldn't help but look at this strange woman. She almost took the hummingbird pendant in her palm. She almost reached out to touch the faint line marking Addie's forehead. By the time she stopped playing, Janice was practically in tears.

Addie Epps noticed the flush.

"Played that one in graveyard tuning," she said. "It's about as mournful as you can get."

"It's so beautiful," Janice said, obviously pleasing Addie. "How'd you learn to play and sing so beautifully?"

"I mostly taught myself. Anybody with a lick of sense can learn."

Addie Epps winked at Janice.

At least Janice thought it was a wink. She wanted to ask Addie about the bone chair.

"Can I show you something?" Janice asked. "Something in the house."

"Not till we learn us a song."

Then she worked to teach Janice the first few chord progressions, but self-consciousness got in the way, and Janice grew too stiff and scared to make a sound.

"Let's start with something easy."

Addie Epps reached and took the banjo from Janice, laid it behind her on the porch, then placed the dulcimer beside it.

"We'll sing together."

"No," Janice said. "I can't. I can't sing."

"Can too," Addie said. " 'Sides, it'll keep your mind off of boys."

"What?" Janice asked.

"You know what I'm talking about," Addie said. "You better use that pretty mouth, that little tongue of yours for some good, before it withers up and blows away."

Addie began slowly. The sweet melody, a balm for Janice's worries.

> *I come from Alabama*
> *Wid my banjo on my knee,*
> *I'm g'wan to Louisiana*
> *My true love for to see.*
> *It rained all night the day I left,*
> *The weather it was dry,*

The sun so hot I froze to death;
Susanna, don't you cry.

"Now follow along," Addie said. "And stay close."

Oh! Susanna, Oh! don't you cry for me,
I've come from Alabama, wid my banjo on my knee.

Janice joined in on the chorus, quietly, so quietly. And hummed along with the next verse.

I jumped aboard de telegraph,
And trabbelled down de ribber,
De Lectrie fluid magnified,
And killed five hundred nigger
De bullgine bust, de horse run off,
I really thought I'd die;
I shut my eyes to hold my breath,
Susanna, don't you cry.

How bizarre, the song, the same song that Stephen had belted out into the night air. Not so completely coincidental, or spooky, given the banjo in the song and the banjo on the porch, and even Janice had sung the song in school, but the strange lyrics of this version, she'd never heard. Felt a little uncomfortable even humming behind them.

Oh! Susanna, Oh! don't you cry for me,
I've come from Alabama, wid my banjo on my knee.

Braver now, Janice let the volume of her voice rise, consciously working to dovetail it into Addie's. Strange, how it seemed to fit. Seemed to belong. Stranger still, Janice found herself singing the words of the verses, the words rising out of unknowing to work the machinery of her larynx, lips, and tongue.

I had a dream de odder night
When ebery thang was still;
I thought I saw Susanna,

A coming down de hill.
The buckwheat cake war in her mouth,
The tear was in her eye,
Says I'm coming from de South,
Susanna, don't you cry.

Janice closed her eyes, and sang louder still.

Oh! Susanna, Oh! don't you cry for me,
I've come from Alabama, wid my banjo on my knee.

She felt the rhythm in her head, the sway in her shoulders.

I soon will be in New Orleans,
And den I'll look all round,
And when I find Susanna,
I' fall upon the ground.
But if I do not find her there,
Dis darkie 'll surely die,
And when I'm dead and buried,
Now Susanna, don't you cry.

And when the last note left her lips, she looked up to Stephen, sitting on his 4 × 4, applauding. Looked over to the banjo. No dulcimer. No Addie Epps. Only the faintest trace of cool damp air lingered.

25

Applause. Stephen Gainy sat straddling his all-terrain vehicle, clapping too enthusiastically.

"Where'd she go?" Janice asked, before embarrassment had a chance to fill the space left by Addie's absence. She immediately regretted asking.

"Where'd who go?"

Clearly Addie must have heard him coming, and left while Janice had her eyes closed. Any other possibility—such as questioning Addie's reality—was unthinkable. But why was Addie so secretive? And why hadn't Janice heard Stephen's approach?

Janice struggled for a quick answer. Something witty and deflective. But Stephen beat her to the punch.

"Have you lost your groupie?"

"Don't mess with me, Stephen."

He sat down on the steps, where Addie had been only moments before. Crinkled his nose and looked around, but didn't comment on what he might have smelled.

"Are you okay, girl? You look like you've been smoking some of my dope."

"Still a little foggy from last night," she said, then noticed the fat bandage on Stephen's right index finger.

"What happened?" she asked.

He held up the appendage, wrapped from knuckle to nail in multiple layers of gauze and tape, so thick it couldn't bend, rusty bloodstains leeching through at the tip.

"You mean this?"

Janice was in no mood for silliness.

"It hurts like hell, I'll tell you that much," he said.

"What'd you do?"

"I don't exactly know," he said. "I was moving one of my stones, and not paying attention. Maybe I tripped. Or maybe something snagged. Whatever happened, two hundred pounds of granite landed on this skinny finger."

He extended it toward Janice, but when she reached out, Stephen withdrew.

"It's throbbing, all the way up my arm."

"Do you think it's broken?" Janice asked.

"At the very least. Mangled is more like it."

"You going to the doctor?"

"Maybe, in a couple days. If the swelling doesn't go down."

"Come in and eat something," Janice said, standing to open the door.

"Thought you'd never ask. What I'd really like is a handful of ibuprofen. I took all mine last night."

When Janice came back downstairs with the bottle of pills, Stephen stood at the mantel with his face inches from the bone chair.

"Where'd this come from?" he asked. No hesitation. Clearly, he didn't make it. And his acknowledgment of the object's presence offered some small proof of Addie's existence. Right?

"I . . . um . . . I made it," she said, with enough lilt to make her answer seem almost a question. Why couldn't she just tell him?

"You did not," he said, with just enough tease in his response to keep his statement from being a challenge.

"Do you think you're the only one in town with any talent," she said, shaking four red tablets into her palm. "Here, eat these."

"Well, it's very cool," Stephen said, not pushing the issue further. "You should make me one. Besides, you owe me, big time."

"Owe you for what?"

"For making me listen to that incredibly racist song."

"How about lunch instead?"

Janice made sandwiches of peanut butter and scallions on toast, and while they ate she tried as casually as possible to ask if he'd ever seen anybody in the woods.

"You mean like hunters?" he asked.

"Yeah, or neighbors," Janice added.

"No. No neighbors. Nobody but us lunatics and possums want to live so far off the grid. I do come across men with guns from time to time. But I don't think anything is in season now. Why do you ask? Have you?"

She started to say . . . what . . . that she'd seen footprints. Said no instead.

"Would you tell me if you did?" he asked.

"Sure. Of course."

Stephen asked if she'd decided to stick around a while. He didn't go so far as to say that he wanted her to, but Janice felt the sentiment clearly enough.

"For a few days, anyway," she said. "The fact is, I still can't find my car key. It makes me anxious to feel stuck."

"I'll make you a deal," he said, wiping peanut butter from his mustache. "I can take the ignition switch out and make the car run so that you're not trapped here, but I'll only do it if you promise not to just drive off down the road and not come back."

She held up both hands and crossed her fingers.

"I promise."

"I need to go home and get my toolbox," he said. "Thanks for lunch."

Janice followed him out the door.

"Be careful with your finger," she said. "Maybe you should walk instead of riding that thing."

Stephen made a don't-be-such-a-girl face, started the engine, revved the throttle, and popped the clutch just enough to make the rear wheels spin in the gravel.

"I'll be back later," he said, blipping the throttle, his bandaged finger bobbing like a stubby antenna.

Janice waved, and watched as Stephen leaned his lanky form to the left, countersteered the handlebars sharp right, cranked the throttle open and spun the ATV in a series of tight circles in the driveway, round and round, the two-stroke engine wailing, pale blue smoke corkscrewing into the sky, round and round, until the rear wheel caught in a rut and the four-wheeler rocketed at full speed across the towpath and over the lip of the canal, with Stephen Gainy clinging, wild-eyed, to the bars.

"Stephen?"

Janice called out, hoping that the silence was part of his stunt.

She stood on the porch, waiting for him to roar up the other side of the canal and wave before disappearing into the woods.

"Stephen!"

"Stephen!"

No amount of hurry would have made any difference. From the lip of the berm, Janice saw the silent vehicle on its side, the front struts buckled from impact with the massive lock stones, saw Stephen Gainy, silent as well, on his back, blood streaming from his nose and mouth, lying on the dry bed of the canal. Felt sure the man was dead, and wept with relief only after she jumped down the bank and laid her head near his heart, and she felt the solid double-thump, and watched the blood bubbles swell and burst as breath escaped his nostrils.

"Stephen! Oh fuck! Oh Jesus! Oh fuck fuck fuck!"

So much blood, on his face, in his mouth, his airway. Stephen coughed, gurgled, choking on his own vital fluid. No first aid. Janice had never learned first aid. Had no idea what to do in a crisis.

"Help! Help us!"

She called out. She screamed for help. Screamed in vain. No one came. No one heard. There was no one to hear. No one but Addie Epps. And Addie Epps wouldn't come. Janice knew this. The fact, the knowledge, was as palpable as her friend Stephen's blood.

"Help! Oh fuck oh Jesus oh fuck . . ."

He coughed again, blood pooling in the back of his throat. Stephen's heel dug into the dirt, his fingers clawed at nothing, gripped for nothing. His limbs moving—Janice knew this must be a good sign. No paralysis. She turned his head to one side. She ripped the sleeve of her blouse off and mopped the blood from his face.

Where was the nearest hospital? The nearest telephone?

A deep gash at the bridge of his nose, a smaller cut in the hairs of his left eyebrow, and a missing canine tooth. The visible damage. Janice, working in stages, got Stephen's head in her lap, his shoulders between her open legs, her hands hooked in his armpits. She grunted, tried to stand, pushed with her feet, and pulled at the same time. Tried again. Tried again. But at nearly two hundred pounds of dead weight, she couldn't even move Stephen's body on the flat ground of the canal bed. She'd never pull him up the steep bank.

Janice wriggled out from under Stephen, laid his head gently on a pillow made from her rolled-up skirt. She crawled over to the ATV, considered trying to right it, trying to crank it. Even if she couldn't get Stephen onto the vehicle, as a last resort she could ride it out of the canal and down the road to find help.

She could, if the front wheels weren't punctured and all but shorn from the axle. And surely the widening and viscous pool of black motor oil and the thinner, more volatile, gasoline trickling from various spots on the engine, surely these weren't good signs. Janice kicked at the vehicle and swore.

She could walk. Could she walk? Which direction? How far? If she walked, and got lost, Stephen might die out here all alone. She had no way of contacting the outside world, and no faith that anyone from that world would pass by. Crisis. In shock, and out of despair, she relinquished any pretense of control. Janice could not solve this problem, not even the new Janice. She lacked both the physical strength and psychological wherewithal. Not so surprisingly, the limiting of options calmed Janice. She'd stay with Stephen until he regained consciousness, then together they'd figure out how to get him out of the canal and into the house. The locktender's house. She sat and watched Stephen as he lay, twitching or jerking occasionally, grunting something wordless, in response to pain. She'd stay until he woke up.

From the house, Janice retrieved pillows and blankets, a bag with all the medical supplies she had, a pan and a jug of water, and clean washcloths. She'd stay by his side. Until he awoke. Until he came back to her.

Janice rested Stephen's head on a pillow. She cleaned his wounds with peroxide, dressed them with fire-orange Mercurochrome. She washed the grit and dried blood from his face, neck, and arms. She tried to get him to sip from a cup of water, but the liquid trickled from his mouth. Janice draped a thin sheet over Stephen's body, laid a damp cloth in a neat swath across his forehead and eyes, then sat cross-legged on a pillow close enough to refresh the cloth every little while.

Janice didn't pray. She didn't know how. Didn't know what to pray for. Didn't know what to pray to. She shooed away the bluebottles and horseflies that gathered where she wiped the blood from his body. Shooed them away again and again. Janice pulled the sheet higher, up to Stephen's neck. She tucked his hair back over his ears; the flies swarmed around her wrist. She swatted, then blew them away. The flies. Bluebottle. Horseflies. Blackflies. Midges and gallflies. They all came to feast. Janice flailed. Janice cursed. In her rage, in her fear, in the madness, Janice laid her body down atop Stephen's, pulled her shirt high up on her back, offered her own back and bare thighs, sacrificed her own body to the biting insects. Still they came, burrowed under, between. Janice tried to form a barrier, a tent of hair, to protect his face, his breath. Janice heard the manifold wing beats, a dull roar in her ears. In her ears. The hum and buzz. The hum and buzz. The dull roar surging like water. Like water.

26

There's a sound, like water spilling around the uneven seals of the lock gates, where swollen lumber meets stone. Janice hears the water spilling through the chinks, sloshing over the shut lock, the dusty canal bed growing damp and muddy. Like water. Rising. Janice atop the unconscious man and the water coming up. His shield. His protector. His anchor. For better or worse. His anchor. The water creeping up through his gray hair. The water spilling over the lock gate, surging around them both. The current swelling, gaining force, rattling the lock against its miters. The splintering gate, and the subsequent torrent. The canal bed comes to life. And Janice, on her belly, on his belly, her mouth to his mouth, she shares her breath, the minnows nip at her eyelashes, the turtles scratch their way up her back, and Janice, through the muddy water rising over their heads, sees it all—the fluid lens magnifies, clarifies, all the bodies coming down the river, the bloated pig floats by with a possum in the ladder of its ribs, mouth full of raw liver, and the man, his crude taxidermy giving way, the man split at his rotting seams, and the filthy ticking and dank clay falling out with each step, trailing behind, and the one-eyed cat on a spinning road sign, and the babies, their hairless heads knocking at the bottom of the canal boats, their fine toes digging into the silty bed, and the man with his stick, he beats her, he beats them, he rakes his stick through her woman's furrow, the splinters, and the pale woman made more captive by her desire for the soft fingers, the warm brown mouth of her sometimes visitor, but the man and his sharp stick always always coming before, the splintering, the flowing water, and blood, and mucus, drops the still warm bodies into the outhouse pit, laughs, like water, like water sputtering over rocks, like laughter, like crows cawing on a fence line, like singing until he comes in, says *nigger music*, says *don't back sass me*, says *open your goddamn mouth*, and the hot pliers taste of rust and charred flesh and chipped teeth, and the little nugget of tongue, her song, becomes a minnow, flopping in the grass, the loss now unutterable, the rage without syllables, the tongue wriggling there until the crow wings into view, pecks at the gristly strip of flesh, the tongue, takes it in the eager beak and flies away, the crow and the tongue, the crow returns—whispers her name in rotten and perfect English—*Janice*—Janice who is naked and drowning and protecting this man in the only ways she knows how—*Janice*—this mutual drowning—*Janice*—the canal swelling with water and the blood of this man beneath her—*Janice*—the crow speaking, in its undertaker's coat, its four-toed boots and clicking heels, its distant whisper—*Janice*—crow mouth—human tongue—speaking softly to her, Janice puts her fingers in her ears—*Janice*—she will not hear it, this crow, this seducer, she will not, she will not—

27

—*Janice*—she will not hear it, this crow, this seducer, she will not, she will not—*Janice*—boot heel to sternum, rib and wrench—*Janice*—the crow, black ratchet of its tongue—*Janice*—the crow—*Janice*—the crow—

"Janice, what happened?"

No, not the crow's voice.

"Janice, I need help."

"Stephen?"

Janice jolted awake. She sat cross-legged and shivering by Stephen's head, with no memory of climbing off his unconscious body. Her back was afire with itching insect bites. When she got to her knees and tried to stand the blood needled its way back into her hungry veins. Night had come and the dense black walls of the dry canal framed a damson-colored sky, a starless and sovereign sky.

"Stephen?"

He tried to sit up. Grimaced. Groaned.

"What happened?" he asked.

"You had an accident," Janice said, kneeling to offer a cup of water. Overcome by gratitude, by a relief that displaced the memory of her dream, Janice cried. "I thought you might die."

Stephen touched his injured face softly, looked at his own arms and hands, felt his trunk and legs.

"God knows, I feel like Lazarus. How long have I been out?"

Janice told him about the accident, of which he remembered nothing. She didn't tell him about the dreams, the crow and the flood and the bad man. Janice said she thought he should go to the hospital.

"Maybe you have a concussion."

"We'll see," he said. "If I'm still seeing double in a couple days . . ."

"Are you? Are you seeing double now?"

"Only when I move my head. No. Not really. Just kidding."

Janice knew he was lying.

"We have to get you in the house," she said. "It's my turn to take care of you."

Stephen didn't argue. Together they struggled, him to his knees, her in the crook of his arm, a living crutch, together they got him up the steep bank and into the front room where, exhausted by the effort, he slept on the settee while Janice readied the upstairs room.

Initially, Stephen resisted, saying he wanted to go home, saying he didn't need her bedroom, saying and saying until it became clear that *saying* was moot. It took half an hour to get Stephen up the tight staircase, but once there, once he was ensconced in bed, Janice nursed and cared for him. For three days, she doled out ibuprofen, fed him cans of soup, water and tea, toast with jelly. For three days she wiped his head and chest with cool wet cloths, changed the dressing on his earlier injury, the swollen and split finger, attended to the healing new wounds, emptied the night jar. For three days Stephen was her focus, her meditation, her practice. But on the fourth day his testosterone-stoked machismo reared its ugly head.

"I'm going home this morning," he said, stoically.

When he stood, however, he stood on trembling legs.

"How you going to get there?"

Clearly, walking was out of the question. The ATV, as well. Janice could cross the river and get his truck, but she wasn't completely sure she could find her way back to Sabbath Rest Road.

"Do you have a screwdriver?" he asked.

Stephen sat in the passenger seat of Janice's Subaru, fiddled and pried at the ignition until it dangled from its copper umbilical. He had to rest a bit, then showed Janice how to short-circuit the switch. When the car sputtered to life without backfiring, Janice applauded.

She drove. Stephen gave directions. Leaving now was out of the question. She had to take care of Stephen. She drove. He directed her to Gesseytown, and to Chunk's Market, where she went in with a short list and without revealing her anxiety, while he lay back in the car seat.

Inside the store, Janice flinched when the door slammed shut behind her.

"That old door's been slamming shut since before me and you was born."

Janice recognized the soft, round clerk behind the register. Hopefully, the woman wouldn't recognize her. Janice walked the store's few aisles, dropping items into a handbasket. Rubbing alcohol. Cotton balls. Antiseptics. Oreo cookies. Beef jerky. *Only the necessities*, he'd said.

While the clerk rang up her purchases, talking the whole while about the scandalous lives revealed in the new issue of *People* magazine, Janice fingered the rack of kitschy impulse-buy items on display at the register. Something about the small doll made of corncob, with its painted face and gingham apron and bonnet, gave her pause. Something about the doll made her think of Addie Epps.

"Have you lived here long?" Janice asked the clerk.

"Feels like more than one lifetime," the woman answered.

"Did you ever know anybody named Epps? Last name, Epps?"

"Sounds familiar, but . . ."

The woman was mumbling when she bent behind the counter to get a bag. Janice tucked the doll into the waist of her pants, coughing to cover the noise. On the way out, the bulletin board by the door caught Janice's eye. The House for Rent ad was gone. She read over the various postings. Nothing of note. A cleaning service: Maid-to-Order. A lost puppy. A missing child notice, cut from the back of a milk carton and stapled to the cork. Office help wanted: Foot-of-Ten Kennel.

"You sure you don't want to go to the doctor?" Janice asked when she was back in the car.

"I just want to go home," he said.

Janice drove, squirming uncomfortably. The rough cob of the doll's body dug into the soft flesh of her belly. The act of thievery itself gnawed away somewhere inside. Who was this new Janice? Who would she become?

Midsummer, and the corn in the fields reached its thousands of green fingers toward the mountaintop. The white bursts of Queen Ann's lace, contrapuntal to the upthrusting purple loosestrife and butter-yellow goldenrod, choked the side ditches. Stephen, a living—if battered—Stephen, talked her back to his house and studio, and she took his breathing presence, his labored utterances, as a meager testament to the solidity and deepening nature of their bond.

"You can't stay here by yourself," she said as they pulled to a stop.

"What the hell is that?" he said, ignoring Janice, and pointing at his studio, where something hung in the middle of the heavy wooden door. Something black. Something feathered.

Stephen brushed Janice away when she tried to help steady him as they walked toward the building. She followed just behind, just in case.

Black, yes. Feathered, yes. A crow, definitely. Maybe even his crow. And without a doubt, that was Stephen's chisel that held it to the door. Someone had hammered the chisel—the chisel Janice had stolen—through the bird's chest cavity and into the plank. It hung, neck drooping to one side, like nightmare's doorknocker, its wings limp and open. A hard mean image against the unfinished wood.

His crying came as a surprise. Janice didn't know how to respond.

"Goddamn ignorant farmers," he said.

"Can I help?" she asked, then reached as if to take the chisel out of the door, out of the bird. As if to reach into the vast chest cavity, empty but for the tempered steel shaft, and pluck out the offense.

"Don't touch him! Don't."

Stephen stepped in front of the door, turned to face Janice.

"I want to be by myself for a while . . ."

"Stephen, you can't . . ."

"It's not a request, Jan . . ."

"I'm not leaving you here alone! You're hurt, and now . . . this."

"Goddammit! Will you just go home! I don't want you here. I don't need you here. Go home! Please!"

Janice cried all the way across the cable bridge. She took the stolen doll from its hiding place, reared back to throw it into the river, but couldn't. Janice cried. She cried, more over the horrible thing that had happened to the crow than over Stephen's harsh reaction. The reaction, she understood. He'd blamed it on farmers. She'd go back to the locktender's house, pack the car, and drive around until early evening, then go back over to Stephen's with something to eat. She couldn't stay another night in that house. Too much. Too scary. He'd let her in and apologize. Janice had no doubt about it.

She played the scene through in her head walking back across the field, caught up in the options for dialogue, for exactly how she'd tell Stephen that of course she forgave him, and of course she knew he didn't mean it, that she'd be happy to take care of the crow's body and the mess, and of course she'd stay. Janice tried the various words on for size, and when she reached the canal bed she barely even acknowledged the damaged ATV. She might even have been gesturing, standing on the towpath, when Addie Epps called out.

"Hey."

Janice looked, tucked the doll under her shirt. Addie stood with her hands behind her back by the front door of the house, stood weaving slightly, as if struggling against a wind only she felt.

"I brung you something," Addie said.

The shift was immediate. One step earlier, her own escape and Stephen Gainy, his injured body and troubled soul, occupied Janice's thoughts fully. The next step, even before her foot had settled into the dusty path, all she could concentrate on was Addie Epps and the gift. One more night. The tectonic shift in Janice's frame of mind so sudden, so complete, she had neither the time nor the energy to resist or question it. She could stay one more night.

"Hey," Janice said. Not, *I'm worried about my friend.* Not, *you must know him, he lives just through the woods.* Rather, "Hey. I brought you something too."

How strange that this odd woman, in her odd dress, a garment that seemed from another time, with her lilting voice and dizzy walk, with her beaming smile and unfocused eyes, this woman who hadn't once asked Janice's name, how bewildering that she was able to command Janice's full attention simply by appearing.

"You go first," Addie Epps said, sitting on the porch step, making sure her own gift was hidden behind her back. "You go first," she said again, closed her eyes and put her hands out.

Such battered hands. Janice couldn't count the scars. Janice wanted to touch her hands, to soothe them with lotions. She pulled the corncob doll from beneath her shirt and laid it in Addie's open palms, noticing as she did that the gingham fabric of both their dresses was identical.

Addie Epps opened her eyes, caught sight of the doll, and her throat constricted. "Hhrrrrrrr . . ." Seized. She gripped the doll tight in both hands. "Hhrrrrrrr . . ." Her eyes rolled up, offered little white saucers beneath the open lids. Breath chipping its way into her throat. "Hhrrrrrrr . . ." Breath levering its way out. Flecks of saliva in the corners of her mouth. "Hhrrrrrrr . . ."

Then it was over. Addie Epps shook her head, smoothed the doll's bon-

net, and smiled as if nothing had happened. Janice smiled back. As if nothing had happened.

"Your turn," she said, holding out her hands.

Janice felt the weight of the gift in her hands. "What is it?" she asked.

A musical instrument, for sure, and very like the dulcimer, the hog fiddle. But both cruder and more complex. This rectangular wooden instrument, the width of a shoebox and not quite twice as long, had two sets of
strings, four each, strung in opposite order near each outside edge. Two
scarred fingerboards, with worn frets, lay between numerous sound-holes
roughly cut into heart shapes, and down the center, the shared sound-
holes were flowers, the painted stems long since scratched off.

"It's beautiful," Janice said, sincerely.

"Called a courtin' dulcimer," Addie Epps said.

"Will you come inside?" Janice asked. "I can make us some sweet tea."

"No," Addie said. "Go get us two chairs. Two ladder-back chairs."

Janice did as she was told; a damp mossy sensation followed her into the
house.

"You know I can't play, or sing either for that matter," Janice said, bring-
ing the chairs through the door.

"Hush," Addie said. "There's always more than one way of seeing a
thing. You looking at this song making through your eyes, trying to reason
it out. Sometimes, some *things* especially, you got to look from a different
place."

Addie Epps placed the chairs face-to-face, the seats a mere six inches
apart, directed Janice into one chair, and sat herself down, heavily, in the
other.

"Take song making, for instance. Music doesn't come from your old
noggin. Real music comes from in here. You just got to remember it."

Addie Epps pressed two strong fingertips into the soft flesh of Janice's
left breast, moved them until she found enough heartbeat to satisfy.

"We're gonna play a song together," she said.

What did she mean by *remember*?

Addie aligned the chairs, took Janice by the knee of her left leg and fit it
snugly between her own two, fidgeted there until her knees, her calves, her
shins, her feet all dovetailed with Janice's. She laid the dulcimer across
their unified laps.

"Tweedledum and Tweedledee," Addie said, grinning.

Janice, unsure of what else to do with them, shoved her hands under her thighs.

"You cain't play note one while sitting on your hands."

So close, this woman and her smile and sweet mossy smells. So familiar.

Addie took Janice's left hand, folded down the pinkie and ring fingers, placed the other two fingers and thumb at three chosen points on the fretboard. From a deep pocket in her skirt, she pulled a fat-quilled feather, showed Janice how to pinch it in her right hand.

"Can you count to four?" Addie Epps asked.

Janice's head spun so that even the simple act of counting seemed a challenge.

"What do you mean?" she asked.

"Can you count to four? One. Two. Three. Four. Like that. This is called the strum hollow," Addie continued, putting her finger, the same finger that found Janice's heartbeat, by a dip near the end of the fretboard. "You rake the feather back and forth over the strum hollow."

Addie, with great patience and much good humor, worked with Janice through numerous missteps and a stubborn arrhythmic streak, sat there, face-to-face, knees to knees, until she was able to produce a fairly steady single-chord rhythm.

"You keep striking that chord," Addie said. "And I'm going to come in on top of it."

And they did it. They played a song together. A short elemental piece of music, but no less beautiful to Janice's ear. Her steady chord laying down the backup for Addie's melody. Janice was so excited by her modest success that she wanted to learn another right away. This time Addie showed her two chords. Both simple and basic, but it took Janice a while to be able to change from one chord to the next smoothly, without pause. Before long, she got close enough.

"All right," Addie said. "You ready to sing?"

Yes! Sour notes and self-consciousness be damned, Janice wanted to sing.

Addie showed her the chord, and where it changed.

"You come in behind me on the chorus," she said, then Addie began to play and sing.

The baby this and the baby that,
The baby killed my old tomcat.

She tipped her head to Janice.

> *What're you gonna do with the baby?*
> *What're you gonna do with the baby-o?*

> *Wrap him up in the tablecloth,*
> *We'll put him in the stable loft.*

This time, Janice was ready.

> *What're you gonna do with the baby?*
> *What're you gonna do with the baby-o?*

> *Wrap him up in calico,*
> *We'll smack his bottom and let him go.*
> *What're you gonna do with the baby?*
> *What're you gonna do with the baby-o?*

> *The baby laughed, the baby cried,*
> *I stuck my finger in the baby's eye.*
> *What're you gonna do with the baby?*
> *What're you gonna do with the baby-o?*

So much fun. So magical, the way the sound spilled from the hollow body of the dulcimer, its eight strings double-teamed by the two singing women, joining with their own mouthed notes to weave the mantle of music. Janice wanted to stay in the yard, in the chairs, in the music with Addie forever.

"Can we do another?" Janice asked, so they worked on a song called "Hog Eye."

> *Chicken in the bread pan, pecking that dough*
> *Sally will your dog bite? No sir no.*
> *Sally's in the garden sifting, sifting,*
> *Sally's in the garden sifting sand.*

> *Sally's in the garden sifting, sifting,*
> *Sally's in the garden sifting sand.*

Sally's in the garden sifting, sifting,
Sally's upstairs with the hogeye man.

Sally will your dog bite? No sir no.
Daddy cut his bitter off a long time ago!

Addie and Janice played the short song over and over, faster and faster, louder and louder, laughing each time at the words.

"Your singing is so beautiful," Janice said, and in response Addie kissed her.

Kissed her. Kissed her full on the mouth. No sisterly kiss, this. Addie leaned across the momentarily silent dulcimer and pressed her lips, lips still warm from song, pressed them into Janice's own lips, Janice's surprised lips. Janice, surprised by the kiss, surprised herself by not pulling immediately away. By letting herself follow Addie's kiss, much as she followed Addie's voice and melody earlier. Harmony. Addie kissed her and kissed her. Not hurried. Not greedy, like the men she'd kissed. Janice wouldn't open her eyes. Knew Addie's eyes were open. Kissing. Janice followed, not fearlessly, but followed nonetheless, and in that kiss Janice tasted smoke, and honeysuckle, cool water, stone, charred wood, Janice tasted moss and clay, tasted the sting of kerosene, tasted the hummingbird's hum, tasted, Janice tasted, maybe for the first time, the weight of her own personal history and its human emptiness, tasted shackles and the sweat of mules, tasted pig iron, coal dust, tasted Addie, this woman kissing her, Addie, so familiar, the tastes, tasted of dreams, of dreams, Janice's dreams, tasted of the man and the brown-skinned woman . . .

"N . . . no!"

Janice pulled back so suddenly she tipped over in the chair, the breath knocked from her stunned lungs.

"No," Janice said. "I'm not . . . I don't . . . it's . . . n . . ."

She scrambled backward, away from Addie, Addie who was sitting still and patient, sucking on her own bottom lip.

"I have to go," Janice said. "Now. I have to go now. Tomorrow I'm leaving."

Janice shut the door to the locktender's house, leaned her back against it, sat there listening to Addie play and hum softly. Sat there until she heard Addie walk away.

28

Stephen would come back and apologize, Janice knew it.

She'd practice a song on the banjo, and sing to him as he walked, or limped, across the towpath. He might even be carrying the letter she'd written him, and he'd probably explain why he never mentioned it. She'd tell about the craziness, about the strange woman who lived somewhere in the woods, about her pretty voice, and the funny slant to her forehead. She and Stephen would eat canned peaches and pound cake, and Janice would tell him how Addie's eyes rolled back when she saw the doll. But if she told him that, she'd have to tell where she got the doll. And why she gifted it. Then Stephen might push the issue, and Janice would have to decide to tell him about the kiss, or not. And if so, how? How would she describe it? Weird? Sweet? Disgusting? Ridiculous! The whole idea was ridiculous. Janice couldn't tell Stephen any of this stuff. He'd think she imagined it all. Maybe she did. He'd think she was crazy. Maybe she was. She had no proof. No idea where Addie Epps lived. No sense of how she spent her days, or nights. Addie Epps, who'd never even asked Janice's name. She had no real proof that the woman actually existed. No proof. No proof, except for the tastes in her mouth, and the searing energy of the kiss that still ricocheted up and down her spine.

My name is Janice Witherspoon. My name is Janice Witherspoon.

Like a mantra, she repeated the phrase to herself. Part immigrant, part exile, she had little else to hold to. Janice's head spun; a carnival ride of emotion. Panic supplanted by desire. Fear and confusion gave way to— fleeting—joy. Back and forth. Back and forth.

My name is Janice Witherspoon.

Had she misunderstood Addie Epps? Had she misinterpreted their inter-action? The kiss? Why couldn't she just leave? Simply get in the car and drive away? Like a child's paper fortune-teller, fingered by memory, the events of her recent past opened randomly and repeatedly in her mind. Danks's death. The dreams. The toll collector. Addie Epps. Stephen's acci-dent. The crows. The music. Janice was too muddled, too stunned to find any thread in the narrative. Were these events linked? Equally seduced by and prisoner to her own unfolding story, Janice lacked the wherewithal to fight against the unseeable shackles that bound her to the locktender's house and whatever would happen there.

Janice boiled water, lots of water, and tried to wash the kiss and its mem-ory from her body and mind. She brushed her teeth, then brushed them again, along with her tongue. But the memory went much deeper than taste. Stephen had to come soon. She hoped he was all right. Couldn't tell him about Addie; he'd think she was crazy. Crazy. Couldn't tell him about kissing Addie; kissing a woman; kissing a very strange woman; he'd think . . . And why hadn't they kissed yet? Why hadn't Stephen kissed her? Was there something *wrong* with her? Why hadn't Stephen kissed her? That was the real question. That was the question Janice took hold of, the question that took hold of Janice. The question stoked the already hot fires of Janice's insecurity, fear, and doubt. Stoked, as well, the unfocused but no less burning desires. And try as she might for the contrary, it was Addie's lips that came to mind again and again.

Why hadn't Stephen kissed her?

Why hadn't she kissed *him*?

Janice brushed her hair. She dug in the bottom of the only purse she'd left Greensboro with until she found, as she'd remembered, a bottle of modest red nail polish, and shook up the separated liquid. It took all the effort she could muster to keep her shaking hands steady enough to paint her toenails and fingernails poorly. Took nearly as much effort to keep from breaking down and weeping as she put on her cleanest underwear, the nicest of her few worn skirts, a button-up shirt, to clean the mud from her open-toed sandals, and walk into the woods toward Stephen's house. She walked and thought, and wondered why she hadn't kissed him. Why he hadn't kissed her. He'd see, he'd know if he just kissed her one time that it was meant to be. They were meant to be. Janice didn't kiss women. Jan-ice kissed men.

Janice, confused and afraid, walked toward Stephen's. She fingered the top button on her shirt. Why hadn't he kissed her? Was something wrong? Was she doing something wrong? Janice worried at the button until it loosened, the air cool against her flushed neck. Janice didn't kiss women. Janice didn't want to kiss women. Janice wanted to be kissed by this man. Her thumb hung at the second button; she worked it free. Why should she wait for him? Maybe that's what he wanted, for her to kiss him first. Would he like that? Janice should make her desire clear, right? It's what a man would want. Right? Janice crossed the cable bridge carefully, her stomach in knots; a wave of nausea followed after she struggled with the final two buttons, the shirttails opening up like wings, her white belly on display, the bra, her nipples pushing against its thin fabric, this new Janice, exposed, bared, strode up out of the woods between the studio and house just in time to see him, Stephen, standing by the Subaru, with his arms around another woman.

Both Stephen and the small birdlike woman who shared his embrace looked at Janice. Janice, who seconds earlier walked with her lungs full of new air, shoulders back, the small moons of her breasts in blatant display, felt that energy drain away instantly. Humiliation swapped seats with derring-do. The power cord severed, she fumbled to wrap the shirt tight around her nakedness. But a thing once seen cannot be unseen.

"Janice?" Stephen said. "What the . . ."

Janice backed up, wanted to turn and run, but had to go on seeing. No other choice. A thing once seen cannot be unseen. She'd exposed herself. She'd been seen by Stephen and the woman. No amount of covering herself up could undo that. But by the same token, she'd witnessed their close embrace. No denying it. The man she'd crossed the woods, the river, to kiss, held tight to another woman.

"Janice! What are you doing? Wait!"

Stephen and the woman stepped back from each other, but remained touching, his arms on her shoulders, her hands at his waist. No denying the intimacy. No need to see more. Janice was finally able to break, finally turned, finally ran. Believing, rightly, that Stephen was still too weak from his injuries to keep up, to catch her, Janice slowed upon reaching the river, but didn't pause—and certainly didn't look up or down the towpath—until she closed the door to the locktender's house.

She paced around inside, going from room to room, trying to reconcile the jumble of emotions that vied for control of her body. Almost, intentionally, kicked a hole in the banjo Stephen had given her. Came to rest, in her spastic orbit, at the fireplace, leaning against the mantel, looking at the bone chair.

"Hey!"

Janice carried the chair outside, calling as she went.

"Hey! Where are you?"

No tenderness in the way Janice handled the delicate object.

"I don't want this thing! I know it came from you! I don't want it!"

Janice heard the outhouse door slam shut, walked around the house, yelling.

"I don't know who you are! And I don't care. I don't know where you came from, and I don't want to!"

Janice paced in the yard, hemmed in by the mountains rising up in the distance, by the dry canal bed, the river, the barren fields, by Sabbath Rest Road. The narrow path between the back door of the locktender's house and the outbuildings defined the boundary of her world.

"I don't want to sing with you! I don't want to play that stupid *hog fiddle* with you! I don't want your gifts. I don't want your . . ."

Janice stopped before she could say the word *kisses*. She couldn't bring herself to open the outhouse door, but she pressed an ear to the weathered planks. Heard nothing. Crossed the yard to the smokehouse. Felt her heart quicken. Listened through the splintering door. Heard nothing. Walked up onto the towpath, the packed earth there strangely familiar.

"Don't come back here again! Please."

The *please* so much softer. Janice set the bone chair down in the middle of the path.

I should crush this thing, she thought. *Stomp it into the earth.*

But all Janice could bring herself to do was snap one thin bone leg. She left the chair lying there and returned to the house to wait. To think.

Stephen Gainy had her car. It was a clear-cut problem, with several solutions.

Addie Epps had an altogether different thing. With the kiss, she took possession of something belonging to Janice that day on the porch — yesterday? A week ago? Months? — but Janice couldn't name it. And therefore couldn't reclaim it so easily. She retreated deeper into herself, holed up in the house and mulled over all that had occurred. She cried, to be sure, but cursed nearly as much. Purged herself of the various incarnations of guilt and shame. Flushed out the residue of desire. The next day, Stephen brought the car back, but left it and went quietly without knocking. Just as well; Janice didn't intend to open the door. Had she lost him? No matter. No matter. She couldn't bring herself to play the banjo after all. Took it up to the unused bedroom and shut the door. Tomorrow. She'd leave at first light. Too dangerous to travel in the dark.

In full daylight, and hurriedly, she retrieved her atlas from the back seat of the car, spent some time trying to orient herself in the world. Found, tucked between Virginia and Utah, the Natural Bridge brochure, which she read and reread, memorizing the entire thing as an exercise to stave off boredom. Janice flowed in and out of logic, in and out of inane fantasy. She imagined herself at her destination, the Natural Bridge. Imagined herself at home there. Pretended for a while to be a Natural Bridge tour guide, making up her script and whole conversations with imaginary visitors, paying no heed to the ridiculousness of the activity.

"No ma'am, we can't allow folks to wade in the river."

"Why, yes sir, I'd be happy to pose for a picture with your family."

"Legend has it that if you walk across the bridge at such and such a time, on this particular night . . ."

She'd pack and leave in the morning. Food for the trip. Water. Clothes. She'd leave it all behind. Stephen Gainy, Addie Epps, and the locktender's house. She'd go somewhere and start over. She didn't need either of them. Didn't want either of them.

But stasis is nothing if not insidious. It creeps in, like a parasitic vine, to wind around and tangle even the best-laid plans. Immobile. Stuck. Slowly, at first. The physical body: too tired, too worried to make such an effort. Then the mind and spirit: too confused, too afraid to even dream of movement. Janice fought the encroaching stagnation with the little energy she could gather. She didn't want this life, didn't want Stephen Gainy, or Addie Epps.

Nor did she want the little basket with three eggs and two ripe tomatoes she found on the porch early the next morning—after she'd sloughed her way down the stairs, through the new day's clinging dread, to the front door—but she ate them anyway, and tossed the basket back out into the yard. Did the same the next day, still unclear who'd left them. Janice felt pretty certain that anything between her and Stephen was finished. She'd seen it with her own eyes, his moving on. And as for Addie Epps, what had Janice been thinking, that she allowed such a thing to happen.

But one fundamental quality of desire is that it functions free and clear of good common sense, not confined by right or wrong. Another, both cruel and merciful, is that over time a body tends to forget the suffering caused by an ill-timed, unseemly, or pernicious encounter with desire. No matter how duplicitous or confusing the embodiment of said desire.

Stephen Gainy.

Addie Epps.

What did Janice want?

She lay in her narrow bed, well after midnight, sweating and trembling. She'd started from a fitful sleep, her body wrapped in a thin nightgown, sticky in the summer heat, her half-awake dreams agitated by discomfort. She'd been dreaming about her dreams. Saw them all, each dream embodied, as guests in a vast, labyrinthine, fleabag motel a little too far from the beach. Each dream, each guest, in a different room. Some truly human. Some wondrous. Others neither human nor wondrous. Saw herself going back again and again to the lobby, saying to the desk clerk, *this is not my key. This is not my key.* As Janice lay in her bed in the locktender's house, trying to figure out what the dream meant, she heard the music. The dulcimer. The hog fiddle, the sweet drone notes chiming into the dark. And before sensibility could get a toehold, she leapt up, practically ran downstairs, and out the door.

"Add . . ."

Goats. The goats startled when she rushed through the door. Kicked up their heels, rattled the bells on their collars. She'd heard the goats. Not music. Not Addie. A heavy moon bathed them all—Janice and the herd of goats—in milky light. She walked into the yard, clucking her tongue, rolling her thumb over her fingertips, and calling the animals to her. Not Addie. The suddenness, the fullness of her desire for Addie's company was irrefutable.

"Come. Come here, boy."

She called the goats as if they were dogs. The goats did not respond. As if teasing her, the animals meandered in a loose pack, just out of reach, around the house. Janice followed, calling all the way. Around the house. Into the backyard. Through the garden. To the smokehouse. They led Janice to the smokehouse. And as soon as she stood near the door, the goats scattered, suddenly and en masse, into the dark woods.

Janice ran, too. Back to the house, back to her room, her narrow bed. Back to her wrestling match with sleep. She lay, forcing her eyes shut, fingers in her ears. But even with her ears plugged, Janice heard the music. And even though she'd been duped once before, and even though she'd cursed and proclaimed her outrage at the woman and her crude songs, Janice jumped up yet again, ran outside yet again. Out the front door. No goats, this time. But no Addie either. She wanted only her company, her presence. Comforting. Soft. Not her kisses. Not her hands. No. Not those. Still, the faint music hung in the unmoving night air. Back, back to the smokehouse. Janice approached slowly. Was the dulcimer, the dulcimer player, inside? At the door, silence. So quiet and still, Janice thought she could hear the branches of the trees up on the mountaintop give way as the moon settled down onto them. The trees, deciduous and evergreen alike. The mountain, Gainy's Knob. Hours to go until morning. Janice could not bear the silence, or its ruptures. Janice could not go back into the locktender's house. Janice reached out and took hold of the looped-chain handle, and for the second time since her arrival, opened the smokehouse door.

29

The smokehouse door—thick planks long without paint, hung in a rough-hewn frame by pitted iron hardware—swung open, a narrow black portal into a high-walled box of knotted, uneven boards, with a gabled roof steeply pitched and made of tin. The yellow moonlight filtering in through the gaps did little to illuminate the small empty room. Nevertheless, Janice stepped over the stone slab threshold. Inside, the shadows compounded with decade after decade of hickory smoke, its foul corpulent history rising out of the firebox, roiling over, around, inevitably penetrating the hams and shoulders and sides hung on meat hooks, penetrating the very wood grain, so that when Janice entered the smokehouse so many years later she could taste the darkness. Empty, the meat hooks dangled from the few rafters like upended question marks. Janice stepped fully inside, let the door close behind her. Lay down on the hard and damp and gritty floor. No pillow. No pallet. Lay down among the countless ghosts of slaughtered livestock, their silent bleats and squeals rising up the stovepipe, a quiet cacophony, nonetheless present. Lay down with the filth, the stench of urine and excrement. Lay with dung beetles and worms. Rested there, with hungry spiders guarding the crevices, with wasps huddling nervously in the joists.

~

—Lay down. Lay down. *Lay down, sweet girl. Let mama tend to this.* The woman. A woman. Brown-skinned and kind, comes in the night. Slips past the padlock. Somehow. *Lay down now. Don't fight it. Me.* Sometimes to take the babies. So many times. So many'babies. *Poor girl. He treat you like a brood-sow.* Sometimes to take the milk. *Be still, girl. Gonna drink you right up.* Sometimes for the babies who cry all the way down the sluice. Who bites the yolk stalk? Her notch spilt wide. So sore. So so sore. And she comes, the brown-skinned woman, to soothe. And brings her own greedy mouth. Greedy hands. A doll for the babies. Corncob and gingham. A dishpan of cool water for her. The babies never stay long. Always gone. Always. Gone. She hides the doll in the folds of her sack dress. But the man who whips her, always whips her. Comes like smoke over the stone threshold. The sack dress bunched at her throat. And the brown-skinned woman. *Gonna drink you right up.* The black lips at her breasts. The woman's lips. When she leaves, like smoke, takes all the softness in the world with her. When she leaves.

~

Lies down at the foot of the mountain. At the foot of the mountain, the heart knits its own cloak of solace. Shhhcck shhhcck, shhhcck shhhcck. Janice, curled on the floor, the moon chiseling away at the darkness. Futile. Janice. In the dream. Or is it memory?—*What's it mean, mama? Nigger blood?*—Alone until, over the threshold, she comes like smoke. Moss on stone.—*Lift your gown, girl*—Is it Addie? And the mouth. And the fingers. Janice, her strum hollow. Each rib fretted. Sings her own drone notes—*This is the body*—whispers the cauterized tongue—*This is the body*—pillow talk. Chock and hammer. A palm full of charred secrets. The skull of a crow—*Kiss this. Here. Now here*—Janice, in the dark. Janice becomes the dark. Or is it the dream? Addie, in the dark. Or is it memory? Shape note. Mouth to mouth, they sing. Focus on the notes. Always on the notes—*Drink me. Drink me all up*—The inviolate night—*Remember. This is the body. Remember how*—Harmony—*Drink me right up*—When she leaves, like smoke, takes all the softness in the world with her. When she leaves. Leaves Addie enraged.

~

Janice woke to daylight crosshatching her naked hip and the ribbed plane of flesh down her side. The thin nightgown, a dirty pillow beneath her cheek. A scrap of gingham fabric bunched in her palm. Janice woke to stiff joints, and sore muscles. Janice woke with her neck cricked so she could not turn her head to the left. Fine splinters in her knees. Bits of straw in her hair. Her limbs, her body, raked and bruised. Soot and ash. Janice woke to the smells of smoke, of sweat, of rust and estrus. To the smell of bodies unwashed and well used. Janice woke, blinked the fog from her eyes, in the corner of the smokehouse. In the corner of the smokehouse, Janice lay, inches from the wall. And what was that? Scratched into the planks at floor level, a childlike scrawl. Familiar. Janice had seen it before. Seen it scratched into the stone at the base of the lock. Saw it scratched into the dirt on the towpath. That name. Two feet reaching up to heaven. Two feet dangling in hell. *Addie Epps.*

Janice woke alone.

Janice woke, however battered, feeling closer somehow to answers, to a *knowing.* Whatever happened, in the dark, in the smokehouse, however horrific, held the keys to Janice's understanding. But of what?

And Janice woke to noise. Loud noise. An engine. A car engine. No, higher pitched. Something pulling, whining. She stood, unsteadily, pushed the smokehouse door open. Morning sun, caught in the dew on everything, blinded her. Janice, still naked, shielded her face and stepped out into the day. Ready. Come hell or high water, ready.

30

Sound objectified, separated from its source, freed from logic or explanation, often plays the trickster in the imagination. For all Janice could tell about the noise coming from around the house—a loud cyclical whining, something pulling, something resisting—it was very possible that gravity's mechanism had been laid bare. Exposed. That she'd walk around the locktender's house and bear witness to the pulleys and cranks, the hoists, the vacuums, all the machinery that kept her and the rest of the human race walking on the face of the earth, that kept the earth whirling in its blue soup, that kept the moon up high, and birds between, that kept the stellar pinball game in play.

Yet it didn't surprise Janice to find Stephen as the source of the noise. He squatted at the front of his truck operating the levers of a winch whose taut wire line disappeared over the lip of the canal. He squatted, shirtless, and focused on the task of hauling up the ATV.

Naked. Janice, bedraggled and naked, could have easily slipped past. Could have gone into the house without Stephen ever knowing. Instead, she clutched the scrap of fabric tight and walked to the truck, the gravel biting her bare feet. With the truck parked at an angle, its hood toward the canal, the winch straining as it retracted its wire, and with each revolution of the spool, the old truck tweaked slightly on its frame. Stephen, at the ganglion of the noise and activity, didn't hear Janice walk up. Didn't know that she stood watching him, stood naked watching him, for several long minutes. Didn't hear her take his shirt from where it hung draped across the rearview mirror, pull it over her head, settle into the fit, and tug the hem down just over her hips.

"Hey," she said, as soon as the ATV skidded over the crest of the bank and Stephen shut off the straining motor.

He turned, as if expecting her.

"Hey," he said, wiping the sweat from his forehead with the back of his hand. Then, "That my shirt?" Then, "Jesus Christ, Janice! What happened to you?"

Stephen unhooked the winch line from the bent crash bar of the ATV. He looked at Janice, closely. There was no way to miss the fact that she wore only his white T-shirt. No way to miss the awkward tilt of her chin, and how she looked at him from the corner of her eye, the head not turning. No way to miss the scratches and bruises on her legs, the dirt everywhere, flecks of straw in her hair, the ash fingerprints on her cheek.

What could she say? That months ago she'd driven hundreds of miles without knowing why, or where she was going, to end up there? That she'd kissed a crazy woman on her porch, and that kiss had somehow poisoned her? That her nightmares were so vivid, so real they left her body bruised, her spirit mauled? That for her entire life she'd felt lost and confused, filled with unasked and unaskable questions? That she'd awakened that morning believing she knew where the answers were to all those questions?

Janice looked him in the eye.

"S . . . sleepwalking," she said. Nothing more.

The pair engaged, for a brief moment, in a silent battle of wills: Stephen, genuinely concerned as well as wanting to protect himself, clearly had more questions about her current physical state; Janice, leaning against the front fender, projected newfound determination and sheer defiance of all possible questions, in spite of her dirty, marred body.

"I have to turn the truck around," he said.

"I have to get some clothes on," she said.

And by the time Janice returned with her face washed and hair combed, with her arms and legs sponged off, wearing her own shirt and a pair of shorts, the muscles of her neck feeling slightly less stiff, Stephen had backed the truck up to the ATV, rigged the line from the front bumper across the hood and roof, down the middle of the bed and between the two wide boards propped on the tailgate and aligned with the wrecked vehicle's wheels. He'd wedged thickly folded rags where the cable contacted the paint job, but when he engaged the winch the tension in the line spat one of the cloths from its position on the roof of the truck.

Janice tossed his shirt into the cab and, without being asked, climbed into the bed of the truck, turning her face away so that Stephen couldn't see her reaction when the muscles of her legs and arms protested the exertion. Janice held both rags in place until the ATV was almost fully into the bed of the truck, then accepted Stephen's help—a brief cradling—over the side so that he could pull it up enough to close the tailgate.

"Thanks," he said. "You know, you left before I could introduce you to my ex-wife."

"I left before you, or your ex, could ask me why my shirt was unbuttoned," Janice said.

Stephen had no way of knowing that she was grateful to learn that the dark pretty woman she'd seen him embrace was his ex-wife. Neither Janice, nor Stephen, could fully know how the previous night would cut and shape their future interactions.

"How's your head?" Janice asked, almost reaching out to the still-visible lump over his eye.

"It's okay, now. She had some pain pills left over from a kidney stone thing. That's why she was there."

"Do you have a few to spare?" Janice asked.

"I do," he said. "Are you okay?"

"Yes. I just . . . I slept funny on my neck . . . if you have a couple extra."

"They're at home," he said. "I'll take you over."

"I'll follow you, in my car," Janice said. "So I'll know how to get back and forth."

Stephen looked her in the eye. He clearly didn't miss the implications of time and regularity, but didn't ask if she'd decided to stick around.

"Okeydoke."

It took her a moment to remember how to short-circuit the Subaru's ignition, but soon she was following his truck up Sabbath Rest Road. He drove slowly. She paid attention. Just after crossing the river, and making the left turn that would put them parallel to it, Janice saw a gravel drive flanked by two small signs. She read the first—WE'RE PRAYING FOR YOU—then slowed enough to read the other in her rearview mirror—FOOT-OF-TEN KENNEL—both routed out of plywood, the letters painted in alternating primary colors. Like the answer to an unasked prayer, she recalled the Help Wanted notice at the store.

By the time they pulled to a stop at Stephen's house, Janice's fractured mind had worked through several scenarios. Something important had

happened in the smokehouse. Painful and terrifying, yes. But too significant to forget. Whether or not she ever kissed Addie Epps again, or
Stephen Gainy at all, Janice had decided that she needed a job. Something to do. Something to occupy her mind occasionally. Something
beyond the locktender's house, or the stone carver's, to connect her to the
area.

"Can I take a bath?" she asked, before Stephen had gotten out of the
truck. "Tomorrow, I mean. Can I come by and take a bath tomorrow?"

"You can take a bath right now, if you want," he said, dropping the tailgate hard for emphasis. "You look terrible, and I mean that with affection.
Why don't you . . ."

"Tomorrow," she said. "I'm going to apply for a job at that kennel."

"Foot-of-Ten Kennel," Stephen said. Then, smiling, "Be careful they
don't brainwash you."

"What?" Janice said.

"They're already praying for you, can't you feel it?"

Stephen fluttered his fingers in the air.

"You know them?" Janice asked.

"Everybody knows the Jimperts."

She watched him unload the ATV, grunting as he pushed it into a bare
spot between two trees. Afterward, Janice and Stephen sat, side by side, on
his deck, their feet dangling, sharing a beer.

"You gonna tell me what happened?" he asked, pulling a strand of hair
from Janice's face. "This looks like more than sleepwalking."

"No," she said. "I fell."

"Okay."

There was considerable silence in their company. Janice had no idea
what Stephen was thinking about. She hoped he couldn't tell how much
she was struggling to stay focused. To fill the quiet space, Janice asked a
question she didn't plan.

"So who is your closest neighbor?"

"You," he said. Stephen tipped the bottle to his mouth, then passed it to
Janice.

Janice blew twice across the mouth of the bottle before drinking.

"I mean besides me."

"By road? Or through the woods?"

"Up the road, down the road, over the river, through the woods? Anybody, Stephen. Epps, for instance? Anybody named Epps?"

A whippoorwill called in the distance. Stephen didn't answer Janice, but clasped his hands together, forming a cavity, a vessel, from his palms, with a small mouth-shaped opening along the metacarpals of his thumbs. Stephen put his hands to his mouth and blew, answering the bird. The whippoorwill returned the call, over and over, from different points in the woods.

"Epps?" Stephen finally said. "No. The name's familiar, but no neighbors named Epps. Why?"

The conversation had already gone far enough to make Janice anxious. She sought distraction. Flicked Stephen hard on his thigh with her finger.

"That's for hugging another woman!"

Stephen set the empty beer bottle aside, turned his upper body to face Janice, who turned in kind, reached out with his stone carver's hand, cradled the base of her skull, and pulled her mouth to his. Kissed her. Full on the mouth. And it was good, this male kiss. The one she'd wanted. Tasted of salt and beer. And the fine hairs of his goatee and mustache teased her lips. Janice welcomed his tongue, both generous and taunting, in her mouth. Good. This man's kiss. The first in a long time. The best in a longer time. Good, but just good. Just. It lacked. It lacked the surge, the core level fire of the kiss she'd shared with Addie Epps. Janice closed her eyes, tried to squeeze the comparison out of her mind. A few short moments into the kiss, and the awkward torsion in her body, both of them sitting on the edge of the deck and twisting to face each other—that twist caused her sore and taxed abdominal muscles to seize and cramp.

"Ow ow ow!"

Stephen jumped down, took her by the waist.

"Stay here tonight," he said. "Take a bath in the morning."

He tried to kiss her again, but Janice pulled away, tried to act playful.

"No," she said. "No. Be patient. Besides, I'm going to be drugged. Are you the kind of guy who'd . . ."

"Absolutely," he said, but didn't push any further. "I want to show you something tomorrow. Come early enough."

Janice promised to do so. She tapped on the horn as she drove away.

She slowed the car to a stop at the entrance to Foot-of-Ten Kennel and read the various signs hammered low into the ground on both sides of the long uphill drive. Cartoonish dog images interspersed with praying hands and platitudes.

Tomorrow. She'd ascend the drive tomorrow.

Back at the locktender's house, for the second time, Janice almost missed the small object on the porch. The bone chair. It was the bone chair, crushed. Janice cried a little as she scooped the broken remnants into her palms and carried them into the house. She'd kissed them both, now. Addie must've known it. And Addie's mouth, so strangely familiar— the mouth of the night? of the smokehouse?—was the one Janice feared most. Janice had to explain some things. She had to find some things out. She had to come to terms with this hydra—now fear, now longing, now joy, now rage, possession, rejection, gratitude and entitlement, desire and denial. Same heart. Same blood. It felt as if she'd kissed Addie before. As if. And, despite the bruising, the raked flesh, the teeth marks that drew blood, if she wanted to *know*, Janice had no other choice. Several hours later, only the waning moon and a herd of goats gathered in the woods saw Janice emerge naked from the back door, scurry across the garden and go, with both hope and trepidation, into the smokehouse.

Nor emerge in the morning, the sweet penance done.
Janice, sunken-eyed, exhausted and filthy, labored up the steps of the locktender's house to gather a bag of clean clothes. What happened in the smokehouse, Janice could not fully remember. Could not point to a mark on her flesh and say, with any real certainty, how it got there. What happened in the smokehouse was almost more than she could endure. Endure. She had to endure. Despite the unknowing, she felt closer—beaten, tired and hungry and sore to the core of her being—but closer to, within reach of, that nebulous and fleeting sense of *understanding* something. Who she was? Where she came from? Who came before her?

"I'll stay," she said aloud. "I'll stay until . . ."

Unable to finish the sentence, she sat on the back stoop with a mug of thick instant coffee, waiting for the caffeine to engage before driving over to Stephen's.

En route, Janice stopped on the shoulder of the road by Foot-of-Ten Kennel.

"I'll stay," she said again.

When she pulled into Stephen's drive, he was in full headstand on the deck, elbows and forearms creating a solid angled base, fingers interlaced and cupping his skull where gray hair met the gray planks. His legs were board-straight and directly over his shoulders. His muscled body bare but for gray gym shorts a little too small, a little too thin for public wear. Janice tapped the horn. Stephen eased out of the yoga pose, sat up slowly and made a slight bow.

"Namaste," he said.

"Hey," she said, more groan than greeting.

Janice set her bag on the deck, reached out her hand, and Stephen helped her up.

She could tell he was looking at her closely. Scrutinizing. Assessing the dark circles under her eyes, the fresh bruises and scratches on the visible parts of her body.

"Janice . . ." he said, more question than anything.

"I'm all right, Stephen. I'm . . . just . . ." Janice answered, wanting to change the subject. "Did you get dressed up just for me?"

"Of course," he said. "Who else?"

"Will you really let me take a bath?"

"Yep." He wanted to push the issue, she could tell. Didn't. "But are you sure you want a job at a kennel? You'll come home smelling like dog pee."

"It's been a lifelong dream of mine," she said. "To come home smelling like dog pee every evening."

"I do like a woman with aspirations," Stephen said. "Now, come on. Before I let you in my bathtub, I want to show you something."

Stephen turned and headed toward the studio. Janice sensed no room for argument. She lacked the wherewithal anyway.

"It's really important," he said. "And I think you'll be pleased."

He paused at the door, and without turning to face her, told Janice he was sorry for the way he'd behaved over the dead crow. She reached as if to put her hand on his back. Didn't.

He led her into the studio and told her to close her eyes.

"Can I trust you?" she asked.

Stephen took Janice by the waist, directed her into the workspace, then patted her—almost—on the ass with both hands.

"Now you can look."

Feigning shock at his—almost—intimate touch, she jerked away before opening her eyes, and bumped into the heavy mass of the stone altarpiece with enough force to make the wooden frame, already sagging beneath the burden, sway and groan under the shifting weight.

"Whoa there," Stephen said, reaching out and stabilizing his work. "I don't know the power of my own touch."

Despite wanting nothing more than a hot bath, Janice mustered the energy to cluck her tongue and wag her finger at him. For the moment, his playfulness displaced her fatigue.

"What am I looking at?" she asked, turning to face the huge stone blocks.

"Step back," he said.

When she did, Janice could tell that all the stones were in place.

"You finished!"

"Keep looking," he said.

Then Janice found it. The face. The once-blank face of Mary Magdalene. Janice's face. More angular, somehow, but still no doubt. That was her jawline rendered in granite. Her brow. Her thick lips.

"Stephen . . . my God . . . it's beautiful."

She reached out to touch the face, but pulled away.

"Go ahead. Please. Touch it."

Janice traced each line of the face with her fingertips, again and again. Down the neckline. The single visible ear.

"It's not quite done," he said. "I need to polish a few spots. And I want to put a crow in the top side panel. I miss that bird."

When Janice turned, tears rolled down her face, carving solid lines in the patina of dust on her cheeks.

"I don't know what to say."

"You don't have to say anything. Let's get you in the tub; you've got a demanding new career to start."

Janice was stunned by his gesture. An apology—or offering, or accusation—in stone. Stone quarried from the canal lock. The time and skill, the attention paid to her face, was more than she could fathom. Did he do it from memory? Why? Why her? What did it mean, her face, Janice Witherspoon's face, cut into rock? A Judas kiss? Irrefutable. Permanent. But beautiful. Janice had the questions in her head, but they were locked away there. Her mouth had no access.

With an exaggerated flourish, Stephen ushered Janice through the sliding glass door and into the bathroom, where he'd laid out fresh towels, a new bar of soap, and little bottles of Marriott shampoo and conditioner. Stephen plugged the tub basin and adjusted the water. He shook a kitchen match from its box and lit a fat beeswax candle on the back of the toilet. The wavering yellow flame cast a magnified anti-shadow of itself on the wall behind it.

"Stephen, I don't know what to say about . . . it's so . . . ."

"Shhh," he said. "Tell me later. Can I . . . I mean, do you need help with the cuts? I could wash your back?"

And while the idea of those strong hands attending to her flesh held no small appeal, Janice wasn't ready. She couldn't let him see her body, not in its battered state.

"Not this time," she said. "But . . ."

Stephen waited until it was clear she wouldn't finish the sentence.

Janice didn't have the end of the sentence in mind. She felt, however, given his generosity, his kindness, and his clearly growing concern over her worsening physical condition, along with her genuine desire to keep him in her life, she had to offer something.

"I'll tell you what, if I get this job . . . if I get this job, we'll celebrate."

"With a bath?" he asked, with forced playfulness.

"Maybe. Maybe not. You'll have to wait and see. Now, get out of here."

With the door closed, Janice undressed, slowly, painfully. She eased into the water, letting herself go into the warmth. The tub, an old claw-foot, was deep and long. Janice settled in to where only her face rose above the water's surface. She listened to Stephen puttering around his bedroom.

"You don't have to babysit me," she said. "I'm more than capable of bathing myself."

She heard Stephen come close, then sit on the floor with his back to the door.

"Tell me again why you want to work at Foot-of-Ten Kennel."

"I . . ." she rose a little higher in the water. "I like it here. But I need something to keep me from being bored to death."

Was that the right answer? Janice felt she had to tread carefully.

"Hmm," he said. "Well, if the job works out, you might want to think about . . ."

"About what?" she asked.

"It's ten miles from where you live now to the kennel. And, you have no bathroom."

"Are you inviting me to move in with you, Mr. Gainy? Do we know each other that well?" She was practically giddy from his suggestion, however tentative.

"Just working through the options," he said.

They sat in silence for a long while, Janice stretched out in the tub, Stephen just beyond, and leaning against, the closed door only a few feet away.

Janice soaked, in the warm water and in the wordlessness. But those noises? What was he doing? Scratching. Soft scraping. It took her a while to realize that Stephen must be drawing. The sounds of pencil to paper, of eraser at work, momentarily filled all available space.

"Thank you again, Stephen, for . . . for my face in your altarpiece. I really mean it."

"You know," he started to say, then paused to attend to his drawing before continuing. "If anyone had asked, a year ago, why I'd left the one face undone, I couldn't have answered. But, then you . . . then we met, and . . . it's not like I made the decision. More like . . . I don't know . . . like the decision was made for me."

He paused again, without drawing or erasing.

"It just felt right."

Janice wanted to cry. Almost. She wrung out the washcloth and draped it over her face. Her whole body ached. To the marrow, and deeper, her very soul was raw. It felt as if she herself were coming through some rough birth canal. As if all the muddled years of her past, time spent gestating in stasis, mired in a dark womb of fear and uncertainty, yoked to both loss and a vague wanting, as if those years were coming to an end. But what would follow? Freedom? And if so, freedom from what? From whom? Soon. She'd understand it all soon.

Eyes and nose peering out of the water, she looked around the bathroom. In the flickering candlelight, on a low bookshelf, a photograph caught her eye. She hadn't noticed it when she was there before. Stephen, a much younger Stephen, and a young woman. They were dancing. Some sort of folk dance. Big, happy smiles.

"Do you miss being married?" Janice asked.

"What?"

"Do you miss your wife?" Janice asked. "I'm looking at this picture."

"Oh," he said, somehow relieved. "Yes and no. I liked being married; I don't miss her."

Janice didn't push. But she waited.

"We weren't really meant to be together. Took us both a while to figure that out. Then she . . ."

He hesitated again, and Janice's impatience got the best of her.

"She . . . slept with someone else?" Janice asked.

"No, no. Well not right away . . . I mean . . . she got sick. She got this illness that I couldn't understand, couldn't deal with. I abandoned her. That's the short of it."

Stephen had stopped drawing. Janice wondered if he regretted the confession.

She added some hot water to the tub. The coughing spigot roared. She had to get to the kennel. To apply for the job there. She had to get back home, to the locktender's house. To the smokehouse. Janice winced, the memory even more painful than the stinging cuts and throbbing bruises. She fingered the oldest bruise, the one on her wrist, the one shaped like a bird. With each tiny movement of her fingers the subcutaneous tendons worked the blood-bird's outstretched wings. As if it were flying. Flying. Or about to fly.

"I'll tell you," he said after a while. "People complain about getting old. But I'm so much happier now than I was as a young man."

"Because?"

"Well, I'm much more patient, for one thing. And much much less at the mercy of my dick, for another."

Janice laughed.

Janice laughed more.

Janice closed her eyes, held her breath and slipped deeper into the tub to stop the laughter. The water filled her ears, muted all sound. Stephen kept talking; she heard the mumbled syllables. Let them swirl around her naked body, didn't try to hold on, didn't try to understand. She needed to get down to the kennel. Needed to get back to the smokehouse. In the smokehouse, things began to make sense. In Stephen's tub, images from the smokehouse played across her mind, and with those images, a flood of contradictory emotions. Shame and rapture. Joy and terror. Hurt and comfort. Guilt and need. So many more. Janice held her breath, lay in Stephen's tub as her body recollected sensations. Her body. Her sensations. The other body. A woman's body. She could not tell Stephen about these things. He wouldn't understand. Couldn't understand. She had to keep the secret. And, more important, she had to keep *at* the secret. There would be answers, soon. Janice felt as if she were about to wake up. As if a lifetime of fatigue and struggle was coming to an end.

—*Come home*—

What? Did Stephen say that? Did he come into the bathroom?

—*Come home*—

In the bottom of the tub, hard metal against her backside, Janice felt the crushing weight of *possibility* settle upon her. She opened her eyes. Looked into the face, into Addie's face. Addie, atop her. Addie, naked.

Face-to-face. Addie's eyes open, her pale lean body aligned with Janice's. Not floating. Not floating. Pressing down. Holding Janice beneath the surface. Holding Janice to the bottom of the tub. Naked and naked and smiling and drowning.

—*Come home*—

Addie mouths it. No sound. The mouth offers no sound.

—*Come home. Come see. My body. Your body*—

Janice wanted to scream. Janice wanted to kick at the sides of the tub. Janice wanted to thrash against the sweet menacing presence. Janice did not want to kiss this woman who was kissing her. This kiss that both takes and gives breath. Underwater. How long had it been? Minutes? Hours? Years? The kiss, she resisted. But only so far. The pounding. The pounding. Her heart? The surge of blood in her belly, in her lungs, in her groin. Pounding. The kiss. Pounding. Give in to the pounding. The door.

The door came off its hinges, slammed against the tub. Stephen, his booted foot, came behind it.

"Janice! . . . Janice!"

Janice bolted upright. Janice sat clinging to the rim of the tub. Janice, alone in the tub, choking, gasping, struggling for both words and breath. The breath whistling in her chest, seizing up her lungs, her tongue. Stephen knelt beside the tub, knelt in the pools of water on the floor, trying to get her to focus.

"Janice? What happened? Look at me, Janice."

Slowly, painfully slowly, the lungs opened to accept breath. Janice cried softly.

"Did you see?" she asked quietly. "Did you see her?"

"Shhh," Stephen said. "Don't talk. Just catch your wind."

He must've seen Addie! How could he not?

"Don't lie to me, Stephen!"

Janice yanked free of his grip and stood, her legs unsteady, turned—naked and dripping—to face him.

"I know you saw . . ."

But he responded before she could finish.

"Jesus fucking Christ, Janice! What happened to you?"

Her body. The smokehouse. The cuts and bruises. The deep bite-marks on her breasts and belly. The fingernail tracks raking her thighs, her throat. Stephen took Janice's arms and turned her gently around to find her backside equally abused.

"Janice . . . please . . . you have to tell me . . ."

Suddenly, Janice was ashamed. So deeply ashamed to be standing there, exposed. Hurt. Stephen had to have seen Addie! Stephen shouldn't have seen Janice's damaged body. Not yet. Not yet.

"I'm okay . . . it's nothing . . . nothing . . . I just fell . . . I . . ."

Didn't matter what she said. Stephen heard none of it. She could tell by the look on his face. Utter shock. Disgust? Janice leaned to get a towel from the toilet seat, nearly fell. She grabbed Stephen's arm; he flinched, as if about to pull away, then helped. Helped her out of the tub. Helped her sit. Draped the towel over her shoulders. Knelt to look into her eyes.

"You need a doctor, Janice. You need to go to the hospital."

"Shhh . . . shhh . . ." Janice shook her head no. "I'm okay. Just help me dry off. Help me get ready."

She took both of Stephen's hands, put them to her breasts, grimaced from the pain, but held him against her. He must've seen Addie. He shouldn't have seen this body. This body, damaged. Damaged by Addie. By the nights in the smokehouse. Stephen tried to pull away, but Janice held tight with surprising determination.

"Just help me get ready," she said. "Just help me . . ."

She forced his left hand down between her legs, began to grind herself against him.

"Shhh . . ." she cooed. "Just do this. Do it for us."

But Stephen jerked away and stood against the door frame. And Janice saw, without doubt, the disgust and pity, the fear in his eyes.

"Janice, I can't . . . I can't handle this." His voice quivered. "These . . . kinds of . . . issues, of problems . . ."

Then it occurred to her that not only was Stephen sickened by the sight of her body, but he also believed her to be, what, crazy? Insane?

Rage. Her weary body could not contain the volume of rage that welled up and spilled out. Shame. All that kept her within any bounds of control, all that kept her from lashing out at him, was the crushing shame that accompanied her anger.

"Leave me alone!" Janice shrieked, covering herself with the towel. "Get out of here! Get away from me!"

He did. She heard the door slam. She dressed as quickly as possible. And still dripping from the bath, still weeping and raging quietly, stormed out to the Subaru, and nearly slammed into several trees as she sped up the drive. Accelerating down the macadam road, weaving, crying so that it was difficult to see. Who cared, anyway? If she died there, along the road, if she hit the ditch, if she left the road and rolled down into a ravine, was killed, instantly, or if she lay there and suffered before death—who would care? Janice drove erratically, cursing her life, cursing the men in her life: her dead, absent father, Danks, Stephen Gainy, others. Drove, cursing the women in her life: her mother, Addie Epps, her mother, Addie Epps. Drove, planned to drive all the way out of the county, all the way out of the state, cursing, the whole way past the entrance to the Foot-of-Ten Kennel, where, as if she hit some invisible inner wall, she skidded to a stop. She'd show him. She'd prove that she wasn't crazy. She'd get this job, get her life back on track. Back on track. That's where the momentum of her upended world was carrying her. Janice knew it. Toward Stephen. Toward a real, grown-up relationship. She only needed to straighten things out, then go back and see him. Proof. Proof of her stability. Proof that she wasn't crazy. He needed only proof. He'd said so himself. Hadn't he?

While the transformative moment happened in a split second—now she is frantic, manic, nearly suicidal; now she is relatively composed and focused—the old car eased up the driveway so slowly it almost stalled. She had just enough self-awareness, in the moment, to realize how bedraggled she must look. Wet, uncombed hair. Damp, wrinkled clothes. Dark circles under her eyes. And enough visible scratches and bruises to give anyone pause.

Janice readied some excuses for her appearance. As if any would be convincing.

She shut off the ignition in the parking lot of the Foot-of-Ten Kennel, and in the absence of backfire heard the dogs barking inside a long low building. It used to be a chicken barn; Janice had seen enough of them in the South to know. But in place of the crate of eggs, or the smiling chicken on its roost, normally painted on the walls, a cross-eyed dog of indeterminate breed grinned at her, the dialogue balloon proclaiming its message:

Dogs Luv Us & We Luv Dogs
Praise the Lord!

A white clapboard house, about the same size as her house, the locktender's house, stood at a right angle to the kennel across the gravel lot. Janice heard the sound of a radio, a gospel station, coming from an open window. Above the only visible door in the barn, at the end nearest her, hung a placard in the shape of a dachshund with OFFICE painted across its long trunk. Janice took a breath, pushed a damp strand of hair away from her face, and stepped inside, into the small windowless room. The off-kilter air conditioner jutting from a rough-cut hole in the cinderblocks near the ceiling worked unsuccessfully to cool air thick with the smells of dog. Years of dog smells, no doubt. In the office, which also served as the waiting room, three plastic molded chairs fixed to a steel beam — probably purchased at a fast food restaurant's going-out-of-business auction — faced an old metal desk piled high with books and files, and hidden among them, an outdated computer. Behind the desk was a thinly padded waiting-room couch, also piled with books and folders, and another door that led into the kennel itself. In one corner, a filing cabinet topped with plaster-cast praying hands and a stack of cheap business cards. In the other, a bulletin board overflowing with cards and Polaroids of dogs and owners hung over a coffee machine.

"Hello?" Janice said, consciously avoiding any reflective surface.

When the interior door opened, the wave of sound and the intensified smells nearly knocked Janice down.

"Can I help you, honey?"

Janice mumbled that she'd come to apply for the job.

The big, pasty, and jowly man, of indeterminate breed, smiled, registered absolutely no reaction to Janice's appearance, and introduced himself as Floyd Jimpert.

"Let me get Mrs. Jimpert," he said. "She takes care of this side of the business."

The equally jowly and pasty, but considerably shorter woman who followed him back through the door introduced herself as Mrs. Jimpert. And while there may have been a flicker of concern — pity or compassion — in her eyes, the old woman didn't make a single comment about the way Janice looked. It was as if they'd become accustomed to, expectant for, the road-worn and beaten down of the world to show up at their door. Come one, come all. Both of the Jimperts were so excited about Janice's presence that there was never any real talk about an application, or any questioning, or discussion of her job skills, or work history. Mrs. Jimpert more or less jumped right into explaining what Janice's duties would be.

"I can't hardly scribble in the record books no more," Mrs. Jimpert said. "Doctor says I got that tunnel syndrome. My arm hurts all day long."

The woman looked at Janice's arms when she said this.

Janice nodded. Mrs. Jimpert kept talking.

"Reckon you can put all our files and records into that computer? Make it so we can figure out how much we spend and how much we take in?"

Mrs. Jimpert perched, a massive flightless bird, on the edge of one of the plastic chairs, and when Janice told her how easy it would be, the woman almost wept.

"I can get you set up in no time," Janice said.

"See, Floyd, I told you if we waited and prayed long enough, the right person would show up. We prayed you here, honey!"

"We sure did," Floyd said. "Prayed you right up that driveway."

They never asked where she was from. Never asked what she did before their prayers got hold of her. Mrs. Jimpert told her all about how they came up from the South after Floyd got out of the army.

"We used to run the egg farm," she said. "Our boy helped us until . . ."

She didn't finish, and before the silence got out of hand, Floyd said he thought he'd heard a little Southern twang in Janice's voice, then took her back through the kennel. The long, narrow room was split in two by a slightly domed concrete walk. On either side, a trough angled down to drains at the far end of the building. Along both walls, divided by chain-link fencing, a dozen dogs, maybe more, jumped up from the cool tile floor, or from their thin foam beds, to bark and bark as Janice passed.

"There're some beautiful dogs here," she said, pausing to scratch the ears of an old bluetick hound.

"Careful honey, you liable to fall in love with all these dogs."

Floyd told her about their clientele, and their busy seasons.

"Mostly folks from the university. They get paid way too much, and do way too little real work."

Back in the office, Janice asked if they had access to the Internet.

"I can download some programs I might need," she said. "Some filing programs."

The idea made Mrs. Jimpert extremely nervous.

"I heard they can steal your 'dentity," she said. "They can take pictures of you when you're not looking."

Floyd told her they didn't know much about that Internet stuff, but he was pretty sure their son had hooked it up.

"Makes me nervous," Mrs. Jimpert said.

"We'll pray about it," Floyd offered.

When the conversation turned to pay, Janice realized her lack of forethought. She had abandoned her only bank account. Had no desire to open another one. But somehow, inexplicably and mercifully, these kind people didn't balk at the idea, awkwardly conveyed, of paying her in cash.

"We'll do it week by week," Floyd said. "You come back tomorrow, and we'll see how it goes."

Janice left, exhausted but ecstatic. It was the perfect job. It was proof enough, right? Just down the road. Paid cash. Easy enough. And both the dogs and people were so sweet. She could stay there for a long time. Stay at the locktender's house. Stay near Stephen, until . . . near Addie. The smokehouse. As she turned out of the drive, toward the locktender's house, Janice goosed the accelerator, almost laughed at the brief squeal of rubber on asphalt.

She went home, without hesitation. Went back to the smokehouse. Soon it would be over. Things were growing clearer, right? Answers were on their way. She went back to the smokehouse, one more night. She could endure one more night. Could allow one more night of being all but consumed by the want and the anger on the hard plank floor. Then she'd tell Addie—*Stay away from his house*—*What we do here*—*What we do here, in this dark building*—*It's different*—*Stay away from Stephen*—Janice went with intentions. Went with expectations. Waited for night, for Addie. Waited for the hunger. Waited for the body. Waited for her body.

In the morning, sore, her legs stiff, all the fine muscles of her back protesting, everything aching, Janice woke with no new bite-marks, no new traces of blood on her belly and breasts. Their absence, the loss, made her sick to her stomach. She readied herself for work, crying all the while.

32

"Hey honey," Floyd said. "Mrs. Jimpert is making a pot of coffee. You want to come feed the dogs with me?"

Janice followed willingly, scratching each eager dog on the head as Floyd scooped the kibble into their bowls. All but three of the ten cages were occupied. The cacophony of barking quieted as the dogs began to eat.

"Oh, she's so sweet," Janice said, kneeling at the last cage and stroking the velvety inner ear flesh of a big-eyed gray and black dog that was more than willing to postpone eating for Janice's attention.

"She is a good one," Floyd said. "And I'm afraid we might be stuck with her."

He told Janice that the dog's owners moved out of state. They were supposed to come back for her once they got settled in, but it had been months, with no contact.

Janice almost said that the dog looked like her friend Stephen, with its gray-flecked black hair. Almost said it.

When she grimaced, and faltered for a second upon standing, Floyd asked if she was all right.

"I think I need a new mattress," Janice said.

"Morning honey," Mrs. Jimpert said, handing Janice a mug imprinted with a smiling Christmas photo of the couple, the Foot-of-Ten/Praise the Lord logo in banners above and below the picture.

Janice spent the first few hours sorting through the chaos on the desk and trying to get used to the constant barking. Mrs. Jimpert took all the phone calls, modulating her voice up and down to overcome the dog noise, and penciling dates, times, and diets into a spiral-bound notebook.

Mrs. Jimpert brought lunch of egg salad sandwiches and sweet tea. They talked, she and Janice, idly. Janice felt comfortable enough to share the tiniest shred of information about her life.

"It's just me," she said. "I wanted to be by myself for a while."

After lunch, Janice helped Floyd run the dogs.

"Now, I don't expect you to do this all the time, honey. We don't want to work you too hard."

Janice told him she really wanted to help. She didn't tell Floyd that she mostly wanted to spend some time with the abandoned gray and black dog. Didn't have to tell him. Floyd handed her the leash.

"You want to walk this old girl?" he asked.

Janice nodded eagerly, and knelt to stroke the small dog.

"Such a nice size. What kind of dog is she?" Janice asked. "I don't know this breed."

"She's a mongrel. The best breed of all."

Janice spun the leather collar up and read the nametag shaped like a bone.

Knobby.

Nice coincidence. The dog looked like Stephen, its hair anyway, and she'd named her mountain Gainy's Knob. The afternoon breezed by, as Janice—grateful to the point of greediness for the distraction from all she'd been through recently—arranged the files in the cabinet, cleaned the computer monitor, and dusted the keyboard. She worked just slowly enough not to run out of things to do.

Late in the afternoon, Mrs. Jimpert said they were done for the day. Asked Janice if she'd like to stay for supper.

"No thanks," she said. "Tomorrow I'll start entering the records into the computer. You'll be technology-abled in no time!"

"Praise the Lord!" Floyd said.

"Praise the Lord," Mrs. Jimpert echoed, with much less enthusiasm.

When Janice went for her jacket and purse, Mrs. Jimpert asked her to wait a minute. Janice wondered if she'd done something wrong. Or if they knew something about her. She couldn't hear what the two whispered about, huddled as they were over by the flea-and-tick bath display.

Mrs. Jimpert turned and smiled at Janice. Floyd disappeared into the back room. The dogs barked maniacally. Janice's heart pounded, maniacally. When Floyd led the gray and black mutt out of the kennel and handed the leash to Janice, she was so relieved that she wasn't being fired, she cried.

"We talked it over, honey," Mrs. Jimpert said. "You need some company, and we want you to have him."

Floyd helped her put the dog in the car; Mrs. Jimpert brought out a bag of kibble, the leash, and a brand-new rawhide bone.

"Thank you both, so much," Janice said from the driver's seat. But even before reaching the end of the short driveway, Janice knew she didn't want the dog. That she couldn't accept it. Too much responsibility. She knew, just as certainly, in that short distance, that it'd be a perfect gift for Stephen. It'd make him forget . . . it'd make him forgive.

Janice wanted to honk the Subaru's horn all the way down Stephen's driveway. She settled for three short taps once she'd stopped and turned the ignition key off.

Stephen came from his studio, with clear reluctance in his gait. By the time he got to the car, Janice could read that same hesitation and doubt all over his face.

"Don't look in the car," she said.

"Janice . . ."

"Close your eyes," she said.

"Janice, I don't . . ."

"Come on, Stephen. Please just close your eyes."

He sighed, but obliged her request.

"And hold out your arms."

She could see Stephen draw back as she draped the wiggling dog over his waiting arms.

"His name's Knobby," Janice said.

Knobby, a little too big to be held comfortably in the arms, squirmed and looked around, the worry clear in its eyes, and jumped to the ground. Stephen held the dog by the collar, between him and Janice.

"I don't want a dog, Janice."

She hadn't considered this response. Couldn't think of a reply.

"He was abandoned . . ."

"I don't want any dog, abandoned or otherwise."

"I just . . . I thought . . . or hoped anyway . . ."

"You hoped what? What's this dog supposed to do? To represent?"

Janice leaned against the car door. He handed her the leash and took a step backward. Janice wound the leash around her fist. Stood, and bore it all. His frustration. His anger. All justified. She took it. She could take it all. All.

"What exactly did you expect this dog to do? Make me drop to my knees and say thanks? Make me think, okay, this is good, she's crazy, but she gave me a dog? I don't know anything about you. I have no proof that anything you've told me is true. I'm not your shrink! Not your priest! I'm not your babysitter! I'm not your lover! Or your boyfriend! I'm not some high school boy you can buy off with a dog, or a kiss. What the hell were you thinking? If you want to be a part of someone's life, you have to let them into your life. And, now . . . it's too . . . I don't want a dog, Janice."

Stephen went back into the studio.

Janice left, the dog whining on the passenger seat beside her. She could take it. She could take it all. He'd come around. She knew it. Sooner or later. He only needed proof. He said so himself.

Night came with its thin moon, and Janice, her thinning body eager, left the dog in the kitchen, in the dark, and went to the smokehouse. Readied herself, in the smokehouse. Lay bare, on the bare floor and waited. And waited. And the dog, in the kitchen, began to bark. To howl and whine. The poor, scared dog, all alone in the house. *Shhh*, Janice called out quietly. *Shhhh*. But the dog didn't understand *shhh*, the dog didn't understand its new isolation, the dog only wanted to be touched and stroked and comforted, the dog knew only *howl* and *bark* and *whine*. *Hush*, she said, almost yelled. Whispered *Addie?* The frightened dog, certain it had been abandoned for a second time, called out its suffering into the dark. No Addie. No body. Could she bear this? And the empty night notched its belt around Janice's waist. And Janice, *shut up*, called to the dog, *shut up*, and Janice, seeing no other way, crossed the yard, naked, to beat the dog in the kitchen. *I'm sorry*, she said, *shut up*, she said, whispered *Addie?* Whispered into the hollow night, and more barking, and no Addie, and Janice, seeing no other way, crossed the yard, naked, put the dog into her car, and, naked, drove up Sabbath Rest Road, drove through shadows, past barren fields, drove without thinking, drove to the market, Chunk's Market, opened the door and shoved the dog, whimpering and pissing, out of the car, drove away. So weary. Janice, wanted, now, only to sleep. No Addie. No smokehouse. Wanted to sleep. To sleep, through dusk, through the angelus bells ringing out in Catholic belfries in the distant valleys, to sleep through bobwhite and whippoorwill, to sleep through blooming of night phlox and moonflower, through columbine, gladiola, and lily releasing their fragrances, to sleep through the mean sound of chisel against stone, to sleep, such welcome sleep, until the goats clattered over the lip of the canal and beckoned.

But Janice, half-asleep, instead made her way to the smokehouse, went in, closed the door. Crawled back onto the dirt floor. Lay down. Opened herself. Waiting. Soon, the morning would begin to nudge the fog up the mountainside. Waiting. Hoping. Needing. The door. The door opened and shut. Opened and shut. The rough frame rocked against the slamming. *Yes*, she says. *I'm sorry*, she says. *Come*, she says. And then, Addie. In her arms. Janice's arms. Dark arms. Whose dark flesh? How? And her mouth to Addie's. And the milk, hot and metallic, and spilling over her tongue, and out of her mouth. So much milk. She may drown. And Addie. And Janice kisses the branded wrist, feels the pulse against her lips. And the brown-skinned woman, her face familiar. The brown-skinned woman who takes the babies, the birdlike cries of newborns. She takes the milk, takes the hurt. Sometimes. Takes. Says *touch me here girl*, says *he don't know*, says *he can't know*. The man takes the babies, drops them in the outhouse. Laughs. Caws. The mules on the towpath, laugh their mule-laughs. Hoofing at the race plank. The mule shoe bites into her skull. Then the man. And all the men. And the buckets full, the bartered goods. And the brown-skinned woman says *don't fight it honey*, says *do this*, says *here, now here*, says *ohhh sweet jesus* and bleats like a goat, Addie smiles, Addie laughs maybe for the first time since, since the scalding steam, says, the brown-skinned woman, *hush girl, hush now, don't want that man to hear.* That man, the locktender. Addie laughs and the sound—so pretty— becomes song. Bleats like a goat, the brown-skinned woman, at Addie's touch. And then the man, the plane of his face lean and mulelike, in the doorway, and swearing, *Abomination! Abomination!* And the brown-skinned woman and Addie, naked and afraid. Cower in the corner of the smokehouse. *Abomination!* he says. The kinked black hair of the brown-skinned woman wound tight in his hands. And Janice, her scalp on fire. The door opens. *Abomination! Janice!* Naked Janice, that voice. *What are you doing? Who's there? Janice? Abomination!* Stephen's voice. Shadows in the doorway.

The door slams. The door opens. Naked, the brown-skinned woman is dragged into the yard. Naked, Addie, ankle chained to the floor. Watched. Stephen backing up and up away from the smokehouse door. Janice naked, writhing, still, then still. Between the slats. *Filthy nigger bitch!* The rope cinched tight. *Abomination!*

Around the side of the house. *Hhrrrrrrr . . . Hhrrrrrrr . . .* Janice fights for breath. *Hhrrrrrr . . .* Shackled, Addie, her plucked tongue, cannot cry out the right words. Stephen, the goats, disappear into the woods. The man, the locktender, goes. Takes his fists. Takes his nastiness. Takes his key. Padlocked, Addie. Stephen. Janice. Light. Her brain fills with pure white light. *Hhrrrrrr . . . Hhrrrrrrr . . .* Padlocked, Addie hears the breach. The canal ruptures. Bottom falls out. No more boats. No more buckets. No more groveling in the mule shit and hay, the rocking boats, the men and their pathetic furies, plowing at her, plowing, boring through the earthen walls. Nothing left. Nothing but the sound of water bleeding from the canal. Then the hiss in the gills of dying fish. Then, light. The pure white light. Obliterates Addie. Obliterates pain. Obliterates. Janice.

33

Janice woke, lying in the doorway of the smokehouse, her bare back against the damp morning ground. Her legs splayed over the threshold. Barely able to move. Stephen? What had happened? What had he seen? And Addie? And the rope? The brown-skinned woman and the man?

Janice crawled to the house, crawled into the kitchen. When her hands stopped shaking, she forced herself to eat, not out of hunger. But need. Fuel the body, or the day would consume her. Janice, battered, avoided all reflective surfaces. When she was able to stand without the tidal surges of nausea and pain knocking her back to the floor, Janice cleaned herself as best she could. Despite the already warm day, already half gone, she put on jeans and a sweatshirt. Brushed her hair back into a tight ponytail. Wished she had a hat.

If she'd had a telephone, Janice would've called in sick at the kennel. But if she'd had a telephone, things would've been different from the beginning. She couldn't fathom staying alone at the locktender's house all day. Going to Stephen's house wasn't an option. He'd asked for *proof*. Janice felt close to the answers, felt that the proof lay in every bloody scratch and bruise on her body, but she knew that wasn't enough. Not yet.

Work. She'd go and do work at the kennel. Mindless, safe work.

But when the Subaru rattled to a stop, and Floyd and Mrs. Jimpert came from the office to greet her, even they—good Christians, more than adept at turning a blind eye, and at making the best of suffering—even they couldn't hide their shock at her appearance.

"Lord have mercy, child . . . can we . . . are you . . ." Mrs. Jimpert said, too flustered to complete her sentences.

"I'm okay," Janice said, practically slurring. "Just not sleeping well. That's all."

Her two worried employers conferred in private as Janice limped toward the office door.

Floyd opened it for her, and Mrs. Jimpert took Janice by the arm, led her to the bench by the window and sat down with her.

"Honey, Floyd and me . . . we think you should take the day off . . . get some rest, and come back tomorrow."

So much kindness masked the woman's obvious concern.

"You folks," Janice said. "I'm just having trouble sleeping. I'll be okay. Really . . . I can get your database up and running by this afternoon."

Floyd sat on the other side of Janice.

"Sweetie, you look like you need the rest a whole lot more than we need to get them old files in order. They ain't going nowhere. How about I give you a ride home . . ."

"I can't . . ." Janice spoke, trying to hide the anxiety in her reaction. "I can't go home right now. Work . . . they're doing some work on my roof . . ."

The Jimperts each had one hand on Janice's shoulders and one on her knee.

Such kindness. Such a wanting to trust what she said. Or, at the very least, to make the pretense as painless as possible.

"Just let me work a little while, and see how I feel," she said.

But less than an hour later, it was clear that Janice was incapable of focusing.

"Janice, honey?"

How long had Mrs. Jimpert been standing beside the desk?

"Floyd's gonna drive you home, okay?"

"No, no," Janice protested. "I can drive myself. Really . . . can I just, if I can just lay down on the couch here for a minute . . ."

"No," Mrs. Jimpert said, stunning Janice with her conviction. "You'll do no such thing, young lady. You're going to come right upstairs with me and take a nap in my son's old room. There's fresh sheets on the bed."

"I don' . . ."

"Floyd will carry you, if you won't walk."

No refusing. No energy to refuse. Just a short nap. Then back to work. Then back to the locktender's house.

Mrs. Jimpert led her through the small boxy house, each spare room spotless and smelling of Pine-Sol and Lemon Pledge.

"You want one of my nightgowns, honey?"

"No ma'am," Janice said. "I just need to lay here for a while, then I'll get back to work."

Mrs. Jimpert stood in the door until Janice stretched out on the bed.

"Them dogs don't need you to hurry up your nap. And neither does that computer."

Janice, too self-conscious to get comfortable under Mrs. Jimpert's watch, smiled and nodded.

"Sweetie," the woman said, draping a wool throw over Janice's legs, then sitting at the foot of the bed. "Floyd's outside running the dogs. It's just you and me here."

Janice didn't know what to say. Didn't know what was expected of her.

"If there's anything . . . I mean, I'll listen to whatever you want to say. I'll pray with you . . ."

What now? Could Janice possibly open up and relieve herself of all the craziness at work in her life for the past year? Could she share even an incremental truth with this soft trusting woman?

"It's my mama," Janice said. "She's real sick. She doesn't sleep. And it's just me to take care of her. I stay up. Sometimes all night."

Mrs. Jimpert looked, looked at the exhaustion in Janice's eyes, looked at the marks and bruises on her arms, at her throat, and laid her hand atop Janice's.

"Okay, honey," she said, the disbelief not registering in Janice's tired ears. "You go to sleep now."

Once Mrs. Jimpert left, pulling the door closed behind her, sleep didn't come as easily as Janice expected. She lay staring at the ceiling. She looked around the room. Nothing seemed to make it definitively a boy's room. Or a man's. Janice had no sense of how old their son was. No model airplanes, no guitars, no posters of either musicians, superheroes, or super-models. The bedroom was as simple and spare as the rooms she'd seen downstairs, unadorned but for the dresser standing—almost altarlike—between the two plainly shaded windows. On top of the dresser sat a large framed photograph of a young man in uniform. A U.S. Marine. Janice got up as quietly as possible, stood before the photograph with the medals arranged perfectly at its base. The commendations. The death certificate. Janice crawled back into bed and cried herself to much-needed sleep with the sounds of barking and Floyd calling the dogs by name drifting through the windows.

Slept—mercifully—without dreams.

She slept until dinnertime.

She knew it was dinnertime because Mrs. Jimpert woke her.

"Wash your hands, honey. The bathroom is right across the hall, and dinner's almost on the table."

"Oh," Janice said, sitting up with a start. "I'm so sorry. I didn't mean to sleep so long."

"Sometimes the body takes charge when the spirit can't do it. You come on down and eat with us."

She had to get home. Back to the locktender's house. Back to whatever was happening in the outbuilding. But food . . . food would help. Help clear her mind. So foggy, so confused.

Janice sat between them. Floyd reached first, then Mrs. Jimpert, and they all held hands while Floyd prayed.

"Bless this bounty, oh Lord."

Their big round hands swallowing hers.

"Bless this child, our welcome guest."

White china bowls reflecting the Formica tabletop.

"Watch over us as we serve you."

White china bowls, beans and corn and perfect chunks of stewed beef.

"And protect our boys in uniform, Lord, while they do your duty."

If only she could stay there forever. If only she could tell them everything. Take back all the lies. Start over. Move into their son's room. Move into their quiet, decent lives.

"Serve yourself, girl. We don't stand on ceremony here."

"How'd Knobby do last night?" Floyd asked, making conversation. "Such a good dog."

"Oh," Janice said. "Curled right up at the foot of the bed. Slept with me all night."

Janice ate until her belly was distended and swelling against her shirt, with the Jimperts encouraging her all the way.

"There you go, girl," Floyd said.

Janice helped Mrs. Jimpert wash the dishes, insisted on it. And when she saw the Natural Bridge commemorative plate in the cabinet, Janice put her hand on Mrs. Jimpert's shoulder.

"What is it, honey?"

"Nothing," Janice said, smiling. Then, "I need to go. Got to get back to . . ."

Mrs. Jimpert folded her dishtowel, then sat Janice down at the kitchen table.

"I'm gonna run the dogs one last time," Floyd said, and left the women to talk.

"You're staying with us tonight, Janice."

Janice shook her head, started to protest, started to mention the dog, or her mother, or some other new lie. But Mrs. Jimpert, solid in her benefi-cence, was immovable.

"That dog'll be fine by herself for one night," Floyd said.

"Okay," Janice said, then accepted her host's embrace.

Okay. Rest would be good. With her belly full of food, Janice conceded that a full night of uninterrupted sleep would help. Would help her gather the strength, the focus necessary for . . . for what? Janice felt as if she were standing on a precipice. No . . . a pinnacle, with many possible sides from which to plummet. Soon she'd know the right step to take. The right jump. The right fall. Soon. She had to make herself ready for the *knowing*. Sleep and food would help.

How could she not stay? It all felt so good. So—momentarily—safe.

"I'll get a jump on the work in the morning," Janice said.

She was about to say that she had nothing to wear, when Mrs. Jimpert said there was a nightgown already laid out for her on the bed.

"I think you'll find most everything you need in the bathroom."

"Y'all are so sweet," Janice said.

From the upstairs window, Janice watched Floyd take the dogs out to the power pole in the middle of the yard, where at dusk the automatic sen-sor had tripped, and the heavy glass light had begun to buzz loudly and glow. She watched the bats circle and swoop.

"Good night," Mrs. Jimpert called through the bathroom door, as Janice eased into her second bath of the past few days. Slipping into the warmth with both gratitude and fear. Addie had found her in Stephen's tub. Found her, and nearly drowned her.

She heard Floyd come up the steps, begin to say something, then stop, not wanting to speak to her at such an intimate moment. Janice heard the Jimperts' bedroom door close. Floyd and Mrs. Jimpert were in bed, with the lights out, and quiet, by nine-thirty.

Janice, despite how much her body longed to soak and heal, bathed quickly; would not let her eyes close. She sat on the toilet, drying herself carefully, slowly, attending to each wound no matter how small. She found and used the various salves, ointments, lotions, and powders in the Jimperts' bathroom. It'd been so long since she was this kind to herself. Janice propped one foot on the rim of the tub, to clip her nails, but got chilled before finishing. She took a thin polyester robe from a peg on the door, and paused to look at what she found behind it. A cartoonish rendering of a tree, on a poster board. At the bottom, around the fat base of the tree, a golden ribbon read: *The Jimpert Family Tree.*

With names scattered all throughout the wide-reaching branches, Janice found Floyd not too far from the top, and beside him the name Marlene. Mrs. Jimpert. One son, Ruben, with a birth date but no date of death. Janice traced the numerous branches of the tree, reading names, mouthing them silently. How wonderful, she thought, to have this history. To know this much about oneself.

The branches near the bottom grew fatter, heavier. Dates way back in the 1800s. Some names too odd to pronounce. Some names . . . some names, surprising. Danks. John Lewis Danks. Janice was so stunned she couldn't figure out who was related to whom. How odd, she thought. How odd.

In the bed, despite the bath, despite the still very present fatigue and awareness of all that had happened the previous night, Janice could not sleep. The room, hot and airless. She stripped and fought her way through the self-consciousness of lying there naked with the good Christian Jimperts mere inches away, on the other side of a thin sheetrock wall. Too hot. She grew more and more anxious by the moment. And, moment by moment, the strangeness of the Danks name appearing on the Jimperts' family tree began to take over Janice's thoughts. Was it merely coincidence? And if so, where did the coincidence stop? She let her recent history unfold in her mind. Months ago, Janice's life in Greensboro had been upended forcefully, unexpectedly. Then, caught up in a momentum greater than herself, she'd made her—seemingly random—way to an abandoned house somewhere in the middle of Pennsylvania: a locktender's house. Met a man, a stone carver, whose father had built the canal locks. On a whim, she'd sought a job at a local kennel. And on the bathroom wall, at the bottom of a drawing of a family tree, the kennel owners' name was linked, by blood, to Janice's past.

She'd met a man. Stephen Gainy. She'd lost him, as well. At least for the moment. All day, she'd kept the guilt and the shame, and the fear of losing Stephen at bay. All day, she'd denied what happened in the smokehouse. What had he seen? What did he assume? What did he know? What did he need to know? What proof could she offer?

Every time she turned over, every time she fidgeted, the creaking bed-frame echoed throughout the house. The Jimperts snored away, oblivious.

Danks. The Jimperts were related to a family named Danks.

Was it her Danks? The Danks who'd struggled futilely with the banjo? The Danks whose blood had spilled into desert sand, thousands of miles away? Was she somehow bound to this family, this place? The not-knowing bore into Janice's consciousness. The not-knowing wormed its way, like a parasitic fungus, into the hours that followed. How? How to find out? Who to ask? Not the Jimperts. Not Stephen. Not, certainly not, Addie Epps. The obsession sharpened Janice's focus. Cleared the fog from her mind. The computer! That was the answer. The Jimperts' office computer had Internet access. In the morning, before work, she could search online for these names. In the morning. In the morning. No. Now. She could sneak out to the kennel office and search the names, now. Danks. Jimpert. Epps. Addie Epps. Even her. The Jimperts would never know. She'd be back in bed within the hour.

Janice was so eager, she almost didn't bother slipping on the bathrobe before creeping down the steps and so stealthily into the office that even the dogs didn't stir. Janice fumbled in the dark with the computer switches until the monitor came on, illuminating her face and the column of lacerated and bruised flesh not covered by the robe.

The dial-up service was slow. Laborious. Janice worried that the hissing, the chittering during the computer's connection would wake the dogs. She fidgeted uncomfortably in the uncomfortable chair. Eventually the colorful Google logo blazed across the screen. What first? Who first? Janice let her fingers play over the keyboard, without pressing anything. She squirmed in the seat, the robe bunched up, the vinyl sticking to her thighs.

Who first? With worlds, vast galaxies of information at her immediate disposal—the portal to it all a slender little box, no bigger than a pencil, and blank—Janice didn't know what to do first. Danks, dead and the name that started the fire of curiousity, was the most logical initial choice. But she couldn't bring herself to enter his name just yet.

Gainy. She keyed in Stephen's last name, but the listings were too broad and numerous. She tried various Boolean searches: Gainy and Pennsylvania. Gainy and stone. Gainy and canal. Beyond a few university webpages, she found nothing she didn't already know. Stephen Gainy descended from a long line of stoneworkers. His great-grandfather helped to build the Pennsylvania canal locks. Nothing new.

Lockhouse.

The entry brought pages and pages of results, including many pictures of houses much like the one she'd been living in.

Her father. Janice wanted to search the whole world of instant information, of history, for some sign of her father. Couldn't bring herself to enter his name.

Danks.

Janice found Private Danks's death announcement, but couldn't bring herself to read the article. A clatter, a sound from outside, startled her. A door maybe. Janice held her breath. How would she explain her presence? But after several moments without the Jimperts leaning their warm, confused-looking faces through the door, Janice continued.

Danks + Jimpert.

She found the connection through the Allegheny County Civil Records website: a marriage two generations back, between John Lewis Danks and Lizzie May Jimpert. She Googled John Lewis Danks and found, after several useless links, something significant: *Tragedy Upon Tragedy*, the headline.

According to the Dunbar Gazette reporter, late Friday afternoon, August 25th, 1898, one Ezra Danks, father of John Lewis, shot himself in the heart on the steps of Dunbar Mortuary, distraught beyond recall after paying respects to the scalded bodies of the poor Epps children . . .

Janice sat back, not sure if she wanted to read on.

Not sure. Her dreams. Were these children of her dreams?

Ezra Danks worked at the powerhouse. Ezra Danks opened the steam valve at six a.m. every morning. Every morning. That morning too, the morning when the four Epps children were boiled to death as they slept in the canal right by the discharge pipe.

Addie Epps.

What did this mean? Addie Epps?

Janice typed Addie Epps's name into the search engine.

Mother Loses Children in Tragic Canal Accident
Human Skeleton Found Chained in Lockhouse Outbuilding

Addie Epps lost her children in 1898?

Who, then, had taught Janice Witherspoon to sing? To play the dulcimer? Who kissed Janice on the porch of the locktender's house? And who . . . all those things in the smokehouse?

The smokehouse. Maybe the answers to Janice's questions, maybe the *knowing* she was preparing herself for lay somewhere else. Somewhere besides the smokehouse.

What was the brown-skinned woman's name? The man from her dreams, what was his name? And what of her own link in this blood-chain?

Janice mistyped, then mistyped again, Witherspoon. Couldn't bring herself to enter it. Without forethought, she entered the name of the boy she'd first loved, all those years ago at church camp, and wasn't too surprised to trace his history along the Web, back in time, to his great-great-grandfather, an itinerant canal-boat repairman, last known location: Central Pennsylvania.

Was every person in her life umbilicaled to this tragedy?

Witherspoon + canal.

At last, she typed in her own name, hesitated, then stabbed the enter key.

Three pages of listings. Janice's heart pounded as she scrolled. Page one. Page two.

There, in the middle of page three, a listing with the two words highlighted.

Witherspoon and *canal*. The sentences underneath the link were incomplete, broken by ellipses. Other key words hanging in plain view, unsupported by details: mulatto . . . midwife . . . lynching.

The screen blurred; a tide of images flooded Janice's mind. Faces from her past. Familiar faces and unknown faces. The brown-skinned woman. Addie Epps. The crazy man who accosted her at PawPaw Landing. In her hurry, Janice knocked the computer mouse from the desk. The dogs startled, but barked only for a moment. She hunched behind the lit screen until all was quiet, put the mouse on its pad, and clicked the link.

Mulatto. Midwife. Lynching.

Power surge. What else could explain the flash, the on-screen blip, then nothing. The monitor hummed, empty and luminous blue.

34

The electric blue light washed over Janice and filled the room. Stormed across her face, through the rods and cones and the vitreous fluid in her eyeballs, bounced back just as blue, just as empty, just as unwilling to give Janice the information she so desperately wanted.

"No!" she said, shaking the monitor in her hands.

What could this all mean? Each person she searched for could be traced back to the canal, the tragedy, the four dead children. Each person connected somehow to Janice. A man named Danks opened the steam valve that killed the Epps children. What then? What happened to Addie Epps? She needed more! More names to search. All the people throughout her life, gone away, or damaged in some unexplained and irrevocable way. Were they all tied through history to the canal? Were they all bound to the poor miserable mother, the widow, Addie Epps? And what about her? What about Janice? What did those three words mean in relation to her?

Lynching. Midwife. Mulatto.

What of her dreams? The things she'd seen and done in the smokehouse?

Come on! Goddammit! Angry whispers. The dogs stirred.

She'd have to wait. She'd have to reboot the computer and wait.

The old desktop machine flickered off, then on, and began a loping series of restarts. Given the sounds, as if the hard drive were eating itself, as if thousands of clicking and hissing insects were battling inside the plastic housing, Janice doubted if the computer would survive the simple process.

It felt, in that minuscule moment, as if a century of fatigue descended upon her. She laid her head on her arms and groaned.

~

—Dreamed the kennel an airtight vessel. Dreamed the dogs pacing sharply in their cages. Herself. Herself walking back and forth between the pens. Dreamed the dogs licking at her palms. Dreamed a windowless room and a purity of light. Dreamed the sluice gate succumbing, giving in to water. Dreamed the water. Water seeks only itself. Dreamed a *knowing*. Dreamed the bitch in heat, teats swollen and raw. Dreamed herself pulling slick pup after slick pup from the womb. Dreamed the whimpering and grateful bitch. Dreamed the kennel an airtight vessel and the water rising swiftly. Dreamed the dogs shaking off first one paw, then the next. Giving in, the dogs, to the water climbing their haunches. Bellies wet. And barking. Dreamed so much barking. And herself. Dreamed herself wading, ankle deep, calf deep, knee deep, a fistful of keys. Dreamed the dogs, in terror, chewing at the padlocks. Digging into concrete. Dreamed cracked teeth and shredded paws. Dreamed hip deep, and the dogs floating at the tops of their cages, black snouts sucking at the air until, one by one, she dreamed the dogs quiet.

~

"Quiet!"

Whose voice? The barking.

"Quiet!"

Then . . .

"Girl! Wake up girl!"

Janice lifted her head from the desk. Light from the computer, the only light, fell across her naked breasts. Indicted her.

"Oh my Lord . . ." the woman said. Reacting to both Janice's nudity and the damage to her bared body.

Janice pulled the robe tight at her throat.

Mrs. Jimpert clutched a well-worn bible to her chest. She stood, in shadow, behind Floyd.

"Oh my Lord . . ."

"Cover yourself, girl!" he said, eyes locked on hers.

Janice wrapped the robe around her as best she could. Didn't understand why they were so angry.

"I'm sor . . . I thought you wouldn't mind . . ."

"Wouldn't mind! We're a God-fearing family, girl! We believe in the Book, and we don't allow that kind of filth in our home! Ever!"

Floyd pointed at the computer.

"It's an abomination," Mrs. Jimpert said.

Confused, Janice looked at the screen.

"Oh my God!"

"Don't you take the Lord's name in vain. Not in my house."

"Oh my God," Janice said again.

There could be no other reaction to what she saw scrolling, in slide-show format, across the monitor, one picture right after another. Every three seconds. The dead. Soldiers. Civilians. The decapitated. Some naked. Some in shredded uniform. The disemboweled. Bomb victims. Men. Women. Children. Half a face. Limbless. Bleeding. Nothing below the waist. Nothing above. Some unrecognizable as humans. Some horribly recognizable as humans. Every three seconds, a fresh picture of death. The banner flickering madly along the top edge of the screen: *Your Gore! Your Gore! Your Gore!* Car accidents. Murder victims. Suicides. Soldiers. Soldiers. Soldiers.

Janice vomited.

"Oh my Lord," Mrs. Jimpert said.

Floyd yanked the power cord from its socket.

"I done put your stuff in the car. You need to leave. Right now."

Janice held the robe closed with one hand, wiped her mouth with the other.

"Right now!"

Janice, clothed in a borrowed robe, cloaked in confusion and distress, stopped at the mouth of the Foot-of-Ten Kennel driveway. In the distance, over the mountaintop, the morning sun made tentative, blood-red stabs at the night. But in the tight confining valleys and hollows, darkness did not relinquish its hold without a struggle.

She turned the car in the direction of Stephen's house. She had things to tell him. To explain. He'd understand, now. It wasn't her fault. None of it. The crows. The accidents. The hurt. She'd tell him everything, and he'd understand, and he'd offer to let her stay the night, the week, the months. Janice wasn't exactly sure yet who, or what, could be blamed. What, or who, was responsible for all that had happened. She was close, though. Terribly, terribly close. And if she told him all that she knew for certain, he could help her figure out the rest. But less than a quarter mile down the road, Janice realized that, whatever she told Stephen, her word alone wasn't sufficient proof.

Stephen would need proof. Stephen would demand *proof*.

Janice pulled to the side of the road. Sobbed. Those horrible faces and images on the website scrolled through her mind. As did the sad, disappointed faces of the Jimperts. And Stephen's. And Addie's. And the brown-skinned woman's. Faces from her dreams. Faces from her past. Janice could not stop the incessant recall. She didn't know what to do.

But even, or especially, under duress, the mind can be resourceful. In that stream of remembered faces, Janice began to juxtapose. People got mixed up. Faces changed. Shifted. Became the faces of strangers, of people she'd never seen before. Never. Except maybe in books. In books! The book at PawPaw Landing. She'd seen her own family name there. Had she imagined some familiarity in the jawline, in the nose, of at least one face? Those photographs. Those faces. Janice knew that there were other photographs in the books. Photographs not on display. Proof.

With only a vague notion of where the park was, Janice drove without haste, and in good faith that when she found PawPaw Landing, she'd find the answers, the proof she'd been seeking.

But for a single park ranger's truck by the main office building—the lockhouse—the lot was empty. Janice hoped the ranger wouldn't recognize her from the earlier visit. She'd driven, lost, for a while, and judged the time to be nine, maybe nine-thirty. Janice parked, opened the door to step out of the car, then realized she was still wearing only Mrs. Jimpert's robe. Almost panicked, almost worked up the courage—or fervor—to go in regardless of her state of dress, but remembered that Floyd had put her things in the car. She stretched across the narrow back seat, wrestled on her jeans and sweatshirt, composed herself as best she could, and stepped up onto the porch of the renovated lockhouse, where the hours of operation were posted in the curtained window: Tuesday–Sunday, 9:00 a.m. until dusk. Closed Mondays.

Janice tried the door, found it locked, and had to knock several times before the ranger answered. The young man opened the door, and stood dead center in the frame, barring passage. His uniform was crisp and clean; the boots and the leather band around his dress cap, the holster and gun, all blacker than anything Janice had ever seen.

"We don't open until nine, ma'am. And the boats are closed today for maintenance."

He looked only in her eyes. Not at her straggly hair, or bruises, or cuts. Only in her eyes. Showed no sign of recognition. His discipline was palpable; Janice could taste it in the back of her throat.

"What time is it?" she managed to ask.

"Eight forty-six," he said, without consulting any watch or clock.

Janice sat down on a bench by the door, heard the ranger turn the lock. She just needed to see the book. The book with the pictures. The pictures inside. She needed to get back to Stephen's house, to tell him what she'd discovered. Uncovered. Her temples throbbed. The bird-shaped bruise burned and pulsed at her wrist. Fourteen excruciating minutes later, the ranger opened the door.

"No tours today. Tours only on the weekends. No admission fee for the lockhouse, or the surrounding buildings. Snack bar won't open until eleven, but there're water fountains and vending machines over by the restrooms. No change until the snack bar opens."

He spoke rapid-fire, was done and gone before Janice could stand from her seat. She eased into the room slowly, quietly, ready for and expecting anything. Janice leaned against the door frame, working hard to control her breath. The ranger came out of the small office tugging on a set of keys that dangled from a retractable spool on his belt. With barely any acknowledgment of Janice, he told her he had to make his rounds and unlock the other buildings.

"Be back in just a little bit," he said, the inexactitude glaring.

Janice wanted to ask him about the books in the case. Could she see them? Could she hold them? She'd expect the answer to be no, but she wanted to ask. No time. The ranger gave her no time. She watched him walk to his truck, tugging out and then releasing the keys over and over as he went. She watched the ranger pull out of sight between the lockhouse and barn. She looked at the glass cases holding the books and photographs in the middle of the room. She saw, on each case, a lock and clasp. She went to the opposite wall, by the cash register, yanked at the Velcro, pulled the fire extinguisher from its harness. Then found the case containing *Canal Life: Legends & Lore* and the logbook, the one where Stephen had pointed out her name. Janice smashed the glass lid of the display case with the fire extinguisher, left it lying in all of its redness amid the shards. She picked the two books out of the mess, shook them off, tucked both beneath her arm and walked, with forced calm, to her car, and drove.

Gesseytown. Knob's Furnace. Dumb Hundred Road. Several miles later, Janice nearly lost control of the Subaru when she whipped off the asphalt and into the narrow, rutted, dirt lane, just before the Dumb Hundred Bridge, that led from the road down to the river. The same river, it occurred to her, that flowed between, that separated, the locktender's house and Janice from where Stephen lived.

She parked, facing the water, surrounded by pines and rhododendrons, in a well-worn clearing littered with bullet casings, shotgun shells, beer cans and bottles. At the center of the site: a fire ring made of stacked cinderblocks and river stones; a faded blue recliner, its arms and seat cushion shredded; the singed, crumpled pages of several porn magazines; and the rotting remains of a field-dressed deer. No matter. No matter. Janice had to see for herself, to see with her own eyes, whatever the books held.

She sat on the hood, oblivious to the engine heat radiating through the sheet metal, the two stolen books across her knees. When she'd caught her breath, when the tremors had settled enough for her to focus, Janice began to read.

Janice found the pictures she wanted to see. Found the stories. She read of the tragedy that killed the Epps children, the tragedy that caused their father to commit suicide. She read of the mysterious disappearance of Addie Epps, and the rumors, sometimes outrageous, of her whereabouts in the years that followed; read of the skeletal remains found in an outbuilding at Lockhouse #33. Janice read the stories, took the time to read the facts as well as the hearsay. She looked closely at the photographs in the books. Studied the faces of the crowd gathered around the Epps boat on the morning of the tragedy. Saw the devastated face of Addie Epps, inconsolable, and unattended to. Saw the draped bodies of her dead children laid out on the bank. Saw the face, in the crowd, of another man, a familiar man. The man in her dreams. The man in Janice's dreams. The man at PawPaw Landing. Janice studied the pictures, turning each delicate page of *Canal Life: Legends & Lore* tenderly. Saw the photographs, the documented evidence of life on the canals, of life in the boats. No less manic, but in a moment of torpid mania, she read the recipes for Turtle Soup, as if in them she might discover something significant about the mess of her own life. Read about putting down worn-out mules. Looked into the captured faces of children playing, tied to the boat decks so they wouldn't fall into the canal. Saw other children caught midleap and grinning as they jumped into the filthy sluggish water for a swim. Janice studied the photographs of the various lockhouses and marketplaces. Their procedures and regular failures. Read of the unending difficulties of surviving on a ten-foot-wide boat. Read of the various maladies and their folk remedies. Read of the complications, the dangers of rearing children on the canal. Of birthing. Of birthing.

Janice read, and reread, about the secretive sisterhood of freed or runaway slaves who came north to work as midwives on the many canal systems. There was little to no proof of their existence. No photographs. Only secondhand accounts. Only a crude drawing of their mark, their emblem, their insignia: a dark silhouette of a bird on the wrist, wings stretched out across the ligaments and tendons.

An hour later, more or less—the conceit of time mattered little now—Janice pressed her foot fully down onto the accelerator, the Subaru spinning and spinning its wheels in the muddy ruts, fishtailing as she climbed out of the woods before finally catching traction on Dumb Hundred Road. No more crying.

She drove, her heart pounding wildlike in her chest, her mind burning, brimming with the things she'd discovered in the books.

She drove to the locktender's house. Drove with the books on the seat beside her.

Poor Addie. Poor, poor Addie.

Fear and resolve. Fear and resolve. And *understanding.*

Janice didn't expect the dark thing curled on the front porch. She got out of the car, unsteady. Held on to the door until the wave of nausea passed, then approached the house. Slowly. A dog? Was it? It was. The dog she'd tried to give Stephen. The mongrel she'd pushed out of the car at the market. It must've found its way back.

Janice clucked her tongue.

"Here girl," she said.

No reaction.

Janice, afraid of being bitten, didn't want to startle the animal.

"Here girl."

The dog did not respond. The dog could not respond. Janice stepped onto the porch and met its open, lifeless eyes, its tongue out, stiff, dry, and curling in on itself.

Janice couldn't scream. Couldn't curse. She understood. But neither could she touch the dead animal. Couldn't even kick it off the porch. Janice, cold, sick, determined, banged at the door of the locktender's house. The door swung hard against the interior wall. Opened too easily. As if it was unlatched.

Inside, the half light of morning revealed intrusion. The gourd banjo, the gift from Stephen, lay smashed apart on the hearth. In the fireplace, between the dog irons, the charred remnants of a letter. To the kitchen, to the cupboard, where the cans and jars had been flung against the wall. Furniture upended. Up the stairs, in the bedroom, in Janice's bedroom, in the center of the bed, the crow's skull on its tether, undamaged. The bed itself, soaked through. Sopping wet. A stinking liquid puddling on the floor beneath it. Janice, angry. Janice, afraid.

And Addie Epps. Poor Addie Epps.

"I'm sorry!" Janice called out. "I know what happened to you, Addie."

She called out, going down the stairs.

"Please! Please! I'm so sorry!"

She called out in every room of the house, in the cellar, in the backyard.

"Addie! Addie, please! Please let me help you."

Her empathy grew. Her delusion as well.

"Let *us* help you, Addie. Stephen! Stephen and I can help you!"

She called out all the way to the smokehouse door. She called out inside the smokehouse.

Janice crossed the yard and slid down the bank of the canal.

"I'll stay at his house. It's close, Addie! Please, I understand everything. I know! I'm sorry!"

Janice. Her pleas echoing off the thick stone walls of the lock. But the stone rebuffed her. Would not acknowledge her. No recourse. No Addie. Janice stood up in the deep lock. Hand pressed to the stone, she breathed heavily, through her mouth. Stepped out to climb the bank, to retrieve the books from her car. Saw the goats. They stood in a line, side by side, at the lip of the berm, looking down at Janice. She walked along the canal, intending to go around them. The goats moved with her. And when she leaned into the bank, as if ready to climb, the big white ram trotted down and butted Janice away.

"Hey!"

The other goats sidestepped into the channel, surrounding Janice.

"Hey!" she yelled weakly. "Stop it!"

The goats crowded her, whispered back with their hot goat breath. They began to push and butt and bleat. Urging, insisting that Janice climb the other bank, the towpath side. When Janice hesitated, the goats nipped at her heels and calves. When she veered to the side, their rough horns and bony foreheads knocked at her hips and thighs. Once at the top, once on the towpath, the animals pushed her, noisily, downstream, away from the lock. Janice walked, and when it was clear that she'd keep walking, the goats dispersed into the woods.

Not far. She didn't have to travel far.

She walked to the big poplar tree, angling out over the towpath, where she'd first met Addie. Addie, who sat against the massive trunk and sang so sweetly. Addie, who sat in the shade of the thickly branching limbs. Now, Janice stood in an altogether different shade.

The body hung from the lowest branch. The body, naked, filthy, and brown. The brown breasts sagging. The sack of her brown belly, sagging. Flies gathered at the white lines of dried milk, Addie's milk, streaking from her nose and over her chin. The neck distended, vertebrae releasing their interlocking grips, the neck so so long, the head bent fiercely over the fulcrum of the hemp noose. The arms dangled, fingers curled into loose fists. And there, at the wrist, the left wrist, glaring against the bloodless flesh, the mark. The bird tattoo. The tie that bound them together. The body. Naked. Brown. Hanging in stasis, at the beck and call of gravity. No wind. And Janice, in the shadow. And Janice saw the crow land on the branch. Saw the crow drop and cling to the dead woman's bloodless shoulder. Saw the crow peck and peck at the useless lids, peck and peck at the eyes.

Janice, driven by needs and fears much older, much more insistent than her weary body, ran all the way to Stephen's. Called his name, with the same fervor, with the same conviction as when she'd cried out for Addie.

"Stephen!"

Janice ran into the house. Through the house. Calling his name in each room.

"Stephen! I know everything! I can explain everything! Please!"

Called his name in the bedroom. The kitchen. The bath.

"I'm so sorry! I'm sorry about it all! Just let me explain."

Out across the wooden deck, the studio door stood open.

"Stephen! Stephen, please! I have proof! You said you just needed proof!"

He must be carving. Must be hammering at the stone and unable to hear.

"Stephen!"

Janice stepped through the door, her eyes wild with hope and anticipation.

"Stephen?"

The finished altarpiece, all twelve stones, fifteen hundred pounds, lay on the floor, their beautifully chiseled surfaces face down, the splintered remains of the frame scattered atop them. And Stephen . . . Stephen lay under it all. Janice could see one hand, a bare foot, and more blood than she thought possible.

"Stephen?"

It was the final, insipid plea.

Crushed. Dead. Stephen, killed by his own work. So still. So perfectly still. So perfect a way to die. Crushed beneath one's own passions.

Stephen. Dead. Like Private Danks. Like so many others. And who to blame but Addie Epps. Janice closed the studio door. No rush. No need.

Janice sat on the wooden deck just off the bedroom. The deck where she'd first seen Stephen, naked and stretching up toward the sun. Now, that beautiful body lay decimated, destroyed, beneath the physical manifestation of its own love and power. The body, useless and abandoned. But what of his spirit? His energy. If Addie Epps . . . if Addie Epps could . . .

Janice stopped. She would not let the thoughts continue. Loss was a familiar companion. She knew its wily charms. Janice left. There was no reason to stay.

Janice left. And where else could she go, but the locktender's house?

Everyone is tested in life. Everyone. She'd seen her mother come up against the test and fail. And fail. And fail again. Most do. And in so doing, perpetuate the legacies set forth in their past. Legacies of violence. Legacies of ignorance. Legacies of fear. Most people carry their histories in front of them; they trip and stumble blindly, and die before they ever think to look around their burdens toward a future.

Nearly evening.

In all the daylight left to her, Janice gathered up the gallon cans of fuel for the cookstove Stephen had given her. She soaked all of her clothes and the few bed linens in the clear liquid and shoved them under the smokehouse. She dragged the lumpy tick-mattress from the upstairs bed through the door of the smokehouse and tipped two half-full cans of fuel over on top of it until the fuel pooled on the floor and dripped between the planks, all the while talking softly to herself. Or maybe to Addie.

"I know who you are. I know what you are."

Janice went to the porch, cradled the dead dog in her arms all the way back to the smokehouse, where she laid it in the corner and stroked its head.

"I know who I am. I know what I am."

The broken banjo, her empty suitcase, the souvenir tomahawk from the trip with her mother, she arranged around the walls of the smokehouse.

Driven. Drawn. Janice knew these things, whether or not she could articulate them. She was not her past. The history that bore her up, that tied her down—she could refuse it. She could. But *desire*, when you're drawn to a thing, when you desire it all the way into your marrow, that want shapes the future. A hard future, from which there is no easy release.

No release.

Janice went back into the locktender's house, searched until she found it, the Natural Bridge brochure. She took the tattered pamphlet, a lantern from the kitchen, and a brick-sized box of matches. Went out to the smokehouse. Knelt at the door. She removed the globe from the lantern and lit the wick. She pulled the sleeve back on her left arm, clinched it tight at her elbow. She put her wrist to the small humped flame, and held it there. Held it there. She bit back her screams. The burning flesh cawed in protest. Wing beats. Hissing and popping, and the stench. Yes, she could smell it. As the sun rolled off the mountain and out of sight, Janice opened the smokehouse door, hurled the burning lantern inside.

35

Janice Witherspoon sat in her car, just up the driveway from the locktender's house, watching, in the rearview mirror, the orange flames swell and leap, swell and leap, into the night, until they began to recede. She loosened the knot on the bandage at her wrist, laid the injured hand in her lap, put the car in gear, and wrestled the steering wheel single-handedly. She may or may not have seen the goats following her, running in the woods. May or may not have heard—over the sounds of gravel crunching beneath her tires—the clappers in their bells clanging madly, or their furious bleats, their little tongues stabbing out in the dark. Janice Witherspoon turned the radio on, raised both legs so that the steering wheel held steady between her knees while she spun the dial slowly. Static and crackling, mostly. But one station, one song made its way through the speakers.

~

Who's gonna shoe your pretty little feet?
Who's gonna glove your little hands?
Who's gonna kiss your ruby red lips?
And who's gonna be your man?
Who? Who? Who?

Addie's gonna shoe your pretty little feet.
Addie's gonna glove your little hands.
Addie's gonna kiss your ruby red lips.
And you don't need no man.

Acknowledgments

Many and much thanks to the following for helping me make possible the book you're holding in your hands: Mike Lucas for his unfailing vision and his unwitting inspiration; my friend (and reluctant role model) Jerry Zolten for his life wisdom and encyclopedic musical knowledge; Laura Ford, at Random House, for her keen editorial insight and undying enthusiasm; Simon Lipskar for his savvy; and everyone else who, knowingly or otherwise, had to put up with me when I was in *writer* mode.

About the Author

STEVEN SHERRILL is an associate professor of English and Integrative Arts at Penn State Altoona. The author of *Visits from the Drowned Girl* and *The Minotaur Takes a Cigarette Break,* he earned an MFA in poetry from the Iowa Writers' Workshop and received a National Endowment for the Arts Fellowship for Fiction in 2002. His poems and stories have appeared in *The Best American Poetry, The Kenyon Review, River Styx,* and *The Georgia Review,* among others. Sherrill lives in Pennsylvania.

About the Type

This book was set in Electra, a typeface designed for Linotype by W. A. Dwiggins, the renowned type designer (1880–1956). Electra is a fluid typeface, avoiding the contrasts of thick and thin strokes that are prevalent in most modern typefaces.